C000224790

KANAGE KANYAMANZA
Copyright © 2021 Kanage Kanyamanza

ISBN: 979-8-4524-8080-8

Disclaimer

This book stands as a work of fiction. Names, characters, places, entities, dates, and events become real either as the products of the author's imagination or used in a fictitious manner. Any resemblance to actual realities sticks around as purely coincidental.

Dedication

To All Times' Learners From Everywhere.

Acknowledgements

First and foremost, praise goes to the power that provided me with health, energy, knowledge and hindsight to start and complete this project.

My deep and sincere gratitude to Nyampinga, whose support was invaluable in the same line of thought. Without her literary guidance, all the resources to edit the manuscript she made available, what the reader has in front of their eyes would have known a different and unpleasant outcome. Indeed, the universe blessed me through her.

My neighbour Dawn, with whom I jog from time to time and who became a source of inspiration, assisted me with critical feedback on my initial draft. It changed the style and the tone of the whole project. She came up with a great insight I highly appreciated.

Louise, another friend, kept me on my toes while she persistently asked how far I got with my work each time we met. She harnessed my accountability towards her about the initial objective I had in mind when the book's idea emerged.

I am incredibly grateful to my parents and other ancestors for their care, preparation for the future and my rightful place in the universe. Their messages convinced me that I came for a purpose that I still try to understand fully even through these pages.

I thank my immediate family. They have been extremely patient with me and allowed me to steal from them our time together. I am overall immensely grateful for their understanding.

Finally, my thanks go to all the people that this book will inspire in any imaginable way. However, its initial purpose was to challenge me and possibly entertain along the way.

I hope you enjoy the story, its landscape, the characters and their emotions made alive.

CONTENTS

Prologue

Hussein Daniel's vegetative state ironically represented one possible conclusion of his past as an abuser of women. I once thought he deserved such a predicament. Time elapsed, and his situation evolved. He eventually fell victim to murder in a hospital bed. He had been planted there, unconscious, for two years.

Dae Kyung Mi, unlucky in her previous relationships, had been his first victim. After each encounter, she felt inadequate, worthless and stupid. I could relate to similar awkwardness. Given her strong personality, I wasn't surprised when she decided to heal her emotional scars and regain control of her life. She lived on number one, close to the lift, on a six-floor building on the second level.

Residents disturbed her whenever they came in or went out. When the weekend approached, she became anxious.

"Today is Saturday. I expect Hussein to come home drunk. Will he curse me again?" Dae reflected on the recurring harassment she experienced. The sadness that these incidents caused in her life horrified me.

"I don't like the ugly woman. Next time I see her in the building, I will kill her," she heard more than once, Hussein loudly saying. I could relate to Dae's situation of the neighbours from hell.

Hussein picked his victims randomly. Unfortunately, none reported him. They suffered significantly in silence. Dae didn't know why Hussein behaved the way he did towards her. She wasn't aware that she was one out of many.

Both had never interacted in a civilised manner. Whenever they met, he only harassed her. I felt empathetic to her plight.

However, he wasn't the only neighbour with a concerning personality.

Haile Mohamed worked as a teacher specialist in mathematics with a complex character, half scientist and half mental.

From his apartment, he could observe the inside of Hussein's place at night, while the light would be on and curtains opened.

"I wonder what that could be! It must be nothing," Haile witnessed, in the middle of the night, an incident that would come to challenge him in different ways. He would get involved incidentally and without any prior intention to be.

At the time, his sense of unhappiness pushed him to look into his own life and eventually seek ways to plan a career change adequately.

"I have arrived at a crossroad. At this particular juncture, I don't see clearly which right direction to take," Haile had reflected.

He wanted to try himself at a career he had dreamed about for many years. He intended to become a collector of ancient artefacts.

Initially, he planned to allocate his time the most effectively between teaching at his college and learning how to go about his new path.

While he had these thoughts about his future, he pursued his regular jogging. Amina Ye, Hussein's girl-friend, who lived in a nearby block of apartments, had never seen anyone exercise in the area. Though she was keen on keeping herself in good shape, she wondered how her neighbours kept themselves fit.

"How should I care the most about my health? I need to eat well and exercise. Doing these two things could be the perfect formula," she envisaged her convenient stay in Vodnak, the city she had settled in a few months before.

She could exercise alone, but she would've liked to practice with others.

"Can I go around in public parks on my own? I am a woman; it could occasionally be dangerous," she reflected on the right time to get out for exercising. However, two other joggers from the neighbourhood went out regularly. Amina, the girlfriend of Hussein, had been into fitness for many years. Dae had talked to her once.

The circumstantial encounter they shared intended to alleviate some anxiety, Florencia Carlos, Amina's twin sister, suffered. The conversation related to Florencia's failed marriage from which she had come out profoundly depressed.

Dae and Florencia went on, strengthening their friendship. However, they had found out that both hadn't been on good terms with Hussein. Their affinity had reached a level of plotting against him together. Once the crime had been committed, Dae's mind often came back to the incident.

With some hindsight, Dae recalled the whole picture of the crime's scene. The related references looked crystal clear in her mind as if this had occurred only one day before. Only some details from her recollection were absent from her painted memory.

They had only disappeared from their safe space because too much water had passed under the bridge.

She had at the time found herself next to her accomplice, near the entrance but inside Hussein's apartment, petrified by the view they had had in front of them.

Florencia had become her accomplice in the attempted murder of Hussein because of their friendship. They also bore a similar hatred towards him. Separately, each one had nourished thoughts of killing him.

"How do you know that guy, who lives on the third floor above mine?" she had once asked Florencia when they had met the first time. Dae had mentioned his name incidentally.

"He doesn't seem normal. He curses women all the time, and particularly when he sees me," Amina had indicated to her sister in a different setting.

"Does he?" asked Florencia. She didn't know that side of her sister's boyfriend. It would take her some time to get to know Hussein, while she pursued a selfish objective of making him his man, at the expense of her sister.

What didn't Dae expect amounted to the fact that several people in her neighbourhood had connections in one way or another to the murder they both planned.

They had accomplished their crime, but the police investigation that ensued and that inspector Sizwe Mtana would lead didn't run straightforwardly. A sophisticated cover-up from an interested party tainted its process. It became marked with twists that created unexpected developments. New interconnections emerged along the way. They took tangent paths on the main journey everyone followed at the time.

After the complete story had unfolded, Dae looked back and couldn't remember how she got into her neighbour's apartment on that critical night.

"How did I end up in this mess? I should have seen this coming. I have been foolish to be led by emotions but not reason," she assessed where she stood while she contemplated the consequences of her action. Although she remembers that, as a solitary agent for vengeance, she had previously planned and executed her slow death mission meticulously, using poisonous injections of food.

She reflected on how much she had to plan to get to the execution of the crime.

An idea to help had popped up in her mind, but she brushed it away instantly. She felt she couldn't do anything. Her legs had become motionless.

"I felt transported in a parallel world, but I couldn't grasp how I got there. It looked strange because I found there people and things similar to those I knew before. However, slightly different," contemplated Dae while she saw herself as an external observer to the scene.

It appeared surreal. Dae felt disconnected from and foreign to the person who died in the room, in front of her.

"Please help, help, help, help!" these words had come out of his mouth as inaudible sounds, like a whisper.

Despite her initial determination, her mouth didn't cooperate once into the action and let her voice shout out loud for help. Her silent call seemed to come from her conscience, which pleaded on her behalf.

The crime that incapacitated Hussein appeared as a consequence of his excessive abuse of women. Unknowingly, Florencia had started on her criminal path when she tried to steal her twin sister's boyfriend.

"I need to protect my sister, at any cost," she decided when she discovered who the person was. In my opinion, her criminal inclination ignored any negative consequence, including imprisonment once caught.

"I can't let my sister be with this scumbag," Florencia characterised Hussein after some time, surprised by the nature of his personality. I admired her decisiveness about taking action to correct the situation, though she would take the vengeance in her own hands. At the same time, I was anxious about what her hot temper would accomplish in the process.

Florencia became highly concerned that she methodically searched for ways to commit the murder.

When the attempt on Hussein's life happened, the victim didn't die straight away. The failed execution caused unpredicted problems for the perpetrator and the potential beneficiaries of the crime. Haile featured among them. As a covert rival who sought as well Amina's hand, any alarming occurrence that would've happened to Hussein could've become advantageous.

Amina had asked him for help to pursue her fitness. They had become close friends as time elapsed. Her body wasn't her only concern; she also longed for her native Occorz.

On my side, with time, where I came from didn't create any sense of nostalgia in my mind. A sort of detachment had gradually developed in my conscience.

Haile hadn't forgotten the memories of his native Wethi. Until he could visit the place of his origins, an absolute void frequently affected whatever he put his mind on becoming.

"I travel like a bird in the sky of our shared universe. In my multiple attempts to land safely somewhere, I don't find any place to welcome me."

"I risk exhausting myself until death while I keep trying," Haile felt hopeless. I suspected him of testing his destiny in persisting.

Amina and Florencia wanted to reconnect. They had left their country of origin while young and after their parents' death. More than the similar roots Amina shared with Haile, they both came to know each other even more as they jogged together. Thus time made them closer.

Their friendship developed to a satisfactory level while the investigation of the attempted murder went on. However, the closeness both had seen flourishing could only get that far.

"I can't promise to be more than a friend. That's clear in my mind," Amina had responded when Haile had tried to deepen their relationship.

At the same period, Haile went miles to cover up the crime Amina supposedly committed when it took place. Though she ended up in prison for a crime she didn't commit, she made the decision deliberately and pleaded guilty for the sake of the renunciations other people had sacrificed because of their unconditional devotion to her.

In return, Amina's willingness to accept her sentence came to represent in her mind a way to pay back her friends and show them that she too cared. I sympathised with her profound, humane spirit.

As the story went on, Dae and Florencia remained the least affected by the investigation. Their official non-implication didn't happen easily because they had a broad criminal experience that had enabled them to perform a nearly perfect crime, far from that.

The Hussein case became their first and last. They were only saved by their predestined fate. It protected them and even cared much for them. That showed undoubtedly long after the story of the crime faded away from the people's memory.

After the release of Amina, Dae reconnects with her family in Niasan and friends from her childhood, including Aimi Aratani she had known during her university years.

A new life, particularly her relationship with Florencia that had also grown out of their complicity in the murder attempt on Hussein, radically took an unexpected turn. The same happened for Haile and Amina.

The investigation team didn't find the right culprit. Though its conclusion helped put in jail, someone who only wanted to protect a twin sister.

The case remained unresolved for the victim as long as there was no sentence for the real culprit.

I suppose the murder of Hussein on the hospital bed hammered another nail in his coffin.

He had spent years unconsciously. Since nobody got apprehended and brought to justice, nobody could know with certainty the motive. An inquiry that would've cleverly scrutinised Hussein's neighbours would have achieved a better result. In the course of the story, life in its different forms had happened, and it had, to some extent, changed everyone involved, not necessarily for the better.

Vodnak
Kanage Kanyamanza
July 2021

CHAPTER ONE - Curtained Off

A Glance At The Crime

Florencia reflects on her deep inner sense of being. Though she isn't in the best of moods most of the time, she felt different on that day.

"Today, and in this particular present moment, I feel alive. That matters to me more than whatever else other people could consider as a joyful life. I would even give up all that I have to enjoy this feeling. What I have gained or came to know and treasure rightly now seems not important in the face of this indescribable but still exciting sentiment I have."

Until a few years back, she didn't feature among the people that only the present preoccupied. Though she was in her current state of mind, there must've been some kind of progression from a different yet undocumented one she experienced for a particular time. The unstable life situations her peers live appears on occasion, clouded by their negative inclinations.

They see the world and their immediate surroundings, only from a particular angle, not always right. Their perspective looks commonly blurred.

It's impossible to see beyond the close and obvious view, no matter how hard they might try to change such perception. In their understanding of one specific area, they share with the majority of other people - success and happiness depend on how they can untangle the intricacies of life. Mastery of the hidden subtleties must accompany any of their supposedly and necessary harmonious expressions to make them shine. Even so, impactful dreams, either conscious or unconscious, can instruct or predict their direction and lack generally from their lives.

An objective observer could testify that she lived an unexciting life.

It resembles a bleak picture of existence without any light at the end of the tunnel, from whatever pedestal one looked at her experience.

A different assessment of their condition - if one could label it as such - should be performed to be clear about their purpose in life, and the results would invariably depend on the standpoint from which the examiner starts. It could be subjective or neutral.

But, generally, such an in-depth approach into somebody's life comes tainted with subjectivity, from the examiner embedded with personal luggage, who cannot ignore its influence on their judgement, whether or not they want it that way. That suggests, therefore, that only the concerned individual knows or feels what their experience entails comprehensively.

She turned twenty that year, the same time as her identical twin sister Amina. Three years before, she had had a kind of a dream. That dream appeared incredibly unclear that if it had become the compass to guide her, it would've instead confused her once she would've followed it. She opted to go with the flow; she chose not to give much thinking and moved in with a man she has briefly known. At the time, she didn't want much of a ceremony. It's as if she doesn't wish to mark or remember that stage of her life.

Strongly tempted to hide from anyone who would supposedly expect to know about her change of social status, she instead enters into that married life quietly. Such behaviour showed confirmation of a real complex, more than the preservation of some privacy.

The husband happens to be abusive. Therefore, a short-lived relationship becomes one of the few outcomes from such a predicament.

To stay with him for even a year looked like a difficult challenge she painfully managed to overcome.

Halfway through, she realised she had made a wrong marriage decision.

After some time, she moves on. She thought she had matured and been strengthened by the experience of her failed marriage.

"With the life experience I have, I think I have what it takes to get a man anytime I want," Florencia makes a fair assessment of where she stands at the time in terms of her relationship with men.

As time goes on, she learns how to seduce the opposite sex. Such skill came to her at the cost of a mental breakdown. Women in her close sisterhood provided her with tips they practised on men and saw them working. Also, through trial and error, unfortunate outcomes had infuriated her and highlighted her hot-temper. Despite that experience characterised by stringent life tests, she somewhat managed to get what she wanted from men.

She had progressively improved her craft while she evolved into womanhood. Reasonably attractive, her irascible character defines her personality. When Florencia decides to approach Hussein, Amina's boyfriend, her manipulative forte at work pushes her into action.

She states her intentions before she embarks on her mission.

"My target consists of my sister's boyfriend. I don't care how she will take it. I need Hussein, at all costs, as an existential quest."

After clarifying the plan to follow in her mind, she realises that she must borrow her sister's identity to succeed with him. She intends to wear similar clothes as hers and imitate her manners. She didn't have to do any work on her voice; both twins sounded similar behind doors.

She used to ask Amina about Hussein.

"What do you think of your boyfriend?" she inquired. She would ask her about his likes and dislikes.

That sort of interrogation happened each time her sister would return from her boyfriend's place. The quiz sessions would become valuable in due course.

Once she mastered the topics both liked to discuss, she felt enough confidence to pursue her plan. When she met Hussein for the first time, while she pursued her goal, she tricked him and made him take her for his girlfriend.

She performed exceptionally well. Hussein didn't get a clue that he had spent three hours with Florencia instead of Amina. Fortunately for everyone in the love triangle, Hussein never mentioned that moment to Amina.

Nobody helped him to find out that Florencia had impersonated his girlfriend. There was only one player aware of the rules of the game. Fate seemed to play on the side of the other sister.

Amina had all along fed Florencia on how abusive Hussein could be. The sisters could usually live on good terms. However, they would occasionally and intentionally hurt each other verbally as siblings do from time to time. At the same time, they would also share their inner feelings and worries. In those moments, Amina would complain about and badmouth Hussein. Her aim seemed to comfort her sister or only feel understood by a close friend who happens to be her sibling.

Initially, Florencia intends to meet Hussein and take advantage of his relationship with her sister. To her surprise, things change drastically and shift her mind when she experiences firsthand what Amina has been living. She becomes angrily disillusioned.

He has an arrogant attitude, and his peers consider him a women's abuser. High-tempered and revengeful, Florencia decides then and unilaterally to end Hussein's relationship with her sister on her terms.

She makes up her mind to kill him.

The motive relates mainly to preserving her sister's future; she considers her plan as an act of love. In her recollection, she pictured what Amina had to put up with because of the excessive abuse. Florencia found it unbearable. She couldn't imagine any reason for her sister to be with him once she realised his character as a person. In a moment of rage, while she wouldn't control herself, she would use a kitchen knife to do the job. It would be her weapon of choice.

However, she had to prepare thoroughly and also needed an accomplice. When the planned action comes, she goes through it all with an engineer's or scientist's minutiae.

All this had happened in the recent past, and it appeared like a neat operation from a professional.

Once the crime is committed, she tells her sister how she performed. Deliberately, she chose not to mention the involvement of her friend Dae. That was how Dae's name would be nowhere in the official police records related to investigating the committed crime. Florencia proceeds that way to take full responsibility since the idea came from her. Despite that consideration, once in Amina's apartment, she feels overwhelmingly anxious about what she did.

Dae had called Amina fifteen minutes before. She announced to her sister how safe she was and headed home. The two accomplices in the crime had completed their mission in Hussein's apartment. They had left him unconscious on the floor of his main room.

While Florencia approaches the apartment she shares with her sister, she sees lights on in the main room. She immediately remembers that Dae had called her sister a moment before. Aware that she probably was waiting for her, she walks into their apartment's spacious area with a hesitant pace.

Given the time, the night sounds uncomfortably quiet.

Florencia glances rapidly at the large contemporary pictures hanging in the middle of the room's main wall. At her right, the chandelier of six ornamental bulbs sheds a feeble light. Without any other thought on her mind than what she experienced a moment before, she goes straight to the sofa, mentally exhausted. She looks like a zombie.

Dae and she had together focused their attention on the suppression of all the evidence about their crime. Nonetheless, Florencia has on her trouser a small fresh stain of the victim's blood, difficult to notice. When she sat down, the bloodstain left a mark on the sofa. Amina questions her several times about what happened. She intends to lead on this and even threatens her sister before deciding to talk about the incident. All the details would be requested, then exhibited.

"Please, could you give me some water first before I say anything?" Florencia asks her. Amina goes to the kitchen and opens the tap.

"Here you go with your water! Can't you see that I am waiting!" Amina, curious, stares at her sister after placing the glass on the kotatsu table. The table has a comforter that hangs down from all its edges. It doesn't allow the view of the space beneath. Its braided electrical part leads to a heat-enabled element located on the underside of the top. Amina had bought it in a local vintage shop visited by many tourists from Pobe.

"You know what! I think I killed Hussein," Florencia finally reveals with the calmest tone one can imagine. She stares at her sister with pale eyes.

"I know you don't have a sense of humour! Your bad jokes can't even measure up!"

"As my friend hinted over the phone a moment ago, I killed someone, and I beg you not to rush and check it out or try to call your boyfriend and or go to his place. You might get into trouble."

"Unless you want to become the primary suspect," she implores Amina and asks her to be cautious because of her deed. In her call to Amina, Dae hadn't hinted any clue about their crime, but Florencia had that impression in her mind that the mentioned interaction had been about what she did at Hussein's apartment. Surprisingly, she was present while her friend called her sister. She couldn't picture out what caused her mental distortion.

"How come! Please, could you at least try to explain; don't make such blatant statements without any evidence to support what you say."

"Listen. After ten in the late evening, I arrived at Hussein's apartment; our restaurant had closed around that time. As I wanted to go and see him last night, when I got downstairs, I saw the lights in his main room and went to knock on his door."

"Hang on! How many times have you been in his apartment?"

"Yes, I have been there before. I think I told you about the first time I went." The conversations Amina had had with her sister, each time she came back from Hussein's meetings or outings, had sounded in her twin's ears as if she too had been with him on those occasions. Telepathy must've played between the twins at those moments. Their remote interactions could be a possibility, as some people believe.

Florencia had always tried to be seen by Hussein as her sister Amina each time they would all be together. As a consequence, even while the tragic incident occurred, she had ensured that. She had worn clothes Hussein had once mentioned as beautiful on Amina, her sister.

"Then, what happened next?" Amina asks.

"I found him alone, almost already drunk. He watched a TV program that I don't recall the name of."

"When I came in, he stopped and invited me to drink with him. He opened a bottle of cognac for special guests, he said. At that stage, he hadn't recognised me. He continued to see me as if I was you. I declined his offer. I told him that I didn't want any alcohol. Instead, I went to his fridge and got myself some orange juice."

"The more he drank, the more he brought up his insanities about women, in the terms nobody else would tolerate. He addressed you and looked somehow confused about me when he thought that I was you, but because of his drunkenness, he couldn't process further his hesitations about who I was."

"Already drunk in his chair, he unknowingly took the drug that made him sleep. The entire scene looked like an unbearable spectacle; he disgusted me to some extent. I thought about you when he visibly engaged in the journey of no-return."

"The way I know you, you must've killed him effectively. Then what now? What do we do? If nobody has found his body yet, the calm atmosphere before the storm won't last. The police will be here soon. One more question: did anyone see you when you left his apartment?"

"I didn't see anyone. At three, in these early hours of the coming day, I think the majority of people must be in bed at this time."

"Did you ensure that we couldn't get linked to the crime? Did you check that you didn't leave behind any evidence that could incriminate us?" Amina enquired.

"After I saw him close his eyes, and after he fell on the floor, I observed him for three long minutes. He got knocked out but was still breathing. Firstly, I tried to make sense of what I had done, and secondly, I thought about the consequences. I realised that I needed to wipe out everywhere in the apartment where my fingerprints might be. When I finished, I switched off the lights and stayed in the dark for nearly ten minutes."

"They became the longest minutes I will ever experience in my entire life. I wanted to make sure that, if someone saw me come out of the building, they could hardly link me to Hussein's apartment," Florencia explains.

"The more Hussein's apartment would look empty from outside, the more time it would take to discover his body. Curtains remained closed, ensuring that nobody could see inside from outside. I concede that in this situation, I acted like any other experienced criminal. I wished and prayed that the crime stayed hidden for the longest possible time," she describes the execution of the operations to her sister.

"I wondered who could be that woman who called me and said that you were safe?"

"Dae has been my friend for a while. She knew that I would be in Hussein's apartment. I had informed her beforehand in case I needed some help. That explains how she joined me in the apartment and later on called you."

Before the incident, Florencia had rehearsed how she would proceed once in Hussein's apartment while in action and immediately after the murder. A particular focus had to be on when she would be still around her victim's unconscious body.

When she got the sleeping drug she planned to use from a pharmacist friend, Florencia opened its container and assessed the invisible powder she had to put in Hussein's drink.

Since she would've to let drops of the drug in his glass, she wanted to ensure that her tools at hand would operate efficiently and not disappoint her. Regrettably, in a moment of distraction, few particles of the drug fell on the floor. She didn't notice and or pay any particular attention.

Something, unclear like a lost thought, clicks in Amina's mind.

Her sister had finished with her story about what had happened to Hussein and her involvement. She realises how mortal as well she could be; she imagines herself in the shoes of her boyfriend. At any early periods of her life, she had never pictured out to herself, as clearly as at that moment, the futility of life. Her parents had died many years before. Maybe too young at the time for her to understand many things; she couldn't grasp the full concept of death. With her boyfriend's uncertain situation, also too young to die, wealthy enough to be the envy of his peers, she couldn't fully realise that his earthly journey would end like in a blink of an eye.

Every time Florencia stayed in Hussein's apartment without Amina around, she always ensured that Hussein took her for her sister. Even on that tragic night when he entered into a coma, he must've fallen unconscious while thinking that somehow he was drunk with his girlfriend. Hussein couldn't have guessed differently.

Florencia didn't notice any sign to alert her that Hussein acted or played her deceptively. Despite what she had on her mind, she couldn't be sure that he didn't suspect her true identity but chose instead not to show what was on his mind. In case he ultimately died, only a visit to him in the afterlife could confirm his exact thoughts before he entered that new world.

"I highlight this in case. You need to think through whatever will be necessary since you never know that death might still spare him. If he survives, I presume he might attest that you did it because, not at any single moment, did he ever doubt your presence in the room. Alternatively, if he ever doubted but didn't show it, that would demonstrate his high capacity to control and hide his emotions."

"So you still deceived him about your identity, even in those final moments of his life?" Amina enquires from her sister.

"Let's hope he has gone for good. Imagine if he didn't die and had to recover from what I did to him by some unfortunate chance for us. You would be in big trouble. He would confirm that his girlfriend had tried to kill him," Florencia replies.

Amina pauses for approximately ten seconds before she comments on her sister's last statement. She pictures all the possible ramifications of what her sister did that night.

"Listen! It's early morning, a quarter past three. We need to rest, though it will be difficult. I will sleep on what you said. In the morning, I think I will have some clear ideas about what we must do. Once we wake up, I advise you to act as usual; we must scrupulously follow our daily routines," Amina tells her sister while she holds her by the shoulders; she slightly pushes and takes her to her room.

By seven in the morning, they woke up and got out of their beds. They quickly get ready for their day of work. On that Monday, Amina glances outside in the direction of Hussein's apartment. She doesn't notice any abnormality in the neighbourhood. Her sister had nightmares related to the crime.

After her bath, she felt refreshed. In her mind, the picture of the crime scene doesn't go anywhere. She has a kind of wallpaper in her brain that whatever is in there seems to hang on.

Amina prepared her breakfast.

"How do you feel?" Amina asks her sister while sitting in front of her.

"Not well, at all. The crime scene looks like an embedded cinema screen from a horror movie that constantly moves in my mind," Florencia explains.

"You have to be brave. We will find a way out. Please go to work and try to clear your mind. I understand that could be a tough challenge right now. A lot has changed last night and life as we knew it might've gone forever. Act normal. Let's call each over in case of any new development. I will leave for the office in a moment, at ten. By that time, someone will have contacted the police, I presume. I will check regularly," Amina counsels her sister. When they finish their breakfast, she sees her off for the day.

At the start of that particular Monday, Florencia's immediate future paints a dangerously precarious outlook. She can't predict what the next hour, day or week will resemble for her. To make predictable what lies ahead, she must control its creation's process through her own will. Nonetheless, she needs to consider a unique riddle.

"As women, we come into the universe and live different and unique lives," she reflects. "Such traits allow us to change our mind from time to time, and nobody has the right to blame us. Nobody should blame lions for being themselves - they are unique creatures -, even while they eat other animals to feed themselves," that unconscious collective conscience prevails around. Whatever the assertion implies, she decides not to let herself totally at the mercy of the circumstances. Within the little space of her existence, she could still manoeuvre freely; she intentionally plans to preserve it firmly and ferociously as long as she can. Under the spell of her intuitive gut, she had committed the unthinkable. The navigation ahead would certainly display high turbulence.

The "Raison d'Etre."

Haile's inseparable friend lives in the neighbourhood of his conscience. The strong affinity that exists between the two makes those who know them confuse one for the other. They have been together for an extended period that he can't remember at which moment of his life their closeness started to take roots. They almost both have been in each other's lives all the time. Without any preparatory hint or a revelatory sign, his friend asks him out of the blue.

"What do you like most in the universe?"

"I love history and enjoy stories, no matter which medium the storytellers use," he replies spontaneously.

"Randomness doesn't exist in the occurrence of things. The way facts about dates, people, places, and events in the universe all connect fascinates me," he adds to justify himself about the things he likes most.

At that time, they sat on one of the many benches of the local park. The weather presenter had predicted a sunny day, and Haile made provisions for spending his entire first half of the day entertained by the excellent sunshine. He didn't discuss his plans with his friend, but as per magic, it happens that he appears unannounced beside him as well.

"But how did he manage to guess that I would be here in this park, at this particular moment?" wonders Haile about his invisible friend but whose presence always remains undeniable.

He didn't have to see him, but he couldn't ignore him either. His appearance doesn't disturb his comfort. When his friend doesn't show up as always without any invitation, that doesn't mean that he has travelled or been busy elsewhere.

His presence, however passive towards Haile's actions it could be, displays its main feature, indicating to be the best closest friend he will ever have.

He lets him be and doesn't interrupt his manifestation, whatever form he might choose to take for his act.

At particular periods of his life, Haile feels the need to pause and reflect on which stage of his earthy journey he has reached. No distinctive element triggers such instants, although those moments' common denominator appears to be the serenity and the cosmic vibrations linked to the context. Such an occurrence could be in the middle of a crowd. It could either manifest in a town hall or on a bus stuck in a traffic jam. This time a public park reflects that required calmness. His friend, who seems to follow him everywhere, would often carry on from where he left the previous conversation.

"I don't get it!" His friend indicates. His comment relates to Haile's interest in history and stories. He remembers earlier when he highlighted how he liked these subjects.

"It shouldn't feel difficult to understand. When it comes to such topics, I suppose I get the same enjoyment as those that a good meal or a night out with friends excite."

He doesn't have to memorise historical facts at all. Their imprint in his mind becomes permanent records once the information of their occurrence flows. He doesn't understand anyone who wouldn't be able to do the same about the past. He compares such difficulty as a failure to take in the nutrients people need for their bodies to grow and live.

"I had a classmate in high school who couldn't differentiate between the important dates of the Small War or Grand War, let alone the politics that could shed light on these human tragedies."

"He couldn't explain the significance of the Nirven Conference of 1838/9 that divided Qarfi among Kivong countries for its exploration and exploitation."

"That puzzled me highly," Haile went on and explained his fascination with history.

However, his interest in history doesn't mean that this subject constitutes his income's source by no means. Like many people, his situation resembles those who do jobs that they don't necessarily enjoy but define their careers. He earns his life from another field far foreign from his hobby.

Haile's friend got this time interested in what type of story could be his, as someone who likes stories.

Although Haile's story was not unusual or incredibly unique, it however featured as one of the untold ones. Like his other neighbour, who devotes his significant time to writing, the life they had both decided to live would be part of the billion stories lived but unaccounted for in the recorded book of humanity. These stories constitute those that time doesn't or wouldn't let come out in the open, whether the protagonists or players live or die. His story would feature among those who remain buried under the wrap of the collective conscience of humankind.

The story evolves initially as an emulation of a great runner with a highly creative mind. Until then, its awareness remains limited to a few people. A radical dreamer brings it up when he uses his imagination. Like other stories, they all originate from the time people started to process thoughts and safeguard them as memories.

Haile's friend comes closer to him and then asks him unexpectedly. The context from where he replies doesn't matter. He can approach him anywhere, as long as he doesn't fall asleep.

"What does all this mean?" The friend refers to the continuous chain of thoughts around Haile's story as it evolves in his mind.

He replies to the question the friend asks.

"The concerned story talks about an experience of compassion, devotion and love that a selected group of individuals opt to display, impulsively or consciously, on one fraction of their journey in the imagined universe."

He adds without pausing, except the time to exhale and inhale once. "These characteristics, they reveal, extend the positive essence of existence through others. While their other nature painted with crime, deceit, hatred, bitterness, resentment, grumpiness, anger, fear, guilt, jealousy, blame, illusion, and so on, raises instead a critical question that sometimes relates to the purpose of people's existence once these features come into the picture."

He concludes with that question on the usefulness of evil among people.

"Needless to say that all these attributes - the list could be broadened - define what makes up the majority of people."

However, Haile judges that he must carry on, reason, and connect the story's dots for his friend's benefit.

"In the described context, portrayed aspects about human nature get found active in one or two people, or even more, simultaneously or subsequently. As a consequence, the highlighted attributes found in action in Dae's and Amina's characters, which, in their case, opposed the logic of things when they appeared intertwined in the way they did."

Though he fears that his friend doesn't grasp the whole picture, Haile demonstrates the story's constraints.

"The representation I highlighted looks like the only one to consider in the particular circumstances. It enables people to understand, for example, why someone would spend tremendous efforts to deceive others or commit a crime, because of love or their ego."

Haile further illustrates the boundaries to consider for the story.

"The same framework could explain as well the way they interpret the world around them. Crimes of passion seem to define what comes to people's minds when love and ego play together, though this doesn't correspond to what Hussein and Florencia intend to experience and translate into action. If they ever plan anything together at all."

Long before and while the events unfolded, or even well after the story gets told, people, Haile included, preferred to spend a valuable amount of their time endlessly preoccupied with complaints instead of enjoying their lives. No matter what characterised the good or bad conditions of their existence at any given time. However, this came to be the outcome of their own choices or uncontrollable events.

The story could've been a non-event for many. However, it did remain uneventful for a long time. The controversy of its encounters concerned intensely a particular group of people that destiny brought together accidentally. One would say that it constituted - or became for them - a significant part of their lives. The strength of the story made it sticky. Their lives became the most talked about at certain moments among those who knew them or found them different through their news exposure. The attempted murder of Hussein, which got particularly highlighted, came to define the relationships of those involved.

The characters whose individualities evolved with time followed the story's narrative, marked by it, as water flows in a river, but doesn't question the reason why it doesn't take a different course.

***

Haile didn't sleep that night. The previous day, he had taken a strong coffee with its full-fledged caffeine while he met and discussed with an acquaintance. Haile doesn't usually like coffee. Even so, he imitates his friends unconsciously whenever he goes out for a drink with them outside his home. He orders the dark or creamy drink once in a while because he has forgotten the last sad effect it had on him.

It had been a while since he had drunk coffee of that kind of flavour. He had ceased to think that each time he did, he stayed awake the whole night. He hopes that next time before he orders a coffee drink, he will remember its consequence on his sleep.

In their meeting, they discussed the literary project his friend worked on at the time.

"Why did you choose to write a crime fiction book?" Haile asked.

"I don't know how to describe the exact trigger! It evolved incidentally. It seemed unplanned, like most of what happens in our lives. Now, I think I remember."

"It has to do with the habits I developed over the years while I read. Sometimes I take notes. Ideas pop up. Thus it happened after I read the DMevotion and X book of Gekoi Nohigashi. I read it in one day. It had been twenty-four hours without any shade of sleep. It appeared dangerously addictive and, at the same time, fascinating. When I finished it, I wondered if I would regularly do my jog around the river's banks, and I wanted it to be central to the story."

"Is there any other element, particular to the area that you find significant for your reader to know beforehand?" Haile inquires.

"Oh, yes! The story behind how the Neptersine came to life and became a leisure destination.

By the time we see things at any given period of their existence, we rarely question how they came to look as what our eyes or thoughts make us contemplate at that particular moment. That place has a long and rich history."

"Please could you explain more?" Haile implores.

"The way the Neptersine looks presently results from several and costly redevelopments made about it from the eighteenth century," his friend indicates.

"The water in the lake gets renewed every four-five months; work to get to this stage of abundant, fresh, but not stagnant water started decades before from a series of muddy ponds spread in the area. It took the human's ingenuity in the writer's mentioned book to accomplish that," the archives of local studies at the town hall highlight the sequence of accomplished phases.

"On top of the physical transformation made over the years, some particular events and occurrences make the Neptersine special."

"Suicide in the waters of that river, of Harriet Brookings in 1826, the pregnant wife of the poet Cerpy Patelle, also happened there; also, the vicinities of the river became the venue where athletes swam in the portion of the Vodnak Triathlon and the Marathon Swim events in August the same year."

"The 1851 Great Space with the lake as its focal point got held there, and the Silver Jubilee celebrations."

"All these things make the Neptersine and its immediate surroundings historically significant," Haile's friend elaborates.

"No wonder you choose to make it central to your story. My final question comes back to suicide."

"Did the suicide of that pregnant woman make you associate a crime with your story?" Haile continued asking.

"By no means. The plot in the named Meng writer's mentioned book became the main influence or reference," his friend replied.

"I can't wait to read the book when it comes out to the general public," Haile concluded.

The impact of the caffeine that Haile took that day with his writer friend lasted longer than expected. He didn't sleep the next two nights comfortably and had persistent headaches. When Haile set out for his routine jog on the second day, his head hurt him because of a migraine. He hoped that when he would start jogging, it would go away with the influx of more oxygenated blood in his brain.

Sadly for him, jogging that morning didn't work out as he expected. He had taken drastic measures towards coffee with caffeine. If it hadn't been for the help received from two paracetamol tablets taken at the end of the second day after the meeting, Haile's misery would've continued; nobody knows for how long.

In the same week, Haile reflects on the conversation he had days before with his acquaintance writer.

"I think I managed to get into the writers' secrets. Did I?" Haile doesn't know how good or bad his comprehension of the literary process comes out.

Haile hoped the questions he had asked his friend had helped him enter the mind of writers and understand what triggers and in a way influences their work.

Though sometimes Haile didn't always connect with those elements while reading, he could once in a while consider authors like friends, because he knew from then on who they look like as people.

At least about the one he had met, he felt that he had become closer to them because of the encounter.

In his spare time, while he commutes on the train or before sleeping, he reads.

"Presently, I have in hand the nth book of the writer Kiharu Mura. I only read the initial pages," Haile pauses and holds the book in his hands and reflects. He keeps such thoughts to himself.

Though he likes books, he doesn't consider himself a fluent but intentional reader, with favourite topics and authors. Nevertheless, he has with books the same relationship he has with food. He occasionally displays a similar attitude towards certain types of books.

He could eat whatever food, but in small quantities and at irregular hours. Food stands for him only as a means to an end. He considers that people eat, and should only do, to live. In front of the food, indifference characterises him.

"Menus are all about food, yesterday, today and tomorrow. I get stunned when I see the extreme excitement some people display while they look at their full plates."

Unfortunately for him, it would be morally indecent to show his astonishment.

"I have to restrain myself from exposing my views openly in front of them because I wouldn't want to appear unmannered. Instead, I have to look considerate." When one shows their feeling - if he said his real thought of the moment - it would make other people lose their appetite.

When he reads books, Haile has his approach.

"I start, spend ten to fifteen minutes reading, then stop. It takes weeks before I finish one book. At any given time, I read several books and stop in the middle of chapters, and that exercise almost goes on forever. I usually come back to any unfinished book randomly."

"But, occasionally, in one day, I can finish an excellent book. Understandably, only when I enjoy the story."

"Smart minds multi-task several activities all the time. They juggle several different things simultaneously, the same way women do," a friend had once told Haile.

The friend had, however, clarified. The latter wanted him to grasp what he meant when he made that statement.

"Only smarter brains among those with imaginative minds complete all their initiatives."

"I don't fall under that category unless others who look at me could appreciate me differently," he had strongly refuted.

He expanded instead on the subject of how he reads.

"I read books the same way thoughts evolve in my brain. It has always been like that. My mind doesn't like to process faster tasks that other people would complete in shorter periods. That portrays my ways about things."

Haile goes on and gives examples of his reading.

"AQ8a, a book from the same writer with its 'little people,' constituted a delightful read. Its title refers to George Orwell's Nineteen Eighty-Four classic. Nonetheless, the similarities stop there.

"I could be wrong," he highlights his opinion about the two books.

"I agree, both writings are somehow futuristic in their intentions," he concludes after deep consideration.

"I enjoy the pleasure and enlightenment that reading provides with little investment and no much sacrifice to get to the top of the mountain. That explains my attraction to that hobby. As well, it happens that I get addicted to certain authors. At the end of a period, I find myself with a collection of their work in my library."

Haile continues with more layers out about his reading. He doesn't want any misunderstanding. He even compares the benefit he gains when he combines his sport activity and writing.

"I would not want to confuse the reader; this doesn't concern the mentioned Kiharu Mura's books. It's about a moment or a spark from a particular experience; I lived it on a personal level, and it came out from my running."

The end line's importance had struck Haile on that Friday early in the first hours that he couldn't restrain himself and not talk about the related story.

"It seems like a eureka sensation when someone makes a significant discovery about something. Yes, after the end of the run, I clearly understood why I had performed the way I did. It felt extremely good, no doubt about that."

"A few years back, I took on a routine to exercise in the morning. It became like a second nature. In those years, I felt healthier and fitter than I had been before. Unfortunately, I suddenly stopped for a reason that I can't explain." With some effort of reflection, he remembers what had happened.

"Winter came, and I strongly blamed it when I thought that it brought an end to my regular jogging. With some hindsight, I found out that this could be more an excuse than a real justification. When the weather became warmer, I didn't have a strong motivation to get out early."

However, the commitment of a neighbour, a regular runner, helped to get back on track within two months.

"It didn't come easy to get fit again and possibly run and allow me to endure the physical plight which results from it," Haile assesses where he stood in his sport at the time.

"Undoubtedly, I enjoyed the whole experience. I wake up at set periods of the day, walk along the same streets back and forth at the same times, and am mesmerised by the beauty of the local parks each time I run."

"My days became even much more productive than before," he concludes his monologue.

Some questions could arise if the concerned shared their story. The interlocutors could, for example, wonder what all this has to do with the end-line suddenly, that each sportsperson has to be aware of and seriously consider.

Think of a person swimming in a wide river, helped in their movement by a massive and floating trunk of a tree.

While that moving object anchors them, that makes their progress effortless. If they imagine in their mind the end-line only, their activity runs more comfortably. That's what Haile noticed that day, a result of his observation. That doesn't mean somebody else wouldn't have had a similar point of view.

He had gone around the Neptersine in his recent running, but he had found that the whole exercise exhausted him to the point that, in his first attempt, he had to stop halfway through. The tiredness he had felt in his legs and their rhythm felt extreme. His entire body ached when he tried to exceed what it could physically bear. Once he had stopped, and after one or two minutes while he walked at a reasonable pace and relaxed, tried to breathe at his usual rhythm, only then could he be able to continue and finish his running!

"At the time, I managed to finish my round of the whole Neptersine. I realised then that I couldn't yet run that distance without extreme tiredness," Haile recollects that, once in a while, he runs with a target in focus.

While his body had felt that way, he promised himself to commit to his preparations before he gets back and does that entire distance.

"I will do regular and shorter runs and perform them for several days. This process will get me where I want to be. I want to go around the Neptersine and run without exhaustion, as I did in the past."

However, what took him through to the end seemed to be more than his preparedness. He had a clear vision instead in his mind of the end-line whenever he started on the distance to cover. He held onto that image of a swimmer helped by a moving trunk of a tree.

The voice

Once on their journey in the Universe, the protagonists each have a friend for guidance about directions. The paths some decide to embark on are the cause of their misfortunes. These negative performances weren't consequent to the guides' incompetence, but only to the inevitability of people accomplishing their ultimate fate.

The conviction and pressure from the instructions they received appear obligatory to the extent that, when the execution time comes, people don't have much room for manoeuvre, whatever decision they take; it only features in a pre-scribed script uniquely designed for them.

A majority of them ended up in their locality randomly. The experiences they lived before their move to the Notgni area, on the Wright's Lane estate in the Vodnak city, characterise a past that haunts them in the present and, in a way, defines them at the moment.

"When I look back, I can't explain how years passed quickly without getting me to fulfil the least any human being of my age should normally have achieved by this time," Haile considers that by his late thirties, he still lives single and on the verge of killing himself because of his overall unhappiness.

Although he appears walking on a crossroad during that period, his distorted state of mind has nothing to do with his career as a math teacher in a boys' college only. Perhaps his background tainted with a traumatic young life he experienced through the war is catching up with him. However, that had happened a long time before.

"You shouldn't take life so seriously. You would benefit tremendously from spending more time with people instead of living indoors and in books."

THE NEPTERSINE : LIMITLESS DEVOTION

"You could try to be more sociable," Haile's colleague teacher, Sarah Cavanaugh, advises him when she notices the depressive mood that he shows at work over several days.

A warm sun period comes to shine in his life when Amina knocks at his door one evening.

The attraction is spontaneous, though its comprehensive expression would take years and tortuous detours and dramas before it becomes reciprocal.

"Heaven hasn't forgotten me. I think it has for me a mission it wants me to finish. That's the only explanation I have for her being sent to me," while Haile reflects on the transformation that Amina brings into his life. Although for a certain period, he experiences it from a distance. He feels grateful. She rescued him.

In his vicinity, there lives Hussein as well. Haile doesn't particularly notice him until the latter becomes the victim of attempted murder. Before the incident, Hussein had been wasting his life instead of studying.

"I might not always be normal. I don't think nobody feels at the top all the time, but I can't help it. I would like to assume unless I might not be responsible for my person," in his moment of lucidity, Hussein reflects on his ways of living. Many of his women victims have complained about him, either face to face or through other channels. Surprisingly, - for the rare cases which passed the offence's police registration stage - he didn't even get convicted. He has enough wealth to get the best lawyers and buy the judiciary system.

"Though I am a bad woman, as an Almighty's creature, there is a minimum of respect that I deserve. I can't let anyone stomp on it as they like. To get them in their place falls into my responsibilities," Dae decides when she teams up with Florencia to give Hussein a memorable lesson for women's abusers.

Florencia doesn't get revenge on him as his victim, but only because she wants to protect her twin sister Amina, his girlfriend. When the operation takes place in Hussein's apartment, Haile happens to witness its occurrence without knowing. He would only realise the following morning.

Once the crime is executed, and later on, Haile suspects Amina. Despite the suspicion, he doesn't dare to ask her straightforwardly.

"I jog with her regularly. How will I put the question to her and find out about her possible involvement?" Haile, faced with the challenge of accusing a friend runner of a murderer, chooses to cover up and protect her unconditionally. Without addressing the issue with her, he instead asks her indirectly where she was during the criminal incident on Hussein.

"While I went out probably at a similar time, I saw someone who could be a possible suspect," Haile came to this conclusion only when he learnt about the approximative time of the attempted murder.

Covering up the crime that Haile planned could get him imprisoned. However, he ignores such a possibility.

"I must protect Amina at any cost," Haile has this persistent call on his conscience that he can't resist. He doesn't even consider that the woman he intends to sacrifice everything for is somebody else's girlfriend. When he starts planning the actions required for his intentions, Haile and Amina's aren't yet even confirmed friends. Nothing could tangibly attest to such a relationship.

The plan to kill Hussein in one go failed. He instead gets hospitalised for an indefinite number of years.

An extended period passes.

"I will unplug his respiratory machine to finish him off," Haile decides at the instigation of Amina to avoid Hussein recovering from his coma.

"Florencia will help you to operate inside the hospital. She will disguise herself as a nurse to easily access Hussein's private ward," Amina had suggested. Her twin sister had already been the leading planner of the initial attempt murder that had got Hussein unconscious. She was still ready to help and finish what she had started a few years back.

"Have you properly checked the hours for visits and rota for the hospital staff in his room?" Haile had enquired from Florencia during the preparatory stage.

"Visits are allowed only between 3:00 pm and 4:00 pm, and doctors and nurses pass in Hussein's ward at 11:00 am and 6:00 pm. Their stay in the ward lasts a maximum of ten minutes. For the last seven days, I did my observation, and nobody from the staff gets into his room at any other time," Florencia reports back on the timing and movements of the people around Hussein's body.

"Let's operate from 10:00 pm onwards. It will be neither early nor late in the night. With the disguise at hand and the rehearsal we did accordingly, the operation should succeed," Haile indicates the best time to enter the hospital.

Over almost twenty-five years, some characters involved in the story navigate back and forth on their journey. Do they proceed that way deliberately or unconsciously? Does such possibility constitute an advantage or privilege on the rest of the people inapt to accomplish a similar exercise? During such an extended period, characters who had remained alive had accumulated a whelm of knowledge.

Fifteen years after Hussein's incident, Haile looks back and assesses the relationship he had with Amina.

After the release, the boyfriend's death, their consecutive imprisonment for different matters, and their life together, though they ended up separating, they remained friends for the sake of the child they had had together.

On the other side, four years before the attempted murder of Hussein, though he wasn't in any way involved, Haile wouldn't have ever predicted that he would become a criminal without any moral conscience. As a college teacher, and for some unclear reasons, he was on the verge of suicide. Haile was as well preoccupied with his students' work, while Amina came into his life. He let her make it upside down but fell for her, and his love for her became transformative in good and bad ways.

Life happens and changes people.

CHAPTER TWO - Where They Were
SECTION 1. Home Of A Kind

Looking Back

Twenty years have passed since the occurrence of the related events. Despite such a length of time, specific memories remain sticky.

"When I look back, I can see now that period in which I grew up as if it happened today," Haile pauses to reflect and remember.

However, some critical details appear to have long faded away or been missed: the stories he and his friend talked about, the clothes she used to wear, how she walked around and what made him feel special in front of her and vice versa, or that one or more traits of personality that defined her uniquely. What disappeared helps him remember what he misses.

"I can mentally visualise the picture. The scars or marks on the legs, and other trademarks specific to her, seem still vivid in my mind," he contemplates as if he watches a movie about a past he knows well."I have to take them with me into the grave. Besides, as the representative signs seem deeply entrenched in my soul, if I try to think of her without them, that would almost destroy her identity," Haile points out for his focused contemplation.

"Beyond her person, all that past that encompasses a multitude of aspects helped to shape who I came to evolve into today in my whole complexity of a particular human being," he concludes.

If given the time and necessary space, he could recall her exact face. She had thin cheeks, a boyish chin, the same height as him, and both had been classmates with similar ages, only separated by three months of difference.

At sixteen, she looked like an adorable woman to be with if Haile at the time could've decided clearly about their future together.

He remembers the communion celebration they had that their respective parents had jointly organised when both were aged ten. They had enjoyed the atmosphere at a restaurant along the beach. They ate delicious fries in abundance, to the point that they couldn't finish all the food served for the event!

"She thinks highly of me. I have good grades all the time," Haile reflects about her and the way she teased him about his school performance in those early years of their lives.

"Was I unquestionably intelligent?" Haile couldn't get the right answer to the question. He looked back and realised with time that what he displayed and that his friend took for cleverness, he could only claim that he stood as the best among idiots.

The beautiful lake close to his hometown laid its waters as far as his eyes couldn't see its farthest side on the horizon. Its long beaches with smooth sand, where to walk on them barefoot seemed most recommendable, or palm trees stood like flowers in a multitude of aligned big vases, were unique in Wethi. Even so, Haile doesn't remember both discussing these things. Alternatively, he must have always selfishly thought about himself first. Then after that, as long as she walked beside him, the surroundings would become meaningless.

The lake had its dark side, but this depended on who talked about it. Fishers found acceptable what others like Haile's family could consider as tainted with a harmful predicament. From time to time, people would remove almost every other six months, one or two bodies with their blinded sights from the water and or end up on its shores. The Haile's lived within less than a hundred meters from the lake. Its water also served in the household's chores, such as washing clothes.

"Which thoughts could've gone through the minds of the families of these victims when they couldn't see their bodies after they disappeared?" Haile tries to understand and puts himself in their shoes.

People who discovered the bodies speculated on the dead's identity and the same went on for those whose family members had disappeared while they wondered if their people had drowned in the lake. His parents believed that the concerned bodies could be victims of the lake's evil spirits, although no particular cause could be crystal clear about their death.

No evidence demonstrated that the found bodies had been in the lake's water before or after death. Also, for that reason, his parents had prohibited him from swimming in that lake. As he grew up, he couldn't swim as a consequence. Therefore, each time he went close to a river, a lake, an ocean, or any other places where other people could've been able to swim if they had fallen in by accident, Haile wondered what would've been his fate if not drowning.

To think about this particular past took Haile back to some of the stories people in his village discussed when they talked about twins. He had heard about the miserable destiny of such children. In the past, not too far back, a curse attached to them requested from the elders' tradition to be killed at birth. If he had been born at an earlier time, he would not have seen the day since he too had a twin. From what he knew from the elders, children born out of wedlock, or those whose top teeth grew in before their bottom ones, or even those who came into the universe as twins, all these innocent souls got merely killed under the village ancient belief that deemed them cursed.

"The thought of having one's teeth come out at the wrong time or in the wrong place in a toddler's mouth, and get killed for that occurrence, seems horrible," Haile thinks of the futility of some traditions.

He had a difficult question for which he couldn't see any answer from the elders' perspective. He couldn't understand on which basis they made their decision about which child needed to die. The parameters used could only be irrational and unsubstantiated. The infanticide that resulted from the elders' traditional considerations and widely practised meant that not to comply didn't constitute an option.

The extreme pressure on families indicated that disobedient villagers could get killed because of it. In the elders of the village's views, their community's overall good depended on everybody's compliance.

***

Around midday, Haile looks at his watch. He closes his eyes slightly at that moment. He intends to enjoy the warmth of the sun that shines from a sky painted blue as far as where his eyes could see. The skin of his face radiates from the reflection of the sun. In his ancestors' country, the sun stood vertically in the sky at that time of the day. He regrets that he can't enjoy it the same way as people in his country of origin - geography matters.

Since he has been far away from home, the sun has never stood vertically above him because he lives in a different part of the universe. The sun that changed its position comparatively has been among the many things that he has lost. He left his roots while very young, and because of that, many of his references got abandoned forever. As a consequence, even the sun appears different. That difference doesn't concern only the appearance. Even the warmth it projects feels dull or insincere.

Nonetheless, he senses a cool comfort like the one that originates from a furnace lit in the main room of a Victorian house from an aristocratic family.

The excellent care it almost injects into Haile skin could be comparable to some elixir. It shows signs that cure the inadequacies he faces continuously.

Two days before, a friend had called him and wanted to visit him. They agreed to meet next Saturday. The friend travelled from a different city, and once in Haile's hometown, he didn't find difficulty getting to his place. Once close by, the friend called Haile, and they met outside his house. Haile stayed with his sister at the time; a month had approximately passed since she arrived. During her stay, she helped out with the household chores.

After the greetings, he and his friend go immediately to a local café situated at the local cemetery's entrance. Haile has agreed with his sister to cook for the guest; he left her some money to buy whatever would be needed and suitable to have a good meal. While Haile and his friend stay out and come home when the table is supposedly ready, her sister cleans the house, goes and buys groceries, and starts cooking. When they arrive home, a delicious meal awaits them.

They all come and sit around the table. The guest digs in and enjoys the food Haile's sister has prepared. He praises her for her culinary skills. He engages enthusiastically with the food on his full plate.

"You've well grown up into a beautiful and skilful woman," he says about Haile's sister. He looks back and realises that twenty years have passed since he last saw her.

"What do you currently do for a living?" he then asks her.

"I work as a pharmaceutical consultant. You can also call it a private contractor," she replies.

"Wow! That's somehow impressive," the guest responds, after some sighing.

"And what does that entail?" He asks additionally.

"I work with big corporations which want to have their health care units for their staff. I help them devise organisational structures that correspond to their specific needs in terms of health care requirements, minimum and practical capacity, necessary medical skills, and operational budgets for their planning.

The conversation goes on and discusses the needed courage to work independently from the traditional pathway, which entails becoming an employee of an institution.

Haile's sister seems to be an intelligent woman. She graduated from university but then dropped out from a specialisation in a top academy. She left apparently because she considered the atmosphere toxic. She decided to change her career's goals because of that experience.

At the time, she came to stay with her brother while she still planned and worked on her next move.

Unlike Haile's sister, Amina has no skills in the culinary field at all. Though a woman on the verge of having her own family, she had a solid excuse for anyone who would nag her for her acute incompetence in cooking.

"I don't want to learn how to cook because I would become excellent at it. In case this happens, I would imperatively try to prepare the menus my mother used to have at home. Consequently, the way I cook would always remind me of her and make me cry. I don't want to find myself with tears every day," she argues.

"I wouldn't want to remember all the time and forget the pleasures of the present moment," she adds.

***

Haile grew up with his aunt's family. It sheltered and nourished him after the death of his parents. A single mother with one boy, Haile's cousin, she received him young in her household.

This cousin, three years older than him, would become his best friend in his teenage years. Though he stayed with this family, he had a younger sister cared for by other relatives separately. None of the two carers could afford to have the two siblings together at once.

"Would you want to wander around or join gangs after school?" the aunt would yell at Haile and his cousin after she packs their lunch boxes in their backpacks.

She would then send them off or announce that last directive of the day while they all stood on the porch of her house's main entrance.

His aunt raised them both as her children. Though he doesn't doubt his origins - nobody had ever told him - Haile would only learn about them incidentally from her aunt's guests. From time to time, they would share stories from back home. "I heard that the Tekele family has also arrived here in the QK. Their mother and two of their children died in the war," he would overhear the guests saying.

Haile knew he came from Wethi while ignoring all the details of him leaving and ending up living in a different country. He wondered about these questions while around his tenth anniversary.

After an uneventful period of his teenage years, he enters university and completes his studies successfully, with the highest academic qualification one can dream of at his faculty. He stands as a highly learned young adult, though his personality and lifestyle come and tell a different story.

After graduating, Haile opts to teach in a college for boys, not because he cannot lecture at the university level. Still, only that's where he finds himself much more comfortable and thinks he can make the most significant impact.

He goes out with friends occasionally for a beer or usual socialising, although many people know him generally as an indoor individual who lives a reclusive life like a monk.

"We shouldn't miss the events of the last Wednesday of the month at the H&I," he tells his group of friends with whom they have become enthusiastic regulars of the monthly program organised at that venue.

He has himself cut off from the permanent tv programs that deceive more than they educate. These are, in a certain way, his views about mainstream television. He considers them intrusive and manipulative.

His material frugality and purchasing habits make him always look for products with discount deals whenever he goes into his local supermarket. Since the start of his career, he regularly saves a significant fraction of his salary. He invests at the same time a considerable amount in selected and stable stock market shares.

With his bank account savings, he can quickly get a mortgage, even though he doesn't want to enrich the bankers.

"I can buy myself a nice house with a loan. The only idea that I would tremendously enrich the banker by doing so frustrates me," Haile reflects on the issue of real estate.

As a consequence, he has chosen to live in a low standard apartment. He pays his landlord only three-fifths of what his mortgage lender would've received as a monthly repayment.

"I will never borrow for a house at any given time in my life," Haile promises to himself.

His hobbies include writing, design and gardening. For years, he has contributed articles to online and printed magazines and participated in discussion panels on climate change issues worldwide.

He discovered his design skills accidentally but managed to sell part of his creations.

"Presently, I enjoy what I do in my spare time as a hobby. But, if I had to make it earn me money, I would have to approach it professionally. Any life pursuit has its requirements," Haile utters for any listening ears. Many who would view his work tended to encourage him to pursue it steadily.

He has to make some decisions about his time management for the next months and years. If not, his hobby can negatively impact his career as a teacher, a job that pays his bills. He could, however, have an excuse to restrain himself from his extra activities. He has come to his hobbies randomly, without initial thorough thoughts and grounded plans, dissuading him from going persistently in such direction.

With writing, as time elapses, he, however, intends to become more serious about it and improve his craft.

"I see the literary expression as the best medium that can make me feel fulfilled," Haile convinces himself at the time he decides to stick with that path for the remaining part of his life.

"I would like to share with the world the tempo of my heart and the views and creations of my mind," he clarifies his pursuit.

"It doesn't matter how what I will talk about will be received. I want to experience total free expression fully," Haile finally adds while showing his strong-mindedness to the extent of stubbornness.

It's not only his conviction, but he can also express himself in unusual ways and often angrily in certain situations.

Even though he was already in his early thirties, he had never taken part in any personal fight. Although he remembers once that he punched someone with his fist.

His victim cycled on the pavement and lost his balance. He came straight to where Haile chatted with a friend. The cyclist struggled to control his bike and found himself too late to avoid the collision. He fell off his bike. Haile got slightly hit but didn't go down. When he saw the cyclist while he tried to stand up, he went for him and punched him hard on his face.

"How could you cycle on pavements? See this accident you've caused. Will you compensate us or pay for our medical treatment?" he shouted at the cyclist.

After the punch that left his fist hurting, Haile got surprised by his impulse. It stood out of his habits. Had he not been involved, he could've won the best long-life award for a well-behaved bachelor.

Like that punch on the cyclist that occurred out of nowhere, Haile's life would reserve him other surprises without any premeditation. There would be reasons to rightly think that human beings appear as complex creatures, with unpredictable premonitions when that happens.

When Amina moved into Haile's neighbourhood, no clue could at the time predict their shared future or its nature, particularly concerning the attempted murder of her boyfriend, Hussein. The incident demonstrated a constant feature of life's unpredictability. The fact that circumstances could influence the emergence in people of their inner characteristics, good or bad, they didn't know about their existence until those particular conditions became tangible to them, and manifested themselves, appeared as a scary reality check. In other terms, given the right occurrences, anyone could become either good or bad in their way. The only difference between them could come from the unique makeup of their personalities.

From then on, Haile would display a trait of himself that had remained hidden without him knowing.

Amina and Haile would continue to travel on their respective journeys in the universe. Nothing predicted that they would ever cross each other's path. If they did, one wonders what someone with some interest in their lives could've for them at the time of their crossing. A relative who might've known their previous interactions could wonder if their experience so far they would share with the interesting side would be about enjoyment, exhaustion or pain.

Once Back Home

To the country where his family has its Qarfian roots, a place he could hardly remember, even often called it home in his dreams, though lived away in exile from his early childhood until now, with references marked by stories he had heard only told by distant relatives, an image of his past but also his present and accessorily his future, Haile returns.

His ancestors' village, which had expanded into a small city of one hundred thousand people, had tremendously changed.

"To some extent, the place bears an unrecognisable stamp of changing times. There had visibly been many regeneration programmes," Haile sets out and expresses to himself the first impressions of the place of his parents for several generations.

The area has public spaces designed for the only purpose to make anyone with spare time enjoy some comfort while outside. In the central park, close to its entrance, a six meters tall statue of Kwame Nkrumah stands. An eighth-floor structure, visible from any part of the city, houses the town hall municipality and its community social services.

Haile enters the city town hall building. The mural artefacts, which represent the local culture, immediately mesmerise him. He wants information about places of interest to visit.

"What can I do for you, Sir?" asks the young woman at the main hall's information desk.

"I would like a map of the city with sites that tourists would be interested in?" he asks the information officer.

"Here you go. This map shows where to find historical places, monuments, museums and parks," the staff indicates to Haile while she hands him a map.

As his tour guide, one remote cousin explains to Haile the significant changes to the city. He had personally witnessed some of them in his early years.

While tangible changes took place within the last two decades, at the same time, the small city's uniqueness remained almost untouched. Anyone aware of its past could immediately perceive its unchanged spirit. The typical "Onkoni" means: let's prosper together, that local people use to greet each individual when they happen to have eye contact with someone outside. In the flamboyant buildings here and there, signs of prosperity were evident.

"I miss these human greetings that have almost a unique, profound sense to our people," Haile explains to his guide - a cousin who shows him around.

The invitation to share food with others anywhere coincided with the way people welcomed those who had been away for some time. Besides, every adult in the community displayed general care towards children outside their homes. Such behaviour made people say that children belonged to the village but not to their biological parents.

"Why did you shout at that kid? Do you know him," he asked his guide, who had scolded the child who had tried to cross the street with a high risk of an accident because he ignored the traffic of cars in that place.

"No, I don't. Didn't you notice that the child could cause an accident because of how he ignores his surroundings?" explains and asks the guide.

Children convey the impression they belong to the entire community rather than to their parents; this comes to light that any adult can scold any child anywhere in the community, particularly when they know the parents, every time they see them misbehaving.

Haile notices that, through the cousin and child's encounter, some of the place's particular traits seem to resist the erosion of time.

Haile's treasured neighbourhood has as well safe-guarded its unique stamp of time. The barbershop situated on the street's left side's curve hadn't changed much on the downhill path. It needed some refurbishment. The old Mekele, its owner, died. This time his son Teodros runs the small business.

A modern restaurant that serves traditional food produced locally has replaced the local pastry. Like its predecessor, it also offers loaves of bread and cakes with similar flavours.

Haile heard stories of young pupils who, after school, run then queue in front of the shop to spend weekly family allowances on their favoured items before they head home, expected by anxious mothers, thinking about the leftovers their mums have finished to prepare. They could've before the last meal of the day, after they have completed their homework, foresee themselves around the dinner table with the whole family, the young pupils in front of the shop waited for their turn impatiently, and exchange a multitude of stories of their day at school and probably their extended lives away from it.

In his hometown, the relatives he grew up with look like middle-class people. They host him. The husband works as a public servant and the wife as a nurse. Their house has all the required minimum standards of a decent family space, with an indoor toilet. Two decades before, such architectural features were lacking in many homes for ordinary people.

He had come back to his roots; this had been an existential imperative for him. It took him time to realise how important this experience would become for his future. At times he had found himself without the competence to know where he stood in the universe.

His conviction consisted in his realisation that it would be hard for him to move forward confidently in life without his two feet firmly anchored on a rich cultural pedestal. Consequently, when he went back where he came from, he tried to fulfil that profound need in him, almost critical to a degree.

While he grew up in exile, and for many years, stories told Haile how his people had been tracked down and killed in circumstances worse than those of hunted animals. Survivors had fled from the North then moved to the West part of their country. They moved into the impenetrable Fakondi forest, where they had initially found refuge.

Others had to hide in marshy valleys after they climbed and went down tens of hills. Crocodiles or snakes also habited their found shelter. That meant danger for them. Sporadically, rebels who pursued them would intercept radio messages among humanitarian NGOs which operated in the area. In that way, they could locate where refugees hid in the Logambu forests. Through such fraudulent use of information between good Samaritans about the needy refugees, the Liberation Front and its allies could quickly locate where they were. Once found, they would be then atrociously massacred indistinctly. Older women and children in the hundred thousand featured among the victims.

The pursuit of a significant fraction of the survivors on distances of more than four thousand kilometres lasted for some years. They had travelled across several countries. Their pursuers looked like they had a license to kill their victims wherever they would go on the planet.

After such tragic episodes, survivors deserved an award similar to those athletes receive after a challenging competition. For his people to survive had to confront an existential challenger: death.

Until then, they had won it over, but their challenger waited for them in their nearest future at the turn of a bush and at a time when they wouldn't be able to escape.

Their status as survivors could hardly be recognised, despite their perilous trajectory for many years. Such recognition would have been an acknowledgement too far for their detractors. Considering them as normal human beings with rights and entitlements would've led to the request for compensation if, in case enough evidence existed of broad complicity or conspiracy in the massacres of Haile's people.

Despite what the survivors had accomplished, however extraordinary it might look, they were not after trophies or rewards. Treated as pariahs, people also perceived them as a stain of the humankind of their time.

Though they had achieved tremendously in survival skills, their tormentors considered that they shouldn't have existed in the first place.

"I remember that I did forty-five miles within seventeen hours while young, aged only between seven and ten years," Haile would sometimes boast to his schoolmates.

He would talk about such a record each time peers around him showed off about an incredible accomplishment they had achieved in their young lives. The distance the survivors had covered all those years constituted an outcome they could've been proud of in normal circumstances. The hunt of his people had taken several years before it finally ended. It left behind a trail of memories that would haunt survivors for many generations to come. Shotguns from the rebels, machetes, and exhaustion had caused the death of the majority of them. They drowned in rivers, starved or ate poisonous herbs.

Sometimes they were eaten by crocodiles or picked by venomous snakes. Some of these stories talked about rebels, for example, who cooked and fed portions of people's bodies to their victims before they killed them.

Another side to the story made yesterday's accomplices, unfortunate victims of the rebels' leader's criminal ingenuity. In his operations to cleanse complete areas of previous populations, he killed all those he had sent to hunt and exterminate Haile's people. After he would've killed them, he would then blame the massacres on his victims or staged their death as accidental. He committed those atrocities directly using his men or indirectly through paid militias.

Seven years had passed since the movement to flee had started. Out of ten people they had left their homes with, only two remained at the end of the journey. Further to the lack of time, the bodies of the dead weren't buried. The rebels who hunted the survivors wouldn't have allowed it.

The survivors had lost their sense or one of humanity in general. To bury the dead appeared as a luxury, not affordable, considering the circumstances. Or to survive and see the next day featured at the top of life priorities every single day. Such misfortune happened because they persistently moved, mainly when they heard the shotguns' crepitations in the distance. They were lucky on occasions when rebels' attacks didn't occur at night.

Inevitably, there would be consequences. Not only concerning people's health but also their spirituality. The spirits would haunt the survivors for long; their anger from the afterlife would result from their bodies' mistreatment. The bodies that wild animals tore apart then ate, and the related overall disrespect, added to that, the lack of decency from those still alive would necessarily lead to some sort of spiritual vengeance.

The way they lived their lives while still living in their respective bodies wouldn't impact their vendetta's cruelty. It would not have any connection with their lived experience. They probably felt miserable because they were left unceremoniously to mother nature without appropriate burial.

They expected minimum decency for their burial like other human beings they once were before they got dehumanised. They had come into the world through warm homes, cared for by people around them, not always in harmonious contexts, but still in families, at least for most of them.

The bulk of the dead couldn't afford proper burials. In places where survivors prepared graves, they were mass graves, without identifying who the dead was for posterity. In such a context, and later years, it would be impossible to trace where the buried victims' remains were. The link between the departed and the living would be therefore lost forever. Survivors had become like diseases nobody wanted to contemplate. Rebels had told locals that whoever would've given Haile's people shelter, would also die. Consequently, they had to be continuously on the move.

Nobody wanted to be associated with these people. Ten dollars per head was the bounty offered to anyone among the locals who would show where they hid. The search for Haile's people became a profitable business. Bands of bounty hunters emerged. They even used door-to-door searches for their hunt. They worked with local authorities to identify hideouts and also threatened anyone local and their entire family if they appeared reluctant to cooperate or visibly colluded with the fugitives.

The ten dollars constituted a lot of money for the villagers in the places Haile's people had been on the move on foot for months. A relative of Haile among them had managed to stand up to the hunters.

At sunset, the hunters stopped their operation for that day, four houses away from where she stayed. Around four in the afternoon, she had seen a mother and her child forced into a vehicle. Both didn't want to go back.

As she had decided not to hide, Haile's relative woke up that early morning and prepared breakfast for her host's whole household. By nine, she grabbed by both hands her sort of colourful sari cloth and tightened it solidly around her waist. While she waited for the hunters to arrive, she felt in her stomach a fear of being forcibly deported. She wouldn't run away this time, no matter what would happen. Instead, she firmly opted to confront them.

She went to sit on a trunk of wood situated almost in the small house's front yard where she stayed. Once informed that they had already arrived in the village, active for the last two to three days before, she had all day long been rehearsing, sometimes whispering, while she fetched water or cooking, what she would tell them. Her mind mentally played all the would-be performances. They arrived in a Toyota pickup with four seats. The team leader came and stood within three meters of distance from a local and older woman, curious about what was happening.

He made his request loud and clear.

"We look for the refugees who came here, and we want to repatriate them to their country of origin, of which safety has tremendously improved as we speak." He looked at Eden Mariam while he made the statement about his mission in the area.

"Please pack your things and get gently in the vehicle." He hadn't paid attention to the two other local women who sat next to the frail woman. They had all noticed the leader's car. To the surprise of the leader of the team, she replied that she wouldn't go anywhere.

"This country made me a resident citizen. It entitles me to live wherever I want. If you want to check out when I settled here, you can ask the Agency of Naturalisation and Home Affairs in the capital. My parents named me Eden Mariam," she explained and used all her energy she could gather to sound convincing. She had been sick for the past two weeks and had started recovering only a few days before the hunters came. They had felt not entirely convinced but left without much room for manoeuvre.

"OK, if what you say comes out as true, we will monitor you. In the meantime, you can't move out of this village. We will contact the capital and verify your allegations. Within three days maximum, we will be back," the apparent leader of the group stressed to her. Hunters got rewarded based on the number of refugees they brought to the local office of their organisation. Aware of all that, the leader decided against that consideration and let Eden in peace for the time being.

He called his subordinates. They had observed his interactions with that frail woman silently. Fate had decided to lend her more days to live as she wished. Eden, happy to remain calm in the incident but internally almost dying, trembled slightly out of fear. She had witnessed the mistreatment of her people once found, without any mercy, despite their conditions.

Eden had been sexually assaulted once during that tragic journey. The rapist had grabbed her hand and removed her from her group.

At the point of the gun, he rushed her away from the rest of his rebel colleagues. He beats her up with brutal kicks then locks her behind the door of a private house in the immediate vicinity. In the deserted house, the rape took place.

The house that had once been the residence of a local chief of the police, with torn and dirty curtains, broken windows splattered across rooms as if the site had been the target of a thousand stone-throwers. In this place, authorities in charge of people's safety had gathered and celebrated in the past not too far back.

Without any more of the youth's glamour or beauty, a frail woman became a victim of the most abject act that shames and humiliates any woman at the core of their soul and body. She had decided to conceal the sexual invasion and humiliation stoically. Her rapist had left her physically and mentally in agony. More than an hour after the incident, she crawled back from where the rapist had taken and left her. She had obeyed and silently nodded only with her head at the rapist's instructions.

Since the rebels had attacked her village of origin, Eden had forcibly left her country to run away from them. She had already passed through two countries and still didn't know where she would settle. While young, Eden had dreamed of going to different places and visiting destinations only learnt from geography lessons. Although her dream became a reality, she had never imagined that she would travel as she did - if her adventures could be called that way - under these dire circumstances.

Along the journey, she had witnessed massive rapes by the rebels where the victims got coldly killed after the traumatic act. In her case, she prayed her rapist would let her live after he had finished with her. Without much energy at the time, she had fainted in the last moment of the rapist performance. When she regained consciousness, she noticed that what remained as cloth on her felt wet and had blood on it.

She had lost a lot of blood that flew from the scars that the rebel's forced penetration into her vagina had inflicted.

It took several weeks and the village's traditional healers' real ingenuity to cure the physical cicatrixes. After recovering, she promised herself that she had to live and survive at all costs to tell her story.

In each settlement, the survivors had managed to connect with locals; they couldn't say their goodbyes. When someone can or has the time to say goodbye from their heart, they can also promise to see their interlocutor another time.

On many occasions, their unprepared departure occurred chaotically at night times. People ran without any knowledge of which direction to escape instant death from the rebels' shotguns.

All those years, there had been few periods of relative peace. In those peaceful times, the survivors could farm and harvest items with a few months' lifespans. These included: beans, peas, potatoes and sweet potatoes. Such periods occurred because their attackers directed their efforts elsewhere before their next rampage. Such a situation appeared precarious, unpredictable to the point that only those not afraid of risks could plan beyond the next day.

In the beginning, Haile didn't grasp the motivation behind his people's plight. He couldn't understand the level of animosity they had encountered in the hands of the rebels.

With time, that pain that resisted its erasure from the memories of the bearers - that each survivor would live differently -, depended on their particular personalities and circumstances; passed from one generation to the next one, it would mark forever, the psyche of an entire community for a very long period.

Even so, as the story went on, Haile learned historical facts that helped him understand.

His forefathers had succeeded to overthrow the rule of an aristocratic elite that had oppressed them for several centuries.

Descendants from that group of oppressors had waited decades to organise, particularly seek foreign alliances and plot to come back.

These alliances, attracted by the determination and criminal zeal these rebels had to achieve total control of the area, backed them because they had shared interests in any new regional power capable of guaranteeing their members' free access to the riches only available in the region. Strategic minerals and other precious products from the soil mattered to these foreigners. The rebels wanted to own all the wealth and the means of its creation in the region. Besides, they aimed equally at sensibly reducing the number of Haile's people conceivably.

Statistically, they constituted by far the majority and always lived as peaceful people who minded their own business for the sake of their families. They differed from the warmonger rebels. While these rebels strategized for their return, they had, all that time, nourished their revenge spirit in such extreme levels that they wanted to exterminate everyone affiliated in any way with the population which had once taken away from them their omnipresent power in the land. They had, for several centuries, exercised such control over Haile's people.

Memories of atrocities the victims had witnessed populated their sleep. These sinister experiences gave them nightmares. They marked the mood of their days negatively. They could hardly reason without that past at the back of their mind. They almost tried to be at peace while they suffered from some persistent pain. However, though the whole experience had radically transformed their look on the world around them, they became more aware of others' plight and, consequently, more empathic.

Haile had come from exile to find out about a part of his past.

Through memories of people around him, told by remote relatives or close friends of the family, he learned a tremendous amount of what he had missed in his life.

Until then, Haile couldn't have yet managed to picture out the context of his origins. His feet this time stood on a pedestal somehow known, not necessarily stable, but for which he could understand the components and essence. He could now grasp the elements he required to move forward confidently in the future.

SECTION 2 - About Thinking

Verba Volant, Scripta Manent

Across the world, languages have proverbs and expressions, hardly understood by foreigners, and for some, even locals find it difficult to grasp their full meaning.

"The statement I would like here to highlight and for which I paraphrase as well the essence goes like this: each incident, be it spiritual or physical, which occurs in somebody's life, or the universe in whichever format it manifests itself, has a meaning, or a purpose. Nevertheless, this would not stand true that everyone, whether not, involved in any occurrence can go along the lines of such a statement," Haile wonders; he reflects on the events that unfold in his life at the time.

"Sometimes, people get broadly distracted to find the time to understand what happens around them or to them. As an excuse for their laziness to think harder about those events, they either become indifferent because they fear to get involved and eventually consumed by their implication or find the justification of such happenings in mysterious causes but don't want to investigate or in the face of which they can only display their indifferent incompetence. On other occasions, they don't need to understand because their situation feels or looks too complicated to grasp. When such circumstances occur, people pretend to understand, in order not to be called stupid," he elaborates for himself while he pursues his internal monologue.

While reflecting on people's issues, Haile took his time to observe the performance and or involvement of fate in their manifestation. He behaved like an advocate of pre-determinism.

"I strongly believe that a significant fraction of people's actions don't depend on their will, but take place while controlled by a nameless order for which humankind has not yet understood its wholeness," he puts definite boundaries to the framework of people's undertakings.

"I consider that when events unfold in somebody's life, most if not all, seem prescribed on two levels. The first one consists of where they involve their personal human experience as a reference, which helps them to understand or interpret what is going on, another one refers to where reality collides with illusion, where they confuse onlookers about what is happening," Haile tries to think for himself and contemplate life around him and through others as an interested observer.

"I have heard stories like the one between Amina that I know and a certain Samuel Kato, at the time of their years at the university," Haile recalls and speaks out, but not loud enough to avoid the involvement of his inseparable but invisible friend.

"Those who, for example, one evening, saw them drink together before the two had their sexual encounter must have thought of them as a couple of lovers; obviously, they wrongly interpreted the situation they had in front of them at the time," he pursues.

"If, as onlookers, they had taken part in the conversation of the mistaken couple they scrutinised, and asked the type of relationship these two had, in their replies, the concerned could've clarified what might've been unclear even in their minds, and enabled a different dynamic to take shape between them," he argued. At the same time, he intermittently assumed his friend's thoughts because he hadn't uttered them out.

The second level consisted of the reality of their actions as opposed to the illusion it projected. Samuel and Amina, as two individuals, male and female, minded their own business in a public place; they didn't fit the concept of a couple in the usual interpretation of the term. However, they gave the impression of intense togetherness. Perception can create its reality.

"I perceive that events that occur continuously give the appearance they happen in a vacuum, particularly for the involved actors, even when they seem, whether or not, to have any connections between them," Haile pointed out.

This time he referred to the same story related to the false couple of Samuel and Amina.

It didn't occur to the narrated story's characters to imagine what it would've been like if the stage would've been changed and made to look more dynamic; if the spectators, for example, had enacted the scene and thus taken part, in front of their eyes. These external entities could've made the whole spectacle more enjoyable or even probably changed its course because of their involvement in it.

Haile regrets that the audience doesn't always get informed about the real act's settings most of the time. They get left out in the dark. The responsibility to get them involved or not doesn't show clearly. They could either decide by themselves or let themselves get pushed to participate. Though the decision will come from their will, their active participation would undoubtedly bring up a better outcome for themselves and others.

In his case, if he had to and been on the scene, Haile could've eventually prepared himself thoroughly to give his best possible performance. In front of the reality of what would happen, he found himself in action but unprepared when he decided to get involved.

He stood accidentally at the right place and at the right time, like what happens to most people in their worldly experience.

Understandably, his pedestal's righteousness and the timing became relevant for the occurrence or fate's manifestation, but not necessarily for the actor involved. Nevertheless, the unpreparedness deprives the audience of the best performances that could ever be. In these instances, the unpredictability of fate becomes manifest. Haile couldn't imagine how grandiose peoples' acts on the scene of the Universe could be if they could all perform fully prepared. For several years, a friend of Haile had contested that idea that considers fate as a kind of normality or accepts the fact that behind every occurrence, a clear or even sometimes incomprehensible justification manifested, however good or bad it appeared itself.

The friend used to refer to an accident a cyclist had caused and in which he got involved. He reflected on some felt joy and pain about it as if he understood whatever went on with that incident. He always brought up that accident when he discussed the concept of fate.

Haile, while he replied to the point raised, argued that, to some extent, there could be more to what he had experienced through that accident and that the friend mentioned.

"Maybe the experience differs totally from joy or pain. Joy couldn't certainly be part of the picture, whatever the angle one looked at it. Nevertheless, sometimes we think we understand what happened to us. Still, in most cases, the whole picture always feels missing. In the same line of thoughts, what do people get from the experience of tragic events?"

"When we survive sad events, where others - sometimes in big numbers - perish, we can only consider ourselves the lucky ones. What we make of our lives afterwards, we stand solely accountable."

72

"Yes, one could be positive after such occur-rences. Such an attitude can be one option, even much recommendable for the sake of ourselves. Imagine if one belongs among the small minority of the survivors of a tragic human experience."

"How they live the rest of their life must be dif-ferent from, for example, another not so deadly incident such as a road accident or an illness. The scale or the context of the occurrence also matters. People survive all the time. Their survival state constitutes the reality worth taking into account. Consequently, there shouldn't normally be any need to call for special characterisation. They all live their lives as survivors of something, as long as not everyone makes it." "Either they admit it or deny that fact and believe that they became immune, what seems important here consists in that they give to their lives a meaningful purpose while they survive."

As the night fades away in the first hours of the day, Haile decides to complain less about fate. He would instead adjust himself to its nature. At least the way he understands it. Ready to compromise, he would be only preoccupied, from then on, by his selfish interests, like everybody else, even those who pretend to be altruistic. At that moment, as another day drew its shapes and colours in the sky, his feelings evolved relaxed towards everything.

In those days, for an unclear reason, he couldn't recall, Haile had stopped from exercising. He became unhealthy as days passed. His body took the toll of those bad habits. His lack of sexual activity featured as well among his areas of concern. He couldn't remember when he had last had intercourse with a woman, let alone a firm and steady erection in the morning.

He felt that he had become impotent at one stage and didn't know what he needed to do. The attentive contemplation of a beautiful woman left him indifferent, without any expected response from his libido. The relative worry in his mind would fade away with time and let him be.

***

Haile has known, for a while, the majority of people in his immediate neighbourhood. On occasions, he would reflect on their makeup.

"People around here generally translate a reflection of the communities they come from in one way or another; they might not be a reliable representation of those entities since their presence in this area results from a construct of randomness. They ended up in this part of the world without any prior consultation between them," he states in his mind while he takes his tea before he goes out for work.

"However, most importantly, I must concede that each individual also carries their uniqueness in their own right. As one would agree, people reflect their inner humanity, willingly or not, no matter what."

"Even when they try to change or pretend to do so, the path they embark on to achieve such personal transformation always paints part of that oneness that defines them. I, like everybody else, feature incidentally among this group of people who stand on the stage here in the present moment," Haile reflects.

For the last seven years, he has lived on the fourth floor of his building. On that morning, he leaves his apartment in a hurry while he wears his grey scarf, loosely rolled around his neck. In the right hand, while he goes to the nearest train station, he holds his black briefcase. Inside, it has the students' papers he took home for assessment the day before.

Outside, the weather has gotten chillier as the weeks passed. Autumn started to transform the landscape with thousands of leaves that fall from trees and or change into unique colours specific to that season. He didn't meet anyone as he headed down to the lift that led outside his building. The elevator got him into the supermarket on the ground floor.

He needed some snacks and drinks for his lunch. Usually, he didn't often take breakfast; a cup of tea at that time of the day sufficed. As he approaches the till the cashier's woman looks at him discreetly; she has eye contact with him. She slightly smiles at his attention and shows in a way some politeness or vague interest in him, but her attitude doesn't freshen up his mind, in case he would have known her previously.

"She somehow fancies me," he thinks, though they've never spoken to one another. She continued to smile and appeared to invite him for a chat. However, he doesn't fall for it, as he doesn't have the time because of his busy day ahead.

Once out of the supermarket, he passes the kiosk of flowers and the traffic lights at the High Street Notgni intersection with Wright's Drive. He moves along Tsobo and Basawi shops before he heads to the underground still on the right.

As he takes the stairs that lead to the station platform, random thoughts come to his mind. They tangle him up to his destination, which takes him twenty minutes of commuting.

"Memory can be a preposterous and impressive concept," he remembers when he read that assertion on an online publication the day before.

"When, at one specific moment, the brain safeguards information to be referred to in the future as memory, concerned people sometimes don't know or realise that they did such things."

"They never wonder how the creation of materials or data held by the memory for future reference or consultation doesn't constitute an everyday routine for the ordinary person. Unconsciously, memories get captured or created," the article Haile read seemed to say. He had had such thoughts while he commuted to his place of work.

On the previous day, he remembered that he had a few afternoon class sessions before going to the college at the end of the morning. He found that he had enough time to walk through the straight paved road located inside the local Old Kingdom Cemetery. On other days, when he didn't have classes to supervise, he could have a lot of spare time at hand. That felt that way on that day.

A few months before, the mortuary place in question had undergone a multi-million-pound project of refurbishment. The Cemetery doesn't get cars that drive in it. Only a few visitors use it at the same time when he does that afternoon. He doesn't remember how many times he saw cars there. The visit he made to the cemetery remained alive and vivid in his brain while he boarded the train and headed to his teaching place. He could see himself step by step - even the pace of his feet - on one of the parallel avenues in that location. Some plants in the middle of graves had as well caught his eyes and even taken pictures.

He saw the word Scripta on one of the graves.

"The word originates from the Latin verb Scribere, which means to write," Haile recalls thinking.

He had learned that and other Latin vocabularies more than fifteen years before while still in high school.

"What motivated people to use unique languages in some contexts. Latin references get frequently used in science, law, and medicine," Haile wonders.

"Maybe early knowledge to be formally codified and widely disseminated needed to use that particular language," he thought. All learned people, especially in the clergy, knew Latin of a high level of complexity.

He remembered that he learned that languages like Latin had fallen in decline with time for specific reasons.

"The disintegration of the Roman Empire had been the main blow to the Romans' language," he assumes.

"Could English fall as well in decline, since the British Empire had ended," such thought crossed his mind.

"Latin, despite its sad fate, has, however, remained present through certain words and expressions. They come to life through other contemporary forms of communication," he concludes.

Expressions like 'ex homine' or 'de jure', familiar to the legal system and that the general public, unfamiliar with Latin, considers as part of the necessary language package any good lawyer must master, have made it almost immortal. The Latin saying, "Verba volant, Scripta manent" refers to written, recorded or marked words or expressions that remain, while only spoken words get lost with time.

Haile comes out as an unconventional scientist and mathematician. If he needs some introduction, this will become his concise but precise description of his person. Occasionally, Haile expresses himself through poetry. Like some extinct languages, unable to mean much in isolation, he leans on other people's lives to live or survive.

He owes his life to Amina, a North Qarfian woman, who unexpectedly came into his existence one particular evening. After that single moment, her humanity meant all that existed for him.

With her, he understood the real sense of the statement that says that even "the mere existence of someone could become the salvation of somebody else."

Thus existing, or only being would be his ultimate realisation once he would arrive at the end of the road. Before he does, he envisages that such an assertion could at some point of his life, while on his existential journey, be the only justification for his life purpose, even and particularly in its darkest moments.

Stories Around

In Haile's opinion, the world revolves around stories. He developed a strong view over the years and shared it among his acquaintances as the need comes.

"I remember family members when they gathered after meals, and the elders told stories to the youngsters," he recalls. These stories shaped the minds of his generation, and probably those that preceded it. The future seemed to remain unchanged in the narratives of his storytelling. In reality, the shared stories depicted how that future would appear, but it looked more like a continuation of the present rather than a different space and time.

His conviction about the world also conveys a better perspective when a collection of stories defines its main characteristics: the stories that people tell and those they hear, while all live as audiences and their producers or presenters from the day they come into the universe, throughout their entire lives, until up to their last breath.

"I should point out that stories don't constitute a privilege of the elders in my family. At school, in church, at the local market, almost everywhere, people use these channels to learn and transfer knowledge, deliberately or unconsciously," hence he concludes when he further assesses the whole picture to pass on whatever the human imagination has accumulated and found valuable from one generation to the next one. And they consist of a diversity of references of real beings and intangible ghosts - things or creatures that humans don't fully grasp nature - related to their past, present and even future existence. These beings have their own lives. They can interact with people as they please or only by invitation. Once in a while, those stories could be mere creations of people's imagination, like fantasies, far remote from their every day's realities.

They could also be like lies to the self and or even others for a variety of reasons. Thanks to the humans' ingenuity, lies could, however, be separated from the actual truths, then these truths consequently used purposely.

"I agree with the fact that memories cover a variety of themes or phases of people's lives. The story about somebody's whole life may constitute a memory on its own held by someone's mind. What one generation passes on to the next one in an oral form could equally be called memories," Haile reckons. These stories, mostly unwritten, generally constitute what people characterise as oral traditions.

A critical question, however, arises in the formation of any memory people hold inside their minds. The answer would undoubtedly carry a hallmark of subjectivity. In truth, once expressed, a memory comes out shaped in tune with the storyteller's main characteristics. Those character traits take form gradually and get strengthened in the early life of the concerned person, which crafts the mould that will give shapes and contexts to the stories heard then shared.

These stories - that one might call memories - play an essential part for Haile because he finds that life would become meaningless without them. They cover every work of knowledge. No evidence proves that people deliberately developed them with an intention for them to find life on their own or exist. Their existence could find its root in a construct of both the conscious and the incidental, without any predetermination.

Memory and oneself couldn't be close in their definition as concepts, but they appear strangely interconnected. Haile remembers some memories for which he has become a lifelong prisoner.

Some daily or regular triggers take him back to past stories, which, though with the force of time, have changed and or lost their initial contextual meanings.

Even so, they don't go away when he doesn't need them. He doesn't escape when his mind takes and forces him to contemplate their happenings. Sometimes, once the triggers have done their job, specific external factors keep him in the confines of his memories.

Like a tree at the top of a mountain confronting the wind that manifests itself or a massive rocky cliff at the shore faces an angry ocean, he forcibly hears those stories, either without alteration by the time they pass through or as transformed. He lives his fate carried by the expression of those memories, like some inevitability along his journey.

The shameful memories or stories people fear to share, or which often terrify them once they only think about them becomes painful, because of the taboos or sufferings associated with their contexts. For such memories to make sense for them, people need to mainly listen to themselves, at the periphery of the deepest intimacies, interpret how one does get healed from such an unpleasant past and put it to rest. Only then can they remain accountable to themselves in their endeavours.

"It might be necessary to perform the exercise of truly listening to the silent voices to regain the self-confidence that those memories hinder when they don't fully get expressed," Haile reflects.

"Stories that get told and the whole process that gets involved in that portrays one of the significant characteristics that defines and differentiates humans from the rest of all creatures with embedded life in their DNAs," he asserts.

"People can't sit side by side and don't tell each other something, in one way or another. Some people score better at it than others in terms of quality and quantity. The champions in that cannot disappoint anyone."

"Others for whom mechanisms of self-censorship don't work, don't either constitute a good company," Haile believes.

People could contribute too little to discussions or display their utter indifference because of an internal self-regulation device, significantly due to their personality. Many consider them as irritating as those who say too much, without any substance.

He asserted that even silence could also be seen as a language if telling, showing, singing, and other visual expressions - namely any known standard form to interact with the world - didn't stand as the only acceptable expression.

"I believe that silence around someone could be a sign of respect, fear, or ignorance. As for any communication made in that format, the silence that emerges from someone could be interpreted differently, from the perspective of the understood recipient," he once argued.

Haile didn't consider the other situation where someone, though when they seem physically present, would be mentally miles away or in a different world concerning time and space. In those situations, they would look indifferent, detached from whatever would be the case around them.

"Silence is one of the great arts of conversation," Cicero one time said. A deaf person through the help of a sign language interpreter had once told Haile. The point raised indicated that "To understand can come from the silence of the person who chooses not to express themselves. At that particular moment, it appears even better that way. When nobody doesn't need to talk to be understood."

Nature generally similarly expresses itself. When that happens, it speaks loudly, sometimes utterly shouts and noticeably stupefies.

It even unmistakably becomes reckless and tragic when it resorts to demonstrate its existence, thus breaking its silence.

***

In Haile's neighbourhood lives an ordinary writer, not well known beyond the area. Being without a famous title associated with his name in the general public's eyes doesn't deprive him of the title's prestige. Every local person knew him.

"The Victims," tells the first fiction story that a local writer named Mustang Dong - had written. Its publication didn't attract much interest from the general public. The narrative referred to the lives of young people from wealthy backgrounds that parents from developing countries send to stay in rich countries like the QK, intending to study and gain western experience. After that, they would return home to run family businesses or enter high-rank positions in the public administration.

The story's novelty resides in that it considers these young people as victims instead of the lucky ones or beneficiaries of the world order as it appears. Such categorisation seemed the opposite of the general belief that wealth or money, in short, shielded the rich from particular hardships, especially emotional ones.

When it came to knowing his neighbourhood, Haile had an acute eye of a Sherlock Holmes-like observer. When he walked along his local streets and talked to different people, he had noticed and been surprised at the same time by the level of emotional issues among the young adults he encountered.

Amina had experienced a different type of attitude each time she tried to connect with people.

She couldn't understand how someone deliberately avoided looking into the other person's eyes, even sparely, when they meet and pass beside each other.

No wonder the place he lived in demonstrated less humanity towards the rest of the world, despite all the official claims to the contrary.

"They have most of the material things that other people from other places around the world might envy, but they lack the kindness to feel attracted to the needy willingly," Haile had concluded after he had closely assessed the people in his new area.

"It's a heart of warmth and affection that brings smiles on the faces of strangers."

"Without such an attitude, these only appear cold-hearted," had he summarised the reason why people from where he lived persistently showed grimy moods in their looks. That could marginally explain their comparative high rate of depression and suicide.

He came to partly understand why countries like the QK and others among the developed ones could wage wars on foreign lands, whatever the official justification could be. While they contribute in different ways to the death of thousands or millions of innocent citizens of attacked nations, these countries can easily disassociate themselves from the plights of the victims that their actions cause. Their citizens can feel detached from the consequences of their governments' military operations, as long as their participation enables them to achieve some national and selfish objectives. Thus, the same manifest indifference becomes observable on the street, in their people's attitudes towards each other.

Amina decided to make the initial step, despite her negative appreciation of the overall context's background. Worth remembering that she came from a different part of the world. Therefore, it doesn't matter that she would behave differently from the locals.

At six-thirty in the evening, she knocks on Haile's door. A whole year had passed since she had moved into the neighbourhood. She had been reluctant to talk to him at first. He looked unapproachable, cold-hearted and unfriendly. He wore clothes without any style; one dark winter coat characterised him. Haile's nose showed a dark indent on the skin where his glasses rested. His tiny eyes planted in a large face made people think of a lion head more than an average person one could befriend. Such a description doesn't mean no woman could feel attracted to him. Lions also have their suitors because of their particular features.

The block of apartments they both live in consists of properties built fifteen years before.

They still look like luxurious places, with a concierge service, an underground car park and a 24/7 CCTV surveillance service. Amina wants to introduce herself to Haile formally.

At their initial encounter, the critical and decisive face to face that would change many things for both, Haile had seemed friendly. They share one similar background, as both were from Qarfi. When she first met him at the main entrance of the building.

"Lucky I feel to see someone from my continent!"

"And which continent do you refer to while you mention that?" Haile had asked her.

"Look at my skin! I think you come from there. Don't you?" she had said, with a surprised but confident face, while she touched her left arm with the right one.

"I can't tell. Your skin looks the Mediterranean type, with its tanned tone. Do you come from Qarfi?"

"Yes, though we North Qarfians consider ourselves more Brabs than Qarfians; I don't know the origin of that perception."

"I will see you around. One of these days, I will come for a cup of tea or invite you for one at my place," Haile said before he headed his way.

"Her face, eyes, and even more, the slight smile on her lips brightened my world instantly, like the mark of a crush from a first love." This description described the stark first impression about Amina that Haile made after leaving. It took less than a minute of small talk while they both stood on the porch of his apartment.

As an introvert, he kept the positive impression of his chat with Amina to himself. The interaction profoundly affected him and changed his overall mood the following days. It didn't look radical but sufficiently perceivable for any close observer.

He didn't mention the reason for his transformation to his rare friends, nor to Sarah Cavanaugh, with whom the relationship they shared remained unclear; it shifted from work colleague to the only friend from time to time.

That depended on circumstances.

Haile had family members with whom he had a detached relationship, particularly after his twenty-fifth birthday. To those among them who called occasionally, he felt that he didn't need to explain himself all the time; once the decision was made to reply to their calls, he often would almost discourage them from contacting him again. The aim was to avoid sharing his intimate affairs, considered strictly personal. He perceived such areas to be private matters.

Except for his professional interactions with his students, he didn't receive any calls for an entire week. He didn't either contact anyone to chat with for the sake of his social wellbeing. This behaviour would occasionally make him fall into depression.

Haile had been a victim of an acute level of melancholic mood for months. A teacher by profession, he interrupted his work.

Although no one at work could explain his deplorable state of mind at the time, even on his family side, there seemed to be no particular issue that could be the cause.

In that period, one night, his subconscious had made him take a step closer to a severe suicidal inclination. In one corner of his apartment's central area, he had hammered a strong metallic hook in the ceiling. It had taken him a great deal of effort and determination to fix it there. On the floor, he had placed a stool. A solid rope with the typical node which would hold his neck tightly until he lost his final breath seemed attached to the ceiling.

In his mind and on the ground, he had well planned what he needed to do. He expected to end his useless life, as he perceived it. The day Amina entered Haile's world, the suicide's set-up hung still in place. Nevertheless, when he saw her, his outlook on life changed completely from then on. She became his inspiration to carry on living.

Every day after that day would be imagined and or planned with her thought in mind. Constant flashbacks about her would populate his mind any single day, without fail.

Haile presented himself occasionally under a negative radar. From time to time, he displayed a pessimistic personality. He always underestimates his worth. Presenting himself that way contradicted his friends' assessment of him. They found him invaluable and resourceful. This portrayal constituted the dilemma that characterised his life. Who he deeply was, his self-perception and that of those around him all differed. Further to how he experienced the world around him, his cautious attitude, even in situations where such behaviour would be detrimental, seemed consequently not recommendable.

It appeared somehow as a depiction of a picture not always easy to read. When others, for example, laughed because of a joke, Haile wouldn't. When someone would observe him, they would think that maybe this constituted evidence of his ignorance about the topic in discussion, but deep down, it resulted from a fear of what could follow if it came out unpleasant and or hostile.

Consequently, he adopted a middle ground and therefore chose not to become overly disappointed whenever that happens. Hence, he had a constant fear of the opposite of the current situation occurring.

After Amina comes and knocks on his door, he intends to find a way to connect with his life saviour at a critical moment of his earthly journey. Remarkably, given that, if she hadn't passed by at that time, the path he walked on would have taken a different direction. From then on, a distinctive track, not far from hope, but still distinct from that, had grown in him as never before. He looked at the present with an open mindset.

He saw plenty of opportunities and value in his surroundings. However, from the start, after they came to interact more, she had told him that they could only be friends. Even with that only promise, that had been an unexpected bonus to be thankful about. Considered the edge of the cliff, his feet stood on at the time.

Nevertheless, his interactions with her, either in thoughts only or in face-to-face contexts, would define the scope or boundaries of their shared particular story. Changes came for Haile and unfolded in complete unpreparedness.

In Maslow's hierarchy of needs, Amina offered Haile a bonus that allowed him to work on and achieve his self-actualisation.

"I will become whatever I could be capable of being," Haile's conscience makes a sort of a firm promise to him.

He had made similar promises in the past. None-theless, this time, his commitment seemed different and more firm than at any previous period of his life.

"The suicidal inclination in recent days has been a serious dent into my potential," Haile indicates to his friend who, as his conscience, does follow him wherever he goes. He counter-argued on the previous statement. He replied to the sort of unspoken question on how he has been performing.

"I do not doubt in my mind that I can go through whatever it takes, with the competencies and abilities I have, to achieve great things, if I put my heart on them," he convinces himself of his unlimited possi-bilities.

The encounter with his neighbour comes out cathartically; Haile becomes a stranger to the person he has been until then. Though the old and the new him still lived together, like Siamese twin brothers. The new Haile appears as if Amina has thrown on him a magic spell of transformation. His name always remains the same, but his mental and spiritual entities have funda-mentally changed.

A different character - probably an even better one - has found refuge in his body. It would've been ap-propriate if he could change his name. However, he con-siders that he should not proceed in that direction be-cause of the practical consequences.

He looked different, but only to some extent. He didn't have to change his external outlook.

The question would've been what people would've thought if they saw him and or had to deal with a stranger in their vicinity. He would've to move back and forth into their lives, unannounced constantly, and remain partially the old Haile. In the case he changed his appearance, he would also have to change his name. That way, the old him would disappear for good, thanks to Amina.

Her arrival in his life would've then fulfilled a specific and unintended goal that would've transformed him radically and created a new him.

A declared friendship from the person who had saved him from himself could make him perform outstandingly, he hoped. Nobody knows if he would ever regret that Amina had rescued him at any given time in his future. Time would tell. In the meantime, he looks as if he wants more from life than previously. He has entered the path of the endless pursuit of happiness, which, when stopped, makes the concerned person feel miserable.

Maturing Unhappy

While the sun shines in the sky, many people have their late lunch in the middle of that afternoon. They enjoy their meal in different spots of the local park behind the college where Haile teaches. On his part, he holds a book of which the leading personality has taken over his mind. He stands as one of those who love that park with his distinctive character, where he leans on a tree and enjoys its shadow.

At the end of that day, he goes home and takes a moment to meditate.

"For the next couple of days, I don't have classes to supervise, nor students' assignments to evaluate," as he assesses for himself his school's obligations.

"I deviated from the usual track that my peers normally follow either by choice or instinctively," while he reflects on where he stands in his life at the time.

"An existential challenge weighs on my person. Questions for which I can't find answers abound. One of them refers to the concept of destiny," he contemplates while he rests in his main room, with a book of which he has closed the pages, in front of a cup of pukka turmeric gold organic, with lemon fruit and green tea flavour. He flips the pages instinctively while he meditates on the philosophical quest his mind carries.

"Does what people call destiny - devised before humans come into the world - resemble at some extent to a linear path, no matter how twisting it can appear in several cases, also called fate, along with people's earthly journey, or exist in reality?" Haile's thoughts follow-through from the announced challenge. That question remains persistently on his conscience.

"Could someone claim confidently without any doubt that they follow their destiny and enjoy it?" Haile queries at the end of his reflection.

Haile used to think that destiny or fate existed until he discovered that people had the power to devise their path in life. Until Amina came and knocked on his door, he had more or less let his existence unsupervised or out of his control. With some luck, he found out that he had some leverage.

"Opportunities for people to change the course of their life come to their attention all the time, and more than often, unexpectedly. To grab them by both hands depends on momentous circumstances and people's readiness to move forward positively," Haile had found out despite his young age. Even so, this came equally as a result of his critical and diverse reading, filled with numerous examples of people whose stories had defied prescribed destinies.

Before his encounter with Amina, his heart had never fluttered for anyone from the opposite sex. The situation didn't presuppose that he had been short of opportunities. Though he hadn't been the most attractive guy around - any girl who would've fallen for him would've been seen as either shameless or desperate -, some women who seek relationships at any cost or careless about the consequences in whichever forms they would manifest could've gone after him regardless.

But Haile didn't give anyone any chance to get closer. Not because he didn't want to, but because he didn't know how to. On top of his ignorance on the matter, Haile found another strong excuse to shut out himself from relationships. He considered that, while he pursued them and got to know his potential partners, he would become stressed, distracted in his work, and eventually miss deadlines for his students' assessments. To catch up with the workload, Haile would've had to do overtime and sometimes work weekends. That didn't fit the appearance of what he wanted to experience from a relationship.

At the time, he wouldn't do any overtime nor any work on weekends. Hence, the root of his acute depression resided elsewhere. He had grown up with a persistent sense of loneliness, away from one only sister he had.

Contrary to the loneliness children encounter when they don't have their parents around, he seemed lucky on that front. He had an uncle who liked him and had provided for most of his study and other material needs. He acted as an adoptive father for him, though he didn't live with him. He had the principal's role in a secondary school, and his wife worked as a civil engineer at the department of public infrastructure. Both highly career-oriented, appreciated schools' benefit where children stay and only come home during holidays. They had helped send Haile to such a school at an early age. Only nine years old, he got put into one such institution. They also visited him regularly.

Though he had a so-called family that consisted of her single mother aunt and his cousin, he felt he had grown up without one because he had lost his biological parents. He couldn't be with them in his critical years of teenagers. War had taken them away from him, and they hadn't been able to be there for him. Nobody could blame them for that. While he remained at his school, deep down, he strongly resented having been sent away from his familiar surroundings. Throughout his university years, Haile didn't get over the resentment he had against those who sent him away and made him learn again about new contexts to adjust. He had never discussed these feelings on the subject with no one, relative or specialist. He only felt not loved. That was the picture of his mindset. He considered himself not equipped to give others what he didn't have, meaning love in himself.

His aunt, a control freak and a little manipulative, had a strict attitude towards her kids. She never tolerated anyone who contradicted her. From her perspective, either you stood unconditionally with her, or you sided against her.

No middle ground or compromise existed. It was imperative for everyone who dealt with her to be on her side if they didn't want to be cursed.

Haile, who had a shy personality, rarely objected to his aunt's orders, even when he disagreed internally. The many built-up frustrations not aired out made him grow up and mature unhappy, without a smile on his face all the time. Hopefully, his encounter with Amina would change all that.

***

Life seems at the time uneventful for Haile. However, he had difficulties separating the ordinary from the unusual. This confusion seemed again to be one trait of his character.

"My days look incredibly ordinary and extra-normal that it makes me worried and expect the worst. It can't carry on the way it is," he reflects upon his situation at the moment.

"I usually rank not among the optimistic guys, nor the pessimistic types, but I think I fit somewhere in the middle ground, still difficult to define," Haile gives an opinion of himself. However, he perceives himself as an ordinary man of every day that one encounters on the street or has as a neighbour. However, he couldn't mislead himself more than that. His peers' teachers had a different and much more positive opinion about him.

His assessment of where he stood at the time had appeared to indicate such an unpleasant picture. A one-year-long interlude came by. He had decided to take it as a sabbatical period to help him move forward.

By the end, he thought he would figure out clearly where he headed.

The time didn't allow him to relax at all. Instead, he worked intensively to change the direction his life had been taking radically. When one looks back, it emerges that the period transformed his destiny. However, if one considers destiny similar to a pre-written script, the year-long period constituted only one phase towards his destination. For the first time in his life, Haile feels that he sleepwalks on the verge of death. He eats unhealthy food at irregular times for several days.

Luckily, such a mild loss of direction for his life doesn't affect his routine jogs. After long periods without any communication between them, friends who see him get surprised at how much weight he has lost.

"I need to do something," as he stands in front of the reflection of his image in the main room; he talks to himself and does an introspection. Two years to the day, he had weighed seventy-five kgs. His weight had dramatically come down to sixty without any sign of serious illness he had suffered in the meantime.

"I think I have lost too much weight; if I don't sort this out properly, I won't need anybody else to help dig my own grave," he also added; he referred to his enormously changed look, with cheeks that looked like those of a malnourished individual. His doctor hadn't found any symptom to alarm him the last time he had consulted him for a general health checkup.

"I don't want to die. Not that I treasure my current situation and feel comfortable in it," Haile asserts while still looking at his skinny face.

"On the one hand, I don't have a special entitlement to life. On the other hand, I wonder why I shouldn't live. Given the situation, I can't leave my fate to continue on its predetermined path, focused on fulfilling its mission, if any."

"I can't let it carry on to play with my life as a piece of chess in the hands of a master on the chessboard," he pursues while angry at the crossroad where he stands in his life at that particular moment.

In this scenario of chess, the master knows the ultimate outlook before the game even starts. Haile seems the only one in the dark, though he plays the pawn's role on the chessboard of which the destination could be even out of the players' control because of the many variables they can't make sense of.

"But I need to explain and understand why I have to live. It looks as if this will not be for my own sake. I have to carry on. I have to. Period," Haile approaches his necessity to live from a scientific point of view.

All the requirements to sustain life appear available. With them in place, there can only be life. If it came to an impossibility, he could consider it a mystery.

While Haile has these thoughts, the sky draws a warm and enjoyable sun on his skin. The outdoor brightness happens after a long walk in the park while he sits on one of the benches located around the three-quarter-mile long pond. His eyes navigate above the trees and buildings on the horizon.

"I don't want to go on with my life to enjoy more of that sort of weather," he looks at the sky, at thirty degrees celsius angle from where he stands.

"This would be a futile endeavour. I have no guarantee that the present I currently enjoy will be there tomorrow or the day after," Haile questions the idea to find justifications for him to carry on with his life.

"Would it be enough if today's nice weather became a permanent feature of my future? I don't think so because life has more value than a constant clear and sunny sky," he concludes.

Haile could find the basis or the justification of his sincere willingness to carry on with his life in the essence of existence itself. While others would want to live and develop a "speculative" better future for themselves or their loved ones, Haile didn't put faith in an unfounded hope. Consequently, he didn't include it in his equation of living. Despite such a view, Haile didn't become desperate either, though he only wanted to be rational. He considers the present as an essential feature of living.

"Once people focus on their present moments - they can live intensively and fully in the now and don't bother about other matters - to carry on with their lives, this then becomes their 'raison d'être.' For them, the present as a gift of the moment, once lived comprehensively, can constitute a memorable and profound past to be proud of," thus Haile defines the motto of his life.

Haile wonders about his memories' weight when one lives the present at its optimum and carries on such a lifestyle for a long time. Memories resemble the roots of a tree which can't resist the wind without them. The more the roots get solidly stretched in the ground, the more the tree can out-stand any wind, whatever its strength or destructive capacity. In his opinion, the past influences the present undeniably.

Before Amina comes into his life, he fails to control his current wellbeing. She rescues him at a time he needs a radical change in his life. His fate becomes momentarily aligned with his determination to carry on living. Though the roots that made him stand up firmly on the ground have, until then, lacked to some extent, they would still appear handy when needed.

***

Haile fears that he gets old. Though he only reached his late thirties. He doesn't yet feature in the aged population's critical bracket that some countries find highly concerning. Some scientists have started to call old age disease. Although that has raised heated debates, someone accused the proponents of that view of economic opportunists or narcissists in denial of mortality.

However, Haile's sentiment about age didn't constitute only his view on the time that passes with years. Particular incidents he found himself caught in became more frequent to remind him about the marks of time on his person.

One late afternoon, while Haile travelled on an international coach, the driver asked him and other passengers to fill in a document with their names and dates of birth. This request featured among the formalities before they got to the border and entered another country.

Once among the last ones to put down their details, surprisingly, when he looked over the other passengers' birth dates, he found out he was the farthest in the past and made him the oldest.

"For the first time, I reflect in front of critical evidence that proves me old," Haile asserts before he puts his details on the sheet of paper.

Arguably, one could say that such an assessment came from a subjective and relative perspective. Though Haile only compared himself with those on that particular coach. Probably in a different setting, that wouldn't have been the case. He was, however, the oldest this time. In the past, he had instead been the youngest when it came to age in particular groups.

"Luckily, I haven't suffered from any of the health failures that become frequent when people get old: no stroke, no cancer, no dementia. I reached my late thirties. As I will become older, I will have to face this challenge where someone looks at years through a philosophical loop and accepts - when these will happen - the progressive infirmities which come with age," Haile portrays himself gradually at an advanced age and visualises the changes his body will go through, becomes weaker and weaker as time passes.

"Will I embark on the quest to aggressively stop or delay that process where the time marks people's bodies with a special stamp when it will come to pass?" he wonders.

He doesn't yet consciously set himself on that path of older adults, though his daily jog fulfils that typical mindset. In his mind, he exercises mainly for fitness and overall to feel good, which comes from it.

To address his old age couldn't notably feature in the picture yet. Nevertheless, there seemed to be another front of his life that he appeared to have neglected.

So far, Haile lived with his wider family and close elders who told him about the right path a true man should follow.

That path supposed to get a good job, a house, a wife, children, then live and enjoy a peaceful and wonderful life. A typical man occasionally supports the rest of the broader family whenever he could.

He seemed to deviate from what society expected from his peers, given where he stood in his life at the time. They had to have accomplished certain things at his age and through a linear path, and any male from the community would almost do similarly.

Though he has tried to be self-sufficient, at the same time - he saved as much as possible for a deposit for his first house -, he has for long thrived to safeguard and strengthen the necessary bond with his community members for the sake of his protection and mental well-being. He could take care of many things by himself, but for the rest of others, he needed generous support from the broader family of human beings around him - call it community, society or nation. He felt extremely joyful when he lived connected with his people.

Back Then

Amina had suffered continuously from a strained and hostile relationship with her extended family from her teenage years. Everyone around her had ostracised her since that period, and as a consequence, she strongly felt insecure. This discomfort on her part happened, though her tormentors had never made any official statement to justify their behaviour.

"I don't want to talk to anybody in my family. It's as if everyone sees me as the one odd out," she told one of her friends at the time. As a result of the feeling, she kept to herself.

She remained only close to those in her family; she felt comfortable to be around.

"Exceptionally, I will attend events such as funerals and weddings for which I will have received a formal invitation to participate," she decided then on.

"Will you need an invitation for a funeral of a family member?" had one of her friends ask her.

"Maybe I won't need one," she replied. Not taking part in such family events would've been perceived in a light she didn't want to contemplate. She considered herself to be still human, also capable of empathy towards the sorrow of others. Furthermore, she feared what her other family members would've gossiped about if she failed to attend.

Michaela Jane, her cousin from a remote aunt, hadn't invited her to her wedding. A few weeks later, when the invitation went formally out to the broader family members, Amina learned that she got left out.

"I got angry not to receive an invitation because she thought of me as the only one who didn't deserve an invitation from the entire family," she told her friend.

Her bitterness, excusable to a certain point, couldn't be fully understood since she hadn't talked to her cousin or read into her mind for clarification. As time passed, she couldn't figure out the justification for the way she suffered from her family.

"I don't get along with her mother, who happens to be my stepsister from my other mother - for anyone to get the picture of the relationship I have with her, they have to know that my dad married my mother in a second marriage -," she remembered. It didn't take her a second to realise the root cause of all the fuss about that cousin's official marriage and her non-invitation.

"She behaves like her mother. I understand why she adopted that attitude," Amina could see then. The mother had requested from the cousin not to send her an invitation. Her aunt always had a hateful behaviour towards certain people, without much justification; she never looked at her positively but rather gossiped or talked ill about her.

Stoically, Amina analysed her overall relationship with her extended family and came to the next compromise instead of her sense of guilt or persecution.

"I don't want to resent them. Preferably I find some relief in the situation. It provides me with some deep and complete consolation and, at the same time, a positive detachment from the bad memories of my past mistreatment. From then on, I will treat the rest of my family the way they have treated me," as she resorted to the tooth for tooth tactic.

For an extended period, she had struggled, sometimes egg-walked and feared alienating any member of her family. Time had come for her to strike a balance. When she looked back, she smiled and wondered how she managed to live under such uncomfortable situations.

After her relief from the created rift with the rest of the family, she felt like a released prisoner. From then on, she decided to enjoy her mental freedom.

***

At times, enthusiastic above the half average of the people, but equally a little introvert, Amina didn't look any different from her peers.

She evolved to become among those faces of women whose beauty featured on the unnoticeable list.

That categorisation didn't, however, take away her attractiveness and charm. Naturally curious, she always asked questions and showed interest in different things, and she used all these qualities to her advantage in life.

At fifteen, she had a bust well-developed and a whole body that featured all the rightly shaped forms expected from a young woman. Sharp in class, she obtained high grades in her humanity's subjects. In the others, such as sciences and maths, she managed only slightly above the average. Occasionally fun to be around, she had a great sense of humour each time she spoke. People around her found her company stimulating. At the opposite of her twin Florencia, she adored her long hair. To make her look fashionable, she wore curly hair girl outfits on days she wanted to feel good about herself and be greedy in that sense. Some people on the street, not many, would turn and have a second look when they passed her. She didn't like to be the centre of interest for anyone, though that happened frequently and unintentionally.

In her high school years, Amina had been close to Michael, a Brazilian teenager classmate.

"I don't recall what constituted the particular characteristic that made me be attracted to him," she had replied to someone who had asked about her first love.

They lived in the same neighbourhood. Consequently, chances existed that they travelled together on their journeys back-and-forth to school.

Nonetheless, this couldn't explain enough the bond which developed between them. Only six months after they had started their regular chats - this was the trend at their school -, they had become boyfriend and girlfriend.

Boys and girls couldn't only be friends. Although only the confident ones among them expressed their feelings openly because to confess that one loves someone requires some courage.

Some inherent characteristics which go with love, such as commitment, loyalty and obligations or responsibilities, demand serious consideration before one engages in such an endeavour.

Michael, born to a single mother, had a stepsister three years younger. Their fathers had separated from their mums when they reached only four and seven. Michael's dad stayed in contact and saw them every other week. Her stepsister's dad was among the persons who had disappeared without any trace. Despite repeated requests from the family to the police, the search didn't provide any positive results after three months, and they had then given up.

***

In her search for a career to pursue, Amina got guided by her gut. While in high school, and even long before, she had felt differently excited each time she went to a local market.

"I enjoy the general outdoor experience that involves visits to the market, while one looks at different displays of items with their diversity of colours, shapes, uses and packages with unique features." At the same time, Amina shared with her friends' things she liked.

"I appreciate distinctively the components and other elements that constitute all the products that I see displayed," she added.

"I feel excited each time I accompany an adult in a shop or a marketplace," she explained additionally. Visits of such places didn't enchant her much, but the attraction to particular items she felt once she found herself in those locations.

"Is there in our brain a device which instructs our eyes to look in specific directions while they respond to definite parameters or variables, instead of others?" she wondered. While young, she didn't have explicit knowledge of such phenomena.

It took her some years to acquire the necessary knowledge on all these issues.

"When I grow up, I will certainly find out," she promised to herself.

"The big question when one goes shopping is: why do they buy this item and not that other one? Should they be frustrated because they can't afford that product if the price constitutes the factor that challenges them? Does the satisfaction one get while buying a product last forever? If it doesn't, how does it fade away? Could people be or remain indifferent while confronted with unsatisfied desires? How do they deal with their disappointing satisfaction?" The young Amina didn't have answers to these critical questions when she finished her A-levels.

Once she became an adult, these questions continued to intrigue her. In the last year of her secondary school, she had started to read more about how the human brain operates in its environment. The more she grew curious, the more she learned how to influence people and get them to perceive things in a guided and desirable way.

To an extent, Amina would study the techniques to make individuals adopt particular behaviours they wouldn't have taken without almost some manipulation.

The most mysterious aspect of her field of interest focused on the apparent psychological impulse that some people have to spend money. In their cases, they spent not always because of how much money they have in their purse or on their credit cards, but the desire to spend inconsiderately and vividly overwhelmed them in such a way they couldn't resist. In the worst situations, they could borrow beyond their credit cards' thresholds to spend as they feel like in those moments.

Haile had a few friends, particularly women teachers he worked with, whose wardrobes contained plenty of new clothing, shoes or handbags they would never wear or carry.

They acquired all those items under the spell of impulse buying while they responded to their ardent desires to fill gaps in their happiness levels or moments of overwhelmed helplessness.

"I want to uncover the intricacies behind that behaviour to help its victims," Amina had seen many adults, while still in her youth, buy almost foolishly.

"Perhaps they have a lot of money that they don't have to think hard on what to spend it on, like those who haven't enough of it, when such people struggle to buy what they want," she tries to understand the unstoppable spenders.

"Shall I call them victims or sufferers, as all these people endured a mental illness without a name?" she wonders.

"Do they only differ from the rest of us, without any behavioural disorder? Those not affected might think about them and consider that they do suffer," she asserted at that time.

However, she had an unanswered question about the extent or seriousness of their situation. Amina would find out the result in many years to come.

In her pursuit to satisfy her curiosity on the matter, she did, for example, find that to buy impulsively originated from some insecurities people who suffer from it have.

"The phenomenon relates to high levels of anxiety and unhappiness. Victims who buy impulsively have their brains wired in a distinctive way to make them behave the way they do when it comes to buying. It's pointless to state that not everyone who suffers from anxiety or unhappiness ends up in shops," Amina learnt this in her lectures.

As far as one knows, two personality traits characterise impulsive buyers; they appear broadly concerned by their image and oversensitive about their social status. When they buy these clothes at once, or other accessories, with the momentous intention to wear them, at that particular time, their mind tells them that others will highly appreciate them.

They buy impulsively because of their incapacity to control their emotions. These emotions translate into their anxiety or the urge to spend on different items. Generally unhappy, their visits to the shops help them lift the mood. Marketers, aware of the triggers for such people, know how to respond to their aspirations when they enter a shop or visualise items online.

At this point, Haile, on his part, had understood and suffered from the strategies of the manipulation of people. Through various communication channels and techniques, mainstream media deliberately instructed viewers or consumers, without them realising, to think and behave in a specific way.

"Since I know this intended intoxication, I have to change and be selective about what accesses to my brain," he promised to himself.

As a consequence, while he doubted television's usefulness, he cut himself off from the tv world programmes. Disgusted and frustrated by the way factual truths he had witnessed and or encountered on a personal level got in many cases portrayed, he contemplated powerlessly the dark hidden agendas of broadcasters or prominent global opinion leaders who used mainstream communication channels the masses to instil their messages. He stopped watching television altogether in a radical move against public communicators' pretence to produce and disseminate truthful news and other entertainment packages.

Previously, he had once thought that when the truth becomes the money of the day, people rally behind it and the world changes. Unfortunately, he came to realise that it didn't. Instead, it adapts itself to that new reality, and sometimes it creates different parameters and paradigms not necessarily aligned with that truth to perform by or around.

***

When Amina turned nineteen, she prepared herself mentally to start her university studies in Needreb City, located in the north of the QK country. To get there, it took a three hundred miles journey by train on occasion. However, deep down, he behaved as if he wanted her desire to pursue further her studies and disappear in the air, as per magic.

"This time, it will be more difficult than usual to find school fees for all the four children I look after," her guardian uncle thought desperately. He had been the only breadwinner in the household, and as a consequence, the burden on his shoulders stood stout. His wife came from a low-class category of people. Her family didn't perceive any particular interest in getting their daughter into some form of education.

She had never envisaged living a life different from that of a housewife.

"Presently, I can't tell what we will do; we can't afford the required amount of money. My earnings and savings aren't enough. I don't see who to go to for help," Amina's uncle pointed out to his wife when the issue of tuition fees came up at the occasion of one family dinner.

It took a while before his family got over the tuition fees' challenge it faced.

To apply for the student loan helped a little. Amina had researched all the requirements to get to the university. Though she did it successfully, she needed more than that loan to live a decent student life.

Her guardian uncle worked in a factory as a low-level employee. He struggled month after month, given the unfulfilled financial basic needs of the family. Consequently, he couldn't commit to fully supporting the strong desire that Amina had of studying at a higher level. Instead, he would've liked to let her enter the labour market after only her A-Levels.

Some hurdles paved her way, and she had to experience them to save some money for her regular costs of living once on the campus.

"I will have to find a way to live in an affordable place and, at the same time, find part-time jobs during my holidays," Amina considered.

She had to share her studio with two other girls. Thus, she also learned to live with strangers, which was new to her.

"I can't afford a private apartment or a student studio with its amenities," Amina reflected while she assessed how she would live as a student. After her registration on the campus, she got directed to a classic non-en-suite room. She found it located among three to seven-bedroom apartments with a communal kitchen and a lounge area.

With a size of two and a half meters on almost four meters, the bedroom had a three to four sized bed. The window opened laterally and nearly entered the wall. It gave a view to an array of houses in the distance. The sight seemed to end only where the Cairn Toan Mountain started. In her three years of undergraduate studies, she lived on the cheapest option, where she paid eighty-three pounds a week all year around. Though her student loan covered her rent, she struggled with her daily expenses and socialising. She couldn't cope financially without other sources of revenue.

With her room in the Autumn Gardens, she didn't have any problem getting to her lectures. Several buses passed near where she lived and had direct routes to her campus.

Her rent included all her utility bills, and this entailed the internet connection available throughout the property and the necessary insurance coverage of contents. Service teams operated twenty-four seven and looked after residents' secured properties. On-site support from property teams and an emergency contact centre opened all-time, added to the residents' comfort.

As soon as she got used to the new academic environment, she enrolled in different student activities. Keen to explore various things and connect as widely as possible, among many other things, she learned about employment opportunities for undergraduates through these interactions with other students. In all her summer holidays, she worked and saved for her daily expenses as a student.

Her personality had made her unable to attract many suitable boyfriends. In her years at uni, the boys she met in her social circles didn't understand her. They seemed either too refined for her taste or couldn't grasp well her character and the cultural background she represented, the one that leaned towards a progressive Islam.

110

Fortunately, her attire didn't fit in the traditional style that portrayed the majority of Muslim girls. Her uncle, open-minded and progressivist in his views on his children's education, didn't find any problem in her outfits. While on the holidays, she discovered her peers, boys and girls, easy to talk to because they all belonged to the Muslim faith.

***

Amina considers that life reserves some secrets to be discovered. She studied the promotion of products. Her interest in learning about people's wants made her apply for a higher level qualification related to personal attitudes towards every day's needs.

"I particularly want to explore products and how their containers get designed for marketing purposes. From there, I will learn how to influence the consumer's behaviour," this constitutes her field of interest in learning, but it won't be the only one that captures her mind.

"The impact of shoppers when they help themselves to get products directly from the shelves, as opposed to the shop staff while they serve them at the counter, will be another area to investigate," she highlighted her intention to broaden her scope of learning.

She appeared interested in all aspects of the interaction experience once a client enters a shop, bricks and mortar or online types.

"I will search for the best way to communicate information about the product. I can't tell yet if it will be different from the present outlook where the manufacturers present it written on the package. Beyond good product design niceties, I want to know if the process would also conjure specific messages when they become included in the design concept itself and how."

"I will seek ways to incorporate some optimism, hope or enthusiasm into the design process of a product," she thinks about all the elements that will convey a different and better message when a customer looks at a product.

The main factors or their combination to consider in the design process and achieve such intended outcome remained. Amina wanted to focus on some of these areas of interest in her studies at that new level. In her stay there, her education didn't shift much from her initial focal point.

"Which field do you study?" had once one of her two roommates asked her.

"I study the people's interactions with the products offered on the markets," Amina replied.

"What interest do you have in that particular field?' the roommate had added while asking.

"What do they do in such studies?" he had also asked to clarify her initial question.

"To answer your question, I would say that I want to be able to influence people's opinions or perceptions when they observe the offerings available to their different senses," she answered.

"As for what we do in marketing, I would invite you to visit your local market or enter an online shop and try to understand what goes on, the insights at play. If you pay sufficient attention, you can get a glimpse of the dynamics in action from whatever angle you start and continue observing. Our area of studies covers one of the main aspects of a marketplace."

"I see! You want to manipulate people, don't you?" her roommate continued asking.

"No, I would like to help people make their decisions more effectively," she argued.

"In the majority of cases, people make uninformed choices and suffer at the end from undesirable outcomes. I want to be capable of helping such people."

"Let's hope you don't become a politician. Maliciously manipulative, they say this today while they paint a different picture in their mind," her roommate elaborated.

"Manipulation doesn't belong among my forte," Amina concluded the conversation.

She researched the variables and elements that triggered in one way or another the different senses' centres in the human brain, towards objects of interest or not, because of their respective functions. A Vodnak Public Relations agency she came to work for, later on, had recruited her based on her dissertation for her last academic year.

Hence she managed to complete her undergraduate studies, despite the initial hiccups she encountered from the drastic changes, especially in learning. Though she even contemplated the fact that her secondary school years hadn't prepared her well enough for that new step in her adulthood, overall, she navigated through it without any painful scars.

***

Of North Qarfian descent with light skin features, Amina carries long and dense hair that covers her whole back. Her hands are always cold like those of lovers, and she likes to wear camel-coats in winter and autumn. Her wardrobe holds several types of that attire with a variety of colours. If she doesn't wear one, her friends would ask her what happened.

Her responsibilities at work entail monitoring local and international news outlets in their different forms.

She writes reports for clients to help them make strategic decisions and move their businesses forward. She gathers precious insights. Artificial intelligence tools her employer has developed empower them. They remove all the hassle that traditional approaches use to achieve similar results.

Real-time inputs help produce automated analytics for any client from any sector of activity, competitors' positions against the client's products, the overall picture of the business landscape, or the industry's brand image. All these constitute information any business would be keen to buy.

Her work could also indicate to clients the impact of their decisions in the promotion of products. Her interest in customer's and product relationships from a young age had propelled her to become an expert in her field. A strong connection between her early curiosity and the work she does by this time undoubtedly exists.

When she doesn't want to feel alone after work or on weekends, she spends time with her female friend who works at the same company. They visit public places, galleries, museums, parks, exhibitions and or attend talks together. They became friends incidentally, drawn towards each other in their company's festive season. At the annual event organised around Christmas to celebrate the staff's performance, they chatted and shared their respective interests and dislikes. They found common ground, which made them come closer in the next few days. They talked about their relationships with men.

While she approaches her late twenties, she becomes Hussein's third official girlfriend with whom she would be together for more than six months. On her side, despite her lack of long-lasting relationships, getting married didn't come from a space of desperation. Instead, she mainly wanted to pursue and focus on her professional career.

She ranked it before any plans for marriage. Her relationship with Hussein evolved slowly but steadily when the unthinkable happened.

Uni Life

In that week, Samuel supervises the apartment's cleanliness, in which he and two girls live as university students. Although he can't unexpectedly apply Marie Kondo's techniques to make their place clean and tidy, they agreed to rotate their responsibilities every week. Certain principles about that shared chore would apply.

One of those made up and unwritten rules focuses on accountability and how far it goes for each resident towards others.

"As long as the person on duty will spend a minimum of thirty minutes per week cleaning the place for each of their allocated days per week, there won't be any complaint."

So far, in the three months that they have been together, nobody has complained.

"I like the way things look at the moment," one of the girls reflects for herself and shares with her roommates, as she refers to the cleanliness of their shared house. She had unconsciously made her fingers check on any dust on the main table. Another roommate had seen her while she moved her finger purposely. All the three residents came and sat, as ready for their dinner. One could wonder if their move was unconscious or intentional. It was as if they gathered together around the main table for a conversation.

"I can't complain," replied the other roommate to the first one, while she thought she needed to give some opinion on the subject.

Though the main table seemed spotless, other aspects of hygiene that needed to be taken care of existed. Overall, their communal life appeared surprisingly dull, without any significant events or stories. Samuel afro-hair hadn't received any appropriate treatment for an entire month.

If he had been a woman - luckily, he couldn't pretend, given that he despised playing women roles when asked or felt uncomfortable around them -, he would've got his hair clean more regularly, like once every week or fortnightly.

It requires special care. Therefore, he would've to budget approximately thirty pounds every month to spend on it.

"Samuel's hairstyle appears uncommon among his Qarfian peers," observes one of the roommates while she tells the other girl who shares the apartment.

"Should we ask him why he combs his hair in such a style?" her colleague responds.

"I don't think it's necessary. Samuel might think you are interested in more than his hairstyle," she answers.

She didn't comment.

Samuel has to go to the women's saloons in his campus vicinity for his hair's care. It was only there that he could find all the ointment and shampoo made for his hair type. Each time he went into a saloon's hair, he came out with a hairstyle similar to that of the Black Panthers' members or Jimi Hendrix of the 60s.

Amina had once heard other students whisper to each other while looking at him that his father occupied a ministerial position in the Pambu government. This government had taken power through a military coup. Luckily, compared to other contexts where such a change of political leadership had taken place, the coup didn't shed any blood.

Nobody knew his connection with the Qarfian State's leaders at that university except two other students from the same country who lived on the campus.

"If it hadn't been because of the military coup, certainly Samuel wouldn't be on his studies here," observed one of the other two Pambuni students.

"If you depict a true picture about his case, what about you? How did you end up here?" It's the turn of the other student to justify his presence at the campus.

"I don't feel any guilt about my presence here, like Samuel, who should, if he has any conscience. I earned my place, and my family pays for my bursary."

"Our compatriot has taken the place of someone who deserved it more. Government money pays for his stay on this campus," he replied.

The Pambuni student who started the discussion didn't reply. He let raised issues remain pending. He didn't want it to carry on. Their compatriot case appeared common among children of the Qarfian elite who studied in western countries. Through nepotism, leaders in Qarfi sent their children to study abroad only because their positions enabled them to do so, without any accountability, at the expense of the ordinary citizens who didn't have access to such privileges.

Samuel always wears a striped red shirt and jeans or a slight variation of the same attire. Except for his roommates, the two other Pambuni students, and later on Amina, nobody else among his classmates knows where he lives or his country of origin. His personality doesn't help much in portraying him as an introvert. He avoids the university's cafeteria and prefers to cook his food. He sources the ingredients through a network of merchants from his country. His roommates have nicknamed him the "Afro" guy.

The two female students stay in one single room with a bunk bed to gain more space. The room has a big framed window and two desk tables arranged to enable each student to concentrate on their studies. The room's design is such that roommates don't disturb each other—bookshelves built in the wall feature adjacent to the tables. One of the roommates had been an ardent advocate of minimalism for some years. She wished her colleagues could embrace it in decorating their space.

"The less we will display in our common areas, the better; if we all adopt a minimalist lifestyle, we could free energy and other resources to pursue the things we treasure most; I found out this knowledge through my reading," she explains to her roommates convincingly.

The other roommate wanted to have on her walls posters of musical celebrities of the Girls Power's era of the 90s and the new Millennium's start. Music groups in that category included Spice Girls and Destiny's Child. The minimalist student demonstrated how they could decorate the place according to their taste.

"Though unconvinced about your theory, please could you take full responsibility for the decoration of our place? We will consequently make you accountable for it. How many days will it take, and what do you need?" Samuel queries, after explaining the minimalist approach's benefits to the interior design of their space.

"Tomorrow, I will give you a small list of necessary items; I think the entire decoration will be complete within five days from now. I shouldn't have to miss my lectures or postpone my assignments to accomplish that task," the roommate in charge replied.

The decoration activity has to take into consideration the voluminous equipment of the household in place. The managers of the block of apartments gave them a refrigerator that the three residents share. Each one has containers for food they have to label with their respective names. They have ten thousand labels to glue on their boxes of different sizes and materials used.

Despite the labels, one of the girls always looks for delicious food held in the fridge, whosoever name was on the boxes. When she spots what she wants, she takes some without any consideration of the owner. Her roommates had complained once when she got caught in the two previous incidents. They had let it pass on the first occasion.

They didn't want to escalate the situation since they assumed it would be a one-off inconvenient occurrence, though the two victims found out later that if they had been tough on her in the first place, the situation wouldn't have come to what it was at that moment.

"I can't point without any doubt at who the culprit could be," Samuel reflected when the incident first happened. He felt, in a way, disappointed.

Though there was no identified thief, there was no guarantee that stealing would stop.

"This has to do with one of my roommates. No stranger to our household would venture into this place to steal only food from the fridge. Nobody has yet reported any complaint about any stolen item," he suspects but also confirms for himself.

A thief doesn't change their habit overnight. In case they did, there has to be a significant reason. Given the situation, Samuel seemed ready to be more patient until he caught the culprit. Then on D-Day, the culprit came to the shared main area, as generally as this could appear, without any awareness of her display of the stolen item. The other roommates could see the homemade jam in question spread on her slices of bread right in front of their eyes.

A few weeks before, the victim's roommate had received six glass jars with jam when her mother had last visited. Only three remained still in the fridge. Two days earlier, she had noticed that someone stole her pots of jam. She had brought up the issue at dinner time when everyone sat around. Unfortunately for her, no evidence existed to put a firm finger on anyone as the culprit. She let it slide.

Samuel noticed it first. He used his facial expressions and eyes and tried to hint to her colleague what he had in his sight. His other roommate sat in the right-hand corner of the table.

He had seen the special jam her roommate had received from home and unmistakably labelled as hers in the fridge.

"I never gave you permission to take my jam!" the accuser asked the culprit calmly.

"Oh! But you have too many containers of jam. I offer you a service when I use them. If I didn't, they would expire and be of no use," the culprit replied, caught unexpectedly. She tries to make it sound like a trivial issue.

"Please don't joke about it. Why are you inconsiderate, as if you don't see that you made our roommate unhappy because of what you did?"

"If this happened to me, I would make you regret your attitude," Samuel reacts angrily to his roommate's arrogant attitude.

The three roommates had ended up together randomly. None had rejected the terms and conditions of the accommodation when they got asked about their opinion. Except that their accommodation requests had been processed simultaneously by a staff member of the students' team in the campus administration, they didn't consider any other particular criteria. No affinity existed between them. The only common denominator they had consisted of being that they all came for their first year of undergraduates.

"I will tell you off to your classmates if you don't stop," the wronged roommate threatened the culprit.

"Oh, right! I will stop," the culprit who wants to preserve her image on the campus replied with some humility this time. The next few days, her horrible habit ended. A visitor who would've come to their place in those days wouldn't have guessed the character of the roommate who used to steal, since everyone behaved responsibly, while they ensured to live in harmony with others.

***

Though the three roommates cook their food, they rarely come together at the dinner table simultaneously. In case this happens, they agree to share whatever each one of them has cooked. It happens that, for that evening, Samuel had announced to the two others that he wanted to get them to taste his special menu from back home.

Once the food was ready, they helped to do the table. On that particular occasion, they had bought two bottles of wine.

"Let's dig in your meal preparation," one roommate says.

"It's delicious," the other roommate highlights.

"Please, could you pass me some wine?"

"I would like to ask a general question about men in a relationship," the first roommate asks while she stares at Samuel.

"That's random as a topic, but still, go ahead."

"What could stop a man in love to confess his feelings? Though the same reasons might not possibly apply in the case of a woman confessing. In a certain way, the variation in motivation depends on the difference between men and women."

"Fear of rejection or lack of self-confidence, I presume. Please consider here that I don't speak for every man," Samuel answers.

"Have you ever experienced those situations?" the first roommate carries on, asking.

"Not yet. I haven't found someone to fall in love with foolishly."

"Can you elaborate?"

"I can be attracted to someone momentarily, but I have never yet failed to sleep because of them. Until that happens, then I will only know that I am under the spell of love. The difference between instant attraction or one's mind responding to the body's desires and love could amount to time."

"It takes time to love someone. Whatever else hangs there before love manifests itself can't be called love. Can it be like a preloved condition?"

"I see," the other roommate says.

The two girls seem close to each other. They had agreed to ask their male roommate the question about how to confess one's love because one of them has fallen for Samuel.

"I believe that you can't control what your heart wants. Though you could resist it, this behaviour would be another issue or frontline to deal with," Samuel adds.

Samuel's answer about the confession of one's love disappointed the roommate who had fallen for him. If she decides to follow her heart, she could be hurt. She learnt at her expense that she experienced a one-sided love.

Samuel had never noticed her interest in him, significantly because she had never expressed it in any form. From that point of view, she accepted that she had been in the wrong and not him. Consequently, she didn't have any right to blame him, in case she did.

"Nobody's life goes as planned. Consequently, some individuals opt to forego any plan for theirs. Although it's still better to have a plan for which directions change according to situations than drive towards unknown destinations from unclear starter points," Samuel drifts into existential matters. They finish their dinner. The girls don't talk much at that moment. They help to clean up the table and do the dishes.

"Next time, it will be my turn to let you taste the food from my beloved Poumanda," the first roommate says while she dries the dishes and arranges them on the shelves where they stay.

"What a delicious meal! Thank you, Samuel," one of the roommates exclaimed.

The time has come to pass nine when their evening togetherness ends.

Samuel didn't use the main room as often as did his other roommates. Each time he wouldn't have his meals there, he would either be in his room or outside. For example, watching the shared television in the living room wasn't part of his routine. Visibly he didn't have any interest in TV programs or news. Their student life together as roommates continued In their first under-graduate year, unaltered by any significant event.

***

As an excellent cook, Samuel offers his rare benefactors or close friends exotic food from his birth-place, thank them, or only socialise. He turned twenty-one. He has no girlfriend. He hesitates about his feelings and wonders if he logically needed one. Whatever he ex-periences in his life at the time, he doesn't feel either emotionally fulfilled.

He doubts that a girlfriend represents his main requirement to address his shortcomings in his emotion-al life.

One weekend in advance, Amina confirms that she would come for dinner the next Saturday. In the af-ternoon of the agreed day, Samuel goes shopping and brings the necessary groceries in the communal kitchen he shares with his two roommates. However, they spend their late afternoon and early night outside, as if he chased them away to have space for himself and his guest.

He learned to cook from his mother. Each time he wants to prepare a different menu, he calls her for guidance.

When Amina arrives, she finds Samuel busy in the kitchen, but the main room's table displays the first pots of food they will eat.

"I can smell your food all over the entire house. It must be delicious."

"I hope you will like my cooking."

"I brought a bottle of red wine. Please don't mind if you prefer it white."

"It's ok."

Once all the plates, pots, glasses and pans with food feature on the table, Samuel invites Amina to come and eat. After the initial look on display, she heads to the main area and waits for Samuel to finish cooking.

"Please, dig in," Samuel says after he places his supposed best menu in close distance of Amina's easy reach.

"Thank you."

Amina offers to serve the wine. She had brought the glasses on the table when Samuel put the last touches on his dinner preparation. Both took their meal in a joyful mood, with plenty of jokes and laughter.

That month of June, summer had come much earlier. The sun had already started to take a long time to die down. By 8:00 pm, when they finished their dinner, they went out for a walk in Kolyrood, the local park.

"Do you mind if I hold your hand!"

Amina paused. A glimmer crossed her eyes when he pronounced the word hand.

"Yes, I do."

"Why?"

"Because I can't hold the hand of someone who has never told me that they liked me, and, on my side, I haven't agreed to any commitment in that direction."

"It's my mistake. I do apologise."

"For what? For the fact that you demonstrated your ignorance?"

"Sorry."

"I hear all the time these types of stories about guys' insensitivity."

"Which stories?"

"Us, women, naturally sensitive, when you don't show and or say openly that you like us, that makes us feel insecure around you if you genuinely do. When your woman - or the one to become - knows that you like her, only then will she walk beside you confidently."

"There must then be a lot of insecure women out there who walk with men like me."

"I state a fact, and I've talked to many women who tried to get into relationships. Believe me or not, that's the reality."

"Good to know."

"And you don't tell her that you like her any time you feel you should say it. You must choose the right moment when she would be more receptive and express her inner feelings about you fully."

"I don't see any right time to confess your liking!"

"You need first to spend enough time together to know her. When you sense you know her and she knows you - here you play your part and help her to know you - you give it a try. Even then, no fact or variable can predict that you will get the wanted reply."

"It's all hard work and complicated."

"Challenges in life are inevitable. At the same time, things also have relative meanings and connections. What one finds difficult, another one enjoys its ease."

"True."

"I think we should head home. It's late."

Samuel walks Amina to her dorm. In their discussion, he hoped to have learned critical lessons about women's character. Samuel regrets not getting much on the subject at school in his teenage years. When it comes to relationships with women, he knows many among his peers who don't have any clue.

After that visit, his relationship with Amina ended unexpectedly. It would be the last time they would be together.

They had been friends for the time of two semesters, while they comforted each other when need be. Their friendship drifted for some unclear reasons, and their destinies diverged forever. Each one got caught in their path, and surprisingly no regret subsisted on neither side for that new direction that their fates took.

CHAPTER THREE - Ordinary Humans
SECTION 1. Friendship And Crime

Ohosh Night

On that Saturday, October 14th, with a clear and sunny sky, but which displayed an unusual coolness for an Autumn day and seemed reluctant to declare its real intentions, Amina had spent exactly one year in her new neighbourhood.

"After this week-long office-work, I plan to get out of my apartment and relax a little," she told her workmate the day before. At least for a few hours, she initially intends not to get her programme for the week-end changed for whatever could be the reason.

In the last two weeks, her employer had given her full responsibility to implement the strategy successfully to enter the Vodnak market. The headquarters had spent months on the planning board and put in many
efforts to make it right. She had allocated long hours on her task and staff meetings and made her team work overtime to respect the deadlines. "I think I de-served that break. This week, we made giant steps for the company," Amina added. She belongs to those peo-ple who live the lifestyle of 'work hard and play hard.' When their goal is to remain human and avoid becoming like robots, one makes a deliberate choice about such life. They both think they should have a few drinks at the lo-cal bar. That place is in front of the Notgni High Street station. She calls her friend and workmate's telephone number.

"Are you free in the evening? Let's have a drink in my neighbourhood today. Please don't disappoint me." Amina enquires but also implores.

"I thought the same thing," the workmate replies.

"I will be there at six," she adds.

"Call me when you leave your place. I will tell you where to meet," Amina replied.

While she waits for the time to pass, Amina gets herself busy before they meet and does some chores around her apartment the whole afternoon. A hate relationship with that activity had developed as she grew up, to the point that she kept her visitors at bay, not allowing them to come into her place.

At times, Amina outsourced specialist agencies to come and tidy her house. This operation had a cost, but she could afford it twice a month. In terms of cleanliness, once grown up, she had changed entirely from the most orderly person she used to be to the worst.

Though she had proactively put her chores among her resolutions for the new year, for the last twelve months, she hadn't gotten rid of articles she didn't use anymore, even from many years before. She bought and accumulated more and more each time. Though these relics constituted the past, that time sank at the back of the memory lane.

No matter how hard she tries. These items include clothes she acquired out of frustration or depression. She had as well books loved or bought only for their titles but had never read. Office accessories from different eras of technological progress feature among the list. Kitchen utensils for which even to wash them have become a sinister task, had also to go, once she would seriously embark on cleaning her space.

At one time, she had tried to learn and play guitar as a hobby. In her tough times of loneliness, she had resorted to disassembling her instrument. She had destroyed it and consequently couldn't play it anymore, but at the same time, for reasons she couldn't understand herself, she had kept all the guitar's parts in one same place.

Until that day, she had looked at them all the time but couldn't dare to get rid of them. She felt firmly attached to them emotionally.

She can't get around that task and clear up all her disorderly amalgam of things displayed all over the place. She usually arrives home tired from work. Moreover, the courage to do her cleaning lacks at such times.

She seemed only to have time to prepare her meals, relax a little, watch a movie and go to sleep, and occasionally this happens while the television remains switched on. Day after day, she waits comfortably for the same routine to unravel for the next day and then the one after. Marie Kondo's Spark Joy would have been most helpful in this area, to declutter and organise her home, given the challenges the whole issue makes her live in those moments.

"I must have fewer hours in my day to go by than anybody else," she finds this as her logical excuse to fail to clean her place.

"What others find time to do around their apartments, I find myself incapable of accomplishing the same," she assesses herself comparatively.

Some of her relatives live spread around the world. This spatial separation adds to her discomfort. They complained that she didn't talk to them much.

"It doesn't bother me if I don't get in touch with them. Although it annoys me when my relatives somehow interfere in my life from wherever they could be," thus she sees the relationship with them and would like it to remain. She would have liked them kept in the dark about her life. While still in the village, she remembers how everyone wanted her to help them. She felt at their mercy. When she entered secondary school - she moved to a different country when her parents died, she promised herself to become freer.

It appears she had many areas where she undoubtedly failed or lacked. She didn't like chores around the house - though she did it well once her heart was on it, she would also struggle to sustain her relationships.

***

Amina and her colleague arrived at the bar at the agreed time. She carries herself and shows off her Bottega Veneta handbag on the left shoulder.

"How do I look?" she turns around in her high heels for her friend to appreciate fully. She didn't say much but showed her thumb up.

"What about me?"

"I like your new hairstyle. It makes you look like a city girl," Amina replies.

That evening, Amina's friend went out with a brown leather pencil skirt, one of her unique and unusual clothes in her wardrobe.

"This handbag came as a gift I got from my last boyfriend of only three months," Amina adds while she looks at her accessory.

She has put on her tulle dress with a neck-tie. Besides, on her left arm, she wears a Channel watch she bought from her first salary after graduating a few years back. To select which shoes to match her outfit took her nearly four long minutes. She wanted to find which pair goes with the chosen ensemble. She has only finished two glasses of wine. Even then, she can accomplish that only when she eats at the same time. Late in the night - already in the full mood of the weekend - they agree to move out of the bar and go on discovering more of the Vodnak night scene. They get further south in the area, at Juju nightclub located on the famous Kwins Road.

The nightclub specialises in cocktails and counts among its clientele celebrities and regulars from the local area. Besides, the venue hosts a variety of events, shows, product launches and live music nights. The two women came to that place looking for a different night out for a change. They get there at half-past eleven. Amina orders straight away an Aeslech Dagger. She likes a Bombay Sapphire shaken with elderflower liqueur, apple juice and a touch of demerara sugar.

Her friend requests the midnight special in Juju, which corresponds to a Stolichnaya vodka muddled with fresh blackberries, apple juice and a dash of bowls of blackberry, served over crushed ice. They enjoy their drinks until their night out takes a different turn.

The time on that Sunday shows one in the early hours of the next day. The girls think it is time to end their outing. They haven't moved from the seats where they have been since they arrived. Two gentlemen approach them. Amina's friend holds her glass, and she sips slowly and visibly enjoys her drink. It remains tightly held in her hands as if she fears to put it down. She seems to think while her eyes closed, but with a gaze in her eyes. She glanced in front of her. Behind the bartender, her sight looks onto the different bottles of wine and whisky on the shelves.

She turns her eyes around. New customers get their cocktails shots on one of the tables in the left corner of the bar. After a moment, Amina and her friend chat with a carefree kind of attitude. Not drunk yet, but they would be soon if they didn't stop. They have ordered another shot of their favourite cocktails.

"What do you have as a drink?" asks the first gentleman, while he introduces himself as Tom to people he doesn't know much.

"Tom, and Dave, a friend from childhood," he adds while he points at himself then at his friend.

"You have here, Amina," she replied and went for his hand, and the gentleman waited to hold hers. Did she forget to introduce her friend consciously? Maybe not. She didn't stop to drink for the last four hours; she has forgotten how to be formal and polite. She manages to get her hand into Tom's one, though she nearly misses it.

"And who could be your gorgeous friend," Tom asks while he looks at her right side deferentially.

"Why do you ask us who we are?" Amina asked as she acted like a big sister to her friend. She looked at her with a severe face and seemed to summon her not to say anything. With her right index finger on her lips, Amina indicates to her friend to zip her mouth. She didn't give her the time to respond to Tom's question.

"We would like to know who will join us to continue and enjoy the night."

"In a moment, we head to a different place much more interesting, with more entertainment than here," Tom pursued, and thus he proved to be the most talkative of the two gentlemen.

"How can it be so?" Amina enquiries. Excited, she asks, while she thinks at the moment that she might carry on with the night out.

"It's in the Ohosh area. We will be there in less than ten minutes at this time of the night. There isn't much traffic right now. Over the weekend, all night long, they don't close," Dave explains with a humble tone in the voice.

Amina looks at her friend slightly. The latter moves her head both left and right, accompanied by a facial expression that nearly says yes to the invitation. She then makes a slight move of her both eyes, like winks, to convince her they should go, although she hasn't found out about or doesn't know much about Dave and Tom. Suddenly she asks.

"Could you give us some moments on our own before we decide?" pleads Amina to the gentlemen.

"Don't worry, we won't be long!" she adds. Tom and Dave looked at each other and headed back to their seats a few ten meters away.

Amina wanted to stay out longer that night.

"Let's go to Ohosh with the two guys who have invited us," she pleads and convinces her friend. That night Amina met Hussein in Ohosh for the first time. They clicked immediately. Though they didn't sit together on that first meet up, they exchanged their contacts.

On three subsequent occasions, they came together for a drink, then on the last one, Hussein took her to his apartment and spent the night with her. In the couple of months that followed, they kept in touch every other week and got to know each other even more.

As time passed, Amina discovered the macho sadistic personality of Hussein. He had this condescending attitude towards women that she could hardly adopt.

Hussein would shout at her or throw insults for no discernible reason, even around mutual friends. At one time, she questions the depth of the relationship they had together. While this went on, Hussein would pamper her with whatever every other girl wanted since he had the means to satisfy it.

Every weekend, they spent most of their time in nightclubs. Hussein's parents' money served him to get what he wanted. He took advantage of the situation as the only boy in the family. Thus he had been somehow spoiled. He couldn't and didn't cook at his apartment, though he was well past twenty years old.

Instead of cooking, he ordered his takeaways all the time when he felt hungry. His female guests who wanted to show him their cooking skills used the kitchen from time to time.

With time, Amina fell more and more in love with Hussein; however, at the same time, she got equally anxious about their relationship breaking up and feared that he might not change in the future.

Best Friends

Florencia had returned to live with her sibling. A few months had passed after she walked out of her marriage. Haile hadn't yet made any connection between her and Amina, he knew. Since he hadn't paid attention to the twins' existence in his area, he must've occasionally taken one for the other.

The conversation he had with Dae was their first, though they had previously seen each other in the neighbourhood.

"What is your field of work?" Haile asked Dae on that occasion. At the time, she chatted with Florencia in front of the main entrance of their building.

"I work in the film sector in the city," Dae replied. She took the question as a formality.

She's a professional Pobean and a single mother who lives in the same neighbourhood as Amina.

"What attracted you to this part of the city?" Haile pursued with some more interest in her person than the question he asked.

"I worked through an estate agent to end up here," she answered. In reality, she had moved there when the relationship with her partner broke up. Her attraction about Vodnak, not particularly the area, came from her readings and the history she had learnt while still young.

"I didn't have any particular preferences. My agent recommended the area for its safety, transport facilities and museums," she replied additionally.

Unintentionally, Dae became involved with the twin sisters because of her hatred against abusive men. On a personal level, she hadn't herself experienced abuse in her broken-up relationship or elsewhere so far. What she lived instead originated from a lack of tenderness that some people not confident enough in themselves suffer.

She felt vulnerable and miserable, each time she considered not to be the centre of attention from her people.

Her repulsiveness towards abuse originated from her life experience with one of her aunts' households.

"Each time I go to visit my aunt, I leave her deeply traumatised in some ways. The violence she suffers and endures in her husband's hands appears extreme from an objective assessment. I don't know how she manages to live with it," she said while she shared her relative's story with a close friend.

However, she got herself served in terms of harassment when she came to live in the same apartment block as Hussein. Things happened unexpectedly. The estate agent had recommended the area, but he couldn't predict the future from what he had learnt about that neighbourhood.

In her early twenties, Dae had fallen for a guy who had considerable wealth but lacked remarkably in romance. She stayed with him for three years in an open relationship. After some time, she tried another love affair with a different man; the relationship didn't go further than a few dates. Heavens seemed not to favour her in the love affairs.

Her parents, diplomats by their career, represented the Republic of Pobe abroad for more than thirty years. They had Dae at the start of their diplomatic career. From the beginning, they gave more importance to their work than their family. Looked after by a nanny until age four, for five years, they decided to leave her with one of her aunts who lived in Kuonl. They had already spent ten years in Niasan when Dae joined them, aged nine. Even then, still focused on their careers, they agreed both that it's in their interests and those of their daughter to enrol her to become a boarder in a private school when she would turn ten.

For several years, they had already saved money. Consequently, they could afford to provide her with the best education in their country of residence.

Once passed her teenage years, she grew up and increased her interest in films as the years went on. She attended the Okyto University of the Arts.

After her graduation, she briefly worked in Okyto; she then moved to Vodnak. Her employer ran a media company specialising in films' production, focusing on oriental traditions. Her Meng education taught her to develop a close relationship with natural surroundings, be sensitive to the change of seasons, and have a deep appreciation of colour. Such a background made her enjoy public parks, visits to museums and other attractions more than the average person.

She ended up in the same neighbourhood as Amina, but her encounter with the twin sister Florencia could be considered accidental. She came to know the latter, apparently because they liked similar fashion styles. She was only three years older. They regularly shopped at the same stores. Though they came from different backgrounds - one originated from Pobe and the other from Occorz - both lived in Vodnak in proximity; also, it was as if an indiscernible magnet had pushed them towards one another.

***

Dae and Florencia experience differently the attempted murder of Hussein. That incident would transform the course of their lives. Both were divorcees, but regrettably, none of them had ever talked openly about their failed experiences of married people for the gossipers.

"I consider my one year of marriage to be a mistake."

"It constituted a worthwhile experience to go through, to do better in my future relationships with men, if they ever happen," she assesses her life with the husband she had left. Such discernment could only be beneficial. When people learn from past mistakes, they grow in wisdom.

"He didn't live up to the expectations I had when I first met him," Florencia blames her ex-husband once she left him. She considers that he didn't love her or show her that he cared about her well-being.

The husband lived in his world; he came home to have his food, change clothes, and sleep.

In the first months of their relationship, having sex with her featured as part of her to-do list. Within ten months of life together, even touching each other stopped. When she left him, the last time they had had an intimate encounter together had been two months before.

Somehow ill-tempered and getting angry quickly, she found that the whole situation had escalated in a short period. Overwhelmingly subdued to the point she had almost given up, she fell gradually into deep and persistent depression. She didn't know what to do. Her twin sister couldn't stand by and let her sink every day to the lowest level of herself. She decided to rescue her from that misery.

Was the ex-husband the only side to take all the blame for the failure of their marriage? Hasn't, at any given time, Florencia looked at her part? They had tried to communicate and talk about mutual frustrations in their relationship but to no avail. Each one continued to blame the other for what visibly couldn't work in their life as wife and husband.

Nobody had tried, however, to listen closely to the views of the ex-husband about their relationship. All the invited and uninvited assessors of their situation had only considered Florencia's perspective.

Still, their analysis didn't guarantee that the ex-husband could effectively be the only one at fault. In the end, whoever could take the blame; separated finally; the two sides had to put aside their past and move on.

Out of the two divorce cases, Dae's one seemed the least her circle of friends knew enough details about. She had somehow willingly avoided revealing much because she had been the one who ruined her marriage.

Though she didn't lack whatever money could buy, she considered herself abnormally inadequate and unsatisfied romantically. She sought a lover outside her marriage to fulfil her romantic desires.

When Dae found the person, unfortunately, their relationship didn't survive.

Since she felt she couldn't go back to her loyal but unromantic husband and didn't want to spend the time and effort required to chase men for romance, she decided to quit men's relationships altogether. Her life stood at a juncture similar to a crossroad when she met Florencia. She discovered that she was in such a situation while she talked to her about Hussein. However, with time, she got surprised when she found out that she felt more at ease with women than men.

***

With the force of time, Dae and Florencia have come to know each other well. It took Dae a while before she could differentiate her from her twin sister, mainly when she visited Hussein in their block of apartments. They became close and best friends. They shared their secrets and public lives more than would sisters do.

"I would like a clear answer to this question I have," Dae prepares Florencia mentally in case she would feel embarrassed.

140

"Oh, no! Please don't be hard on me, but go ahead," Florencia pleads.

"Between you and your sister, who has Hussein chosen as his girlfriend?"

"It's complicated; I mean difficult to explain."

"Please could you elaborate? Has he confessed to you, or did you? What is happening? I see you and your sister coming out and going to his apartment separately. Still, I've never noticed all three of you together," she presents Florencia with the picture of a puzzle for their love triangle. Dae, visibly, doesn't know the exact position of each different piece.

"I can't answer your question with certainty at this time, maybe within a week. I will be more accurate on where things stand by then," Florencia replies.

Dae didn't try to put pressure on her. She could only guess what could be her burden at the time. The twin sisters probably competed for the same man. Dae didn't dwell on her unanswered question, and it didn't alter their friendship.

In their spare time, mainly on the weekends, they would go out to have coffee or for walks. They would visit people and places they knew or wanted to explore together. Dae became aware of the toxic and twisted relationship between Hussein and Florencia, where the latter had to pretend to be her twin sister while in front of him. With their body features and looks, they seemed like identical copies. Anyone who didn't pay closer attention to their differences could effectively get confused.

Dae has had as well her share of Hussein's abuse for women in general. Each time they would pass each other, either near their building, or elsewhere in the vicinity of their apartments, or even on the high street, he would not miss the opportunity to harass her.

There seemed to be some devilish attraction between them, of an undesirable nature. She described him as a despicable person.

One day, Florencia comes to see her in her apartment to seek some help. She wants to confront Hussein and make him stop his abuse of women, and particularly her sister. Still, she can't argue more on how to go about it. Her friend appears to be more resourceful than her.

"I told you several times how unmanly Hussein is. Though he behaves the way he does, particularly with his abusive attitude, my sister doesn't consider him a bad person. With such an attitude, I understand more the statement that refers to the blindness of love. In my sister's case, that gives me the reason to make me badly want to end their relationship, and I need your help," Florencia explains and pleads strongly.

"Don't worry, I will come up with a plan and let you know," Dae replies.

A few days later, she came to Amina's place when her sister had gone out. They planned together what they needed to do about Hussein.

"Whatever we do with him has to be when he is not sober. Alternatively, someone will have to make him drunk. We must also drug him to make him unconscious," they gave the impression that they agreed on this latest approach.

"I will drug him, and you will kill him," Florencia explains and elaborates on the ultimate and decisive solution to end Hussein's abuse of women. She coldly suggests this plan, to the extent that her friend didn't recognise that side of her. However, they had been friends for some time. She couldn't understand where Florencia's toughness came from. Understandably, she had had an unenviable life, but to get to where she envisages killing someone, this seemed new for Dae.

Florencia had experienced a traumatic marriage. In a way, this could be why to the point of rage. She couldn't wait any longer. The time had come for her to decide if it was still possible for them to plan their future together.

"We need to talk," Amina calls Hussein and summons him for an urgent matter. She didn't want to discuss the topic over the telephone.

"I will only be available tomorrow, and from 4:00 pm onwards. Let's meet at my place," Hussein replied.

"OK. Then I will see you tomorrow," Amina responded.

Hussein couldn't think of what could be the topic of their conversation. No severe or unsettled issue existed in his mind that he needed to sort out between him and her.

In the morning only, he attended lectures, but part of the afternoon, he would usually be at the university library. Though he is considered an irregular student, he surprised people when he behaved like a normal one. Consequently, he would be on time for lectures, put in the necessary effort to complete some of his assignments and use the library for that purpose. Other days, he would go wild, disappear, and spend three consecutive days or a whole week without any trace of him. In that period, he would therefore miss the lectures listed on his curriculum.

While he grew up, he repeatedly heard that he would inherit his father's businesses and sometimes this would go over into his head. To study or not to study, that didn't constitute a serious problem for him. No academic demand on him mattered as a consequence.

"As the only male heir of my father - Hakuna Matata - whatever I do, to study or not, it's up to me," Hussein would go on and reflect in his mind whenever he got frustrated by the expected academic work from him.

These negative ideas came around when he had been drinking or found it hard to cope with studying pressure.

On the agreed day, Amina headed straight home from work. She arrived at Hussein's apartment at 4:00 pm exactly. At her job, staff could choose to work flexible hours daily, as long they clocked in seven hours each day. She knocked on the door of Hussein's apartment, but nobody replied. She called him, and his phone rang several times without anyone on the other end responding. Two minutes later, she tried again with the same outcome. Then she texted.

"Where can I find you?" Amina asks him.

"You aren't home because your apartment looks empty."

Though she's his girlfriend, she didn't have the keys to her boyfriend's apartment. Hussein had deliberately avoided giving them to her because he expected to cheat on her occasionally. Such behaviour characterised him, unreliable as one cheater could be.

She received a message after thirty seconds.

"If you don't mind, please could you join us in the usual local pub?"

She texted back.

"Can you talk?"

"Let's talk another time," his message said.

"Listen. I told you that I wanted to talk to you privately. I understand today you don't want to. We will find another time."

Amina felt desperate to make Hussein more considerate of her and stop his constant abuse towards her. She didn't want to lose him. On the issue of peoples' characters, she forgot that they don't generally change unless she had some magic spell to use on him.

Some common knowledge stipulates that one must agree on how others portray themselves until they prove themselves wrong.

This statement says that if someone pretends to be truthful while his actions show the opposite of what they say to be, they have established themselves as liars in that particular instant. Consequently, one has to consider them as such.

Hussein's girlfriend, Amina, knew that people considered Hussein a womaniser. Hence, she had to watch or police him constantly or live with that vice about him. For example, she feared that when Hussein went to a pub on that day, he could end up home with a different woman either at his apartment or in a hotel room. To have a girlfriend served one purpose for him, and when such an arrangement didn't work for any reason, he turned to another woman.

They had already been together for six months. Hussein had been crazy about her the first month of their relationship. He had managed to be with her in all her free time away from work. Soon after, Hussein had started gradually to distance himself from her. He avoided seeing her when they had agreed to meet. While she would wait for him, he would flirt instead with other women.

***

On one ordinary day, Hussein has a drink and a meal with a group of friends. He had had so many similar occurrences in the past, but he would face uncontrollable circumstances in the foreseeable future to enjoy anything.

In the discussion which went on in the group, one of the participant women despises him profoundly. In the past, she had fallen victim to his bullying on two occasions.

Despite that dark relation they shared, she didn't keep herself away from the group. Instead, she stayed put around him at the same table, actively engaged in the discussion. She seriously warns him about his abusive attitude towards her peers.

"Don't you ever think that these women you humiliate all the time could one day come after you?" she angrily asks him. Hussein had initiated the ongoing discussion on a theme of particular interest for women.

"I don't care. I will ignore such women the same way I see you as useless," Hussein had replied with some degree of nonsense because he was already drunk. Seemingly, though the woman had warned him, it was as if he wasn't listening. The warning didn't connect at all with his reason. Instead, he continued with his drinking.

His circle of friends knew well that he didn't often select who to abuse or not. He treated women similarly without any distinction. On any single day, every woman he came across could be his target.

It didn't occur to anyone to assess if Hussein, to abuse someone, needed to have known them for some time. Not at all. He had a sort of allergic reaction to women in general. Probably he felt some uneasiness about being nice to them. That characterised his personality. Unfortunately, that behaviour would become fatal at some point.

"Are all the men in his family like him?" Amina had once asked Ahmed, a cousin of Hussein, to talk about him in his absence.

In his family, nobody else behaved like him towards women. If there had been someone, therefore, Hussein's manners could've been genetic.

Such an incomparable attitude only became manifest when he moved away from his family to live independently. Freedom can cause damages when not managed adequately.

"The family context must've been the factor which enabled him to contain his expression of abuse," Amina had then argued at the intention of the cousin. While his direct family was around, Hussein must have found it hard to control his behaviour. Understandably, he had to think carefully about how his father would have taken it. That possibility existed, and it could impact his inheritance.

Nevertheless, no definitive conclusion on the issue stood in view. It seemed uncertain that the family acted as a buffer to keep an explosive element locked inside its container. There must've been a root cause to such an attitude; one would wonder if this had been the case in his family's environment.

"How could they dare, as incompetent as they appear? I will crush them with my fist," he had replied to the woman who had raised the question from the group. His eyesight had a worn look. His reply had come minutes after the woman who had asked the question had long left. He had spent two hours and drank heavily strong brands of alcohol.

Another woman among his victims, who happened to be in the same group, had addressed him directly and menacingly. She had almost taken the place of her colleague, who was not there anymore.

"Wait and see. Women don't always use poison to defeat their enemies when they strike. It's a matter of time only. You can't continue this way without consequence for your inappropriate actions against other human beings," the woman in the group told him angrily, at the same time as she looked him straight in the eyes.

On this occasion, while a little drunk and intensely irritated to the extent he had become speechless, instead of his usual talk-backs and shouts, he forcibly pooled up the table the group sat around. Whatever was on the table, from bottles of beer and wine to glasses and cutlery, food, fell on the floor.

Luckily, nobody got hurt by the broken glasses. However, two of the group members got their clothes dirtied by soup and sauces that had been on the table.

When the plot to kill Hussein emerged, none of the women who had been with him that day got involved. Despite that, Dae and Florencia's criminal plan, though not directly linked to his angry behaviour at that time, had become like a logical but extreme step to address the uncomfortable situation Hussein had created. Whenever and wherever it might be, he couldn't help but mistreat every woman in front of him.

"The attempted murder on him has to be a carefully planned operation," the executioners thought. The two accomplices held several preparatory meetings before D-Day. The plan involved three stages.

If all these steps went well, Hussein would die within hours. Nobody wanted his death to become a thorn in the neck for some of the people whose involvement was inevitable. Firstly he had to be drunk, secondly to be knocked down - whatever means the perpetrator would use - and finally stabbed to death in the chest.

"I need to do this. I can't let my sister down. She might not rightly appreciate who she would be marrying. What I accomplish here represents the only option that could end their relationship completely. Before I get there, I need to think through a lot to execute the plan well," Florencia reviews in her mind from different angles her criminal action plan. Understandably, she doesn't see anything wrong in her undertaking.

For several days, the idea to get rid of Hussein navigated in Florencia's head intermittently. She felt no way to turn back. Dae, with whom she had discussed the plan - at least in its initial and unfinished form -, seemed as determined as she sounded. Florencia could count on her without failure. To work out the details constituted the tricky part.

It's her first time to get involved in a criminal action of such a scale.

On the one hand, she didn't know who to ask for help. On the other hand, she didn't want anybody to see her as a criminal.

She felt that she would be disappointed if her twin sister disapproved of her action. She only expected some understanding from her, given that she did that for her.

"I will work with Dae only. If she wants to seek support from elsewhere, I don't want to know, as long as we execute our mission well," Florencia concluded for herself, while in her mind, she referred to the plan for the operation.

"Please don't ever talk about this secret operation to any of your friends or your family members. We must take the details of the mission to our grave. Unless we fail and we get found out, then we would probably be imprisoned. The only person to know about it will be my twin sister, even her, and she doesn't have to be aware before its completion," Florencia guides Dae on who to take into the loop of the plan and when.

They devised the operation in absolute secrecy. The two accomplices took extreme measures to avoid their eventual incrimination by potential investigators.

"A week before the day and another one after, we can't use our telephones," they decided.

"We can't utilise any means of communication that could leave traces of any sort after their use," they agreed. During the concerned period, they were meant not to communicate even in writing using messages or emails.

On the day of the incident, they worked on their alibis meticulously. They ensured that people they knew saw them in certain places, some minutes before the crime.

Dae lived on her own, and for that reason, her alibi, which indicated that she was at home, could only be confirmed or strengthened by the people who would have seen her moments before the incident. On the other hand, the two sisters could quickly fabricate their alibis which stated that they were together at home at the right time because of their supposed implicit complicity as twins.

SECTION 2. Close To Friendship

Enmity In The Air

That winter, on a Monday midday, Haile's flight landed at Wortheart International Airport. Once he arrived in the airport's lounge area and muffled in his coat, he searched for his colleague Sarah. He finally finds her. She had waited for thirty minutes.

Before he boarded his flight a few hours earlier, he called her to ensure someone would be there for him when he arrived. He had a limited circle of friends; one could even doubt if such an entity existed in his case. Except for Sarah, who didn't seem by then to qualify as a real friend - the type of person someone shares things and secrets with - he didn't have anybody else on his list.

Haile lives a thrifty life. As a math teacher with a few years of experience in the role, he earns a good salary, well above the national average. He saves a significant fraction of his income, contrary to most of his peers who live in the present.

He overly trusts public transport for his travelling, whereas others have their cars. When he returned from his trip, while he got down the airport's escalators, Haile thought of the difference owning a car would've made and then leaving it in the parking lot and being able to drive home. He stopped himself quickly from such thoughts on the issue.

Sarah had replied and promised that she would come and pick him up. Haile had attended for a whole week an international conference of maths' teachers. He skipped his early fitness routine in his entire stay at the hotel; he struggled a little to get over it while he was away from his familiarities. The conference's organisers also had a tight program which didn't offer free time to the participants.

Although others prefer summertime, he enjoys the breeze of the winter period. It makes his brain function at its full potential capacity. He reckons.

When he looks back, he believes that it's in such periods that most of his career's successful accomplishments took place. The final push for his academic work, his best essays that reviewed new developments in mathematics, or the planning of competitions in maths between colleges while he was in charge all occurred when the temperature stood close to zero. These activities had propelled him to become a kind of celebrity in the maths world of his country.

Sarah spots him first, whilst he carries his black rucksack on the shoulder, in the national passengers' arrival area. Sarah waves both arms to get Haile to notice her; it doesn't take long for their eyes to see each other. With a quick and unaffectionate hug, they exchange their greetings. Sarah wears black leather gloves and a neutral dress for work under a beige feminine winter coat.

"Good to see you back," Sarah says in a neutral tone while welcoming Haile.

"Me too. It's great to be back home," Haile replies.

"How did the conference go?"

"I met new and many people of great interest. They do significant work in our maths' field."

"Undoubtedly, our school will tremendously benefit from your participation."

"I agree. If you want, I could confidentially share my debrief with you once I report back to the headteacher."

"No. It's not necessary. That will be for your chief of the department and the hierarchy of the school."

Sarah has taught in the same college as Haile for more years than he did. After some time, through informal interactions in their mutual free times, she became his only female friend at that school.

152

Way back, Sarah doesn't recall what made her be-have friendly towards him. She couldn't see any particular aspect to explore further about him.

Sarah stands now at this timely space when one questions how they ended up where they momentarily stand, without any logical explanation.

"What about we shared a meal tonight instead since I returned?"

"What do you try to say?"

"OK. Right! Indeed, you don't know me well."

"How dare you provoke me that way? You called me out of desperation to come and pick you because you don't have friends. Frankly, I despise you, now that you challenge me through an invitation for a meal!" Sarah displays an ironic tune while she tells Haile off about his gesture of kindness.

"I must appear too complicated! Though I experience the opposite daily," Haile replies and adopts a conciliatory voice.

"You mean you would like to be discovered, like the hidden gems that the explorers surprise themselves with and wonder why they couldn't find them much earlier?" Sarah asks.

"Without any pretension, I would want people to learn to know me instead," Haile calmly asserts.

"I think you should learn about your social skills properly. I don't find that we became close enough to do that. Maybe that will be for another time, but not today."

"Please calm down. Let's forget about the invitation."

"Gosh! No wonder you're consistently depressed. You will end up in a mental institution."

Haile didn't respond and tried to remain as calm and composed as possible. They had already done a few kilometres from the airport.

With Sarah's VW New Touareg's comfort and performance, Haile seemed to enjoy the company despite the fact both didn't talk to each other much.

The thought of a personal car comes back to his mind. If he had had one, he wouldn't have suffered the uncomfortable company of his friend. Haile attempts to introduce another topic to talk about, but this doesn't work out either. He couldn't understand the attitude of his colleague. Hence Haile stopped even trying.

In the last ten minutes before he arrives at his apartment, a total silence between them prevails. Apart from the music of a Michael Bubble tune that plays in the car, they don't exchange any words. Both instead immerse themselves into their worlds.

Haile looks out of the window at the multi-million complex apartments they pass by. He glances at the dark clouds in the distance. The TV broadcaster had announced some rain for the next few hours. He thinks about all the rare friends he had in the past, from childhood to his adult life. He acknowledges that he doesn't know what they have become.

"How does Sarah compare to them?" he reflects without uttering his thoughts.

"Was there anyone among them on whom I could count on without any affinity between us?" He wonders mindfully on that matter.

"I don't see any. Maybe Sarah stands special to me in her way," he concludes about the relationship he has with his colleague teacher.

From his internal monologue about the type of friendship he has with Sarah, his mind takes him nearly ten thousand miles away and more than twenty-five years in the past. The river passed through his village. He crossed it every day and ran to school with other children from their hilly neighbourhood.

He remembers the tall guy who looked older than he was, given his registered age.

There was this particular way he facilitated their football sessions. Haile played the role of a referee for the matches they had in front of their classes. Though all were in the same year group, his role added an essential part in their sport activity's smooth supervision.

While Haile had let his mind drift into his past, Sarah, in that time, tried to block out any other thoughts from her mind. She doesn't want to be distracted while she drives.

All the way home, from time to time, Haile indicates the route to take, while he points his finger left or right, given where they arrived, be it in an intersection of roads or on a side-road they needed to take from the highway.

She had never been in that area of the city. Within three to five minutes, they would be in Haile's close neighbourhood.

"Don't you think that was harsh? What you said a moment ago!" Haile asks and tries to clear any possible misunderstanding. He paused and waited for Sarah's response.

Sarah doesn't reply.

"Whatever! I will see you tomorrow, but please make an effort and improve your mood. I will reiterate my invitation," Haile adds.

She pulled her car into the parking lot along the main road.

"We have arrived there. The house number you told me, I think, can be seen over there," Sarah points her finger towards the block of apartments where Haile lives. She had stopped the car. Her overall mood hadn't changed at all since they left the airport.

Haile got out and took his luggage from the car boot. He then waved goodbye. Sarah didn't even look, but her attitude seemed to say and show that she was relieved.

THE NEPTERSINE : LIMITLESS DEVOTION

It's noon. The main street in front of the block of buildings Haile lives in seems empty. Only, a group of pigeons on trees without leaves, on the left side of the pavement and in some distance, proves there might still be a sort of life around. When he opens the door of his apartment, a dog barks in the background.

"What could it be that made it bark?" he wonders. He goes to his balcony, while unconscious of the reason he heads there. At a neighbour's house, Radio Ten plays a tune of Bobby Brown. He gazes above the homes in his neighbourhood.

All appears peaceful, without the noise that usually pollutes the area, though he came to be accustomed to it. Even the usual traffic on the nearby intercity roads conveys a rare contribution to a peaceful mood of the moment. At this particular time of his life, no pointer would've predicted he would become an indirect witness and actor in an attempted murder that occurred in his immediate neighbourhood within a couple of weeks.

***

Sarah's father was a Presbyterian pastor. His ministry had taken him and his family to several countries where development still lagged behind and at the bottom of the world list.

"What do you want to be when you grow up?" her father would ask her at dinner time while the occasion would gather the whole family.

"I think I will be a teacher. Ms Thompson excites me when she teaches the class to read good stories," she replied.

When Sarah grew up, she witnessed poverty in its different forms. She objectively understood what it meant to live disenfranchised. Her personal experience made her an unintended observer.

156

Her father's ministry managed the service of feeding the urban poor. In her teenage years, she even volunteered to serve at mealtimes.

Many years later, she became a teacher, and her family's ministry abroad ended. They returned to Vodnak, and she found a teaching role in the same college as Haile.

On one occasion, she and Haile had got drunk the night before. For some reason they don't remember, he had slept on the couch at her place. Both wake up that morning, ready for their breakfast. He had been the first to have his bath. The night spent at Sarah's apartment had been accidental. He hadn't brought any spare clothes to change those he wore the previous day.

"Could you pass me the bread, please?" Haile asks Sarah, who sits in front of him on the opposite side of the main table. Sarah finishes spreading butter on her toast.

"Did you know that the majority of people in the world don't eat breakfast, not that they don't want it, but only because they can't afford it?" Sarah argues.

"What do you mean?" Haile asks.

"I have known folks who struggle to find one meal a day because of the conditions they live in and the incompetence of institutions supposed to help them," she explains.

"I understand. If it wasn't for the corrupted structures which generally control everything, such conditions could change. The problem consists in the support local leaders receive from external partners, without any requirement of reciprocal accountability, as long as the donors get their interests served," Haile argues.

"In your opinion, the external partners would be to blame while the poor remain poor, or their condition occasionally worsens," Sarah counter-argues.

"You are partially right. The external partners shouldn't be the only scapegoats of that poverty situation. There is a saying which states that nobody develops nobody, and further indicates that people develop themselves. In the context in question, if the concerned people can't find a solution to their problem, whatever would be imposed on them as the solution won't necessarily alleviate their plight," Haile elaborates.

"Listen! This topic of poverty covers broad areas of issues and knowledge. Therefore, one can't discuss its different aspects over one breakfast. Let's pursue the debate another time," Sarah concludes the discussion.

"I agree. Please note that I've only paved the path of the place where I was born. Much of that will come another time."

They got ready and headed to their place of work together. During their breakfast, the hangover soup they took helped them face their students in the morning sessions while in the right mood.

***

It's on Friday at 11:00 a.m. in the college where Haile and Sarah teach. Their second intimate encounter takes place at the end of the second term of their academic year. It's after the school assembly. The headteacher has now wished the school members, staff and students, to spend a holiday of total rest for everyone to come back fully refreshed.

While the headteacher addresses the audience, Haile scrutinises; then I will go to Spangon for the rest of our time. How about you?"

"Relatives in Miugle want me to visit them. Please let me know if you will have time for me before you travel."

"I won't pack much. Tomorrow and Sunday, I will be home. Please pass any hour at your most convenient time."

"Let's make it on Sunday at noon. We should have lunch together."

"See you then until that time."

What happens between them when they meet on the agreed day? Would it change their relationship's nature? The occurrence called for an assessment in its own time. One could wonder if their different backgrounds constituted a barrier to their closeness. Will they become intimate, though they seemed to struggle on that other front? Life and the universe, in general, have their mysteries, and they only let people discover them with a pinch of patience.

Worth Protection

The cat saw him first. Haile had come across it on the street along his block of apartments. He had stopped incidentally to observe its stroll. The felid had no distinctive feature or characteristic, except that it had imitated him while it looked in his direction. It continued its errant walk as if the encounter didn't stir up any significance.

Surprisingly, while his thoughts shifted from the cat's act, Haile noticed that he breathed, his feet headed towards a specific direction, and his eyes looked at an object well defined. As if these actions were not part of his unconscious routine.

He realised that moment of awareness one doesn't get conscious about all the time. The power of the present, within which no other fact or occurrence mattered.

"Can such moments be meditation, or living in the present? While forgetting willingly about the past and also forfeiting the future? The logical and final step means to be more specific on the moment one chooses to focus on?" He wondered with some degree of uncertainty.

Whatever it was, it looked like a moment of discovery. Though still an ordinary day, on the street without a famous address, it became special in some sense as well.

Haile and his colleague, Sarah, the history teacher, had agreed to spend their late hours of the day together at a local pub. Way past six, he had felt more friendly than usual. Much earlier in the afternoon, he had initiated their conversation. Sarah had finished her session and headed to her office. In the corridor, she nearly passed him.

"Hi, Sarah!" Haile says without insisting. He doesn't wait for her to complete her supposedly expected response when he carries on.

"What will you do this evening? We can grab one at a local place," Haile attempts to block her way and make her slow her pace to listen to him.

"I find the after classes' period most convenient. I will be in my office until then. You could join me there, close to the time you want us to go. We could then leave together," Sarah replied while she thinks of the reputation Haile had as an intelligent teacher at that school. He made his students score high nationally in the subjects he taught and supervised.

"In a moment then. I will see you later," Haile replied.

With clear intentions, they both had ended up in that pub. They didn't go there regularly. The place at the end of their day became a one-off. Sarah didn't think she would ever repeat their encounter the whole time Haile would stay at the school. He didn't fit her type. There won't be any other invitation she would accept from him until circumstances would take him on a different life path. Each of them had willingly decided to be there this time, probably incidentally, or bored of the way they spent their time after work. Or for Sarah, it had only been out of politeness. They had had a few drinks and chatted beyond the usual school subjects they taught.

"So you've been into sports all your life?" Sarah had asked him after a sip from her glass of a martini cocktail. Haile had earlier explained his jog routine.

"I wouldn't say all my life, but the truth is that after my university years, I actively pursued my body and mental fitness. I have so far enjoyed it the same way others enjoy going to a pub every other day or don't miss a soap opera on television," he replied.

"But on top of that, a health element exists that I don't deny. It keeps me going. Each time I stop to exercise, I feel as if I betray the needs of my body. I won't stop until I die," Haile elaborates on his fitness' habit.

A minute of interlude passes. Neither Haile nor Sarah wonders what the other thinks and tries to self-censor from what comes to their minds and struggles to come out.

"Do you want to listen to a story I heard about, which appears hilarious, given where one stands on its main issue?" Haile asked.

"Please tell me."

"It's about girls who lose their virginity?"

"What about when men lose theirs? Do they never seem to be virgins? In their manhood, they appear to supervise how or which girl has to lose their virginity or not," Sarah argues.

"I think that assumption is implicit. When girls lose theirs, they lose it either to boys who could also still be virgins or not. Probably, when people talk about the loss of virginity, in the case of girls, that gives the story much appeal in the psyche of the majority of men," Haile counter-argues.

"But, couldn't there be also sexy boys? In that situation, could then these boys become the prominent subjects of the story you talk about?" Sarah argues while she refutes the focus Haile puts on the girls.

"You know what? I think more stories about girls who lose their virginity than men's similar stories exist. You know why? Because men dictate the stories, the general public tells and those it should ignore." His argument confirmed a well-documented narrative that the victors write history; in this particular case, men being physically and generally stronger than women, even stories that glorify their manhood - whatever aspect they portray - appear to be popular.

"The whole concept of even a loss sounds negative. Why don't people say losing childhood, youth - while referring to the teenage years -, or maturity? If all these steps constitute the normal stages of personal growth, negative association to them should be necessary," Sarah argues.

"Do you still want to hear my story or not?"

"Ok! Go ahead. I hope I stated where I stand."

"It happens on the night the newlyweds get together alone to consummate their marriage."

"One could object that there shouldn't be an issue if the loss of virginity occurs on that occasion. As if it couldn't logically take place at any different time. I would contend that effectively the loss of virginity should occur only at that time."

"Though, in my view, to lose or not someone's virginity, for a mature girl, should not be a big issue. As long as it does happen, it becomes an enjoyable experience, with good memories for the future. The wish of every parent with conservative ethos consists in that it only happens on a special night. But, the way the night gets experienced, the story focuses on that only. When the groom and the bride get into their room, the former doesn't know how the bride looks. The same goes for the bride. They don't know each other. Understandably, both knew for some time that they would get married and had to get ready for the occasion. Not being like animals while being taken to the butcher for slaughter, the newlyweds might not be aware of what goes on since their relationship has been an arranged marriage between two families. Even so, what the groom and the bride only know relates to the fact that the former will do whatever is necessary to make the latter lose her virginity on that particular night. On the other hand, the girl will do whatever she can to protect it for the sake of the honour of her family."

"The two families, which agreed to marry their son and daughter, bring together two individuals who haven't been in any relationship with each other before that day. In this conceptual context - and in most cases - they have not had any intimate and personal encounters with the opposite sex. Despite the agreement between the families, they look like strangers to one another until their special night. To abide by each side's demands, lose or not lose the bride's virginity, becomes a critical challenge. To protect her virginity, sometimes the bride resorts to extreme tactics."

"She puts an oily substance on her entire body to make it difficult for the groom to hold her still in any particular position."

"If the bride looks more physically apt than the groom, sometimes the entire night ends with a failure to consume the marriage."

"As the couple struggles to overcome the challenge, in such times, peer boys and girls positioned outside the bridal room try to listen to what goes on inside secretly. When the groom wins over her bride, sometimes loud applause rises from the hidden audience."

"The next day, after the groom's feedback about his unsuccessful night, the two families go back to the negotiation table to ask the bride to bend her guards down to let the groom get her to lose her virginity. She would then abide for the sake of the relationship between the two sides."

"What an incredible story!"

"Effectively it is, and it's a reminiscence of the past of certain communities. I don't expect to see such practices these days with the liberalisation of sex."

"Truthfully in the past, the culture valued and safeguarded the fact of remaining a virgin until marriage, but the question which arises concerned when could be the right time to lose one's virginity?"

"That's a tough one. I can't be the right reference on the subject. Though I highlight that, the pressure from peer groups, one finds themselves part of plays a critical role in the timing."

It got late. Although both Haile and Sarah had classes only in the afternoon of the next day, they needed to go home and rest. A little drunk but still able to stand up independently without much difficulty, both could walk in a straight line. Sarah could hold her drink much longer, but for Haile, three glasses knocked him down. When they left the pub, she helped Haile walk properly and not cause an accident on the street.

Sarah called a taxi and invited Haile to get the last one for the road at her place. Once at her house, she quickly prepared some food to eat; then, they continued drinking. Past midnight, Haile, totally drunk, voices some nonsense related to their lessons at the college and his feelings for her.

"I will get a bath, and when I come out, we will see if I can lose my virginity to you. It's a game I invite you to. I hope you can live up to the challenge."

"You can't still be a virgin, Sarah! I don't believe you could still be at your age."

"How do you know? It's up to you to find out. I will put on enough oil to make it difficult for you to check me out. I will be ready in a moment."

***

Weeks had passed from the day Haile had told Sarah the story about the newlyweds. Their friendship evolves.

He arrives at Sarah's place at the agreed time. She offers him some wine that they sip on the balcony of her apartment. The lunch she prepared consisted of a mixture of dishes Sarah learnt about years back when she travelled around the world with her father.

Haile finds it delicious since he doesn't have good culinary skills. Haile puts his glass on the table and pauses a few ten seconds. He calmly looks into Sarah's eyes.

"Do you have a boyfriend? Despite our last - I would also say accidental - intimate encounter, this question remained unanswered in my head until today." Without introducing a topic of some sort, Haile asks Sarah with a severe look on his face.

"Do you want me to be the one?"

"Please answer me first, and then I will tell you where I stand."

"No, I don't."

"What do you mean?"

"No, no-no. You aren't allowed to cheat. You haven't answered my first question, though I replied to your pre-condition."

"In that area, I behave like an explorer. I could be one if I find that we can stand compatible and some reciprocity prevails."

"I can't figure out how to explain my situation when it comes to boyfriends," Sarah carries on.

"Do you want one?" Haile continues to ask.

"I can only give you the same answer as earlier. It's difficult for me to pinpoint what I want in that sensitive area."

"Now I can honestly answer your question. I want to be your friend. I suppose I already was, but I would like to seek formal recognition unless you don't know either if you need a friend."

"Look, Haile. Listen to me carefully. For years I struggled with the different labels attached to human relationships. I prefer the simplicity found in the world of natural life, humans excluded. Within it, I don't think you have labels like friends, girlfriends, divorcees, separated, you name it."

She pauses for a few seconds, then pursues.

"And I consider that, as our society evolves, we get close to the original animal purpose to mate and or to reproduce, which means that people would meet only for the sake of it, given who among the parties demonstrates interest in this unique aspect of their interaction. The world needs these encounters for intimate relationships to sustain the species. People normally sense in themselves an emotional need and seek its satisfaction. That would be it. Forget about the ceremonial rituals. In the animal kingdom, the only ritual relates to the partner's seduction before mating, no contract between the parties, no witnesses required, no commitment to one partner and one only, and no paperwork or court order in case of divorce. If this happens to be accurate, one could also have several partners."

"Nonetheless, because I don't have any expertise in the intimacy between animals, and neither an animal myself, so I can't speak from experience and with enough authority on the subject. I can't, therefore, confirm the validity of these statements a hundred per cent."

"All this to tell you that I don't believe in labels and contracts in humans' relationships," Sarah elaborates for Haile to explain where she stands in terms of man's and woman's relationships.

They don't finish the discussion. Haile excuses himself and leaves a few hours later. He needs to evaluate and mark some students' work for the next day. He couldn't figure out clearly what Sarah wanted after her long diatribe.

SECTION 3. A Painful Path

An Irrational Marriage

In their teenage years, Amina and her twin sister Florencia develop and demonstrate adverse attitudes toward cleanliness and tidiness. Their opposite personalities in that specific area of their characters contradict the commonly accepted similarities between twins.

Identical twins generally and supposedly behave similarly, beyond their physical resemblance. Even so, no aspect of their characters could be as untrue as in the highlighted case for these two. Amina's space at home looked as sanitary and hygienic as a morgue, while her sister's one reflected a disorderly mind.

"Nobody who knows them for a long period and their family's background can understand their behavioural differences," said one of their aunts.

People wondered why the sisters could be so different. No explanation appears certain about the root causes. When one looks back, no specifics in their early development would have predicted such irreconcilable attitudes in their day-to-day behaviours.

The filth in Florencia's room horrified anyone who happened to come across it. Empty boxes from ordered takeaways, sometimes with their leftovers from several days, would remain beside her bed for up to a week. From time to time, her sister scolds her because of that, but she wouldn't change. While these food remainders started to rot, they would give off a stinky smell in her room.

"Please, can you join everyone at the table for our family's meal?" Would sometimes implore her uncle-guardian!

As often as possible, he wanted to have his food while every member of his family would be around, eat and share whatever was available to eat. She would respond and pretend to be busy or not hungry.

"Could you go and plead with her to come and eat with others?" The uncle would request Amina to insist and get her sister. But, in her utter stubbornness, Florencia wouldn't budge for anyone.

She had left her native Occorz only aged ten. Six years had passed after the death of her parents. In all those years, she had had a "rebellious behaviour. Nobody could tell if this resulted from the early loss of her biological family. Her guardian had sought no expert's assessment of her abnormal attitude. Contrary to her sister, Amina had led an exemplary existence far different from hers. There must've been an element with a dark spell specific to her genes in her DNA.

She rarely swept her room or put in a bin her used cans, card boxes, or plastic containers from fast-food deliveries. Clothes with bloodstains from her periods would pile up, and she won't appear to be bothered. Her uncle would only enter her room from time to time to check if there weren't any insects or wild animals flourishing while they fed themselves on the leftovers or took advantage of the dirt and dust that accumulated there.

Her uncle rarely took the initiative to help clean her room. He didn't want to create precedents. Florencia experienced her prime teenage years at fifteen.

"Can't you understand the importance of tidying up and being clean all the time and around oneself?" her uncle told her off sometimes. At some stage, tired of scolding her, he had stopped getting angry because of her. He didn't bother anymore. In the past, once he would scold her, she would react unpredictably.

Her teachers considered her as an average student.

"I hope fate will be on her side. I don't need to plead with Allah for him to take care of her. I believe more in her inner abilities than the capacity of prayers," reflected her uncle-guardian. He despised people who relied uniquely on prayers to overcome their misfortunes. Time and time again, he had seen them go downhill in despair and hopelessness until they died.

Amina's room, on the other hand, constituted an example of immaculate cleanliness. Spotless and aired every week, with an orderly table for study and even curtains washed every month, whatever in the room seemed professionally looked after. Everybody in her family held her in high esteem. Despite their praise, they also said of her that she suffered from excessive decluttering. They teased her and said that she had the characteristics of people who suffer from obsessive-compulsive disorder. While they referred to her cleanliness, nobody believed or understood how far she represented her sister's opposite. On that matter, their differences resembled those found between day and night.

Thus the twin sisters constituted two extremes. Without any clear indication of how much even twins could appear so unlike. When they both passed their twenties, their differences in the highlighted aspect of their respective personalities didn't change. Although it could portray minor variances, given the particular circumstances of each one, it remained fundamentally the same.

***

Florencia ventured into her marriage as several people do. Many get into it irrationally. In the process, they become couples and experience lives for which they weren't ready, and when pain and despair pack their days and or nights more than anything else, they end up miserable.

"Love occasionally makes people look like crazy creatures and come to live or behave unwisely," a friend told her when she confided in her that she planned soon to go and live with her husband.

The speed at which she moved in with him, from the time she got to know him and her arrival at his house, took only a few weeks.

"She looks like someone who takes strong and untested pills for a dangerous illness, that they consider that they would undoubtedly die if they don't take them", the same friend reflected about her attitude towards her rushed marriage.

"Nobody can predict the outcome," she deduced from her reasoning.

In that initial period, many questions she had would've made her not stay a whole year of agony in her marriage if she had given herself the time to think them through and found answers. She appeared like a traveller who starts on a journey with no direction or an exact destination, while unpreparedness would guarantee non-completion.

When the time to look back on her life with her husband came, she had only regrets about many things which happened in that period. She blamed herself for what she didn't do or did, which got her in such a situation. That would be her story. Although she would keep it to herself for a particular time, those who would have known her would also share it in their own time, as a gossip topic.

However, the question would have been to wonder if the story would tell the whole picture, either of herself or her husband. Understandably, that would be only about their relationships. No other parts of their lives would feature in the narrative, whatever way it would be shared or preserved. The accurate recollection of the story - at least what could be traceable about it - would be in her head and nowhere else.

It would be far from their entire story since their relationship as husband and wife consisted only of a small fraction of their lives.

There would be particular triggers of the memories of such a story. The voices Florencia heard invited her to remember where she had been. External factors could also prompt her to get back to her past.

Those signals would remind her why remembering becomes necessary. It was a kind of medicine to access a stable present and build her future. Given its importance, how much time or required effort to allocate to such exercise could be why the ordinary person didn't usually ask themselves.

Haile, interested in history and memories, had never come across any study to clarify that question satisfactorily. For example, it would've been of some interest to know that when one spends indicatively one or two per cent of the national budget on remembrance activities, a list of tangible outcomes would be gained and recorded in their monetary worth for the public to contemplate. Besides, nowhere existed any resource indicating objectively past aspects of the collective memory to ignore without any future negative repercussions.

On the way memories get formed, he surprisingly noted that, for the general public, he couldn't find formal techniques taught widely in classrooms or private settings, which showed how people create and safeguard memories. Even where such endeavours took place, the ultimate purpose and circumstances to keep and retrieve one's memories didn't always seem explained or fully understood on individual or broader levels.

At the end of that year, Florencia had moved out of her husband's house. That constituted an end of a chapter in the book of her life. New chapters got written and took shapes soon after - to think about them might have started even before her leaving.

The same way the previous chapters had started unexpectedly, nobody knew when the current or new ones would end. How long she would dwell on her past would be up to her.

Florencia hadn't had an easy life so far, though she wouldn't compare hers to the one of those who lived more miserably than her.

"She doesn't look like a person immune to pain, given her background. She is a survivor. More importantly, she has evolved into a completely mature individual."

"She grew through the pain she encountered. Such an experience appears to be her nutrient for growth," someone from childhood had told her. They had assessed her situation that way after the failure of her marriage.

Without Amina's dedicated support, it would've been impossible for her twin sister to be where she ended, out of the bondage of her husband's abuse. Throughout her life, Amina had played the role of a comfortable pillow the sister relied on to overcome any huddle she came across. She had been an exemplary model in that role. In the marriage of Florencia, if it hadn't been Amina's insistence and sometimes threats for her to move out, she would've, for instance, stayed in it, and probably ended up with a suicide, as she had once felt before.

She mainly lived in the present. Though she occasionally thought about the past, she had a faint picture of the future. With such a personality, she couldn't be afraid of things she didn't know clearly. Such an attitude could be harmful or beneficial. Though ignorance might be immensely costly in specific cases - if not all - her lack of awareness came to be occasionally advantageous. Though the longer she would remain ignorant, the harder her downfall could be.

***

At one time, Florencia thought that all house-holds had abusive husbands. In her dark moments, she felt suicidal. Still, a lack of courage stopped her from killing herself, despite the repeated silent call in times of despair to end her life.

While these thoughts visited her mind regularly, she considered that one needed some publicity at the occasion of such a send-off.

In her world, nobody she knew had resorted to suicide as an escape from the disappointments of life.

She considers that confronting death's challenge requires the same amount of courage - if not more - as the requirements necessary to live or survive.

The difference resides in the possibility or the misfortune of not having the time to contemplate the result of the action taken in the situation when the pro-tagonist ends up dead.

"To consider the after-death experience, the pos-sibility of contemplation seems absent. The representa-tion that could paint clearly in people's minds space and life as they occur after-death, nobody has come back from death to tell such a story. Thus, such consideration should not be put in the balance, if someone decides to die as a deliberately chosen option," had Haile reflected once Amina had shared with him enough her sister's life.

But Haile also has a different opinion. His never-changing view was that death featured as part of living. It would be absurd to imagine life without it. Maybe that explains that people who use their human experience of living don't perceive life in heavenly places where time seems infinite, or things appear to have no beginnings or ends.

"The two concepts of life and death appear inter-twined, one that implies the other per their essence," he firmly indicates.

"People who want to live, die by the thousands. Though I want to die, look at me so alive. Life can be unfair," Florencia once rumbled to herself when nobody around could hear her. At that time, she had dropped three inches lower on the scale of unhappiness.

"If I don't wake up, it will be my wish come true. I wouldn't want no one to cry for me," a thought that comes to Florencia's mind while she lies on her bed, embedded in a cover of intense sorrow.

"When fate grants me what I've asked for, I would want people to be happy for me."

"Though I won't be around to police them and find out how I contributed to their happiness," another thought that follows up from the previous one. The process could've been a mental game she played in her head to ease her mind.

The remote contemplation of death, where she traded the idea of suicide mentally that Florencia had, could be seen as a repetitive feature in her married life.

"I feel depressed, and I don't sense any hope. I think I need some, so I could continue living," each time she felt low, what kept her from the final solution seemed to be some vague expectation of a better future, away from her husband.

She seemed to play with death, and that occurred whenever she recalled her husband's abuse.

"What did I do to Heaven to deserve this?" At times, she wondered why she had to continuously face her anxiety that could take her in the precipice unexpectedly.

"Can it be all my fault? I know whenever we fail, we always find excuses or scapegoats. It can't all either be my husband's doing," on the one hand, she doesn't blame her partner for her misery. He hadn't put a gun on her head to make her move into his house. Even so, on the other hand, she couldn't have predicted the level of abuse she would face once there and become his victim.

The whole year she spent with her husband, smiling while around him, happened rarely. Even his jokes sounded dull in her ears. The most straightforward thought about him darkened her mood instantly. Dazing was a common trait of her days.

However, nobody could tell if her occasional sleepwalking at night featured among the consequences of her miserable married life. Absent-minded while shopping, her basket of groceries missed items or could have those not required. Frequently forgetful appointments to attend, guests to host, or friends to visit became extensively mixed up in her mind that her ex-husband decided to take her to a specialist. Her twin sister Amina once came to see her and noticed that her life seemed to take a difficult path.

"What goes on, sis? You know you look frankly unrecognisable beyond reason," she angrily asked her.

"I know you've had some serious issues to deal with, but you need to decide soon before I lose you for good. As my only close family, you know without you, my life would not be the same anymore," she summarised her concerns about her.

For days Florencia had lost her appetite. Appalled by whatever around her, she spent her time in bed. Disinterested in reading, entertainment from the television, even sex, misery kept her unfit for nothing. When tired of staying indoors, getting out and wandering in the neighbourhood and sitting for hours on benches in local parks, it helped her mental state to remain sane.

Her periods of sleep got at this time, populated with nightmares. The dreams she had could be senseless, difficult to remember or interpret, but similarly being highly intense experiences. They displayed plenty of wonders and colours.

Though they could be sketchy for her, they could be more so for whoever would listen to them. She could hardly describe the details from her dreams to her listeners.

The horror dreams she had would take her back to her childhood, in a gloomy forest close to the village where she had first seen the sun, as the only important gathering element.

All the four other children she came with into that open space in the middle of the forest, she doesn't know any of them. They seem to mind their own business like everyone there.

She looks up and sees tall trees where the view of the sun looks like a lit candle, of which the frame fades away soon. Another night, she dreams about being in the middle of a football pitch.

Her body lies in a cross' form on the ground while her eyes look up in the sky. The blurred light makes her think of hope despite the hopelessness she feels around her.

As in an attack formation, giant monsters with dangerous looks made out of dark clouds descend towards her speedily. Before they get to her, she wakes up from her dream. She sweats and becomes anxious. It takes her time to realise that it represented only a dream.

Sometimes, she felt that drinking alcohol could help lock out her nightmares in her sleep. After she swallowed a few drops of whisky capable of knocking down a lion, she would go to bed. Still, this hadn't a positive effect on her, and headaches constitute some of them. Each time she managed to get deep into the unconscious world, the dreams that came to her grew even scarier. The supposed cure hoped for transformed itself into a trigger to invite multidimensional monsters into her dreams.

Amina doesn't fathom how the same creatures persistently come into her sister's dreams on different nights on a practical level.

"Had they found her mind to be a comfortable and pleasurable place worth for regular visits?" She couldn't make the correlation at that point.

"Did things in her unconscious world behave similarly as in the conscious one?" She wondered.

"Would it be comparable to the dreams which visited Florencia' mind each time she entered into a deep sleep?"

Amina had these tricky questions on her mind while she thought about the situation of her sister. In the meantime, she and Haile had continued their regular fitness routine in particular spots of their local parks. For the sake of Florencia, would Amina one day have to move away to a calmer space to live a much more comfortable life? She didn't have an answer to such a question? Many others, she reserved a different time to bother her and kept her mind busy all the time.

Honey, I Am Sorry!

Three months before, Amina had noticed a severe deterioration of her sister's health from her last visit. When she saw her in that state, she shed uncontrollable tears. Although she finally managed to calm down, she had paused for a few minutes, avoided looking at her, fearful of showing her how internally distraught she felt, at the same time angry and disturbed.

"I can't cope with all this that you are doing to yourself. I will return within three days. Today, I only came to assess the situation. From what I witnessed, you don't have to stay here any longer. In the meantime, I would like you to pack all your belongings. Either you pack today or not, on the day you will see me again, I will not let you remain," she utters at the intention of her sister before leaving.

On that day, they didn't hug each other. Without "how have you been?" When she arrived, her sister had only a quick look at her. Florencia didn't comment at all while her sister stayed at her place. Once there, Amina had started sobbing only a few minutes after, when she reflected on her sister's plight.

Florencia didn't wait for her sister to come back for her. As she had advised her, Florencia had packed whatever she wanted to leave with once she left. The next day, it was D-day to leave her husband. She arrived at her sister's place with all her belongings, the ones she considered precious.

When she looked back, deep into her relationship, surprisingly, she noticed that she had started to find ways to accommodate her husband's abuse. Like a person who faces some existential cruelty of life but feels that it must be their fate without any means to escape it, she had instead tried to adjust herself and found a suspended line over which she could hang on while she breathed painfully.

However, in her moments of clarity, she felt compelled to never give in to her mind, which whispered to her: "does it matter?"

One day, she had calmly and coldly assessed her situation and understood that such a life wouldn't be worth her sacrifice and not bearable for a long time. Doubts that had started to cripple her mind evaporated instantly. She could see without much ambiguity where she headed. It's only then that she decided to pack her things and go back to live with her sister.

Her couple had come together, not as a consequence of a kind of love. Instead, on the part of Florencia, she emotionally feared her loneliness, for a woman in her prime years, and with a great desire to be dependent and feel protected by a man.

"Once I get married, I will feel less lonely. I will be a different person in many regards, on a personal level and from others' perspective," these constituted some of her assumptions and justifications that she put forward to get married. A better argument for entering a married life could've been the possibilities of personal expansion it enables. She had responded in nearly similar terms to a friend who asked her why she rushed to move in with her boyfriend of a few weeks.

"I hope the difficult moments I experience now will disappear after I change my social status and become a married woman," she had finally added.

Her feelings and hopes defined part of who she had become. Nobody could look at them differently; without them, she didn't feel like herself. She would've instead been a different being. In her view, she seemed like a piece of an artist's creations, for which the public couldn't perceive all its details to appreciate its wholeness. It would've been illogical and, in some ways, unfair if that wouldn't have been the case: not to see her the way she indeed featured in her entirety. This view came again from her understanding.

In particular cases, couples living together define love as their intimate and other positive emotional interactions.

Florencia and her husband, officially unmarried, shared a roof, a bed, sex encounters, breakfast and bills. They pretended to agree on all these things. Or they stood fully in harmony with them. Beyond them, a restricted privacy area existed where the partner couldn't access or trespass. Truthfully, not much love characterised their couple.

When people in a couple love each other but can't share and get fully involved in their partner's life, they become lonely. When Florencia once reached that level in her marriage, she felt confused and lost. That's when she looked back on her past with a lot of regrets. She believed that she might've lived as single people do if alternatives to her issues existed.

She dreamed of having a lot of money. She expected it in the form of greed she set up to her standards. She hoped to see it through, not necessarily by herself but with others' help, as the easy path to greatness, but without all the required personal sacrifices to get there. Some people dream of great expectations from life but want to see them fulfilled by others on their behalf. On the other hand, she craved friendship with other women and men from time to time if she could. Not one man, but as many as possible, she could physically and emotionally bear. When she felt close to a man's body, held tightly by an intimate embrace, she perceived herself transported alive to heaven, as she imagined it. As a devoted Muslim, she thinks such intimacy with a man could correspond to the highest heaven among the seven her Quran teachers taught her.

Florencia worked in a small restaurant and didn't earn much, but looked happy all the time with her co-workers. Her exceptional skills in that sector made her enjoy her career.

To be fair to her, she got more interested in the profession than the money it brought her.

She could cook either paid or not anytime. She had met her husband of one year on one of such occasions.

Her woman's abuser of a husband came as a regular client to the restaurant where she worked. On one occasion, when she had started to become friendly towards him, after some small talk, she addressed him casually and looked firmly into his eyes.

"What do you think of me as a woman?"

He smiled without a clear and definite facial expression of some sort.

"Why don't you join me if you need a husband? I could become yours now, but don't delay your decision for long."

He looked neat, well dressed all the time, and somehow educated. Overall, a nice guy externally.

"Well, whatever! As long as I will be able to leave as soon as I don't feel happy," she replied and spoke out her harsh truth in his face.

Within three weeks of that conversation, she took her things from her sister's and moved in to live with the man.

***

In those days, Florencia displayed deep sadness from the gossip going around about her life. Three days had passed when her aunt tried to find out.

"Where can I find Florencia?" Amina's aunt asks while she looks at her anxious.

"I heard her in her room," she replies.

"Why doesn't she help in the house as you do?" the aunt pursues, instantly as she talks to Amina about her twin sister. Florencia, from their room, could hear her aunt who badmouthed her.

Before her adulthood, Florencia had had problems with a lack of parental affection. She had difficulties engaging with other people.

Such inadequacy appeared to originate from her parents' absence at an early age. The twins had lost their biological parents while young; Florencia thought that even if she didn't perform as well as Amina, they could've loved her the way she wanted to be loved.

In her teenage years, she kept to herself in class. She had no friends, and her unfriendly attitude made her a victim of bullies. She had difficulties picturing love in her mind. She had never learned what it meant or encountered its real manifestations in her personal life.

When she got married, her emotional problems worsened. The husband would occasionally express his frustrations unreservedly to her.

"I might be unromantic in many ways. You can blame me for that. If you didn't have your body, there won't be any other likeable part of you that would make anyone come to you," Florencia's husband told her once, while he didn't look in the right mood to appear affectionate in her eyes.

Undeniably, her cognitive deficiency in love would affect her relationship with her abusive husband. Such insufficiency on the part of his wife became a justification for more abuse. The abuser enjoyed that situation. It had more of the burden gloom attached to the life of a husband who loves their partner in a standard family setting.

Florencia would not have been involved in such a toxic relationship if it hadn't been for her problem of loneliness and a strong desire for affection.

"Don't people with behavioural deficiencies deserve to be loved or some kindness?" she once wondered. At least she acknowledged her lackings.

And these persisted as real human issues that required serious consideration.

Before Florencia decided to be with her man, she felt she would not cope if they remained unresolved in some ways.

"Am I condemned to live on my own because I lack in many aspects?" she has asked herself but couldn't find a definitive answer.

But at the same time, she didn't want to start a family and add children to the equation. She didn't know yet if she had chosen the right man to become her children's father. She didn't want to burden herself further unnecessarily, not before three years with him at least. Within that period, she assumed she would've seen or experienced a man's and wife's relation enough to assess if her family's environment would be suitable for kids to grow in happily.

Emptiness characterised her true self. She hoped that having a man by her side could solve her problem of deficit in affection. As a plus on her side, she looked beautiful enough. If fate hadn't deserted her, she could've found a better man. Her limbs, thighs and hips stood all delicate and curvy shaped where necessary; to watch her undress appeared fascinating. When one looked at her, that seemed magical and aroused erotic desires. She had a body that gets some men unwillingly hypnotised and prompted unstoppably to do the unthinkable.

"I can't stop myself from looking at her. How can someone be as beautiful as she is?" her future husband had reflected for himself when he first saw her in the restaurant where she worked. He would, later on, realise that he stared at her unstoppably. From then on, she started to look at her more discreetly.

Their relationship took only a few weeks to develop, get to know each other and live together as man and wife. Within such a short period, nobody could pretend to know someone; however, intense could be their interactions!

The man enjoyed the fact that he didn't wait too long to have all the pleasures that Florencia's body could provide to him.

Despite all the abuse he projected onto her, he would try desperately to hold onto her when she realised she had to end the relationship. He failed. He, unfortunately, let her go.

When she went to live with him, she thought that would solve some of her hidden problems. She hoped she would be less lonely and somehow fulfilled in ways different from how she lived before.

She believed that her marriage would be initially for a short period, a sort of test for the water before she could get in and swim. It is meant to last until harmony in the couple prevails. She planned always to be prepared to pack her belongings when the circumstances would push her to.

Unfortunately for Florencia, none of the positive expectations of their relationship materialised. She even felt worse than when she lived alone. At least while she stayed with her sister, she could count on her unconditionally. The loneliness she experienced with her abusive husband became a compounded and lonely hell. Before, she lived her loneliness uneasily, but her husband had replaced it with a persistent sensation of insulated anxiety and fear of the next moment, whenever it would come.

She lacked love from a young age, and as a consequence, she didn't know how to give it to others. Her external beauty constituted an empty shell and looked like a flower without a soul. Before she went with her man in her everyday life, she didn't learn to practice the little social gestures or manners that once looked at as a whole encompassed the expression of love.

Even in bed, her abusive husband would have to make tremendous efforts to enjoy their intimate encounters.

185

She behaved incredibly passively without any initiative to call the entire act enjoyable. If it hadn't been for the husband's guidance, evidently because of selfish interests, their love encounters would've also become only grounds for abuse. She uniquely responded to requests from her husband and executed as he asked.

"Though she feels incapable of love, her body longs for pleasure. Her emotionless eyes try to tell me that, from time to time," once thought the husband. Indeed, he wanted more from a woman's body. That explains the reason he let her go without too much drama.

Surprisingly, her husband didn't love her, either. He could caress and admire her as a prerequisite to getting what he wanted from her. Nonetheless, deep down, this couldn't be appreciated as an expression of love.

A definite and convincing doubt existed and showed that he couldn't sacrifice himself for her at all, whatever the circumstances. Fate had brought together these two individuals, but they lacked enough affection for each other, to the extent where none of them could die for the other.

Florencia despised her abusive husband initially when she noticed that he didn't love her but used her for his selfish pleasure. As she starved for recklessness, she wondered where she would find another man.

The little pleasure she enjoyed to being with him had a mysterious connection with his abusive attitude. It seemed like to have erotic excitement further to or because of the fall of deadly bombs, but, under normal circumstances, such life would've then been or seen as insane.

"Will you throw me out when you won't find any more pleasure to have me?" She asked her husband one day. He didn't reply immediately.

"I won't have to. Life will take care of everything. You will see," he finally answered her question after one long minute.

"I won't have any say in what will happen," he added with a lowered tone.

"Time answers most of the difficult questions of life," he finally ended his contribution to the conversation she had started.

That evening, she sat in the corner of their main room and gazed outside at a point in the sky she couldn't tell what it might be.

They had finished their dinner throughout the time of which she had received her usual lot of abuse. Her heels supporting her body, her hands on her cheeks, and while she leaned forward, she then started sobbing slowly and more loudly. At times, she blamed herself for being treated the way she felt mistreated.

"It could only be my bad blood to attract such misfortune," she cursed herself. In her view, there couldn't be any other logical explanation. She felt that way.

Through her only will, she thought she couldn't change much in her circumstances.

After a few months into her marriage, confronted with the harsh reality of a couple's life, she came to realise several things.

"I don't think relationships suppose or demand the expression of passion or empathy towards each other every day," she reflects for herself.

"Those who perform well in relationships of husbands and wives could only feel completely fulfilled for a couple of months, but no more," she pursues her reasoning.

"Life of a couple doesn't exist where no one hurts no one; to hurt others comes as a second nature to the human condition," which became the conclusion of her assessment of relationships within their couple.

However, though all these statements characterised the ideal of anyone who enters a couple's life, every aspiration doesn't mean that it always has to be achievable or attained.

***

This time, Florencia, without much thinking about the purpose of what she ended up saying to her husband, appears to appeal to his soul and seek forgiveness.

"Forgive me, honey! I don't know what I would become without you. Sincerely, I am sorry," Florencia said this while she still cried after a mental recall of the sad recent moments she had experienced.

She sat on her own in her main room when her husband came from his studio. He approached her. Her tears dampened her cheeks. He brought both his thumbs near to her face and wiped it gently. He embraced and kissed her on the left cheek.

"Please don't go. Let's stay like this for one more minute," Florencia hugged him tightly and didn't let him go until it hurt.

During their embrace, the husband tried to read her heart. It beat faster and louder. She looked anxious. On the one hand, he felt sorry for her. On the other hand, his level of love for her increased by an inch in that particular moment. He started to wonder how far he could go to sacrifice himself for her. He realised he had a degree of love for his wife he hadn't noticed until then, though it didn't feel enough.

"I regret not having loved you as you expected. I don't even know if I had any contribution in that area. I struggled as well. I couldn't give what I didn't have," Florencia's husband summarises his love's point of view.

With time, he had come to love her absence of passion in their relationship. It appeared inevitable, in uncertain times when her mood would be at its lowest level. He enjoyed seeing her vulnerable. With his selfish mindset, her wife's loveless life didn't bother him at all. Life appeared distorted by many parameters, some more out of the couple's control than others. At once, Florencia entertained and even begged to let it go on forever that way. In the right moments, she felt unhappy, whilst others would've felt excited.

Five days before she meant to leave her husband, she got injured.

"How will you leave with an injury? Please, can't you wait until you get healed? Do you want people to think that I caused it?" her husband queries.

She doesn't reply. They chat in their shared bedroom.

Regardless, she strongly wants to end the relationship. The pain from her wounds still felt intense when she called a taxi to move her luggage. Her husband didn't try to stop her. He got angry at her in a self-centred manner because she took away her beauty which provided him such enjoyment. He had never loved her beyond her incredible body.

Before they separate, the abusive husband wanted to ask Florencia one last question, which had hung on his mind for a long time. The entire period they had been together, he hadn't found the right moment to raise it out.

"On some occasions in bed, I have sensed you to be emotionless. At one moment, I thought your mind flirted with other men in our intimate encounters."

"I wondered if they constituted men in your past or those you got involved with at the time. I didn't get any answers to those questions; I kept them to myself. Please, could you give me some clarification, as we now part in different ways? I tried to search into your eyes and question your heart, but I couldn't see anything. You always had something inaccessible to me, no matter how hard I worked to find it out. What could it be?"

Florencia already put together the luggage she meant to take with her and leave him forever.

"You've been nice to me. Despite that, I still have one unanswered question about why men always think too much when it doesn't matter anymore?" she replied. While she converses with her husband, she takes her clothes from the wardrobe.

She added a full stop to her answer. The husband, on his part, would have found it unusual that her wife that he would part from in a moment would have wanted to explain her true feelings in those circumstances.

The taxi continued to wait outside their house. She took her bags and didn't say goodbye. Within twenty minutes, she buzzed at her sister's.

"Can we undoubtedly say this now comes to an end this time?" Amina asked her.

"Hell! It ended finally," she replied.

"You could say that you are free now from your prison; I feel deeply relieved for you," Amina concluded.

Once in Amina's apartment, while she unpacked her things, she checked into the drawers, cupboards, and wardrobes, where she intended to keep them. It had only been a year since. Not much had changed in her old room: all the fancy sunset curtains and the blue sky wallpaper seemed to say that she had never left.

Her unofficial marriage had ended. She had to deal with how she would cope with the emptiness that would invade her with its full force. Such uneasiness had affected her before her time with the woman's abuser.

She couldn't figure it out immediately, but fortunately, the time came to her rescue. She didn't spend much of it waiting, though the solution it offered her didn't match her expectations.

She regretted that her ex-husband didn't make any effort to dissuade her from leaving. On the other hand, the husband appeared uncertain if he would have succeeded to stop her if he had tried. The biggest challenge concerned him. To save her or not, whatever he needed to accomplish looked too much, according to him. This situation would become real in case he chose to do anything in his power to make her stay with him.

After a few days, while she felt a little settled at her sister's place, she called her ex-husband.

"You behaved cowardly. Why didn't you try to stop me from leaving? You should have killed me instead after I had been with you without love. That way, nobody else would be fooled by my body," she explains to him with a voice tainted with regrets.

"You don't seem better than me, but an utterly selfish being," she adds.

"If you can't make somebody else better, you personify a worthless being. You noticed I couldn't love the way you wanted. Maybe your love would have saved and transformed me. Who knows! But you showed your strong interest in my body more than any extractive engine could do. You wanted to play with that part of me."

"When its useful life expired or satisfied you with the outcome, and after that, your excitement faded away, you let it go. What you did, you escaped yourself. You despised how I felt, but at the same time, you picked from me what excited you," she elaborates.

"I don't think we planned what happened to us. Fate used us for its purpose," he retorts.

"That seems like nonsense! You still try to avoid your responsibility," she reacted angrily.

She cut him off. Since she knew him the whole time they had been together, she predicted that he wouldn't respond constructively. She didn't expect the impossible to come out from their conversation. She started to sob and cry in a faint voice. The blame game started playing. She took him responsible for her misfortune. On his part, he got angry at the fate that had made them meet.

Everyone seemed to have found their respective scapegoats. Nobody wanted to assume their responsibilities in what happened. Could they both be, at the time, ready for the burden put on their shoulders? This sort of question fell in the scope of their possible answers that only the future would solve. Florencia would unexpectedly find alternative ways to deal with similar situations when she incidentally resorted to a radical and deadly solution. However, her primary intentions consisted of her strong desire to help her sister, Amina.

Moving On

Once separated, Florencia couldn't help keeping a few things from her life as a couple. The only reason she held onto them came from the fact that she had felt attached to them with time. They, on their turn as well, had become part of her existence, as the skin can't detach itself from the body that nourishes it. Conversely, the body could provide cover and protection.

She considered those souvenirs as mementoes. She didn't have as many as she would've liked. Some had great value from her perspective and justified their worth for the pain to preserve them. They stood like some sentences assigned to her by the court of time because she had existed. Others mirrored representations or symbols that kept a trail of traces displayed everywhere, places her journey had taken her so far.

The contrast of these features' portrayal was that once exposed to the inevitable erosion consequent to the weight of their existence, they could fade away and or get shelved in the backyard of history. They could therefore become hardly traceable. Since, at some given time, people might not remember them, and consequently, the memory might risk not keeping any of their traces.

"I don't want to remember," Florencia would hear an inner voice telling her. That insider knocked once in a while when sadness from the past grieved her.

Nonetheless, she still vividly remembers the last day she left her husband with some bitterness in her heart, difficult to describe.

"I should've told him more thoroughly to bugger off. I let myself down and gave total power to my emotions for guidance," Florencia assesses while looking back. Nevertheless, she has a clear image of all the things she couldn't handle appropriately because of that day's events.

"I didn't know that he hated me so much. From day one, I presume he found me stupid. Further to such assessment on his part, he could treat me the way he did, as he liked," she did an evaluation long overdue of her married life. One could wonder if that exercise from her part had some significance once done at that point. Maybe it could only be her mind that played some tricks on her.

She needed some peace for her conscience, whatever the way she could achieve such a state of mind.

It didn't seem easy for her to measure how much her husband hated her.

"How could he let me leave unceremoniously as a nuisance someone gets rid of?" she couldn't understand.

"How could he ask me such a stupid question at that specific moment, on my way to the taxi, when he knew well that it would be the last time we would both have a conversation as husband and wife? A question on my bad performance in bed!" she couldn't believe it.

The question appeared to the ex-husband so critical that he couldn't uphold it. It seemed like a must-do, the ultimate item one puts in a bag to go somewhere and ensures that it doesn't stay behind.

Luck, however, appeared to be on Florencia's side. Fate generally accomplishes people's subconscious wishes unexpectedly. When she thinks back to the whole situation, she doesn't imagine how long it would've lasted living without any affection from her husband.

A six miles' distance she did in her taxi returning to her sister's apartment lasted forever. While she travelled back, she felt lost in an unstoppable recollection of her now ex-husband's life. She weighs now how miserable and pitiful she had been. "If someone had lived the married life I endured, they might strongly regret what they went through. Regardless, that's not my case. I take it as fate that needs to happen somehow to someone.

That I became the chosen one to roleplay it in the universe, I think I got to perform the character because I suited it best."

"Imagine people refusing to take up their role or place in the universe; instead of being at their best in the position they hold! The world would be full of unhappy individuals and, overall, a sinister environment. Negativity invades people's way all the time, and I learned these harsh life lessons along my journey. They taught me a different path for the next steps of my fate. I suppose my journeys have the useful purpose of getting me out of the direction I had taken. Certainly, or I hope, the part of my life that remains will be more fulfilling on a personal level and broadly for the people around me."

While she travels back through her past, she tries this time to think of happy memories, the ones that make her look forward with some confidence, and she wishes to recreate if possible.

The only night she had felt somehow loved also came back to her mind in a flashback. Surprisingly, she could only recall that single night she had appeared happy for three hundred twenty-six days spent in her marriage.

"It must've even been an illusion of happiness, far remote from the reality of the terrible relationship I lived in during that entire period," she realised.

"It has been a mistake even to feel that way. Happiness can't be random; its manifestation has to be justifiable. My momentary happiness of that night seemed different. Retrospectively, I couldn't see any practical reason for me to be happy. On this, and I am not exaggerating anything. At the time, the level of affection I had from my ex-husband was dangerously low, and my assessment can't be any more objective," she concluded.

"If I hadn't left my sister to get married in the first place," Florencia feels guilty. A year had passed.

The perception of guilt comes back occasionally to haunt Florencia, especially on rainy days. These constituted some unpleasant times. She couldn't walk out; the newly washed laundry wouldn't dry quickly to be ironed.

The dog would appear anxious and look as well outside the rain's drops. Even the coffee in her hand tasted awful. The only element that could appease in some ways her sadness came from the tune of the song "They don't care about us" arranged by Michael Jackson. It played on the radio she had turned on when she came down to the kitchen for her breakfast. If it hadn't been for that song, her whole day would've felt sad. The melody settled an uncomfortable section of her path's life.

***

Florencia's time to move on had come. However, memories continued to weigh much on her mind.

"I shouldn't continue to dwell on the past. Related memories won't get me anywhere. I have to force myself to forget, for me to get somewhere safe," Florencia finally decided almost a year out of her marriage.

"I have to navigate in an emotionally stable context and feel alive again if I ever did," she promises to herself. From where she had been or the experience she had been through, one could put a question mark on the place where she would've liked to be. She didn't have a clue.

Her past established her kickoff to start and paint a different and better picture of where she might be in the future. She internally agreed on the sequence of actions required, though some people believe that the past should remain where it belongs.

She wouldn't escape hers and thus avoid standing on it and or look forward confidently. Instead, she partially stood as her prisoner's past. Undoubtedly, it would influence - either she liked it or not - her future decisions.

She needed to know for sure where she headed this time. One lesson she had learned from her unfortunate experience consists of the importance of patience that she had to integrate into her decision-making process as an initial step to know.

In those moments, she wondered for example if she had to be the sole assessor of her situation or seek the help of somebody else for the next stage of her journey. In the past, she had failed to trust herself; this time, the challenge she had to overcome could even be more prominent. She had to change radically and become a trustworthy individual, not for the sake of somebody else but herself.

Before even she thought to trust anybody else, in case she needed them for the journey ahead.

"From now on, will I live without anybody else in my life? I should calmly address this issue while I ride to the right zone and get ready for action. I will give myself enough time to think about it. It could be months or even years before I become confident enough about the next trajectory for my life," Florencia assesses, where she stands by that time.

She wouldn't have to partner with anybody to bring onboard unless she has thoroughly tested or checked out the lucky candidate for their overall worth as character.

"I think the time has come to depart from the naivety of dreamers who embark on journeys without directions or destinations. I have experienced shortcomings after my stupidity at her own expense."

"This time I have to become ruthless with reality and use a tooth for tooth approach for whatever I might receive from the universe," she sets a firm pedestal for action with clear guiding principles.

Her past unpreparedness had enormously cost her emotionally. As the proverb goes - those who don't want to endure life's challenges and uncertainties avoid coming into the world. People could also rightly add that such a statement constitutes the appropriate ground for testing for whoever questions the worthiness of life.

"I have fallen once. That past failure shouldn't restrain or stop me from taking measured risks," Florencia looks back and sees in past mistakes positive insights.

"This time around, I will ensure that things become different. To be knocked down again might still be a possibility, but if this ends up happening, that will overflow me with some confidence. I have started developing a strategy to endure and overcome any challenge," Florencia could visualise the path she would walk on more confidently.

She had to make better choices or be an efficient decision-maker. It would be a new skill to learn. Unless she mastered it, she risked being capable of believing in the unbelievable. Despite the reality of uncertainties in human behaviour, she aimed to give less room to beliefs or have faith in people. Her new standards would have to have tangible facts as a pillar - the more there would be, the better. This modus operandi would prevail before she made any critical decision. She had decided never to surrender anymore, not to put her trust in nobody else's hands. Living that new approach and a fresh start with a no-reverse mechanism. First, to be a better person, work on herself to build trust in her character, and never surrender whatever the circumstances. She would consciously and continuously challenge herself to remain in control of whatever seemed controllable around her.

SECTION 4. Stories With Men

An Old Acquaintance

That Monday, Amina's last lecture of the day ended at 11:00 am. Though she didn't see herself as a loner, she doesn't have many friends on the campus, but she wants to be alone at lunchtime. She has always been sociable in a certain way. Nevertheless, at the same time, she doesn't belong to the type of girl who seeks friendships aggressively with new people. At the time, she usually took her lunch at the university's cafeteria. But for that day, she opts for an average and private restaurant situated in the vicinity of the students' dorms. She doesn't have to commute to get there.

The weather forecast of that day predicts some sunny spells in the late afternoon. It features a typical autumn morning's early November characteristics, with a high temperature of only eight degrees celsius. In the air, it drizzles, but it doesn't require carrying an umbrella. Amina wears her long and grey Alpaca blend cardigan, square toe leather boots, striped relaxed fit shirt, and cropped mid-rise jeans. When she had come out from her house, she had only found out later that she had forgotten her scarf. Already on the main road, she hoped that she would cope without that accessory to keep her neck warm.

Within ten minutes of walking, she finds herself in front of the restaurant. She gets into the building. The windows on the main roadshow's side bore massive posters with the restaurant's specialities. On top of the entrance, a luminous sign indicates the name Simba's Chef. That sign can be seen from more than thirty meters at night, from either direction of the street. The interior design features an antique style and is uniquely distinctive.

Clients who come in pass beside the cashier's desk, located on the right side, characterised by a colossal ficus plant, which looks dark green. In its natural environment, the plant would not have appeared any different. Amina suspects it to be human-made.

She doesn't pay much attention to the manager who comes towards her, though he indicates to her the available table where she could sit. She didn't let him finish his show of customer care. Amina goes to an isolated table from where, in a way, she could easily see outside and doesn't have to turn her head.

"Please, could you give me a glass of water, to begin with," she asked the manager who had followed her since.

After she sat adequately on one of the three chairs available that surrounded her chosen small table, she observed the people who walked outside. Across the road, she sees a shop for sex toys. A young couple in their twenties passes by, glances furtively at the items in the shop window. The couple seems to enjoy their time out. They giggle and hold hands. They looked like employees of a corporation in the vicinity of the restaurant.

Before the waiter comes around, Amina gazes on the outside again, and she doesn't fix her eyesight on any particular point of interest.

"Those sex toys must be like paracetamol tablets when they fulfil some necessity. I should not be surprised about them," Amina thinks about how useful the items in the toy shop could be. As an adult, she exudes what could be in a sex toy shop. Nonetheless, she has never envisaged entering such a place.

Her thoughts get back to the sex toys.

"How have I been sex-wise lately?" The sex shop had made her as well think about her own sex life. She planned to let it take its natural course and have sex only with a human being.

"I don't want to disturb the natural order of things," she concluded her internal discussion back and forth with an invisible interlocutor.

She didn't have any specific thought or topic to keep her mind busy waiting to be served. She had decided to come, mainly for two trivial reasons, but she has been motivated by some nostalgia.

In the small town she came from, close to home, a remote relative ran an eatery - that's what her uncle had let her know. It gave some sense of familiarity. She had been there many times with her adoptive parents. The restaurant reminds her of the comfort and security that she felt in her hometown. Things that only a family and or a community can provide.

She can afford the day's menu, and it seems of a high standard for someone on a student budget. With ten pounds, she will pay for the lovely meal she ordered. It consists of a bowl of noodles, topped with slices of seared chastu pork belly, bamboo shoots, an onsen egg, and seaweed. She doesn't pay for the water she drinks at her table. In the meantime, the waitress who had come and taken her order now brings her the food.

While she has her head down and focused on her plate, a group of three students enters the restaurant. They go straight to the table opposite where she sits. Michael de Souza came with them. After they sit down, they pursue their conversation.

"I watched the last football game of the Rhinos. If their striker Migui had played better, they would still have a chance to top the championship," one Michael friend says.

"Sorry, I didn't have time at all. I had a five thousand word essay I had to complete for Monday," the second friend replies, with some regret that he missed the performance of the team that they both support.

They change topics and talk about several other things, some more important than others, like the controversy that a new welfare bill had created among MPs. It pointed out the importance and difference of classes in one society.

"Have you managed to flirt with the blonde girl? I mean, the one who always comes to sit next to you in the auditorium." The student recipient of the question doesn't reply. His mind had travelled far while he seemed physically present. As if he didn't hear his colleague ask him, he brought a completely different topic to the discussion.

"I haven't finished the science project; I will need some help from you when we go back to the campus."

"Last holiday I attended a classical music concert. I didn't know how enjoyable it could be beforehand, but I was positively surprised when it ended."

"What are you talking about?" another student in the group asks the one who previously spoke.

Five minutes pass. The conversation among the two friends jumps from one topic to the next one in random order. It went on while Michael appeared preoccupied with a different matter. He isn't mentally with them.

Michael looks around the first time; he moves his head from left to right, then from right to left and scrutinises rapidly, but cautiously all the restaurant people as if he is searching for someone. He doesn't expect to find anyone in particular. Even so, his gut tells him that there must be someone he knows in the room.

"Please pass me an extra copy of your menu? There seems not to be enough for all of us," Michael asks the waiter who stands near their table, where he expects an eventual order. Before he directs his eyes to the menu that the waiter gave him, he looks in the direction of Amina the second time.

By this moment, he strongly thinks that she must be her friend from secondary school who sits alone at the table seven meters away from his group.

He can't wait to talk to her as he quickly places his order. He then stands up and heads towards Amina's table. His friends don't have the time to ask him where he is going. On second thought, they didn't bother. Nonetheless, when they see him while he stops and talks to Amina, they think he must've been her acquaintance. They plan to confirm their initial thoughts once he returns.

"Do you mind if I sit on this chair?" Amina raises her eyes to look at the person who talks to her.

She finds that Michael de Souza stands at her right side, with his athletic body of one hundred and eighty-five centimetres and a lot of muscles, nicely held in a light blue shirt he had received from his aunt as a Christmas gift.

"Yes, you can," Amina replies inadvertently, with her mind lost in distant memories, which, if brought into the open, could've looked inconvenient with the context. She has such moments of gaze at occasions, where her immediate surroundings vanish and get replaced by an imaginary world in her head.

"Are you Amina?"

She pauses up to ten seconds before she replies while wondering if she should be polite or not towards her interlocutor.

"Yes. Do I know you?" She doesn't recognise him immediately and thinks of ignoring him. She imagines him as one of those guys who always think that a woman alone in a public place needs someone to accompany her all the time for her security.

"What did you order?" Michael asks while he has his eyes on Amina's plate.

"Noodles and seared chatsu pork belly."

"It looks delicious. I should try it next time."

"Sorry. Please, could you help me remember you? My brain gets fuzzy sometimes about people I've met in the past."

"It's Michael. Michael de Souza."

For a few seconds, she went back into her memory for help.

"Yes, it's Michael! You looked like someone familiar, but I couldn't figure out who it might be. You've changed in seven years."

"Am I right about the last time we saw each other?" She asks Michael, somehow happy a stranger hadn't mistakenly approached her.

"It's time which changed, not me. Years pass, I remain the same person."

"Are you the Amina I used to know? You don't imagine how you've changed as well. You look beautiful, though. I don't recall that I used that characteristic when I referred to you at the time. You also seem to have matured. Even if you don't say anything, your face has that strange look of seniority that only time brings about."

" I don't exaggerate. I have always been the same, and I hope I will remain. However, I consider that time changed me. I find it difficult to resist and overcome."

"Do you study here? You look like a student, though I imagined you somewhere else."

"I do engineering."

"What type of engineering?"

"Video games. Paintzle stands as an innovative video game. A friend and I came up with its concept. One or several players start and create an online designed picture or painting. It doesn't have to look like a Picasso type or a Kandinsky. Once they finish, they choose one option between three suggested types of tools that cut puzzles into pieces people buy."

"The next step of the game consists of making the pieces of the created puzzle available to anyone who wants to put them back together in the shortest time. Once you start to play the paintzle, you can't see the original you or another have created. You can play solo or in an online group. The game can be played either by characters in video games or anyone with access to the internet."

"That sounds exciting."

"Yes, it is."

"How did we stop in those years?" Michael asks while he tries to get back to their shared past.

"Does that question even matter now? At the time, I remember well that no closeness existed between the two of us. In those years, I got unsettled. Romance or relationships, in general, appeared as a luxury, given my circumstances. When I look back, I consider myself lucky to have managed to pass through that period unscathed," Amina explains.

"Remind me, if you need to, about this guy you used to hang up with most of the time. Many of us thought of you both as an item," Michael tries to get Amina deeper back into the memory lane.

"I considered him only as a friend, no more than that. He had insisted that he wanted to be something else more intimate towards me. Though I had explained to him that I had other priorities in my life at the time," Amina dismisses past speculation about her.

"Hey, Michael. The food has arrived. It will get cold," his group of friends calls him to rejoin them. Instead, he takes one or two minutes before he leaves Amina's table.

"We should meet again. What about the day after tomorrow, at 1:00 p.m. at this same place," Michael suggests.

"I would like as well. I will be available at that time. OK, then in two days.

He didn't say goodbye. This behaviour resembled him from what Amina still remembered about him.

She finishes her meal before Michael's group of friends. She stands up goes to the cashier and pays her bill. Before she leaves the restaurant, she has a look in the direction of Michael. They have distant eye contact.

Once outside the restaurant, she realises Michael has not given her his telephone number. He neither asked hers. She doesn't want to go back to the restaurant to ask him. She fears that he might take it as a sign that she has a particular interest in him. Consequently, she lets it slide, and expects Michael to most, turn up at the suggested time and venue.

Two days later, at 1:00 p.m., Amina comes back to the agreed restaurant to meet him. He doesn't come. She calls Michael's faculty and hopes to know where he might be.

"Excuse me. Does Michael de Souza have lectures this afternoon? As a close friend, we had agreed to meet this afternoon, but unfortunately, I can't get a hold of him."

"Please give me your telephone number. I will call you after checking," the receptionist replies.

Amina doesn't receive any call from the faculty; thus, Michael becomes untraceable. Her afternoon gets ruined by a series of disappointments. With some hindsight, she couldn't picture his old friend as a likeable person. Though she knows him from a past they share, she remembers not to tolerate him for his unreliability. She decides to put behind her all the blunder of the day and carries on with her student life.

Oh, Men!

Amina has many stories from her relationships with men. She occasionally shared them with her closest workmate. One example relates to her neighbour Haile as a male candidate to connect with, but in the same realm of thoughts, her mind takes her back to revisit her years at university.

Samuel had been a classmate. She got close to him in unconventional ways. His colleagues knew well that he - the shy guy - kept to himself. Physically attractive and athletic but not exceptionally intelligent, Amina had a short interest in him.

She had incidentally stayed in front of the lecture room that day. She hadn't any reason to rush home or anywhere else. Samuel had joined her a moment before. The lecture had already finished a few minutes earlier. Both seem not to have specific plans for the next few hours.

"How are things, Samuel?" Amina asks him. She had come straight from a lecture on the effective use of social media for product promotion. They both studied that same topic.

"If everything depended on me, I would've wanted to see things improving!" Samuel responds with a disinterested expression in his tone.

"How has your family been? Any recent news!" Amina pursues her enquiry. Like others close enough to Samuel in their class, she had learned that he had lost a sibling in the recent weeks.

"I've tried to get over the bad news as best as I could," Samuel answered with a similar detachment in his deadpan voice. Amina and he know each other only as acquaintances. They shared greetings when their paths crossed on the campus' avenues and corridors. From time to time, they also attended the same class for most subjects from their respective syllabuses.

"I will check your availability and take you out for a drink to cheer you up one of the coming days," Amina offers.

"I will let you know," Samuel replied while he went his way. Nobody presumed at that stage if he too would be in any way interested in her. Samuel has two male student friends with whom they go out together. He generally displays some acute indifference towards girls or women in general.

Amina and Samuel don't get attracted to each other instantly, but gradually. She had reached out to him only per courtesy and out of compassion. Amina intended and tried to comfort someone who experienced the loss of a relative. On his part, Samuel, for him to appear polite further to the kindness she had demonstrated towards him, responded positively to her invitation.

He called on Thursday evening.

"I am free next weekend. Though Saturday would be better, pick the time, and I will come with my car to your place."

But Amina doesn't expect him to honour his promise. While he informs her when he would be available, he wants to be out that weekend. Though the outing doesn't constitute his first occasion with a girl, Samuel doesn't have any particular plan for Amina. In his mind, he pictures himself as a subject of attention from her because she wants to comfort him for his loss.

They went out together in a local pub close to their campus. They found out incidentally that they both liked to play and watch basketball. The screen in the central area displays an SNBA match. From where they sit, they can still see which teams, on that day, compete for the title of the Suan championship.

"Do you mind that we move closer to the screen over there?" Amina asks Samuel and points at empty tables not far from the tv screen.

"Are you too into basketball?"

"Yes. The coach of the university women's team selected me at the start of the year. I have been practising since I was nine. My uncle used to take me to a local club for youngsters. I got my love of the sport from that period."

"I should come to support you one of these days."

"I would appreciate it if you came."

"You must be good if you practice at the university team's level. I have always liked basketball as a sport. I practice from time to time, but I have never taken it seriously. I don't even know the reason I don't invest myself fully into it. Probably the lack of family support or a strong push from someone close could be the cause of my detachment."

"What about your family?" Samuel asks Amina. He wondered why her uncle, instead of her parents, got her to like and practice basketball.

"I grew up as an orphan in my uncle's household. He works in a textile factory in the Lower Country. Unlike me, he always spends his time with his machinery while breaking up tools then putting parts back together, using a range of equipment. He has been watching Formula One since I first saw him in front of the television. That means way back in my childhood. As far as I remember, he likes action movies and soap dramas. He devours history books about human inventions from ancient times and from around the world. He doesn't earn much. He only graduated with an A-Level education. His family counts the least in his priorities."

"Despite all that, didn't he support you to get to the university?"

"I managed to go to the university because I did apply for a student loan. If I had waited for my father's support, I mean my uncle, at the same time, my guardian, I would not be here today."

"God knows when I will reimburse the money I borrowed. When I thought that I could go to university, I longed for freedom and was excited to live independently away from my family."

"I had this burning thought that I would spend my time without them around. However, I got worried at the same time because I would've to live in a city about which I didn't know much."

"I chose to sleep in the dorm to keep my expenses to a minimum. I can't afford all the niceties of the student life that children with wealthy backgrounds enjoy," Amina explains her family background comprehensively.

"As I understand, money has significant importance in what you said. You mention or refer to it several times, but if you had been wealthier, would you have taken any different path than the one you walk on today?" Samuel asks Amina.

"I don't mainly complain about money as such, but the type of hardship someone encounters when they don't have enough of it," Amina replies.

"Furthermore, I pursue the type of studies I've always wanted to do, though I feel sad that I don't enjoy the company of my friends nor share a beer on a night out, as often as I would like," she adds.

"Sadness doesn't typically define those who lack money. Your sadness shows as the least painful occurrence compared to the one experienced by those students that you unconsciously envy if you do. They have their devils, not worth befriending," Samuel explains.

"I agree. Relativity lies at the core of everything. I share my sadness while I think that no other situation compares with my life at the moment. However, I stand in a better position than any others who also suffer more than I do, for a multitude of reasons," Amina expresses her assessment of her comparative state of things.

"Does this express the nuance I intended to highlight properly? Not sure. Money doesn't stand on trial in my story. It became a critical issue for me, although some students didn't feel the same way as I did without it. They appeared comfortable. Unless they lived in denial."

The day ended on a negative note because of the topics' nature they had discussed, but their knowledge of each other increased.

They both got out together the next Saturday, for the entire evening. They got drunk and went home in a taxi. The morning after, they found themselves naked in Samuel's bed. They realise they had sex together.

As they observe each other, still lying in bed, not fully awake.

"Are you awake?"

"Yes."

"How do you feel?"

"Fine. I have a little of a headache, though it shouldn't last after I take a bath."

"I think we did it."

"For sure, something happened."

"Every encounter in our lives has to have its first-ever moment. I experienced my sexual one then."

"I did as well."

"I never thought it would happen this way."

"What do you mean?"

"It happened randomly. Previously, I fantasised about it. I know myself well not to be an easy girl who sleeps around."

Samuel had watched many romantic movies and seen live how lovers behave towards each other. He imagined himself in similar situations, nervous and ignorant about what to say or do.

"I agree we got drunk. Our hidden sexual desires took the upper hand. One intent or thought led to the next, and then we got fully into it."

"Do you regret it?"

"No. That's not what I meant. I tremendously enjoyed the intense feelings I experienced."

"On my part, I only regret that I couldn't be fully conscious. A dream - a joyful one - had visited me. I don't, however, recall how the visit ended."

"I think we got attracted to the act like two magnet fields which can't pass close to each other without colliding."

"Our mindset couldn't fully comprehend and or appreciate the action at its worth."

"I hope you enjoyed what we did. Except for the slight caveats I pointed at."

"Can we safeguard it in our good memories?"

"Why not?"

"The way forward seems blick. Time will tell."

Amina sums up her assessment of their sexual encounter that night.

That morning, without much consideration or particular thoughts about what had happened between them that night, each one prepared themselves their breakfast. Their chat came out at its lowest frequency. They had had sex together, half-drunk, without the usual romance that generally accompanied it between lovers. It had been very casual; one would say similar to feeling thirsty and then heading towards a water tap and opening it. Perhaps, this appeared as one way for Amina to cheer up heartedly someone from the opposite sex.

With and after that one-off sexual encounter, each of the protagonists returned to their usual academic routines. It was as if it had been a breath of air pumped from the atmosphere and then had become available. Besides, once its momentous usefulness was achieved, it landed in the dustbin of memory, despite its nearly noble initial purpose of somebody's well-being.

The encounter took away from Samuel's mind the weight of his grieving. Thus it positively alleviated the sadness about his loss. On her part, Amina increased her sense of fulfilment, while her conscience told her that she had contributed to someone's happiness by her almost charitable act.

***

That day, the second one after her sexual encounter with Samuel ended, Amina woke up in a bad mood. The more she thinks about it, the more she feels awful and miserable. The way it happened seemed the total opposite of what or how she had ever imagined or idealised.

The two lectures of the first half-day have finished nearly at lunchtime. Only at 2:00 pm would Amina have her next scheduled class. She spots Samuel in the lecture room. He caught her while looking at him from three rows behind. When the lecturer ends the session, she hurries fast to get to Samuel.

"Hi. We need to talk." Amina tells Samuel on the go.

"You mean now?"

"Yes, if you don't mind."

"OK. However, you took me off guard. You could've called to get myself mentally prepared if need be, in case you want to talk about serious issues."

"Sorry, I can't tell beforehand if it's serious or not. It all depends on how one looks at it. Whatever, I need to get it out of my head. That's the only way I will feel calmer."

"Go ahead."

"Let's go to the park; it's less crowded."

They walked side by side and tried to be as relaxed as possible, mainly Samuel, who didn't know what to expect. The five-minute walk to get there doesn't take time to finish.

Once in the park, they seem both tense and don't talk much until one of them reduces the pace then stops.

"Could we sit on that bench?" Samuel points to the second available space they pass. Amina goes straight slowly. She sat down and waited until Samuel sat too comfortably.

"I start."

"Yes."

"Our encounter the other night, I think about it a lot since, unfortunately not in a positive way. As I told you previously, it came as my first and I consider it as an accident. Before I carry on, please would you agree with me on my perception of our actions. Do you find that for you as well, it constituted an accident?"

"I agree with its unplanned reality. Still, unless we consider every unplanned occurrence as an accident, I will then concede that it was," Samuel replies.

"However, I would like to point out some nuances in what you say. The fact that if an unplanned accident happens to be pleasant, I wouldn't insist and call it an accident, but a pleasant experience. However, such appreciation depends on how the person who lives that said accident felt while in the act," he adds.

"I agree with that. I got drunk, and you too, I suppose. Consequently, if we both didn't have all our minds, evidently with different levels of drunkness, I presume that our actions, therefore, didn't feel all pleasant. I regret now what I experienced. I would've preferred it to be fully conscious while I go through such an encounter."

"You heard my point of view. I don't think I would need to repeat myself."

"I feel disgusted that I had to get drunk to have my first sexual experience. Regrettably, I would have liked more romance. I feel doomed that my second and other subsequent encounters worry me. Will I have to get drunk to be in the right mood for sex?" Amina elaborates for Samuel's attention.

"I suppose you will need some adjustments. Your imaginary initial encounter simply seems to be fantasy-like. Your conscience should guide you if you need to drink to get rightly ready," Samuel advises Amina.

"You sound inconsiderate. The whole encounter constituted an unfortunate experience. I will ensure it doesn't ever happen again," Amina concludes.

A few days pass, and the incident belongs already in the past. Amina makes an extreme resolution about her drinking. She decides to stop it altogether, exceptionally when her future boyfriend, husband or lover isn't around to take care of her. That way, there wouldn't be any risk of getting drunk and ending with unplanned sex. She convinced herself that with some strict discipline, she would never go through a similar experience.

She has already gone to see her doctor check if she got any urinary infection or pregnancy since Samuel didn't use any contraceptives. The one-off sex encounter she wants to forget forever refuses to let her in peace. At the end of her conversation with Samuel, though she doesn't find the whole incident pleasant and the way both discussed it, she senses some relief.

Up until they greeted each other, Samuel had been for Amina, a relative stranger. However, both attended a few courses together. Did their fates cross at that moment? It's possible. One can confirm that, but without complete certainty.

If they did both mean to get to know each other more, they couldn't stop their momentarily shared destinies.

Fate came on stage to perform what it excels at its best. The trigger had been the death of Samuel's relative. His friends on campus talked about it. Though he couldn't come top of the popularity's challenge among the students, his typical shyness had made him well known in circles close to him.

What if Amina hadn't been in the same class as him? Probably what happened between them would not have occurred. Even in this scenario, nobody could tell since not such encounters happened uniquely among classmates.

Truthfully, no element indicates that they couldn't have been able to meet in other circumstances. Only speculation here could sustain that such eventuality would've been impossible.

Regardless, the sexual encounter Samuel had with her in a moment of half drunkenness and half-asleep navigated in his mind for weeks, as a bridge someone crosses for the first time, as the incident provides a new perspective of the landscape. Either one crosses that bridge once or several times afterwards, the perception it gave the initial time will fade away with the increased familiarity of the crossing. That embeds the essence of experience.

Once Amina graduates, she stops playing basketball as a regular practice. However, she later found out that sport would help while she would be in prison.

Her imprisonment occurred in her prime years, the late twenties. It shut down the expectations she had for her future. She consequently fell into a prolonged depression and other related mental illnesses quickly. Without the help of sport, it would've been more challenging for her to rise again and be back to life once released. Her fitness got sustained, and her mental health gradually improved. Despite the harsh circumstances she lived under at the time.

SECTION 5. Dreams, Haile and Amina

Knock-Knock

The knock-on Haile's door that Amina did on one ordinary day triggered an unpredictable trajectory in his life. Like the majority of the happenings in people's lives. He had, however, to assess the righteousness of the path objectively, his earthly journey would take as a consequence. After a long internal back and forth evaluation over several months, Haile chooses to make the irreversible decision. He believed that once one had set clear goals, life became easier for everyone. Though there was no guarantee that he and those that his mission or plan of actions would make him come across would sail smoothly through difficulties if any.

"If I don't accomplish this right now, that will never happen at any other time," he reflects on his strong desire to embark on a writing career.

However, he will not be able to reverse the decision once related actions start unfolding. No matter how risky this could be with a range of varied outcomes.

"I will save more if I live a more frugal life than ever," he decides to become more considerate of how much he spends to face his financial shortcomings once he starts to work only on a part-time basis.

Though this constitutes a big move - despite that, it doesn't seem existential - the decision looks measured and cautious. Haile would teach half of the time available. To concentrate on his all-time passion becomes his ultimate motive.

In year four, he recalls this particular teacher who miraculously transformed his attitude towards learning. He was then nine while he attended primary school.

"Young man, you become whatever you want to be when you set all your will on your objective and maintain the necessary focus as long as it takes," his teacher had told him and the rest of the class.

That teacher made him improve drastically on his grades. His parents had previously been worried about his future. Any reasonable and fair parent would have. Suddenly, he became their pride, though one would wonder if that came from the teacher or the child's fate. Overall, his early life got transformed.

"What happened recently to our child?" his father had positively wondered in those years when he saw him perform well in class.

It would be challenging to assess rightly, mainly if you don't believe how much luck contributes to how people's lives end.

Haile has a strong desire to change lives.

"I would like to impact children's lives as my teacher in year four changed mine."

He went to teach because of the transformative experience he had that particular year in primary school. He wanted - and in his present position of teacher - to motivate children to enjoy and learn new things and to be curious all the time.

"If children get encouraged to experiment, explore and be bold enough and not be affected by failures, therefore they can engage with the world in a positive way that rewards them and adds value to humanity in general," Haile thought.

His consistent conviction stemmed from his belief that failure is part of the journey to success. Such a path means that someone has to overcome one or many challenges to stand proud on their pedestal. A toddler on their feet - after weeks or months of a multitude of failed trials - could testify to that truth.

It took him time to decide and reduce the days he taught, not that he felt reluctant or scared of the unknown in the new direction. Other priorities had crocked up into his way and taken a toll on his life until he felt ready for the next move.

He immersed himself into his new role and became a writer, a novelist, to be more precise. In a nutshell, his time off from his classroom's interactions with students would then focus on his future readers' entertainment through his literary creations. He thought he could still impact other people's lives that way.

"All these years, I wrote in my dreams, now the time has arrived to become real," he expresses his inner determination for himself.

He didn't, however, know how to get started. Despite that, he felt he couldn't have a fulfilled life if he didn't overcome that challenge and realise his dream. He remembers how his adoptive parents had dissuaded him from pursuing literature studies.

"To get an income in that field stretches even the best. In our broader family, nobody stands as a reliable reference to motivate and encourage you into what you want to do," they argued for Haile's attention.

For him, however, to venture into that field had its origins in the ways he intended to revisit his roots. He felt, to a certain degree, that the universe had unwillingly cut him off for a certain period of his life. However, the time had come to immerse himself into his origins.

If it hadn't been for his parents, through their persistent request, he would've become a historian instead. Unless he responds this time to his mission in the universe, he considered that his life would be miserable and full of regrets, he said to himself. Moreover, he doesn't want to experience any of that at the end of his earthly journey.

Nonetheless, he would have to overcome the financial burden consequent to his decision. He needs to work harder in that new-for-him literary field to maintain at least his current standard of living.

His full-time career provided him with a decent salary so far, plus long holidays not found in any other profession. Indeed, he will have to struggle and indulge in living on a part-time teacher's small income.

While Haile works, that will be the case. He would wait and improve to earn a good income from his new craft.

"I refer to him as a journalist," that's what a Suan radio commentator, who regularly read his notes, had once referred to him as in the comments section of an online journal he edited.

At first, he's surprised but silently enjoyed the title. He embraced what the new title projected outside for him unintentionally. He can at least count on the positive image he had felt from a particular target community of followers. He has already published in some well-known newspapers.

"Friends who read my articles introduce me to their peers as a writer whenever we get together," Haile translates the sense of fulfilment once he reaches the goal of his literary pursuit.

Though he enjoys his pieces written in different formats and styles: opinion articles, poetry or essays, he never considers himself a writer. Such an attitude could be one of his weaknesses since he doesn't portray or project himself correctly to the outside world. He underestimates his worth.

While much younger, Haile had followed a different academic route from the one that generally characterized most writers. Those with a particular interest in history, literature and writing, usually studied humanities.

Besides the statement, some famous writers appear well-grounded in professional areas utterly foreign to the general literature as ordinary people know it.

Reccobe Slooti features as one of them. She became a renowned writer though she started as a biologist in her professional life. A piece of advice from her teacher of creative fiction sustained her into her new career.

Although she still struggled between her job as a scientist and her initial fascination with literary work, her teacher explained to her, "When you let go of a goal, this doesn't mean you've failed, as long as you have a new goal in place. You didn't give up anything; you only changed directions, and this constitutes one of the important things you constantly do in life."

"I didn't study literature in particular. I graduated with a good university qualification, one can imagine. For the part of my formative years, I studied classic writers and thinkers such as Plato, Shakespeare, Orwell, Hemingway, Socrates, Cicero and others of a similar calibre," Haile once introduced himself to a group of would-be writers. It was asked to participants to indicate what had inspired them.

He had never participated in any literary competition. Instead, he had been active in advocacy. He gave talks on concern issues whenever he felt the need to advance his favoured causes but was always unrepentant about his radical views on some of the themes he addressed. He has seen his online presence makes him perceived as an expert. Consequently, broadcasters invited him to contribute to their talks or interview him publicly on particular topics.

***

In his mid-thirties, not married, Haile was not yet a confirmed long-term bachelor. Graduated from the Kyutsu University in Fukuoda - Niasan, he holds a PhD in mathematical engineering. Haile teaches that subject at a Vodnak college. He has had several incomplete research projects he works on for many years. He considers them as work in progress on his computer, where he keeps them as encrypted files,

Maths' departments in the universities he expected to partner with had their budgets cut. At the time, the government where he resides pursued policies based on austerity. Funds to major social projects - community centres, housing, welfare, and the number of public civil servants were reduced.

This political orientation happens while, at the same time, privatisation wherever this out-performs the status quo gets actively implemented speedily and mercilessly at a broader scale.

Amina, on her part, doesn't fall among the typical beauty pageants. Those that everyone would want to talk about with their colleagues at work or on a night out. She believes that perception about her in a way that she would ferociously argue with anyone who would depart from it. She wouldn't like to be fooled by those who qualified her as a beauty.

However, she has an incontestable charm, only fully appreciated by those close to her and interested in her personality. She once caught Haile's eyes. At that occasion, since the interest seemed mutual, she thought of him, for a slight moment, as a potential life partner. Although she immediately brushed off the idea from her head.

"I don't want to invest any time and try to know him better or win him over," she had decided at the time.

Haile, on his part, doesn't have the look of the usual handsome guy. However, he had his own opinion about her.

"She doesn't fulfil the prerequisites of my type," he thought at one stage. This portrayal from him pops up in his mind before they had had a chance to interact.

But when she knocked on his door, her impact became permanent.

"She looks too good for me even to consider that I could be in a relationship with her," that became the first thought that crossed Haile's mind when Amina formally introduced herself.

Both Haile and Amina would greet each other on the street when they happen to cross their mutual paths. As neighbours, this will become frequent.

Only thirty meters separate the doors to their apartments. Both live on the fourth floor of their building.

However, their greetings don't ever go as far as for them to have a cup of tea together. In a nutshell, they don't know each other well.

To a degree, they both come out as introverted sort of personalities. From time to time, they express themselves in monosyllables wherever and whenever they converse with other people, different from their familiar audiences.

Despite Haile and Amina's particular personalities, they happen to spend more than the usual time together for an unknown reason one day. It's outside their local supermarket. They talk about things they do when waking up and before going to work. At that moment, they somehow click. They discover and rightly appreciate the benefits to run together in their neighbourhood as often as possible. Haile had noticed before that to run on one's own could look odd when one could exercise with a partner.

"But where will I find that sports' partner," he had this question once convinced that to run with someone would be ideal.

He could feel more motivated and didn't have to exercise alone while he worked on his fitness.

Though still young, Haile wants to remain fit as long as he can, at least until his late seventies. Or as far as his body will allow. Amina aims to lose weight. On a recent visit to her doctor, her body's mass index characterised her as obese. Hence, she had to address it if she didn't want to damage her health further.

Since they both work in different fields with specific set times of the day, they agree to synchronise their availability to run together. That way, they won't miss out on their individual and daily schedules. The Neptersine becomes the area of preference where they meet and embark on that journey of fitness. They discover their now-familiar unexpected universe. Along the way, life takes them by surprise. It makes them shake up their past. It came to define a new present. As a consequence, their encounter enables them to start on an unpredictable future.

It became full of twisted devotion and compassion that challenged the strength of their relationship.

Dreamed In Childhood

A few days after Amina came to see Haile, he had a dream. The dream takes place in his childhood. It brings about a strange sensation where he bonds with his parents, that he has not had a chance to live with, because they died before she could go to school. He wakes up while the dream feels unfinished, at the moment where he promises Amina that he will cherish her whatever the circumstances they will encounter together.

The strangeness of the dream stands in the fact that he meets Amina while she looks still young. Though they appear as children in that context, Haile doesn't mistake her for anybody else. In their real life, they only meet when they become both adults, but the dream makes it possible for a much younger Amina to come alive in his childhood. He has never seen a picture of Amina while still young. It can surprise how the subconscience operates like an automated studio of creativity.

Haile realises then that he stands awake. He doesn't feel like he would be able to fall asleep again immediately. Haile leaves his bed and goes to the kitchen. He takes from the fridge a bottle of orange-coloured drink and pulls it in a glass. While he still reflects on his dream, he tries to make some sense of it.

"Is this a prophecy or a particular message that I need to take care of?" he feels surprisedly concerned while reflecting. By the time he goes back to bed, Haile knows well what comes next with his dream. Nevertheless, unknown variables exist that he must deal with as they emerge.

For a long time, he has not had a vivid dream of which details he could remember clearly the day after. He had been separated young from his parents. They had died in a war conflict.

It ensued that he had struggled to understand the full sense of a relationship with another person, whoever that could be.

He had a vague recollection of the concept of love. He can't remember if he had ever learned formally about it, in its different and possible formats or contexts. He had no explicit references at all.

From the dream, the message seemed to explain why Haile lives alone even in his late thirties. He could've had probable tangible excuses to still be unmarried at that age, but his dream appeared to indicate the root cause of his challenge in relationships. With a fair assessment of himself at the time, he rightly admitted that he lacked in that particular area, although the problem consisted in what he would do about his deficiency.

In the dream, Haile sees himself imprisoned because of a woman. The next dream sequence tells him that he will get married to the same woman after his release.

"Do the fact that he meets Amina in his neighbourhood and the dream has any connection?" he wonders. If any relation between the two elements, this puzzled him to think that his new neighbour could get him imprisoned. While he doesn't believe in superstitions or dreams, he can only wait and see what his hidden roadmap in the universe will be.

The picture of Amina he had kept after his initial and formal contact with her showed an ordinary attractive woman that he thought he probably didn't deserve because of his self-depreciation. She looked unexceptionally beautiful. At that moment, and despite the dream, he couldn't logically imagine that she would become his wife one day. The vision showed that this would occur only after his imprisonment because of her.

In the meantime, unfortunately, Amina would experience an abusive relationship with Hussein. Haile didn't know how events would unfold. He chooses the enjoyable part of the dream and leaves out the rest.

Despite his inclination, the vision appeared to be a full package; either Haile took all of it or left it and forgot about the benefits. He felt that fate played him a cruel game. He couldn't refuse to play unless he agreed to die single.

The process would be long and unpredictable. Some pointers stood like mountains on the horizon that he needed.

On the other hand, he thought about the deterrents which might destroy any relationship not solidly anchored on a reliable base. Mistrust, betrayal, selfishness, lack of care or empathy, and or manipulation are featured on the passive list. There could be others, but these came straight away to his mind. He had never experienced a proper and deep relationship with anyone. In the past, he might've had one, but evidently, he didn't preserve it as such in his memory. His character's nature could partially explain why he couldn't sustain a long relationship once he entered one.

"Maybe if I had my biological parents around while growing up, would I have performed better in a relationship? Uncertainty prevails, but what the intuition seems to tell me is that I would have had some tangible or even credible references in what to do or not to do. Besides, my behaviour would've been a consequence of how my parents would've performed in their relationship," Haile falls into a nostalgic corner.

"In my case, and those similar - for people who grew up or came into adulthood without their parents or in a single-parent household - the relationship's world seems like a landmine field."

227

"When someone comes from a broken family, to expect them to evolve into a functional couple comes out as asking an elephant to hatch an egg," Haile profoundly reflects on the challenges he has faced for a long time about relationships.

"One would wonder if any alternatives exist to remedy that challenging deficiency for most young people, single or married - both male and female. They find themselves in families not conducive to building healthy relationships with future partners. Also, those from already constituted couples, who belong to the same demographic, face the same problem," Haile wants strongly to help himself in that regard if it doesn't look too late in his case or those in a similar situation or much younger.

Faith institutions tended to fill the gap left by broken families and develop relationship skills among the youth based on religious teachings. Even so, the ideal environment or long-term boot camp for stable familial relations is, as one would expect, one of a functional family. Foster parents have also been another alternative for a long time, but the concept's positive and negative elements make it the second-best solution. Despite highlighted inadequacies, the path to follow came clear this time. Haile decides to move forward.

"I would observe her from a distance from time to time. Hence our connection will be silent in those moments. Though it could be for a long time," Haile opts to deal with what the dream appeared to tell him.

One would wonder the reason he chose that attitude towards what would be their future relationship. As one of his character traits, he pursued one goal while seemingly disinterested, but at the same time showed steadiness and humility about it.

However, his undeclared love for Amina will do the talking. Though he speaks to her from time to time because of the intertwined circumstances they both go through together, their brief and occasionally intermittent chat doesn't make them come closer. They only enable the development of a specific format for their relationship.

When the time came, he felt compelled to move mountains for her sake, to make her feel that he cared. She will lean on him in desperate moments. Despite the distances or other factors between them at different moments of their interactions, many people would remember them after being gone.

On her part, Amina couldn't be with Haile to pursue a special connection with him. From her point of view, the guy didn't have any particular feature to make him attractive.

"I want to be a good neighbour," a thought Amina had while she prepared her visit to Haile. When she greeted him, she only returned a welcome and friendship Amina had experienced when she had first encountered him.

He didn't fit among her type of guys, on top of his unique physical unattractiveness.

Haile's repulsiveness transpired in how he carried himself, the clothes he wore, even the way he talked, or lacked any confidence in himself. Amina wondered how he could be a charismatic teacher if he didn't project his confidence into his pupils unless he became a different person once in front of them.

Their encounter constituted only the start of a story with many chapters or twists. No element could predict the end's contours at this stage, nor the characters in its climax.

In Their Middle

That night Haile went to sleep exhausted. The next day he had to wake up at the usual time, fifteen minutes before six, to go on his jogging. Despite the tiredness, this time, his sleep was without nightmares to trouble his unconscious journey. Once he woke up and was ready for his fitness routine, he got out of his apartment and walked downstairs of the building. Still dark. The stars in the sky weren't eager to unveil their brightness. They might also have been hiding under their heavenly covers.

"I need to wait for Amina to come down; in the meantime, I can gaze outside the windows. I don't have to necessarily focus on any particular spot as far as my eyes can see," Haile stands close to the stairs of the first floor and is not wholly awake.

Amina and Haile had an agreed time - it could change each season - they both set off to the park together. A delay of a few minutes could be acceptable, then the one on time would make a call and enquire about what would be going on. She came on time but not in her element for the run. At a distance of nearly twenty meters, they walked side by side silently. He envisaged censoring himself before he utters any sound out of his mouth.

"How do we dream while asleep," he suddenly asks Amina. He focuses on the question because the dream he had that night seemed not to make sense. He had only kept pieces of it. While he struggled to remember all the details, he felt more interested in the how of the whole process of dreaming.

"How do we make up our dreams?" this initial question had come to his mind, and when he spoke it out. He raised it because of his uncertainty about any conscious intervention in the way people shaped their dreams.

His doubt made him change the formulation of the question. He left out any human power in the dreams' creation.

He hadn't even greeted Amina, who seemed familiar with that. Other than that such habit, he usually displayed kindness and politeness towards her. He had his ways to compensate for his rudeness. While they left their apartments or came back from their jog, he would politely open for her the different doors between corridors or lifts that connected their apartments to the main road.

"Though uncertain on my part, I suppose people might randomly dream," she replied without any hesitation as if she wanted to make sure her interlocutor understands that she doesn't know much about that topic.

"I have an even more serious question about dreams: do our body and soul or conscience all together stay in one location when we dream? In those moments, do people not get separated from their body and the element which triggers and supervises the process of dreams' development? Or do those two elements act, if any performance to talk about, and or separately exist?" he pursued.

Amina doesn't answer immediately. She struggles with any alternate response she thinks of providing for the different asked questions. Her portrayed confidence in highlighting her ignorance could've kept her away from her anxiety. By any means, she didn't have to respond since she had acknowledged her ignorance to Haile, who had asked the questions to someone who appeared to be proud of not knowing. The person in question could be seen as the odd bloke since she didn't understand the matter. Instead of answering, she went on a different tangent to the topic.

"At the start of the day, when we wake up or any other time after some sleep, and we explain that we had a dream, do we at that time make any difference between ourselves and our conscience which momentarily speaks out about the dream? Or do we express ourselves as one compact entity? People's conscience and their bodies constitute one thing, of which components, if any, act all the time as one unit," Amina convinces herself of such reality when she replies that way.

It might be a personal point of view, not necessarily shared by everyone in her circle or beyond.

Amina argued that if one of the parts in action separated, it would've been impossible for the unit to function as before. While dreaming, conscious or not, in her view, people dreamed from inside their bodies. Such a line of thoughts constituted the opposite of Haile's beliefs when it came to dreams.

"People's conscience inhabits only alive and expressive bodies. This statement bends towards certainty. Once asleep, the said conscience could be in their body or not. It might even travel to places they can hardly imagine," Haile states his belief on the matter.

Haile had raised the questions about dreams, not that he wanted definitive answers, but to share with Amina his concerns about a personal experience. After he explained his previous night's encounter with dreams, and while he couldn't figure out whether or not he felt whole with his body and mind while dreaming, he became transformed further to the discussion.

The next night, he revisits his world of dreams. He goes places with the least mundane distractions, away from the inner city where he lives and works. Mainly on weekends, he can afford long periods of free time. With a basket full of provisions for a picnic of one or two - occasionally, he asks a friend to accompany him - he takes the underground from High Street Notgni and heads on to Debden.

He arrives within an hour of commuting.

In the open area generally used as a campsite, he spots a place further away from the rest of the visitors who also came to enjoy the location. He sets his mat and picnic provisions under a shady tree. He laid down on his back and then closed his eyes to dive into himself as deep as possible.

He uses his hands and thoughts to navigate in the new space. The stiff landscape which moves around safely demands him to be cautious. In the blink of an eye, he falls into the abyss beneath him, and at the moment, he can't figure out how deep the hole goes.

He rumbles around for more than an hour. He doesn't meet anyone he can talk to and ask a question. Though the dense air he moves inside could hardly allow him to open his mouth. The place appears unfamiliar that he doesn't have any picture to compare with, from all the visited sites. All around him, as far as his eyes could see, an array of rocks with dark algae abounds. The view appears not hospitable, and he can't escape from there. He decides to continue to explore since he cannot turn back.

A bottomless void appears. Haile can't imagine what might be in that distance where he sees clearly, but at the same time features a blurry horizon. Any possibility might be there. His mind goes into what it does best: it creates its representations where it can't spot the real ones. He can't fathom what the place stands for. He dives even deeper intending to uncover himself through memories unveiled through his dreams. He only appears to get feedback on his visit as a gentle wind tries to take him away from the spot his feet stand firm. He doesn't want to be swayed away, given that he ignores where he might end up. He resists. As the wind gets stronger, he appeals to more energy inside him to stay where he is.

If he doesn't immediately go back where he came from, he fears not returning. As he uses more strength while the wind pushes him in the opposite direction, he finally emerges from his dive. Unable to rationally interpret what his thoughts told him, he decides to let it all go. He grabs a snack from his picnic basket lost in his mind, eats while absent-minded. The overall rollercoaster of thoughts had taken, in real-time, less than ten seconds to navigate through his mind.

While they travelled back and forth in his subconscious, it seemed he had done a few hours on a fast jet that took him to an indefinite number of places.

They had arrived at the place in the park where they usually start their jog. The whole journey in his dream had taken place while Haile walked beside Amina, but she hadn't noticed that his mind had travelled far away.

Each one makes their moves to stretch their feet, arms and other parts of the body before their run. That day, Haile didn't feel in as good form as the last time. No clue could indicate if that dream experience a moment before had any link with his energy level for the run. Three weeks had passed. He had given himself a pause after a year-long of regular jogging. There had been an interruption of a few weeks from time to time, but he had embarked on a fitness routine he wouldn't trade for any other physical or mental practice. From a health perspective, he had started benefiting from it. Besides, he enjoyed his overall exercising.

CHAPTER FOUR - Experience A Crime

SECTION 1. The Profile

A Birthday In Disau

When the summer holiday came to a close, Hussein's family and friends gathered in his parents' spacious and luxurious villa in Disau Aibara to celebrate his twenty-one years' birthday.

"As this important anniversary for my son brings the family together, I need to get the whole preparation perfect and right for the occasion," Hussein's mother instructs the team she has put in place to prepare the event.

Among the many gifts, Hussein got offered a set of keys for his special day. They can open an apartment in Vodnak that his father bought him for the occasion. After the birthday's celebrations, a week later, he flies back to Vodnak. He has lived in that city for two years already. Officially he returns to pursue his university studies, to do his second undergraduate year. Although he came to the QK, he spends his time in nightclubs with young people from his social class and Aibaran origins. His parents insisted that he needed a European education because of the myth of excellence it carries worldwide. However, governments from the broad South challenged that myth. They had opted for their youth to study in the local institutions. Their argument consisted in that once these young people graduated and returned home to their respective countries, their knowledge and application to the local reality carried critical dissonances.

They contributed to the distortion of local reality from its normal evolution since they imposed new schemes to solve local problems but didn't consider the context's particularities.

In the end, the applied medicine didn't work because it didn't respond to a correct diagnosis of the patient in need of a cure.

Hussein's circle of friends consisted of young heirs in their twenties and early thirties. Some spoiled children from these wealthy families don't generally care much academically. They don't have any reference to hardship, things such as homelessness, hunger, or statelessness. Their financial future doesn't depend on how well they perform in the campuses' theatres. Logically, they won't lack much while they live.

Sometimes, these youngsters consider that their wealth doesn't fulfil them. They then travel to foreign countries with the least luggage to experience the thrill - if any - of those less fortunate than them, or even only to discover the world their families' wealth cannot provide.

Immediately after the celebration of his birthday, Hussein didn't say goodbye to his parents. They learn about his trip only when he calls them from Vodnak. It's two days after his arrival. He lives on a reasonable monthly allowance that his father gave him as an agreed arrangement because he doesn't work yet.

"I will give you this allowance for a limited time only. There will be a time you will need to work hard to earn a living. That will be sooner than you expected. If you don't want to be surprised by what will happen to you, you need to change. Don't blame me for loving you this way, as my only son. The way I ended up as I stand today, I had to work hard," Hussein's father warns him and demands from him to become more serious about life. In whatever way, the allowance Hussein would stop when he turned twenty-three. Contrary to the other foreigners who came to the QK and were obliged to do two to three jobs in one day of twenty-four hours to make ends meet, Hussein didn't have to worry about work.

If his family disowned him, he could only agonise about earning an income, but he couldn't imagine how that would happen, considering the high family's pedestal he stood on.

In the Summer of that year, Hussein boarded a flight from Cairo International to Vodnak. One hour later, within the confines of his seat and its security belt, he senses the limited freedom to move around. He tries to make himself comfortable despite that. He manages to have a nap for a few hours. On top of his preparation for that trip, he had felt exhausted from a long night out. He had spent long hours in a nightclub with friends the day before. The flight doesn't take long from departure to the destination: five hours and thirty minutes in total. The sky over Wortheart International Airport looks clear, the pilots of the Airbus A330-300 manoeuvre to approach and land.

Once in the airport's lounge, a dried sound of an Etab ballad 'Basharouni' flows from above in the speakers. The melody reminds Hussein of his Aibaran heritage. It makes him nostalgic for the things and people he might never see again for as long as he would stay in the QK. They will be gone for a while, unreachable as he would like, or die forever. Not that he couldn't return to Disau. Such an eventuality had a probability close to nil to materialise. However, destiny always has its plans.

In his case and the nature of his country's politics, fierce resistance to change seems embedded in the elite's core that rules in Disau Aibara, this since immemorial times. Contexts within which politics play in his country and become the norm for society, as far as he could remember, evolved uniquely in their unfolding.

The time he spends in that airport's lounge brings up feelings he experienced once in his lifetime.

He feared they might never get repeated any time soon or in the distant future. That's the thought which crosses his mind while he listens to the musical melody.

237

A CHBS billboard states the "Welcome to the QK" in bright colours subtle to the eyes. At that time of the morning, clouds in the sky have become more menacing and predict an imminent rainfall.

Street vendors and even taxi drivers aren't in the right mood. This didn't stop him, within thirty minutes, from managing to get to his apartment in Notgni and Aeslech.

A whole year has already passed since his first landing in the QK. He tries hard to belong; he will, however, never feel integrated within this new human setting. Regardless, he counts on his steady determination to stay in that place as long as he can. Though he had this indescribable sentiment that seemed to indicate that Hussein would persistently feel like a foreigner, looked down on by the natives, no matter how much wealth he could display or friends he could list as close contacts among the nationals.

"Have you had a nice trip, Mr Hussein?" asks the Eastern European concierge, who mans the block of apartments he stays in.

"Yes, I have, and thank you for asking," replies Hussein with an indifferent tone and an inexpressive face. With his eyes' blink, he doesn't take time to look into the concierge's face while he greets him. Hussein"s attitude disappointed the concierge after his benevolent display of politeness. Despite that, Hussein has straightaway changed his attitude of indifference because he needs to ask him a personal question.

"Has anyone come around and asked for me in my absence?" Hussein enquiries.

"No, Sir," the concierge answers.

When Hussein returned to Vodnak with keys to his new apartment in hand, he decided to stay momentarily in his previous studio. He planned to organise a party to unveil the new place to his friends.

Rebellious as his typical behaviour, Hussein had demonstrated that he had no interest in studying from the start. "Why does he have to be like that?" Once Amina wondered when she began to get closer to him and get to know him a little. He portrayed the behaviour of some children from wealthy or elite families from developing countries.

These children, while they rely on their origins and stay momentarily or study in the West, they think that the wealth of their parents constitute a permanent fact that time couldn't alter.

Amina, as far as she was concerned, had had difficult university years. She had enough motivation but financial hardship impacted negatively on her studies.

Hussein's parents wanted him to be studious and become a child that deserved their inheritance for which they worked hard to develop. Any parent would expect that from their offspring. Nevertheless, their expectations would end up unfulfilled for other reasons than their child's unwillingness to study.

Amina once thought that Hussein's negative attitude towards studying could be down to his disobedient personality, probably developed from the rebellious teenage years. At the same time, she wondered if there could be any other explanation. His mother liked to compare him to his remote aunty. If that came to be the case, some of their respective genes could be a complete match in that regard.

That many people found undesirable some of his character traits; nevertheless, they had undeniably made him who he had ended up being or perceived to be.

However, this would become irrelevant in the days or weeks ahead.

Hussein would fall into an unexpected vegetative life after attempted murder on his person.

The sudden dramatic turn in his health cut short any issues about things that affected or explained his life. However, those who suffered from his attitude could somehow feel relieved, while the criminal assault put him in a state of a permanent coma.

The universe pushes some people to rest, and they get enormously missed because of their deeds while they stayed alive. How far people would remember Hussein positively remained to be seen. He would not die immediately, but while he still lay on a hospital bed, what feelings would have the people he had mistreated and left with scars they couldn't easily discard?

A Typical Weekend

Late in the afternoon of that Sunday, Hussein wears a cotton jacket and a polo shirt. He didn't wear his pyjamas when he last came home and fell asleep. A painful migraine and an acute hangover after a lousy weekend made him feel miserable and kept him indoors. He has not eaten at all for the preceding twelve hours. His fridge looks nearly empty. He needs to get to the grocery store nearby to buy takeaways to alleviate his hunger.

"How do I get up? I feel awful," Hussein manages to show his already negative mood while still half awake. Already four o'clock, and he hasn't dared to open his curtains. He has lectures to attend and assignments to complete for the next day.

He spent the previous night in one of the night-clubs along Greek Street in the Ohosh area. He left past midnight, completely drunk. He also flirted with women from different nationalities and backgrounds. With two friends from Disau Aibara, he doesn't miss any opportunity to go out to dance and drink. A few times, he doesn't invite them, but his friends do. He has known for many years, and they all come from his country.

"Let's play hard," Hussein had adopted this motto for his life. However, he had left out the first part of the usual principle, which implied to work hard before they think to play hard.

Naturally attracted to women, as any normal and handsome man in the prime of their youth would, Hussein finds it hard to get attached to any girl for long periods. For a couple of weeks, he hasn't had any woman in his bed. Before that, one of his friends has agreed to arrange an overnight pass. He had been out for the chase game at that time but didn't remember how the hunt went the next day. He had woken up alone.

"What a night!" Hussein thought when he woke up the next day and didn't feel awful as usual after similar outings but still doesn't remember much about what had happened.

In one of his memory repositories from the previous nights, among the most recent ones at the back of his head, he saw himself, but not a hundred percent certain, in a pub with a glass of cognac and coke cocktail with ice in it. He chatted with one of his friends and looked at two girls seated alone at one of the tables on their left side. They appeared to expect someone to join them, as they always kept their eyes on their watches and the place's entrance.

"Look at the one with long black hair and visible curves!" Hussein's friend had then told him while he pointed at one of the girls in one corner of the pub.

He and his friend had decided to go and ask them to join them. The girls told them that they waited for their boyfriends, who would arrive soon. Hussein and his friend had come back and appeared walloped in their mind. Though they only left the girls until they noticed the arrival of their love partners.

He doesn't even remember how he got back to his apartment. The last souvenir he recalls relates to the fact that he passed out in a restroom somewhere. He would be reminded well after that he got home in a taxi. He has a vague memory about the people he met or went out with that night, if any. He decides to call his friends to find out what happened the night before. He takes his phone and flips his finger on the screen. As he moves down his middle finger on its screen, his mind connects some names to what he did the night before. He calls Ahmed, then Mustaffa. None of them replies. They also seem to experience their misery or are busy in their places. In the late evening, precisely at 11:00 pm, one of his friends calls.

"How are you managing?" Mustaffa asked.

"Alright for now, but I had a bad day because of the drinking. Can I get a favour from you about yesterday?"

"Yes, go ahead."

"What happened to the girls we wanted to have last night?"

"When their boyfriends came, we had to give them some space."

"Did we stay in that same place until I came home?"

"We went to a nightclub. The place looked crowded. When a waitress came to ask if we could share our table, two girls came and joined us. They seemed to be the same age as us. When we asked them about who they were, they indicated they were students. We chatted with them, and the mood seemed great; you had a particular interest in one of them and looked excited about the prospects of the night ahead. However, the nightclub had to close at 1:00 am. Sadly, none of us could've any of the girls. They wanted to return to their hostel. They had come out to refresh their heads after a week-long of assessments," Mustaffa explained.

"That's the picture of our night yesterday, but you heavily drank. In the end, it became even more difficult to have you leave the place, so much so that you seemed unstable. At one point, you even passed out before you got into your taxi. I put you in the passenger seat and told the driver your address. I feel surprised about how he got you out of his car," Mustaffa went on.

"I don't remember any of those details," Hussein replies.

Hussein attends university and is proud of himself to be the son of a well-to-do Disau family. His parents inherited and increased their wealth year after year through connections with the kingdom's royals and business acumen applied into trade transactions."

"His father owns an airline company that serves Disau Aibara and all the neighbouring countries. He would like to pass it on to him when he turns thirty.

Hussein's father met his QK wife while studying in Vodnak in the second half of the 70s. With time he became enthused by QK for its multiple attractions and its people's lifestyle. He decided to invest in properties in the QK capital.

Among his assets, he has two-bedroom apartments he bought in the wealthy borough of Notgni and Aeslech for his two children.

Though he lives and looks after his business interests from Disau, Hussein's father spends half of his annual holidays in the QK. He owns another five-bedroom apartment in the south of the borough, near the Squoll river, where he stays and hosts his guests when he spends time in Vodnak.

Very westernised, Hussein's family appears somehow to occasionally meet in these private gatherings convened by the royals. These relatives resemble the conservative royals from Disau when they mistreat women and or seem religiously and traditionally strict. Their women don't drive cars or go out independently without their guardians' permission, who always happen to be generally male.

His parents got him registered at the Vodnak School of Economics. While he doesn't concentrate on his studies, he uses his time and takes advantage of the freedom that living away from home allows him. With such a way of life, understandably, he doesn't perform well academically. Hussein could've considered himself lucky. Unlike most of his peers, his family didn't plan to arrange his marriage. If this were ever to happen - somebody else selecting which woman to marry -, the sealed relationship would tie Hussein to the chosen woman for life, though she would've been matched to him almost randomly, him without any say in it.

He was aware of the situation and the position of his father on the matter. His views about women didn't differ from that of the rest of the male youth in Disau. He enjoyed the unequal conduit between men and women that the Disau social system's patriarchal status favoured. He would treat them un-decently occasionally on his numerous nights out in Vodnak. He found such an attitude typical since this featured in the tradition of the Disau people. Amina had fallen for him and unconsciously ignored that side of some of his people's culture, which doesn't view women as men's equals.

She has widely read about some Aibaran women's conditions, but she couldn't imagine that Hussein would be among the active enforcers of such unprogressive practices towards women. Given his family background, his parents' level of westernised lifestyle, and the way Hussein abused her, time and time again, in a way, Amina understood the power of culture over individuals. She couldn't think that she could only be a victim of her boyfriend's personality or failed family education as a well-rounded person. Her conviction told her that some influences existed out of people's control. They impacted the way they behaved, even them not knowing.

Among Hussein's many friends, mainly those he went to pubs with or clubbing, some wondered about the ultimate consequence of his extreme abuse of women. From time to time, they dared to confront him and even discouraged him since they could perceive that it would not end well.

The Bullying Side

Not naturally alluring, but with some effort on her body and appearance, Amina has that magical ability to transform herself into a nicely built queen. However, she complains that she needs to make serious attempts to please when her peer men don't have to. In her view, men who pamper their bodies as women do, have lost part of their masculinity and manhood.

In her opinion, men could look ugly and still be attractive. Other than handsomeness, the male characteristics that portray them as protectors or dependents compensate widely for other shortcomings related to the overall look they might display. Such a view constituted her assessment of male attractiveness.

Like any other woman in a couple whose members behave still as new into their relationship, Amina tries to know more about her partner Hussein. This occurs at the start of her unforgettable journey in somebody else's life, and it wouldn't be highly recommendable.

"I take it easy and not consider this relationship as my must-have to fulfil my life destiny. By the simple fact that to assess the reality of things objectively, I would be foolish to think that without him, my world would end," she tells herself at the time.

"When I look at my relationship with him that way, that attests to a sign of maturing, I suppose," she reflects.

Only six months had passed. They had embarked on their journey of dates. The casual openness or the little desire of them to be alone together lacked still at that stage of their relationship. They continued to observe and scrutinise each other cautiously, whatever they shared or exchanged between them or means used.

They struggled on the basics required to develop their relationship, preoccupied with their right foundation about a future together. Amina appeared concerned. Hussein only considered their relationship as another venture out of the many he had already lived on his part.

Nothing indicated that he would change in the future.

"Shouldn't we have our relationship in order?" Amina asked Hussein once after she spent a night with him.

"What do you mean? Do what about what!" replied and asked Hussein with a surprised look on his face. This conversation occurred the day after he spent a good night out while he heavily drank with his friends and Amina around.

His infatuation with Amina didn't seem to bother him. The input of Hussein into their relationship's growth; I resembled one of a careless contractor assigned to a site. He wouldn't care much how the construction project he works on would appear in the end once all the work would've been completed or left unfinished for whatever reason.

"I would like to know our relationship's future," Amina asked Hussein that morning, after a breakfast in which she did little to make it memorable.

"What problem do you have? What do you want me to tell you? I still feel young, and I don't want to promise things I can't guarantee to fulfil in the future," Hussein replied. Despite the disappointment from such an answer, Amina decided not to give up quickly on their relationship. She would stick around him as long as it would take to win over his heart.

Though Hussein was in a relationship with Amina, he cheated on her with other women but ensured she couldn't be caught.

She would only get vague suspicions from the way he behaved while they went out together. He ignored her presence and would openly show interest in other women. The women he would flirt with would be much younger than Amina. Apart from their younger age, no other distinctive characteristic would've justified that he could cheat on his girlfriend; this came from her analysis of their relationship.

These women seemed not better than her in many respects. Amina didn't come from a noble family or a rich ancestry, and her peers at work considered her highly refined.

There might've been other personality differences, although Hussein didn't care much about that aspect. Any woman who could be able to be or behave in a submissive manner could be convenient for him. Greedy or careless, uneducated or without a solid background, as long as she could accept his abusive character and be beautiful enough, she could become his woman.

At the early stage of his adulthood, he doesn't think starting his own family to be a good idea; but would he seriously ever plan to have one at any given time in the future? To his peer young and wealthy friends, he claimed that he would only settle for one woman when the latter would have demonstrated that she could help him plan his future better than he could do. His view would let him think that he had more interest in mature women who could instil some discipline in him. Such a scenario would probably occur once he would be much older.

Abusive and arrogant, in any group of friends or peers he participated, they saw him as the only one whose opinions mattered. He looked like he led a talk show; he distributed time to talk to the members. He interrupted anyone he wanted or brushed off their views in impolite ways that humiliated his targets.

He persistently ensured to take a central position while in discussions. All the time, the tone of his voice was one decibel louder than the rest, insensitive. He didn't care about what others thought of any topic they discussed or him. His jokes or remarks demonstrated the narcissistic and sarcastic sides of his character sufficiently.

He intelligently brought up issues he mastered well for discussion, with the only purpose to crush the views of anyone who would intervene.

He created spaces and opportunities for self-glorification. For him, debates looked like games without clear rules, where he wanted to be an indisputable constant winner. He enjoyed them very much. While arguing, he despised silences because he perceived them as time wasted when he would be shining. He monitored interventions for that reason, steered conversations, and ensured that everyone could express their views he could counter-argue and win over.

Despite his bully tactics as a vital aspect of his character, his friends enjoyed his company. He mentally abused them without any doubt, but surprisingly they didn't dislike him as a consequence. Instead, they found some sort of comfort when they gathered around him. From their perspective, he made them grow their character under the influence of his personality. He victimised them, but they loved the result, like sufferers of Stockholm syndrome. He had this ability to make those he interacted with as friends or peers feel good about themselves. They believed that their lives increased in their worth when they stuck around him.

His wealth and the generosity he projected with it made him look sociable, though, indisputably, he didn't have any sense of social responsibility.

Interestingly, his generous actions always came out in pubs' confines, where, once drunk, he would pay, for example, for everyone in the room a glass of whatever they would be drinking. He had many friends if one could call them such, given that they navigated around him, mainly because they purposely pursued what he did for them with his money.

Hussein didn't complain like the people who whine that they don't have friends. At least he had somewhere to start related only to the gifts he gave out; his satisfied entourage found him as a person of great charisma to be around.

***

At five forty-five in the morning, Haile and Amina, in their exercise outfits, pass near High Street Notgni station. That supposes they left their places much earlier to get to that location. It's a one-mile distance from where they live. Early workers already enter the underground to commute towards their different destinations in Vodnak city and even beyond.

"They spend day after day with their strict discipline to wake up in the morning, get ready each time to go to work, eat their breakfast sometimes while they sit uncomfortably or stand, and work with a boss the majority doesn't necessarily like, and on every other day he abuses and humiliates them publicly; the victims can't stand it, but they feel powerless. Though at the same time, this didn't constitute someone's life experience, through choice or by fate, they hang in there and decide not to complain, for reasons they don't know clearly," discusses Haile with himself in his mind, and wonders if these people he observes who head to the underground ever question the purpose of their lives in the Universe.

He monologues without any sound out within the confines of the silence his co-runner offers him unexpectedly.

The Basawi takeaway restaurant Haile and Amina pass by has not yet opened. When Haile happens to be in the area around lunchtime, he doesn't resist getting in there and buying his salmon teriyaki with brown rice. It's a delicious menu of marinated salmon with teriyaki sauce - brown sushi rice - sesame oil - avocado - red cabbage - roasted butternut squash - edamame - cucumber - sesame seeds - red onions - mixed salad leaves - hives and Pobe dressing.

Ten meters from the restaurant, the newsstand owner at the station's entrance already has his items arranged for sale. The day's display features same-day editions of The Tunes, The Guards, The Freed, The New Squoll Times, La Maison, Le Citadin, and other tens of newspapers and magazines.

In the last ten years, Haile has noticed that newsstand. It must have been there even many years before moving into the area and coming to know it. He can't recall if any aspect of that kiosk has ever changed all that time. Some things time doesn't format them anew. Understandably, content in the news sold through the material displayed in that stand changes every day or regularly.

As they walk toward the park, Amina talks about the visit she did and other places she went with her nephew over the weekend.

"My nephew has this new game one finds on Nintendo. I observed him while fully immersed in it. Without much noise, his only facial movements expressed whatever the game demanded him to perform," she explains to Haile. Thirty meters before they get to the entrance of the park, they cross the street.

Supermarkets, big brand shops and stands align on either side of the section of the high street. Located less than a hundred meters before one gets to the park, these products' display outlets will only open later in the morning. It seems too early at the time. Some early bird staff already stand in front of the entrance doors, where they wait to get in and prepare displays for the day. In case they didn't arrange them the day before. These big shops usually open from 8:00 am onwards. The majority open up even an hour later. Those who sell snacks, soft drinks and sandwiches begin sometime before allowing commuters to buy their daily's provision.

Meng House, on their right-hand side, displays selected items from Meng. Pedestrians could see them from outside, but they couldn't rightly appreciate these artefacts because they appeared in their miniature sizes.

The day before, that institution organised a talk to present Meng theatre to the QK audience. Haile attended. Kojo Toshinobu, the Meng playwright in the spotlight on that occasion, talked about his four plays, including Dilemma.

The play touches on significant social aspects of human behaviour, morals and the concept that highlights the impulse to accomplish the right actions when someone struggles to overcome impossible challenges. After a nuclear tragedy the Meng country experiences, government officials interview a college student, a rice wholesaler's wife, and the Nuclear Security Inspection Office's deputy chief inspector. The play's fundamental question hangs on being virtuous when specific actions become unavoidable and personal sacrifice too subjective.

"What went through your mind in the first moments of the tragedy your area experienced?" the interviewer had asked one resident, as highlighted by the presenter.

"I didn't panic exceedingly. By not having any personal references to compare it to, I couldn't guess how the situation could seriously be dangerous. As I followed the news on television, I became afraid of what might happen. I couldn't think of what I could take with me before the general evacuation of the population. The whole picture appeared scary," the interviewee managed to reply.

Haile and Amina arrived at that Notgni High Street station ten minutes earlier than usual. As they wanted to gain even more time, they decided to start their jog at the Notgni Gardens entrance instead of the Pond, situated one hundred meters inside the park. It wasn't the first time they proceeded that way.

Haile sees a homeless person who has passed the night in the park, still asleep on one of the benches at the entrance. The rough cough he heard from him had raised his attention. He brushed off from his mind any concern he might have about him.

Once they arrive at the Pond, they split, and each one goes in their direction because they run at different paces. They seem both not to want to, and neither feel that they compete against each other while jogging.

Thus there is no pressure on anyone to run at somebody else's pace; it would also be physically draining for whoever would move slowly or faster to accommodate the other partner.

***

At that time, Haile and Amina have been into their sports activity for the last ten months. The Pond - a local artificial lake -, in Notgni Gardens and the paths around the Neptersine have been their grounds for exercising. Though both participate for fitness reasons, each of them has specific individual and specific motives.

"I want to address health issues and lose weight," had Amina stressed to Haile while she explained what she pursued in her running.

"I have a particular interest in the side effects of regularly exercising. I have noticed an overall improved level of good health exempt from inclinations toward depression. It will be down to my consistency in my exercise routine to feel that way all the time," Haile points to Amina about how he valued his regular sports activity.

In that whole period, their exercising has been interrupted from time to time by other life's priorities or elements linked to the weather, but soon out of the way, and it would become possible for them to get back into their routine. They have given themselves a target to continue without any interruption through the winter season and see if they could do a whole year of jogging. In the end, they plan a celebratory event for such an achievement if they manage to get there. Sometimes they fell behind their programme. One might have had to go away for a particularly personal reason or when the day's clarity diminished. On these occasions, new arrangements took place either individually or jointly. Haile happily enjoyed the run, to the point that it had become second nature to him. He always looked forward to his run any other day as if any other aspect of his life depended on it.

He had been for some years not disciplined about his minimum daily food requirements. He somehow skipped his meals, mainly his lunches, and didn't feel excessively hungry until dinner in the evening. Understandably, these unhealthy food habits could lead to illness, especially for his overall body's immune system.

Since he didn't eat at set times of the day, this became detrimental to his health because he also exercised regularly.

On her part, Amina had noticed that her consistent practice of fitness could get her to the body shape she wanted, but she occasionally let herself off and did not stick to her effective diet.

Within six months of regular exercising, Haile had lost a lot of weight. From a high start of 92 kgs, he had declined to 75 kgs. The drastic shift resulted from a self-imposed discipline of jogging, exercises in the gym sometimes to work on his muscles, and meticulous control of his diet. He had become a handsome, tall guy whose attractiveness had been a hot gossip topic among his female colleague teachers. His previous ugliness of some sort had faded away through the transformation. His acquaintances, who had noticed the change, thought that he had hidden his handsomeness in an undefined space that his new sports' activity triggered and revealed itself.

He looked like a different person, not bony at all. Instead, he displayed an enviable attractive and athletic body. Amina wanted to tell him how much he had positively changed, but she couldn't find a way to say it correctly. She didn't want him to think that she seduced him.

From the beginning, she had fenced their relationship inside a place she didn't want out for any reason. At that moment, such an idea was far away from her intentions.

This attitude seemed unusual on her part. She always had comments for most of the topics they discussed when they exercised together for their run along the Neptersine. Suddenly, she had decided to censor herself for that particular topic for some reason.

Since she didn't want Haile to think wrongly about what she would say, she referred to his weight loss through an indirect speech.

"What do you eat for breakfast?" Amina asks Haile.

"I take cereal and a glass of squeezed orange juice every morning," he replies.

"And what do you have for lunch?" she adds.

"It depends on where I stand when this happens, but I take a light lunch which consists of vegetables and fruits. I normally have my main meal in the evening, always before 7:00 pm. If I pass that time without my dinner, it becomes difficult for me to jog the next day," he replies.

"I think that way, my digestive system has helped as well and sent me warnings when I don't respect the normal meals' schedule," he adds.

On the same morning, they exchanged about Haile's diet. Like at any other time, they walked outside together. They were out together at any time; he moved a half feet ahead of Amina since the pavements they used looked narrow and could hardly allow more than two people to stride side-by-side at such an early hour. When they paced that way, Haile found it easier to pass and give space to any walker who would come from the opposite direction to pass them. There must've been another reason for him to walk that way occasionally, if not all the time; he wanted as well to stand, as a shield, able to confront any danger that might come from the opposite front.

That protective way while they walked together focused on the safety of the person behind. Most of the time, Amina would be talking, while Haile would give the impression that he listened attentively, though this wouldn't always be the case. He would only intervene sporadically.

For some reasons and days, Amina changed suddenly and talked to a minimum of her usual standards. There could be one to three minutes of silence before she said anything. That made Haile uncomfortable for all that time; they had been together, while each time they went out for their jogging.

"What has been happening? Today, you seem not talkative as much as you used to. You look like a different person while you behave that way," Haile complains.

"I have been the talker for far too long, and you haven't been helping," Amina replies.

"But I never complained. I don't understand your need to talk less since you don't annoy me at all! The topics you cover always bear some interest. I don't often intervene, but that doesn't mean there can't be any interest in what you would be saying," Haile explains his position further to the displayed and unusual silences of Amina in their walking.

After the observation Haile had made previously about Amina's deliberate silences, she returned to her usual frequency of chats the next few days. Her co-runner didn't bother to ask her why she would talk because he didn't have to complain at all.

Changes in their early sport routine became occasionally inevitable and somehow necessary. Personal circumstances or external and uncontrollable factors were the root causes. The momentary interruptions couldn't deter them indefinitely. All the time, they both returned to their programme at some stage. The running started to feel like part of their life, unconscious as breathing.

SECTION 2. From A Distance

One Jog At A Time

Haile lies on his bed, half-asleep. His conscience digs in its repository for excuses for not getting out of the bed.

"Let me check the time," this came as a flash thought that crossed his mind at that time of the night.

He had to stretch his hand towards the small table beside his bed to keep; his mind seemed to indicate. When winter came, he discontinued his running. When it became much warmer, he didn't resume his jogging; another habit had become a new routine. On this, he resembles anyone who doesn't enjoy change.

"I need to assess how it looks outside," he instinctively glances through the windows, and this follows a recurrent instruction from his brain each time he gets up to be ready for his running.

An enthusiastic at times and in heart, he occasionally and consciously creates his picture of the day as he would like it to be. It would then represent his perfect day as he could imagine it. He used this technique as one of his ways to go through his immediate future, not hindered by difficulties along the way, and even if they arose, he could overcome or challenge them more easily. In any case, it worked for him, though some doubted it.

The night's darkness has gradually given place to a favourable horizon with a clear sky. The process moved slowly but steadily. Dawn has nearly come.

"Soon, it will be the time for the early birds to be fully awake and start their daily undertakings," he thought. Rainy clouds from recent weeks have disappeared.

He continues with a gaze at the outside space.

He lives in one of the apartments in a five-storey tall building located on Wright's Drive. The storeys line up one after another. Local authorities hadn't allowed developers to build new apartments in the area. Consequently, the architecture had remained unchanged as far back as many residents could remember.

"This means that one day my place will fundamentally change once one of these applications for the redevelopment of the area will be approved," he concluded. His mind comes to that conclusion while he looks at his local area through the window. Though still dark outside, he could see some cranes in the distance, at one uncompleted development nearby.

The traffic on the main street outside sounds dangerously loud. It took Amina time to get used to the noise of the area. Windows, generally closed, insulate the interior of most of the apartments from external ruckus and cars' pollution. The general public's traffic passes by the building's main entrance, located next to a busy bus stop.

Residents from the three top storeys had a lift to get to the ground level of the building. At this level, a private pharmacy store, a coffee shop, and a supermarket opened seven days a week. They occupied the entire front of the estate from one street to the next one. The courtyard hung on the third level between ranges of apartments. Spacious in size, which depends on individual considerations -, it has small trees and bank benches. The picture would be incomplete without the children's area in one of the corners of the courtyard. All the apartments were built in a c-shape around the square.

Hussein and Amina live in apartments situated on the same fourth level but opposite the residents' courtyard. Anyone could see Haile's studio on the same side as Amina's but in different blocks of apartments.

Dae lives in the same block of flats as Hussein, two floors below him. The lawn in the courtyard looks natural, but it came from a factory. It gets hot when the sun shines for long periods. The gated and spacious area served for parking cars and spanned from one end to the other outside the c-shaped built space.

The concierge service of the buildings appears inconsistent, and the overall maintenance somehow underperforms. Residents' complaints about poor service fill the workload of the buildings' managers.

On the premises, they represent the private company they work for. It has been many years that residents have been in limbo.

They don't know what to do to get services improved. The majority of the complaints get ignored. The last one that many had raised concerns the outdoor lights in the courtyard, which didn't work correctly on the fatal moment when Hussein got stabbed. If they had, Haile would've been able to identify the person who walked in that space and that he saw that night.

This time on a different day, at dawn, he goes out for his jogging.

He hesitates to call Amina, his co-runner while waiting for three to five minutes. She texts him.

"I couldn't sleep properly at night. Sorry I can't run today." I have had such nights recently. Unfortunately, that would characterise overall how they both lived their sports activity.

"It's ok. Don't worry. We will go together next time."

Haile decides to leave and go jogging on his own. The air outside feels still warm, and it predicts a fresh morning. The new season has not yet announced its colours, nor brought its full chilliness. Nonetheless, in those days, everyone already wears items from the autumn collections.

He opts to wear shorts with bare legs; on top, he has only a black t-shirt. Once in the stairs, he goes down but stops instantly halfway to wait.

"I forgot my water," he realises. He runs back to his apartment.

The moment seems to be another fresh start of the day where he will run without Amina. From his apartment to the Notgni Gardens, it's a three to five-minute distance with a pace of a military march. Where he does his jogging, it's only two hundred meters away, inside that vast park.

While walking, he thinks about the writer who lives in the block of apartments adjacent to his. From time to time, they meet in the local park while they do both their jogging. They have been acquaintances for many years since college.

One month before, he had suggested to him the book title 'The Neptersine' the writer worked on while he ran together and enjoyed the sight of that artificial river.

The writer had explained to Haile that his recent project had been motivated and inspired by a book of Kiharu Mura he had finished reading, *'My Thoughts When I Think About Jogging.'* He indicated that Mura's initial approach to his literary work got him excitedly energised. The Meng author started his first novel, but he couldn't guess what he planned to write about. This intrigued him first.

At the same time, that idea to go forward, not guided by an exact planned destination, but advance still without disenchantment, solved in a way the unease he had experienced. In the past, he had felt seriously challenged by that situation. He had struggled in his several attempts to make ideas flow naturally.

A brisk wind blows on his face, as he remembers.

Tourist boats for hire appear still attached in the perimeter close by on the river's waters. It looks too early for anyone to venture out on the Neptersine scenery for a contemplative purpose.

He had settled for the title suggested to the writer when one day he passed two women runners. The apparent shy one avoided looking up in front of her at a distance of approximately thirty meters.

"Could it be her shyness that makes her not look straight in front of her?" Haile wonders. He didn't have an answer, though he had observed her from afar for a moment.

Two male runners had come from her opposite direction. He saw her make a move sideways, unexpectedly; it looked as if she feared to fall into the trap of a tropical and hungry lion. Alternatively, she had remotely sensed these male runners carried hidden weapons that would harm if someone came close. As evidence of that premonition, when she became sure to have made some distance between them and her, she returned to the leading runners' track.

Without any prior clues about the book's plot, Haile censored himself and avoided questioning what the writer had in mind and what would be the dominant theme for the story he intended to tell.

Incidentally, the project had started when he went back into his exercise's routine. This occurrence happened at the same time when the doctor's writer also had recommended him to exercise to address some health issues his body carried or could suffer if not dealt with in time.

"Have you seen that kind of shy woman over there?" Haile points in the runner's direction.

"She translates or defines a particular human character," Haile highlights to the writer.

"However, I don't intend to portray such a personality or concentrate on shyness, but I would like only to look at it as one trait of a particular individuality out of many," on his part, the writer explains.

"I want to make that characteristic stand out as a bold statement about individuals," he adds.

"Likability doesn't come with strings attached in my mind," he concludes his interaction with Haile on one of the characters in his book.

Groxy Rane in *Feminist Gone Bad* talks unhindered about her relationship with the characters.

"In my writing, I favour unlikable characters, to those who carry themselves in socially unacceptable ways, say whatever they think, and are action-oriented whatever the consequences of their behaviour. I make my characters do unthinkable things and go on unscathed. I instruct their imagination to create ugly worlds where they decide unimaginable actions. I want them to be like humans making mistakes and being as greedy as one can think," Rane says.

The writer had appeared to be at the same wavelength as Rane, while he lets people - that he chose as characters - aspire to become who they wanted to be, even unconsciously or unintentionally.

"Likability appears to be a complete lie, and more radical than that writer would qualify it differently, since he considered it a luxury," Haile had reckoned on that day when they discussed his friend's literary project.

"If one looks at it rationally, the whole human experience appears not likeable," the writer had then boldly indicated to Haile.

"I bet with anyone, to find me, one only likeable person, without any ugly side, from their background or physical outlook. Focusing only on likeable characters would be to miss the point since the world doesn't consist of them only."

"The most powerful narrative capable of winning a prize would have a complexion of more human characters who appear equally as likeable and as unlikeable!" he strongly argued. He tried to explain to Haile what he genuinely thought about the expression of the human character.

"At the end of the day, that's what characterises our humanity. It doesn't consist of only likeable people and the rest of us, like you and me. It would represent different humanity if it only consisted of the good ones. Would those seen as foes have to find their world and live there so that they don't spoil the good humanity? I don't know. I think the characterisation or definition of such humanity with only good characters would require a different name," he winded up.

At the time, Haile brought in the discussion his ultimate view.

"If we consider the fact that likability or the opposite, both evolve with time, today entities - an object or a person - could appear likeable, but they might not have any guarantee that they will remain the same tomorrow. The same goes for what appears unlikeable at the moment. No substance seems permanently constant, and even when it does, when its surroundings or context change, the whole picture changes while it keeps unchanged some - if not all - of its main components."

***

Old enough to look like Amina's oldest brother, Haile and her had eight years that separated them. Amina had told him once that they could only evolve towards friendship. She had her eyes instead on much younger bachelors with bulky pockets. That explains in one way how she had become Hussein's boyfriend.

At one point, Haile had considered her materialistic, but he seemed unsure about that. The things she wanted from life could make anyone think of her like that. However, her views on what mattered the most appeared to change over the years.

"We became friends, right?" he suddenly asked her, almost from nowhere, as if purposely and at the back of his mind, he wanted to hear that they had between them more than their friendship. In some instances, people say things in one's life, but deep down, they want to mean or wish to hear much more enjoyable feedback from their listeners.

"Yes, we are, without any doubt!" Amina replied with an air of surprise.

"What bothers you?" she went on with a lower tone.

"What a silly question!" she added and asked with a changed expression on her face. Haile didn't respond. He couldn't and didn't want to because he felt embarrassed by how she had asked the question. Haile had made himself look vulnerable.

He went for her hand and held it tightly, in such a way that he wouldn't let her take it away, in case she wanted to resist. Amina let him hold her hand despite telling him that they could only be together as friends.

They walked side by side to the pond.

"Promise me that you won't forget me," Haile implored Amina. The request sounded as coming from a space of desperation.

"Don't worry, I won't," she replied in a near whisper. They had arrived at the place where they usually go their ways and start their runs.

Her reply calmed him down for a moment. It reminded him of some of his early encounters with Amina when he began his first round of the pond. Many years had passed since she had moved into the same neighbourhood.

He regrets that his memory has grown dim with time. Many things get lost as the years fly by. It makes Haile feel some painful anxiety. Somehow it hurts a little or feels sad. He wonders if he has forgotten the relevant bits. When people lose something, they simultaneously block or prohibit their ability to objectively evaluate what they have lost. In a way, these critical memories unduly turned into mud or got left to sink into the sewer of time.

There came a time when Haile struggled and tried hard to wholly grasp what the concepts of memory and contours of history meant. In his understanding, history appeared broad and applicable to a group of individuals, a nation or several nations all together as one, whereas memory applied only at personal or community levels.

"Can memories as a collection, or a sum of individual recollections of the past, whatever the format they got presented in, constitute or become perceived as history?" he wondered. He couldn't give a definitive answer because of his lack of expertise in that domain of knowledge.

While he rumbles over these concepts, Haile believes that people can hide their memories. The process can seem voluntary or forced for different reasons. He believes in the view that highlights that someone can suppress them.

"I don't want to think about my ex-boyfriend, wife or husband," one example of voluntary suppression of a souvenir from the past that Haile thought about when he referred to what someone might say concerning an issue in their history. Haile had his interpretation of people's connection to their past.

"This statement sometimes could look like an illusion or a lie to oneself, to feel at ease. Although reality always presents itself differently from such deceptive justification. "

"The basis of memories consists of facts embedded in history, whatever its format, lived collectively or as an individual experience part of the collective one." However, Haile doesn't seem to agree with such an assertion.

He had strong convictions in particular areas.

"The paradox in the field comes from the fact that someone could act on their memory, hide or suppress it, but it remains impossible to erase the roots' history that created those memories. Memories define what someone's mind or brain keeps from the past. The history behind those pieces from the past lives somehow independently from what the individual memory keeps saved for posterity. People's minds don't have any control over it. To erase or change history appears like to destroy oneself. It seems as if to cut a branch of a tree one sits on," Haile asserts.

But to keep on living, he made a promise to himself.

"I have to go back to the mere remains of my past; however, blurred they seem in my memory." He remembers how and why he had struggled to go back in time.

"I want to capture these moments of my life in the moments they happen and preserve them for posterity, even though their importance and intensity at this particular time overwhelm to the point that it looks impossible to distinguish what to keep or what to leave out. To arrange them whenever necessary constitutes the challenge: should it come out by calendar dates as markers or as key events or phases of personal history."

Now that time has elapsed, with some hindsight, Haile could only understand what happened then. His past events' recollection was related to that period when he learned from his diverse surroundings and involvement.

When Amina had entered his world, Haile didn't recall much of the things they talked about during their initial interactions. He couldn't presume that she had never loved him. That's somehow why she had told him in a near whisper not to worry. She knew that with time his memory of her would fade away. On that matter, she appeared wiser than he had so far demonstrated.

Seen At Night

Haile, glued to his television, watches the Pobean drama series, Mr Yong-gi-shine. The series follows the journey of a Pobean young boy who, with the help of a Christian missionary, travels to the SU in the 1871 Shin-miyangyo SU expedition to Pobe. Once adult and natu-ralised, the young Pobean returns to his ancestral coun-try as a Suan lieutenant.

He had escaped from his native Pobe because he feared premeditated death on his person. He remembers that, while young, he had to run for his life and hide from his parents' killers, who beat them to death. His mother, in agony, helped by her last breath before she died, whilst she looked at all the blood from the wounds of family members that assassins had killed, she had loudly ordered him to run as far as he could. Only that way could he not end up with the same fate as her peo-ple.

The young Pobean returns home after more than two decades. Despite the lapsed time, he still recalls and resents the nobility's people from the elite who killed his parents. At times, he subconsciously and forcibly feels pushed to take revenge but resists in extremis. Despite his resentment, he falls in love with a Pobean woman from the nobility whose lifestyle and love for her country match his.

At one time in Pobean history, members of the lower class of society consisted of slaves. The young Pobean boy's parents belonged to that category. They had been punished, tortured, then killed by their master for some unclear wrong they had supposedly done - that he can't recall with total certainty. While he returned to Pobe, he intended to sacrifice himself to help the Pobean woman freedom fighter he had initially connect-ed with and towards whom he had intimate feelings.

269

While he watches films at home, Haile doesn't switch on the lights in his apartment's central area. He relaxes in front of his television from that spot.

On the tv screen, the light reflection doesn't interfere with alleviating the on-air programme's quality of visibility. Also, from his room, when Haile uses his long view spectacles, he can tell what happens in the apartments opposite his in the distance, mostly when occupants have not closed their curtains. He acts in those instances like a voyeur or a spy.

On that silent night, a calm wind that he feels a moment after he went to his local grocery store blows in the air. Almost forty meters ahead in the distance, he saw the profile of someone that would emotionally consume and alter his life forever. The woman he perceives in Hussein's apartment differs from the one he thinks it to be.

Early on, around ten in the evening, he had seen lights on in Hussein's apartment. Though he wouldn't tell the identity of the person he chatted with at the time, he had undoubtedly seen at least two people in that apartment. By the reflections or profiles he sees from afar, he thinks of them as a man and a woman. Uncertain, he wonders if the woman could be Amina. Even so, everyone in the neighbourhood knew Hussein and Amina as a couple. However, they ignored all the details of how their relationship had evolved. The couple involuntarily made their relationship known to interested outsiders because they lived in the same vicinity. From time to time, they would hold hands confidently in public.

Midnight had passed when Haile thought of eating. He has only a dozen eggs in his empty fridge. Luckily the supermarket at the other end of the block of apartments opens 24/7. Haile rushed and picked two bottles of fresh orange juice and some milk for his breakfast. He equally grabs some avocados.

By the first hour of the early morning, Haile returns to his apartment carrying a pack of groceries in his hands. At that hour, he assumes to be the only person around to walk in the block's shared public space. He guessed wrong in that space of approximately one hundred square meters in terms of people there.

Somebody else walked into that location at that moment and ran away from something. The person in question hopes to keep her night walk hidden as long as it would take.

A silhouette similar to Amina heads anxiously towards her apartment. It moves at the other end of the alley, opposite the set of apartments where Haile lives. He doesn't pay any particular attention to that individual's specific shapes, carries on, and goes to his apartment. He doubts that that other person saw him. It appears that the light at that central courtyard inside the c-shaped blocks of buildings doesn't have enough bright street lights. Recognising faces from afar makes it difficult, if not impossible. One could misread a person on a walk-in that area at that time of the night, mainly if they don't move in the right direction to enable better visibility.

Haile has known Amina for some three years. He thinks that even without much light out in the night, he could recognise her silhouette. One of the apartments in the block where the person's shadow appeared to have come from still has some light. Haile, back in his apartment, drinks some juice, then gets into bed. Before he does, he glances toward the window in the direction of Hussein's apartment. Could it be that his instinct pushed him to check if Hussein still talked to that woman he had imagined to see him with earlier? The apartment looked in the dark by that time.

When he woke up the next morning, a team of paramedics from the ambulance service had their car and a stretcher in front of the block where Hussein lives.

271

Around nine-thirty in the morning, Haile, on his way to work, asks onlookers what happened.

"Whose body's these paramedics came to pick?" he enquiries.

One of the few neighbours who had gathered around gave him some answers.

"The Disau young man has been badly injured. I don't think he will make it."

While Haile heads to the underground station, he reflects on the previous night incident where he must've seen Amina while she came out of the block in the early hours of the morning. Straightaway, he doesn't think of any connection between her and Hussein's state, where he was said to be seriously injured and close to death.

"I don't remember if the light I saw last night came from Hussein's apartment? No, I think it came from the left side of his place," he wonders, uncertain. When he commutes to work, he leaves aside that thought and carries on with his day's plans.

However, he becomes more and more anxious for Amina. Before he arrives at work, he calls her.

"Please would you mind, can I ask you a big favour? You told me once that sometimes you take your laundry to your agent when you want it cleaned faster on the same day. Could you also take today all the clothes you and your sister wore yesterday evening? I will explain later. It seems to be extremely important. If you do, you will be helping." Haile couldn't stop thinking about her after seeing the ambulance service and learning about Hussein's situation. His brain continuously played a multitude of scenarios in his head, some more complex than others. He tries to figure out what possibly happened that night and what it came to be as a consequence.

"For you to help me, please could you update me regularly on the situation," he added at Amina's intention.

He presumes a few hours later that Amina would be interrogated in the next hours if the police had already invited her. He decided to offer Amina some advice to prepare herself.

"When you go to see the investigators for interrogation, please respond confidently, only focus on what you need to tell them, to succeed," he elaborated.

Amina turned over its head Haile's request for her to understand what he said and the motivations behind it.

She immediately realised that effectively, if Hussein had been a victim of a crime, she could as well be seen as a primary suspect. In the eyes of everyone who knew both, he stood as his boyfriend. Therefore, she would be the first person the police would want to investigate. On the other hand, if Haile hadn't witnessed the crime from afar, he could as well have her already portrayed as the culprit. Understandably, what he asked went along the logic his mind had imagined: how to erase as soon as possible evidence that could incriminate her.

At lunchtime, Haile's mind brings him back to Hussein's case. The more he tries not to see connections, the more he suspects Amina of possible involvement. He has seen them together several times in the last six months. Also, even Haile and Amina had, on different occasions, talked about Hussein. He considered both as close friends since Amina hadn't revealed more to help characteristically define their relationship's nature. He decides to call Amina again to determine if she knows the whole picture of what happened to Hussein.

"Hi Amina, can you talk?" he asks while assuming to know already where she would've been on the night of Hussein's attempted murder. As another option, she ignored who he thought he saw since it had been her sister who had been in her boyfriend's apartment that night and not her.

Haile doesn't want to make her feel uncomfortable; he hides his straightaway suspicion about her probable involvement. Uncertain about the person he saw that night when he came from the supermarket and guessed to be her, he adopts a cautious approach and stops accusing her prematurely.

"Today morning, when I left our block, I saw an ambulance in our place. I suppose that by now, you know the person they took to the hospital! It's Hussein, your friend, who got badly injured. He could even die," Haile explains and waits to assess what would be Amina's response.

"Oooh, no. Please, can you confirm? Nobody has told me whatever yet," she enquires, with a spoon full of sadness in her voice. She pretended not to know. Her sister had indicated that she had left Hussein dead. The information Haile shared constituted another surprise when Amina learnt that they took him to the hospital for care.

"Yes! As sure as it could be. I asked the neighbours who were present at the scene when I passed them on my way to High Street Notgni station. Moreover, I could see that the paramedics moved up and down from Hussein's apartment," Haile explains.

"I will find out in which hospital he has been taken and visit him as soon as possible. I call one of his cousins to find out in the meantime," she points out innocently as she continues to pretend not to know much about what happened with Hussein.

Haile can't make up his mind about Amina's involvement in Hussein's misfortune that night. He decides to find another approach to confront her.

"But you know what! A moment ago, I received calls from tv journalists; they wanted to know about the incident. What shall I do?" Amina implores Haile for help. She knows he can't refuse since he has offered to help without a prerequisite condition.

The fact that journalists got interested in Amina's side of the story, as Hussein's girlfriend, confirmed in Haile's mind that she could get caught if she didn't take any precautions. She needed to think about how well to handle the situation, given that now she has to protect her sister.

The situation gets more and more complicated: the police and now the journalists all want to know the truth. Consequently, Amina has to be consistent in her narrative of what she knows or what she wants them to take as the truth.

"Try to be consistent, whatever you tell those who will interview you or interrogate you. As long as you show confidence in whatever you have to say, and it appears logical, stick to that, and you will be fine," Haile advises her.

"If you show some hesitation or inconsistencies in your answers, they will pick it up quickly to see you as the culprit," he added.

"I only wanted to let you know, if you didn't already, about the events of today morning. I know you leave our block much earlier than me. Also, I saw the paramedics around ten. I didn't have time to ask about how his body got discovered or what had happened," Haile also adds, simultaneously as still some suspicion of Amina's involvement builds up gradually at the back of his mind.

"OK. We will catch up another time," Amina replies.

"I told the journalists that I would talk to them only after I have seen the police inspector in charge of the case," Amina also explained to Haile.

"Thank you for letting me have the update," Haile replied.

"That's kind of you," she concludes the conversation.

***

Haile had the habit of sleeping late. Like any other night, on the one Hussein gets deadly assaulted, he went on his balcony. Summer, already around, had cool nights.

The air was neither cold nor hot but fresh. It was tenderly inviting, to stay out for a moment and enjoy it. While he scrutinised the night in some distance of the same building block, the light in one of the apartments opposite his got switched off; he then told himself, "Another late sleeper." That apartment, located almost thirty meters on the left from his and one floor below, switched off its lights in the block where Hussein lived.

In the morning, he remembered the apartment in the dark the night before he learned about his immediate neighbourhood's fatal incident. At that moment, he also recalled that he saw a couple in Hussein's apartment before midnight of the previous day.

When Haile got interviewed about Hussein's incident the next day, he explained that he hadn't seen or heard anything. He manifestly lied because he wanted to cover up Amina's potential involvement. He and another witness constituted the only people who saw the likely murder's suspect that night.

Amina's interview by the investigators came late in the afternoon of the day Hussein's body was discovered. The police went to the company where she worked, but she had left much earlier. They got told that she had gone to the hospital. Hussein's body ended up there. Policemen asked for her phone number and wanted to invite her for an interview.

"Hi Ms Amina, Inspector Sizwe. Please, would you come as soon as possible to the police station for interrogation in the murder of Hussein? We will expect you at 4:00 pm," Inspector Sizwe indicated to her.

"Hello. Though present at the hospital, could I come after checking which state Hussein is in?" Amina implored.

"I will wait for you, please don't take too long to come. We need you urgently. My team will be there soon to help in case you need transport to get to the police station," the inspector replied.

"I don't think you need to send me a car; mine can get me there as well. After I visit the hospital, I will come straight to the police station," Amina replied as calmly as she could, instantly as she avoided showing any anxiety in her voice.

The inspector has gathered enough information about Amina's profile and the characteristics of her car. From her workplace, colleagues told him that she went to the hospital in her car. In the meantime, he had dispatched one police car without official licence plates and a police officer in civil clothes to watch over Amina's movements discreetly. He informs Amina that he sent her a police car since he wanted her to feel that the police insisted on seeing her interrogated as a primary or essential suspect.

In due time, Amina drove to the police station and was ready for interrogation in a murder crime investigation. In her understanding, she went there not as a suspect but as a critical witness. Though she thinks that, on the police's side, she already features as the primary suspect.

The first person the police had interviewed had mentioned her as the victim's girlfriend. Many witnesses confirmed to have seen her with him on several occasions. Not yet the primary suspect in the full sense of the term, but inspector Sizwe had deemed urgent to interrogate her as quickly as possible. Amina's work colleagues had been surprised when they learnt that she got involved in a criminal investigation.

She stayed at the police station for forty-eight hours while the investigators asked her what she did at the time of the attempted murder.

Her apartment was thoroughly searched in her absence; the police looked for evidence of her probable involvement in the crime.

After she conspired with her twin sister the time of their breakfast on the day Hussein's body got found, they had both agreed to vacate their daily routines as usual.

She had also talked to Haile before she went to the hospital. Once at the police station, she called her sister to tell her not to panic because what she had done, she did it for her sake. She didn't voice it as clearly as such because she feared the police monitored her communications. As a strategy for the interrogation, she decides to confront the investigators.

Amina hated the overall look of inspector Sizwe. Not that he looked ugly physically. On the contrary. He stood as a tall guy, intelligent from a Nganzi middle-class family who had made it after a democratic government post-colonialism. Confident enough, he behaved, however indifferently, towards whoever didn't benefit him. In normal circumstances, she wouldn't usually and visibly have enough reasons to dislike him.

Emotionless and impossible to read, his intentions looked malicious at times while interacting with people. It was broadly untrustworthy, which made Amina dislike him to the point she did, despite his external attractiveness.

The first session of the questions had ended inconclusively. Inspector Sizwe had left the room, visibly frustrated in the face of the answers Amina had given and shown her that he would come back, but he hadn't indicated within which length of time. Amina must've dozed off in the interrogation room - she hadn't eaten adequately in the last ten hours - because she didn't hear inspector Sizwe open the door.

Here he stood on the opposite side of the table and stared at her. While still handcuffed and at the same time raddled, she noticed him when she slowly raised her head and gradually opened her eyes. She couldn't tell how long he had been there. Presumably not long enough because the policemen's workload doesn't allow them to waste time, and Amina supposed that he came there to carry on his interrogation. He had brought her a cup of water that he held and waited for her to pay attention to the new session.

The light in the room didn't sufficiently brighten. However, it couldn't be an obstacle to enable and read facial expressions or features of whoever would be in that space. Amina didn't or couldn't guess how old he looked. He had these types of faces which conceal forever any mark of time on the skin. He had recently had a haircut, but from a distance, she couldn't tell which aftershave he used if indeed he did put on any.

His voice had no accent. Neutral instead. Impossible to pin him to any specific geographical spot. Without any hint to point to what had to come next, Sizwe pulled a picture out of his jacket.

"We found this photograph of Dae and Hussein. As you notice here, they both seem to sit in a restaurant and somehow celebrate. Did you know about any of the relationships that existed between them? From the time it was taken, and now, the picture appears to be one year old."

Haile had told her to be cautious while she answered the police's questions. When on her own in the police station's cell, she had thought about that, but she couldn't come up with a well-thought-through strategy to adopt. She decided to stick with any narrative she could repeat over and over again.

"Yes, I know. Dae and Hussein, though not in any formal relationship, knew each other before he became close to me." After he sat opposite Amina, inspector Sizwe pushed the picture in front of her.

"What could you tell me about the two of them today? Have you seen them together recently?"

"No. I think I won't help you." Inspector Sizwe couldn't read any clue on the expressionless face of Amina.

"You haven't yet come clean about the stain of Hussein's blood found at your apartment on the sofa."

"I've explained the only possible probabilities because Hussein hasn't been to my place recently."

"I know you got your hand in his attempted murder," Inspector Sizwe had suddenly stood up from his chair, and now he leaned over her. He shouted, somehow irritated and frustrated. Except for that circumstantial evidence of bloodstain, no other substantial element proved that Amina could be the murderer. This view coincided with the pure truth about her involvement.

Sixteen hours before, he had called Amina for this second interrogation at the police station because of the photo found among the pieces of evidence collected from Hussein's apartment. He had expected to hear from her if any glimpses of suspicious relations between Dae and Hussein existed. He was disappointed. He had to release her because he didn't manage to get what he wanted her to tell him. Would there be any new evidence that could compromise her further? He wasn't sure.

Florencia brought the bloodstain found in Amina's apartment without knowing. She hadn't realised on the night of the attempted murder that she didn't get rid of all incriminating evidence. A forensic lab was sent the bloodstain for analysis.

Furthermore, the investigators had found another substance in Amina's house, but the inspector Sizwe team hadn't yet assessed its overall importance in the murder case.

SECTION 3. Scenery

The Murder

On an ordinary Sunday, at night, Florencia enters Hussein's apartment past eleven. Once there, firstly, she aims to distract Hussein and put Rohypnol, also known as a rape drug and used on the streets, in his glass. Close to midnight, the woman manages to accomplish that task. She made him take the disempowering tablets unknowingly; consequently, he becomes unconscious after some time.

Florencia and her accomplice had planned that the stabbing would come after Hussein fell unconscious. After she had ensured that he couldn't harm her or anyone else, she then calls her friend Dae. Thus the plan goes in full motion and on track as initially arranged and agreed.

The crime occurs after a few glasses of wine that he takes while Florencia remains sober. She has opted to drink orange juice instead. The cognac he had brought on the table to share when she came in remained closed.

The perpetrators of the crime had planned that it would occur in the early hours of the next day. Hussein would be knifed several times in the chest. That would make him enter into a coma hours later, further to the inflicted wounds.

"You, useless brat!" Hussein had uttered toward Florencia. His words didn't come out correctly but dragged on each syllable, like those pronounced by a drunken man. At the moment, he thinks that the person he talks to looks like Amina, his girlfriend.

"You've been out with other men and pretended to be busy at work," he adds. Florencia doesn't reply immediately. She occasionally displays soft tempered behaviour when nobody provokes her.

Sometimes, it doesn't, however, take much time to get or make her angry.

Suddenly, Florencia recalls that Hussein has repeatedly insulted and cursed her before. She got lost in her thoughts while meditating on what a friend had had to endure because of him. Florencia now looks at him and pretends not to hear anything from him; she fixes an imaginary point on the wall behind him, like seeing through his face. If Hussein had had all his mind in order, he could've thought that she was staring at him. She contemplates quietly on how to respond to his abuse.

"Not again. We've been here before. I can't convince you otherwise," Florencia managed to say after a short period of only around twenty seconds.

"I can't take it this time. My patience has reached its expiry date. It's your time to reap what you sow," she shouts with more agitation in her voice.

Suddenly, she leaves her seat on the left side of the sofa they both shared. On her far left, within five meters of distance, the kitchen featured in the perspective of her eyes. One could see a range of kitchen knives from the main room that vertically bent and hung on an IKEA stainless steel wall rack. She briefly forgot what she had agreed with her friend Dae, the plan of their revenge against Hussein for his abuses. She then immediately restrained herself from the impulse to go for the knife at that moment. After three meters from her chair in the direction of the kitchen, she stopped. She turned one hundred and eighty degrees and looked at Hussein.

"Sorry, I let myself be short-tempered. I sincerely apologise," Florencia significantly lowers her voice to show her deference. At that particular moment, she stands not to face Hussein nor the kitchen where she heads. Instead, Florencia looks sideways at the wall in front of her.

She knew that Hussein liked such an attitude from women. That immediately reduced his anger, but he accompanied his change of demeanour with a firm slap of his hand on the face of Florencia.

She accepted the humiliation stoically and didn't shed any tears. Such behaviour from her seemed to calm him down, as he felt in control.

The drug took between twenty and twenty-five minutes to show its impact on Hussein. While he sinks deeper into unconsciousness, at the same time, he fights hard to remain awake. Although his fight to keep his eyes open constitutes a lost cause. The administered drug seems too strong to allow him any resistance. He can't control his fall into sleep mode. Florencia watches him closely while she assesses the responsiveness of his reflexes.

Hussein has put his head on the table where he sits. His arms support it to make it feel more comfortable but without much success. He can't remain in one specific position. After thorough verification that he has become unaware of his surroundings, Florencia calls Dae, her friend and neighbour.

***

"Please could you come up quickly!" She almost whispers on the phone, at the very time that she fears that Hussein - or anybody else in the adjacent apartments -, though visibly deep in his sleep, could listen to their conversation.

"I got in his apartment. Please come quickly and get ready for your part of the action," Florencia tells Dae over the telephone.

"Ok. I will be there within five minutes," Dae replies.

From then on, Florencia and Dae had agreed to make the least noise they could after Hussein would fall unconscious. She finds the door slightly opened. Florencia waits for her. Dae had deliberately avoided knocking on the door to minimise noise. They had discussed all these small details of their operation while they planned each stage.

When she came into the victim's apartment, she talked to Florencia, who welcomed her in, almost whispering.

"Please give me the tools?" Dae asks Florencia, at the same time that she refers to the knife and hands' gloves she had brought for the occasion. They had discussed them in their planning. Florencia had taken care of everything necessary for the operation. All the tools that would be needed fit in her handbag. She proceeded that way not to raise suspicion either of Hussein or anybody else.

Florencia had come well prepared. She had a pair of gloves that she passed to Dae. Anyone who might've observed a hospital's operation room would've thought to be in the presence of a surgeon with their assistant.

"Here they are," Florencia handed them to her. She had kept them in the main room, not far from where she and Hussein sat side by side a moment before.

Dae had agreed to kill Hussein. She had her reasons. She had requested Florencia to have her phone on silent mode as soon as she entered Hussein's apartment. As long as they would be in that space, Dae recommended having all the phones on silent. She explained to her that they didn't want to get disturbed in their deed.

"Don't worry, you will be able to remove the restriction once we finish," she added while her friend showed an inquisitive look. While they stayed still there, and Hussein's lifeless body on the floor, Dae implored Florencia as she whispered.

Dae hurried to take instantly one of the blades Florencia presented her. She grabbed the biggest one among them. It happened to be the sharpest. Moreover, she swayed like lightning. That knife came surprisingly from the set Amina had gifted Hussein once he had told her jokingly that he could cook delicious meals. Florencia knew the origin of those knives; she had selected and brought the set, mostly because of its background.

She wanted almost a reverse spell to strike Hussein since he had continuously abused Amina, and no element indicated that he would stop at any time in the future.

Hussein had had a habit of insulting Amina, her twin sister Florencia and Dae unashamedly. The three women in his neighbourhood connected to him in one way or another. He treated them like low-life creatures. By that time, while his motionless body lies on the floor of his apartment, he can't guess the nature of the unexpected that hits him. Though he looks unconscious, Dae starts to stab him repeatedly.

While she stabbed him with a kitchen knife, Florencia, a few meters from the scene, looked with an inexpressive face.

Hussein's spirit seemed to observe what was happening to his body like a stranger who contemplates a scene he doesn't master the entire meaning. His consciousness gradually drifted from the present reality and tried to speak to him in a certain way. With his eyes closed and the rest of his body, except his heart, don't show any signs of life, he doesn't feel in the right mindset to realise the full extent or magnitude of the incident where he plays the central role. His mind and full attention, all distinctly, operate at a different level from his body and observe the entire scenery from a distance close to the room's ceiling.

"You kill someone!" Hussein's consciousness which talks inaudibly manages to utter to Dae, who is busy and stabs him, holds the knife menacingly. He realises that essential aspects of the scenery have changed. He looks up in the direction of Florencia from above, outside his body. With his eyes, he tries to open as widely as possible, but without much success. His face displays a strong expression of surprise. The knife points to his heart and strikes steadily and forcibly.

Hussein has not the force nor the right body balance to stop her. His conscious mind outside his body makes a person's noise seriously hurt when the first and second knife's stabs hit him. Unfortunately, nobody hears the sound of his suffering.

From the perspective of the two accomplices in the crime on the scene, he looks unconscious. The next knife's strikes don't come with any significant pain. The evidence of his hurt seems absent as if the victim wants his pain not to be known. The assassin strikes ten times before she realises that Hussein's body doesn't show any sign of life anymore. Blood covers all her hands, arms and the top that Dae wears.

Hussein's blood was tainted with a high rate of alcohol. Consequently, he had lost his sense of coordination and couldn't, therefore, manage to stop his murderer and protect himself from the stabbing. On top of that, Florencia has tampered his drink with Rohypnol to get him unconscious.

"End now, idiot. I can't tolerate you anymore. Thus you are finished with your life. You did as you liked; you treated us, women, as trash. Your freedom to insult me all the time, abuse and humiliate me anytime, stops instantly. I must recover my dignity," Florencia talks inaudibly to herself in a long monologue while she looks at Dae when the latter stabs Hussein with an internally angry voice and a little lousy.

It happens that Florencia didn't talk loud enough to be heard by anybody else but herself.

"Ooh! You hurt me! Please stop," a ghostly voice that sounds like Hussein appears to ask Dae, his assassin, in a faint whisper at the fifth strike of the knife. She doesn't let herself be distracted by that noisy thought while she also forcibly stabs Hussein several times in his heart. She chose to hit him at that part of his body because she sincerely wants him dead at that very moment. As she strikes with her right hand that holds the knife, her left hand leans on the left side of the chest to keep up with her necessary balance.

Vengeance and hate had merged, and she somehow acted blindly; she couldn't reason at that particular moment. However, it would've been of interest to get a deeper understanding of the rationale that made her act the way she did.

The two women carefully cleaned the place after they had arranged Hussein's body on the floor. They removed any shreds of evidence that could incriminate them.

They concurred that Florencia would tell her twin sister that Dae had stabbed her boyfriend. She would as well inform her as soon as they confirmed Hussein's death. However, it was Dae who finally made the call.

"I inform you that your sister got involved in a slight accident. But, please don't panic. It's not serious. She will be safe with you in less than fifteen minutes. I strongly recommend you not to call anyone before she arrives. Please be patient for a moment, as she will be on her way and soon with you. She will explain with all the details; don't worry, we came out together," Dae briefly elaborated for Amina with a white lie about what had happened.

Dae put her phone close to Florencia for her to reassure her sister.

"I'm with her. I will be there in a few minutes," she managed to say, while she too ensured that her voice didn't get heard beyond the room.

In a ten-minute long period that resembled an eternity, both women stayed in the dark of the room where the body of Hussein was. They intended to wait and mislead anyone who might've watched the apartment from outside and at a distance. Florencia and Dae had discussed that, as a prudent measure, she would have the curtains closed as soon as she would get inside Hussein's apartment. She had done that immediately once there. In their moment of inattention, Florencia left Hussein's apartment as the last one forgot to close the door. She hurried to get to her sister's place and explain what had happened as Dae had told Amina.

On the other side of the block of apartments, the murder of Hussein went on. In the distance, Haile stood in front of his windows, looking outside in the direction of Hussein's apartment. He knew that Amina visited Hussein regularly.

Haile didn't and couldn't see inside Hussein's apartment. When the light got switched off while he looked, one unusual incident momentarily took place behind the curtains - he couldn't guess what it might be at the time -, in the same direction where his eyes focused. It would get darker in the hours and days that would follow. At the time, it was only in the early hours of the next day.

Wethian And Nganzi

Haile and inspector Sizwe had unexpectedly met in the neighbourhood where the attempted murder on Hussein had taken place. They knew each other from before, some years back, while both were doing their university studies.

"Hi. Haile," Haile does a slight bow of the head as he greets his guest Sizwe.

"Hi. Sizwe," Sizwe replies similarly at the intention of Haile.

The first encounter these two have at the university of Kyutsu seems casual. The group of black students at that campus - only sixteen individuals out of a thirteen thousand student population- constitutes the smallest minority out of all the minority demographics. On that occasion of their outing, when they both meet, their group consists of six members.

Sizwe looks older, and Haile considers him his senior. It appears that they have many things in common. Though they both study subjects far remote from their respective hobbies, they similarly enjoy visual arts from whichever part of the world the pieces of their interest belong. They can talk for hours about the differences and similarities between Hindu and Yoruba traditional dances or oral stories; the same can go on for western paintings of the renaissance and spiritual content of the Bakongo kingdom's masks. As they start to get to know each other better, they organise walks together on weekends along the Eboshi pond. Whenever the weather allows, their small group also arranges picnics in local parks.

"Someone told me that you come originally from Wethi," Sizwe informally enquired from Haile in one of the walks they do together in one holiday afternoon.

"Yes. My ancestors comes from there. Despite that, I stand as a first-generation QK Wethian. If I had been one year older, Wethi would be my country of birth. I first saw the sun in the QK."

"My mother came to the QK while heavily pregnant, but she died while she gave birth. She suffered from health complications. She had arrived further to war back home in those years. Perhaps she died as a consequence of things she had gone through in the war," Haile replies.

"Sorry to hear that. What about your father?"

"I had one, but we separated. Hence I became an orphan. I always prefer to say that I don't have one. However, I can't say with total certainty that he died. If I ever get confirmation of his death, will I know when he died? I prefer not knowing and consider him as dead."

The little information Haile knew about his dad consisted in that, during the war back home, he got separated from his mother. Until his mother managed to leave for good their country, she didn't know well if her husband had died or not. Thirty-five years had passed. Haile's relatives had told him all those circumstances through which he came into the world. He tried to make sense of that complicated situation.

"But this doesn't mean that if I had a father around only, I wouldn't feel like an orphan," he adds.

"You see! I have a different mastery of the concept. I consider orphans who, as a consequence of deadly circumstances, sees one member of their nucleus and normal family was taken away," he elaborates before he lets Sizwe respond.

"Sorry. I will not ask how your father died - though no related story can be a hundred per cent certain -, I suppose that happened in that war you mentioned. Sometimes most people prefer not to talk at all about such a tragic past and its victims. That becomes one of the ways to make things rest."

"It's OK. My father died effectively at that time, I suppose. I grew up with my uncle's family. What about you?"

"I come from Nganzi, from the Ludzu tribe."

"What do you think of Nosfum Muntu?"

"As a Nganzi, don't be surprised if I tell you that back home, we consider the guy as a sell-out to the white hegemony."

"But the entire world praises him for his Nganzi fused pot and his stand on the harmonious life together of different communities in our country."

"If that life together could be sustained at the expense of correct alleviation of the wrong from the past, how could it be right, whatever the praise he gets?"

"What do you mean?"

"When the segregation got abolished, the economic inequalities it had created over the years didn't go with it. The majority of the Nganzi economy features still and will for a long time remain unfortunately in the hands of a white minority and their new black allies, while they all exploit the black masses."

"I understand," Haile finally says. He could only pretend to understand since he couldn't be a Nganzi. He doesn't have any lived experience of the natives, the frustrations transmitted from generation to generation, for which no light at the end of the tunnel seemed to shine.

"You need to be Nganzi to understand," Sizwe argues.

"Why do some people consider Nosfum a saint, an icon or a role model, particularly in the west?" Haile asks.

"The west has put him on a prestigious pedestal because he stood for a status quo in his country, where no major foundations had to change fundamentally, while the real power holders remained the same."

"What about Wethi? What outlook do the prominent politicians there project?"

"I have not had much interest, except about the country's history."

"While I learnt about Qarfi in my A-levels, I found out that Wethi stood as the only Qarfian country that colonisers didn't conquer and occupy."

"It had also seriously defeated the Italians at the Battle of Dawan in 1896, and the humiliation of the invaders made them forget to think about or try any future attempt."

The bond - or interaction only since they never became close friends - between Sizwe and Haile lasted the time of one academic year. Sizwe completed his studies the same year. Haile stayed longer in Niasan. He only saw Sizwe again in the investigation of Hussein's attempt murder case.

They had briefly known each other ten years before and under some happy circumstances. Nobody knows if this time, while the investigation of the murder case goes on, Sizwe would be influenced by the shared past.

Haile lives in the vicinity of where the crime took place. He could've been or not been involved. Sizwe had concerns about trusting Haile's knowledge of the neighbourhood or their past friendship to unveil the crime's suspect. These questions and others go through Sizwe's mind when he sees Haile close to the crime scene and learns that he lives in the same building block as the victim.

***

The police inspector graduated three years before Haile from the same Niasan university. He did a different academic programme.

After his graduation with a degree qualification in law studies, he practised criminal law in Amsterdam for several years before joining the Vodnak metropolitan police.

Sizwe and Haile, when they meet again because of the attempted murder case the inspector investigated, in their brief exchange, they introduce themselves as alumni from a similar Niasan university. They shared and stressed how difficult it seemed to live a decent student life and make new friends in that environment. At least, that had been the case for both of them. They featured among the few black students of their university.

After graduating, Haile, on his part, went into math teaching. On the side of his career, he also wrote as a hobby. Over the years, he produced stories that his readers enjoyed.

"When I first read your pieces of writing, I thought of you as a professor," one of Haile's friends had told him once. The friend couldn't be far from a right guess because he taught as his career. In his writing, he played with concepts.

He likes to think and what goes with it and self-censors when he processes his thoughts. Around related activities, he seems to organise himself well. He becomes extra-selective about what he ends up speaking out or putting down on a paper with such a process. One would wonder if he sets things that way intentionally or unconsciously.

Inspector Sizwe has known him briefly while both studied at Kyutsu in Niasan. Though they belonged to different age groups and majored in separate subjects, they had ended up in a circle of friends where, regularly, they all went out together for a drink at a local pub.

"You seem introverted. You look in a way inaccessible to anyone you don't like - most likely unfamiliar with you - or with whom you don't share any possible interest," Sizwe told him once while they both stayed still at their university.

"I might be wrong, but for the little time I've had to know you, that's what I came up with," he adds.

"I think that's an almost fair assessment from an intelligent guy like you," Haile politely reacts to Sizwe's statement about him.

Haile had all the time been a free thinker. He expressed himself without considering who would be his interlocutor, directly in the face to face situations or indirectly through his writings. In parallel to his lessons to his students at the college where he taught, his literary activity constituted his favoured hobby as his peers went on different paths in their university years.

"Though introverted as I could be, I often proceed with selective manners, not as a way to satisfy a particular request or recommendation," Haile had pointed out in that same conversation.

"Selfishly like anybody else, whatever I do, whatever ways I do it, deliberate or unconscious, I only have in mind myself as the focus. That's my way to connect or not interact with my social surroundings. I find that it would be even harder if I had to be somebody else and act distinctively to please someone else than myself most of the time. Or if I had to be in other people's shoes to be social," Haile asserted then where he stood in social interplays.

Suddenly, he wonders what these other people would do in his place. He agreed that only people with shortcomings didn't reflect - which constituted a famous axiom -, while he believed that thinking was a privilege. He concedes that not everyone has access to it.

Indeed, that's how things are. On such a matter, he didn't mean to think for only the sake of it, but with an intentional thought process that manifests an occurrence in the brain to serve a specific purpose.

On the one hand, one requires a particular environment and a conducive mood to think rationally and comprehensively. On the other, a specific collection of people makes an effort not to think. This latter category justifies its laziness in the fact that to feel intensely seems to drain some energy. At times it exhausts like labour work. Like people who don't enjoy labour work, Haile could not enjoy what he likes while he processes his thoughts, even though he persists and doesn't complain much about it. He loves to read and write. To dream appears as well part of his landscape. To jog regularly helped in these activities he adores. He didn't know much yet about Amina, his neighbour. She appeared to like and be around different people, but simultaneously, to have her own private space.

Haile remembers. At moments, she had explained to him her preferred columns in the popular newspapers she consulted regularly.

Haile didn't indicate her how much exercise helped him enjoy what he liked most. The fact that both pursued their fitness programme showed some evidence that it worked for them. Once in a while, they even gave themselves more difficult targets for their jogging.

For Haile, from then on, all seemed possible. He wants his fitness routine to help him achieve whatever his mind envisions on the horizon. In recent weeks, as he liked thinking, he had found himself capable of putting on paper the equivalent of one thousand words of thoughts every day. He wants to maintain and even exceed such performance.

With such a level of accomplishment, he could every month produce at least twenty-five thousand words of good thoughts worth sharing with the general public.

"I've noticed that with achievements, it looks like an unstoppable rollercoaster, where achievers live in a world of constant new challenges. Such life goes on through exigent goals, sometimes set by oneself, others by others, this until one dies," Haile reflects on some of the characteristics that gave sense to living. Another side to his statement is to be able to achieve whatever he sets his mind on existed. Though this one piece of evidence related to his relationship with Amina proved that he had at least once failed. Until then, this didn't constitute the only failure he had known in his life. He had plenty he could talk about if the panel of assessors ever called him to testify. Either the statement stood untrue - which meant that some objectives seem impossible to accomplish -, or he didn't love Amina or intended to accept her love if it manifested itself. That had to be one or the other. He could rightly appreciate that reality. He would not continue to ignore it and pretend it didn't exist. It looked like he deceived himself into feeling good, like one who feeds themselves with drugs to feel momentarily happy. The illusion to be an achiever put him on a pedestal that gave some value to his life. However, this represented a phantasm uniquely. Would he continue to avoid facing his reality? That he could fail or that impossible things to achieve existed!

The Caretaker

Everyone in Hussein's apartment on the night of the crime found themselves there for a purpose. Unconsciously or willingly, each one has a role to play. A direct perpetrator, an accomplice and one victim constitute the people on the scene.

To plan the murder appeared completed and almost perfect, but its execution partially fails. Had Dae prepared adequately for the stabbing, she would've reached Hussein's dangerous heart's parts without significant problems. If she had done, for example, her rehearsal in a forensic lab and trained herself on dead bodies, she would have succeeded once in the actual operation. She could've made fatal cuts which would've finished her target in a matter of reasonable time.

No unforeseen phases in the execution appear as they go through the operation. Dae goes for a sharp knife from the victim's kitchen. She selects the medium one, as she finds it easy to handle for her average hand. She knows that Hussein has a well built young man's body in his prime years. He attends the gym regularly even though he drinks above the average person. When he has not drunk, he doesn't miss any of his fitness sessions.

Florencia managed to get him to take a tranquilliser without him noticing. He had collapsed half-drunk when the murder attempt occurs.

The effect of the drug knocks him down and makes him lie on the floor. Despite the drug's impact on him, even though Dae stabs him several times in the chest, this doesn't damage his heart enough to kill him instantly. The cuts aren't deep sufficiently. His blood doesn't flow out of his body speedily to provoke his instantaneous death. At some point, the flow stops.

That explains how in the morning, several hours after the stabbing, Hussein was still alive - understandably not in the best of conditions - an ambulance took him to the hospital.

"Though he got stabbed, this hasn't worked out as expected," Dae thinks with some anxiety when she sees the ambulance. She doesn't dare to get out to look closely at the body. Although she can't get all the details from her main room, particularly the state in which the victim seems like after he stayed unattended in his blood for hours. While unseen, she observes through the curtains of the window of her main room how the paramedics handle Hussein's body.

Undoubtedly, in the mind of the two accomplices, when they leave the victim's apartment, they think of him as already dead, but their lack of experience in the crime world would show later. They don't have the guts of professional criminals. As their first time, they forget to check on Hussein's neck the flow of blood in his body. Given the amount of blood that came out and still spread on the floor, none of them thought to check his breath when they were about to leave. That would have alerted them about the time he would finally die.

In the morning, they were surprised when they saw an ambulance that took him to the hospital. They felt anxious when they realised that he didn't die. Several questions popped into their heads. They needed to get answers quickly. They had to deal with the consequences of their crime as cleanly as possible. In their plan for the operation, they hadn't thought hard enough about the possibilities of such an outcome. They hadn't envisaged that scenario.

Dae wants to talk to Florencia and discuss the new developments, although she remembers that she can't use her telephone as agreed previously. She doesn't want to risk herself out while the ambulance and the paramedics have not yet left.

At that time, a few neighbours still ask or find out what had happened. Unprepared, this scenario seemed new to her. She opts to wait.

"How do you feel? Have you seen the ambulance in front of his house?" Dae asks when she arrives at Florencia's apartment around midday of the day of the crime.

Yet, she experiences a little anxiety because of where Hussein's body had ended, not in the morgue but on a hospital bed.

"A moment ago, I only heard an ambulance in our neighbourhood; from our place, I couldn't see his apartment. How does the plan for today look like?" Florencia had led in the preparation of the crime, and she wants Dae to take over the management of the aftermath of the murder.

"I agreed with my sister that we should carry on with our routines. Doing that will reduce possible suspicions from the investigators," she adds for Dae to be aware of arrangements at that moment, in case she had some to suggest.

"Let's meet every other day at 10:30 pm after you finish work. I will come to your restaurant, and we will update each other on our way home," Dae adds.

"I might visit you unannounced in case an emergency arises. If I don't come on the agreed day, that will mean that there won't be any new development to report on," she concludes.

***

On Monday, around 9:00 am the caretaker of the block of apartments where Hussein lived discovers his body. He sees what he thought initially to be someone on the floor, not manifestly in a conventional way. The body faces down in a flask almost full of blood.

He immediately wondered why the victim could be in that unusual position. Unmistakably, the victim hadn't gone to that length to find a container and put their face in it; but the murderer intended in some sense to mislead the investigators. The caretaker found that the door stood slightly opened. Even so, he restrained himself from entering the apartment.

Careful enough not to touch the door's handle, he had learnt all the things from the CSI series about not contaminating a crime scene. Instead, he pushed the door cautiously and slowly to have an exact look inside.

That morning, he calls the police station, and the inspector, Sizwe Mtana, replies. The inspector sits in front of a hot cup of coffee he brought from the office kitchen a moment before. The caller reports on his office desk about a murder incident close to Wright's Drive in the borough of Notgni and Aeslech.

"A person in apartment no.75 at Wright's Place looks dead. I can't tell how long he has been there, without any movement. Blood spread all over the floor's room, mainly around the victim. I passed and swept the corridor near the door when I found the latter somehow slightly open. When I didn't notice any sound from the apartment, I stayed put for more than three minutes, checked and waited to hear any sound or movement. When I glanced inside without entering, I saw the body on the ground. In the past, I have witnessed similar cases; that's the reason I became suspicious," the caretaker indicates these details while he describes how he discovered the body.

"If you haven't entered the apartment, please don't. In case you did, I hope you didn't touch anything. I would like you to get out of that crime scene immediately; I don't want to have the evidence tampered with," the inspector explains and requests from the caller.

The caretaker obeys the instruction and moves away from the apartment entrance, where he called the inspector. While on his way down the stairs, he meets a woman in her late twenties with a black rubbish bag. He sees her while she heads to the big container that serves to recycle waste outside the building. She doesn't walk confidently with a suspicious look towards him; it looks like she didn't want anybody to notice any abnormality in her attitude. Her apparent behaviour could be understandable; she lived in the same block of apartments as Hussein.

"If that night, a tragic incident happened in the building, she could be an important witness. She must've heard or seen something," the caretaker thinks of her as connected to the crime.

Thus he had already qualified the incident as such. She came straight back into the building while she left the rubbish outside. The caretaker saw her from the apartments' main entrance, where he waited for the police to arrive soon.

The police inspector, Sizwe, replied quickly to the call. It took twenty-five minutes - the average fast response from the police - to get to the area, given the distance. His team of investigators cordoned off the crime scene immediately once there. They arrived at the same time as the ambulance.

"Where can I find no.75?" asks the inspector Sizwe, visibly in a rush to have the initial impression of the crime scene. The caretaker had approached him once he saw the police car and stopped to greet him when he got out and came towards him.

"That way," he replies while he pointed in the direction of Hussein's apartment.

"And your name? You sound like the person who made the call about this case," Sizwe adds.

"Morino, Morino Kendo," the caretaker answers.

"You don't need to come with me, but don't go too far because I will need your statement," the inspector Sizwe explains.

"I will be busy with my work in these different blocks of apartments," the caretaker replies and points at the nearby buildings. Residents from adjacent apartments to Hussein's got directed to a particular pathway for their way in and out to limit any contamination of evidence. Nobody from farther apartments in the neighbourhood has permission to visit those near Hussein's apartment for two weeks. Residents from adjacent apartments to his, considered as potential suspects, get dealt with differently.

Logically, this assumption couldn't, without any reasonable doubt, exclude them from the remit of the investigation, though potential suspects could've come as well from afar.

Once inside the apartment, with their specialist tools and some hindsight, the Sizwe team starts their job and scrutinises the crime scene. Straightaway they notice the absence of any messy struggle that might've taken place there. The victim appears to have fallen on the floor from his seat. After that, bloodstains came out from the inflicted wounds. That induced the fact that the victim must've been familiar with his assassin.

"They must've known each other," concurs Sizwe in his mind.

The paramedics from the ambulance service made the initial observation that Hussein's heart was still beating. He had lost a lot of blood, but they had only found him unconscious.

Nonetheless, they found it crucial to rush him to the hospital. They consequently gave three minutes approximately to the investigators to collect all the evidence they thought would be necessary before they took the body away.

"Please, make sure to take pictures from all the pertinent angles, collect fingerprints on any object that hands might've touched - glasses, bottles, cups, utensils, computers, doors and cupboards' handles -, don't forget any hair, traces of blood, and any other physical evidence that could help in the investigation," Sizwe demands from his investigators.

"Prepare me a leaflet to be sent to the neighbours and ask them if they didn't see or hear any unusual thing, please get any helpful information on what happened, from every source you might think of," Sizwe adds at the attention of one of his team members.

"Don't forget to check out the victim's last calls and emails, plus the contacts of people he might've been in conversation with recently," Sizwe instructs.

"The paramedics were categorical that the victim had entered into a coma after the stabbing. His brain lost oxygen because of the insufficient flow of oxygenated blood."

"Please make sure to retrieve the knife or any other deadly tool used on his body, and preserve the fingerprints carefully on them," he explains to another member of his team.

Within forty-five minutes, the investigation team had finished its first initial visit to the crime scene. It had collected all the evidence the investigators could think of at that stage.

"Please cordon off the area to prohibit anyone from entering the scene. Close the apartment and get the key once every team has completed assigned tasks."

All the time the investigators had been inside Hussein's apartment, two policemen from the same case had stayed outside, where they ensured that nobody from the general public or onlookers forced their way into the crime scene.

Once the initial facts about the crime are in his hands, inspector Sizwe decides to interview the caretaker who had called the police station. The interested onlookers were also briefly interviewed on the spot. The investigators asked everyone if they didn't hear or see anyone unusual, possibly connected to the incident the previous night around 1:30 am. Local journalists on the scene also pitched and asked residents their questions.

Further to how the caretaker had described the crime scene, Sizwe had judged it appropriate to have among his team a pathologist to look into possible seminal material from sexual intercourse, if any. As the victim appeared dead, further to the call the inspector received, the expert would also help determine the time of death, if that constituted the victim's state. In the end, they found that Hussein still breathed even after many hours from his stabbing.

The investigators collected, documented and preserved all items of evidence they could find.

They tried to assemble any material with possible DNA or fingerprints, but some fear persisted that they could be affected by the "CSI effect" if they ignored other exculpatory evidence.

If they proceed the way they had started, they could only end up with someone accused guilty or innocent based on the false evidence.

To consider the observer's bias from the analysis of evidence collected, inspector Sizwe decides to extend the collection of forensic evidence that included the fingerprints and DNA to more people in the vicinity of Hussein's apartment. He did that after his team scrutinised the CCTV tapes around the block of flats.

The inspector knew well that DNA evidence from the crime scene could help, though the technique also had its limitations. Sizwe wouldn't only rely a hundred per cent on that technique.

He was well aware of the problems of cross-con-tamination of DNA, their mixed-up in some labs, and how they hid human errors.

"I will use a combination of different approaches of investigation to determine the right perpetrator," he reflects. Though the technique has contributed and solved many complex cases, some police force colleagues still didn't believe in its efficiency.

Much more supportive of the approach of direct witnesses of crimes, they argued that a fleck of blood, saliva on a cup's rim, or a piece of hair didn't weigh enough in the identification of the culprit.

The perpetrator had forgotten to close the door firmly while they left. The caretaker had found it suspi-cious when he came around the apartment in question.

That morning, Hussein's classmates at the univer-sity, unaware of what had happened, had called him sev-eral times. They had tried more than three times. He couldn't be reached either on his mobile or landline. The day he entered into a coma, he had to do a presentation at 11:00 am. The assignment consisted of applying a software programme that modelled the management's restructuring for an imaginary company.

Hussein was at the time working on such a project. He had developed its prototype.

Bad for the tutor responsible for his study pro-gram, the said presentation would not happen.

After the caretaker's call reporting the crime, the police intervened. It would've been challenging to stop it. The perpetrators had considered such presumption. Hussein's death at a given time and its timing played a crucial factor in the execution. Once collected all initial evidence, would it have been possible to expect a smooth investigation followed by a clear identification of the culprit? That wouldn't be the case.

SECTION 4. Evidence's Search

Gushed Out

Hussein's blood had long gushed out of his chest wounds. The shirt he wore at the time of the incident had turned bright red. Almost arty and tender to the eye without the tragic story it represented. The nurse in the ambulance vehicle had tied several bandages tightly around the wounds to contain the blood that hadn't flown out yet. The car had come from the hospital located approximately ten minutes away from the crime scene.

At the reception of the hospital, people looked at the wheeled stretcher that carried the body of Hussein and probably assumed the victim to be another casualty of human violence or the cruelty of nature. They couldn't tell the difference between both through their quick observation and not necessarily intentional at Hussein's overall appearance. Victims of murder cases and other fatalities could come in a multitude of shapes.

The medical team assigned to his case consists of two doctors and two nurses. A heart surgeon was in charge of mending internal cuts through which the victim's blood had flooded out of his body.

"Please help, please help, keep him alive," Hussein's cousin pleads with the doctor who appears to oversee the operation. He would've liked to go with the body in the operation room.

"Stay here. You can't go in the operation room," the chief nurse urges the cousin who accompanies Hussein's body. She has to restrain him physically since he tries to force himself into the room.

The police traced and contacted the cousin when the victim was rushed to the hospital. Hussein's official records showed him as the next of kin the authorities had to inform in an emergency.

Like inseparable brothers, they were often seen together in major night parties across Vodnak.

After he signed the hospital's admission form and the permission that authorised the operation to go ahead, he stayed in the corridor. A friend with whom Hussein and his cousin shared many and lousy nights out had rushed there as well. He wants to know the outcome of the operation. Though Hussein had lost nearly a third of his blood, immediate infusion had instantly alleviated the risks of death.

After three hours of intense operation, the doctor in charge comes out of the surgery to announce how it went.

"The vitals didn't get seriously damaged. The operation went extremely well. However, the patient remains unconscious. At this stage, I can't tell if he will come out of the coma. We will keep him under observation for as long as necessary; we hope that he will recover soon," the surgeon in charge says to the family and friends who rushed to the hospital when they heard the bad news.

"Thank you, Doctor, for saving his life," Hussein's cousin replies with a degree of relief in his voice.

"Is it possible to visit him now?" he asks additionally.

"Not now, but within three hours. Though you should ask for permission from one of the nurses who will be around," the doctor indicates.

"Good to hear that he still has a chance to survive. What happened bothers me. When you called, you didn't give me all the details or enough to come up with my assessment," the friend asks, a little angry at Hussein's cousin. They both sit in the hospital's corridor and wait for the three hours to pass before they get allowed a visit to Hussein."

"In the meantime, the leading surgeon had moved him to an after-operation ward.

"He has been seriously wounded. People don't know who did it. I saw that the police had started their investigation. No item seems missing from his apartment.

Further to the rumours in his neighbourhood, his girlfriend features among the prime suspects," the cousin's victim replies.

"Where did all that originate? What would be the motive? Could it be jealousy? I remember once that Amina changed her mood, and her face became angrier than necessary when one or two girls she knew chatted with Hussein while their couple had come for a night out. He had responded with undeserved kindness towards the girls, although Amina was present. Such an attitude on his part appeared unbelievable to her; she presumed that he took her for granted. Needless to say, nobody knows until the unthinkable becomes possible. I know a great number of women who show great interest in Hussein," the friend explains.

"Maybe Hussein didn't realise and behaved somehow indifferently. How could he be so inconsiderate of Amina's feelings to that extent."

In that particular moment, he had rightly role-played the typical Hussein.

***

Amitaf, Hussein's sister, starts to wrap up her school books. Within a few minutes, her afternoon's class will come to an end. The school bell rings. She puts her phone on her ears to answer a call from her family. She learns from her mother about the attempted murder of her brother.

The mother couldn't help it. Probably she didn't realise that her daughter could still be in her classroom. It would take time for her before the bad news sank in.

Five thousand miles away from Disau and two hours of difference separate Hussein's mother from him in real-time. For that reason, she cannot see him immediately. On that day, she had received a call about her son's incident from a relative who lived in Vodnak.

"Please be there for me while I prepare myself to join the rest of the family," she had replied, imploring. She had been agitated for the whole afternoon, called several airlines and tried to arrange a flight. She finally managed to book one for the next day.

Amitaf and Hussein appear close to each other. However, they display different individual personalities. The sister immerses herself willingly into the brother's shoes more than the latter does when he tries to show empathy towards her. Between her and her brother, she seemed more grounded and mature. They were different, and that's how they were. The way she processed the terrible news would become, however, problematic later on.

Amitaf had occasionally watched murder cases in movies. In her mind, these crimes always referred to the human imagination keen to entertain. Even when she read related stories in the newspapers, no hint about these stories indicated that similar incidents could ever come close to home.

The day she got informed of her brother's incident, she had a friend's birthday party she couldn't miss for any reason. She went to the event and tried to avoid thinking about her brother's condition, while her attendance at the celebration became a temporary strategy to blackout her mind.

Once home, although she relaxes on her bed and was ready to fall asleep, she couldn't avoid any longer relating to what her brother went through in the incident.

While her mind worked out its crime scene and script, she fell asleep.

"I can see Amina when she puts a poison in Hussein's glass," she whispers to herself while half asleep before she drifts into a deep sleep. She suspected her. She had once met her brother's girlfriend. Although she tries hard to speak louder or move around in the room, she feels strangely unable to do so. On top of that, nobody appears to notice her.

In that space, Amitaf feels and looks invisible. In her conscience, which must've been a dream, she witnesses the attempted murder of her brother. She doesn't seem to know who the assassins are. In an ultimate effort to check on Hussein, she gets away from the forces which held her in one place. She comes and runs towards where Hussein has fallen and now lies on the floor.

In her sleep, she sweats and her heart races. When incidentally she steps into her brother's blood, she wakes up almost out of breath, unsettled and anxious. Since she sleeps independently in her room, she doesn't have anyone to calm her down immediately.

Though she had experienced nightmares before, they generally related to unfamiliar events or situations. She couldn't picture her brother's attempted murder as one of the horrors that her sub-conscience would play her once sleep would take her. Alone and scared, she couldn't experience any more peaceful rest in the room next to her parents. Nobody in her family knew what she was going through at the time. The parents didn't see the health's implications of Hussein's incident on their daughter.

Amitaf leaves her bed and comes to knock on their door.

"Mum, I had a horrible nightmare. I stepped into Hussein's blood on the floor. I can't sleep alone."

"Come, my baby. You can sleep here."

Though already sixteen years old, her mother invites her to spend the rest of the night in her parents' bed. Sadly, her mother's kindness doesn't stop her from continuing and, unfortunately, enduring her ordeal.

With her parents, Amitaf ultimately manages to sleep. They wake her up at the usual time to get ready for school. They get their breakfast all together as a family. The family driver takes her to her school. In the lessons, she has difficulties concentrating on whatever the teacher says. She gazes off and fixes imaginary spots in front of her in the distance.

When she gets called to answer a question, she looks absent-minded. Such abnormal behaviour went on for the whole day. In the recreation times, she became unusually irritable, with frequent outbursts. Her friends have difficulties in recognising the paused and reflective Amitaf they have always known.

The first weekend after Hussein's fell victim to attempted murder, Amitaf went to Vodnak to visit him in the hospital. For five days, her brother had still been unconscious. She walked into his ward cautiously. Afraid to wake him up. Though he remains in a coma and unable to hear anyone, she faints within less than five seconds while looking at her brother. She wakes up three hours later and asks what had happened. Calmer than a few hours earlier, she returns to see Hussein in his ward. This time while she observes him, she manages to hold it together and stays calm. She approaches the bed he lies on and touches his lifeless hand. Many thoughts cross her mind, some more hopeful and sinister than others.

***

By the time Amina and Hussein's cousin visited him on the day the ambulance took him to the hospital, a surgical operation had repaired his heart's damaged parts.

The knife used to kill Hussein had repeatedly reached his heart into the right atrium and left ventricle. That's where his blood had flown out from, and the overflowing affected the lungs.

While they operated on him with an intense focus to repair damaged nerves, the surgeon and his team continuously sucked blood that had invaded parts of the body, including the lungs. In the operation team, the doctors and nurses considered it a miracle that the rescuers found him still alive when they arrived in his apartment. If a delay in the body's transport had occurred by an hour maximum, he could've died before reaching the emergency room.

Though the operation succeeded, the doctors hesitated to pronounce their verdict on whether he would recover his consciousness sooner or later. It had been sixteen hours already that he had been in a coma. Although the state of his pool and other vitals showed his willingness to stay alive, that didn't stop his fall into unconsciousness.

After his surgery, some of his family members and friends feared that he could carry on and only live on life support for the rest of his journey on earth.

While in the coma, he wouldn't be able to hear or talk, though there was some doubt that he knew deep down in his mind who had stabbed him to near death. The perpetrator wanted him dead. Moreover, that person would walk from time to time in his ward for visits. Officially, and among Hussein's circles, everyone considered his girlfriend to be the culprit. The couple had been together for a long time.

Many people feared that the culprit or an accomplice could do it again, given that Hussein hadn't died immediately. There was no indication that the direction of the investigation could move away from the girlfriend.

That situation explains why nobody among the investigators had yet supposed that a male murderer would have committed the crime.

Once Hussein would luckily come out of the coma - if he ever could -, the dilemma for him to confront his assassin persisted. He would have to have a serious chat with his girlfriend. Such a possibility didn't feature among the thoughts of those who wished him a quick recovery. Their most urgent preoccupation appeared to get him his consciousness immediately.

After a month, with Hussein still in a coma in the hospital, no signs show that he will reconnect soon with the outside world. In the meantime, his family and friends pay him regular visits of support that he can't unfortunately acknowledge.

Sadness crips in people's minds when they realise that he couldn't hear whatever they said, particularly when they comforted him. Some of his visitors who come to his ward seem desperate more than others about his health. They ask tough and existential questions to the doctors who operated on him.

"What did you do to my son?" had asked Hussein's mother to the doctor who happens to be present in the ward, three days after the surgical operation ended. That afternoon, that doctor was on the late afternoon shift and, at the time, he performed his last tour of the wards, meant to finish soon. He had thought he would go home peacefully without much trouble for the day. It happened that incidentally that evening, he had a birthday party for his elder daughter aged six.

"From the beginning, we did our best to save your son. Surprisingly, you give the impression not to appreciate the work the team did and continue to perform here for him rightly," replied the doctor while he hammered his words with added anger.

"Please, excuse me. I have other patients to visit. I can't afford anybody else to ruin the time we spend to see, nurture, and talk to our patients, all this to speed up their recovery," the doctor additionally explained to Hussein's mother while he found his way out of the group of the present visitors in the ward at that moment. He then turned towards the entrance and left.

Amina, on her part, had also come regularly to see Hussein. As the days pass, she falls into a depressive mood. Though visits were every other week, deep down, someone didn't want to see Hussein in a state of total recovery. If she could even have a few minutes of her own in the hospital ward where his body lies, she said to herself that she would as well end the victim's life for some reason. The question prevailed to know if, to kill him for good, she had enough guts to unplug the respiratory machine that the hospital had put in place to make him stay alive.

Profiling

For a couple of months, the investigation struggles to find the individual who committed the crime. The murder happens inside Hussein's apartment, around one-thirty, in the next day's early hours. Somehow, the victim and his assassin know each other. The inspector Sizwe in charge of the investigation came to that initial observation.

Given his crime scenes experience, the inspector assumes that Hussein's murderer doesn't look like a professional criminal. He made that deduction after his first impression. It appeared that the murderer couldn't be cautious enough. If things didn't happen this way, he wouldn't have left behind any evidence that would become later on incriminatory.

The murder showed at first the signs of a crime of passion. In such situations, most people don't reason. Inspector Sizwe's team had collected every piece of evidence they thought would help to catch the culprit. He even sent genetic material such as skin cells, hair and bodily fluids collected on the crime scene to the general police laboratory for analysis. The laboratory featured among the top three labs in the country. The inspector intended to compare the DNA extracted from the collected evidence against the national database and match them to check the owner's identity.

The task to collect every possible evidence extended even at Amina's apartment. Once the inspector made up his mind about her possible involvement, he went for it. Thus the search of her place for clues of Hussein attempted murder became among the priorities of his investigation. Though he hadn't declared publicly any indication to incriminate Amina as the prime suspect, he had suspected her from day one.

There was no evidence so far that she had been in her boyfriend's apartment on that fatal night because no physical and indisputable proof existed.

However, phone conversations between the couple showed that they experienced those difficult moments when they hated each other. They hadn't spoken to each other in the two days before the incident.

Hussein's phone had been among the evidence collected at his apartment in the first visit by the Sizwe team. They had tracked all the calls made recently, particularly those intended to people they could suspect, Amina included.

Further to assessing the calls Amina and Hussein made to each other in previous days, it emerged that both stood at the brink of a breakup. Their relationship seemed at the time strenuous, as each one blamed the other for the uncomfortable conjecture it experienced. Even so, from there, to end up with attempted murder, nobody could see any direct and apparent link. A piece from the puzzle was missing. Even when one read between the lines, there was no evident motive for the attempted murder. No element from their conversations could indicate the possibility of the incident.

They have a heated exchange.

For Hussein, all features in the past were out of reach.

"We can't go on like this. I don't plan to see your parents. On top of your abuse, you dare to claim that I need you more than you need me. I even heard your friends say behind my back that I gold dig. If you hadn't flirted with me - remember you intentionally approached me on different occasions in that pub -, I wouldn't have ever accepted you from my initiative. Shame on you!"

Thus Amina said in one of the calls that the police had managed to trace.

Based on those calls, the investigator had been able to obtain a search warrant. To support his request, he had argued with the public prosecutor office that if he didn't deliver the summons, Amina could cover up her tracks and destroy all evidence about her possible involvement.

Before even the planned interview that Amina had to attend at the police station on the day the caretaker discovered Hussein's body in his apartment, inspector Sizwe had called her at work. The time indicated one in the afternoon.

"I suppose by now you know what happened in your neighbourhood early in the morning. Hussein was almost killed. We need some evidence that could help identify the perpetrator. I called to inform you that I will visit you soon," he already had a search warrant for Amina's apartment.

"My team will arrive there soon. If you want to wait there while we do our search, it's up to you," Sizwe to Amina.

Investigators arrived at Amina's apartment before she did. They opened her door and started their search straightforwardly. They were particularly interested in the traces of Hussein's blood components and other remains of the drug used to make him fall into unconsciousness.

They managed to pick the bloodstains Florencia had left on the sofa the night before. The sponge used while Florencia checked the drug was also found and taken away for examination. A drop from the poisonous medicine had fallen on the table she sat next to, and she couldn't wipe it out properly because she didn't notice it. Consequently, microscopic traces had remained on it.

Among the pieces of evidence collected from Amina's apartment, two albums of photographs had attracted the inspector's attention.

One of them featured a picture of her, her sister, Dae and Hussein, on a picnic in a public park. Another one showed them both in a restaurant.

Inspector Sizwe, through the case, had now become familiar with everyone in the pictures. His interrogation of different people had helped, but nobody had mentioned the odd person he didn't know yet.

During the interrogation of Amina, he put the pictures in front of her.

"Do you know this person?" the inspector asks Amina and points at the face of Dae in the picture.

"She has been a friend of ours for some time. She lives in the same block as Hussein," answered Amina.

"Does Dae know Hussein? What type of relationship exists between the two, if any?" Asked inspector Sizwe to Amina.

"Apart from the fact that they both live as neighbours, I don't think that there could be any interest between them. I have never seen them together or heard anyone mention that they could be close friends," replied Amina.

Dae, a beautiful and top manager in one of Vodnak city's renowned film production companies, while in her late twenties, had decided to help Florencia in her criminal act for her reasons.

Once they had finished their joint intervention at Hussein's apartment, she had gone home. She put the clothes and other accessories she had used or wore - from gloves to underwear -, while at Hussein's apartment in a black plastic bag. On her way to work, she had thrown the bag in one of the furthest rubbish containers around the apartments' block.

Inspector Sizwe wanted to find out more about the Dae's lead for his investigation. She appeared in two photographs found in the albums from Amina's apartment.

He had learnt that she lived not far from Hussein, in the same block. In the picture where she seemed to enjoy a meal in a restaurant with Hussein, they looked like people having a good time together. Maybe there could've been some sort of jealousy that could've prompted the incident. Sizwe ordered two of his investigators to look more into the Dae's file. With the two pictures that feature Dae in their hands, they went back to the crime scene and started to do door-to-door interviews with Hussein's neighbours.

"We have two pictures with Dae on them. She is one of your neighbours."

"We would like to know if you've ever seen her with Hussein, either when they went out or came home together?" The policemen went around and asked that question. Nobody in the neighbourhood seemed to have ever seen them together. That assertion looked like a mystery for the inspector. The picture from the restaurant implied a different story. It represented two people visibly happy to be together in a public place. The date on the image indicated almost eight months before the incident.

"She must've been intimately linked to Hussein before he decided to have Amina as her new girlfriend," assessed inspector Sizwe while he spoke to himself. He wanted to know how their relationship had evolved and the reason it stopped. She lived in the same apartment block as Hussein, but chances existed that there could be a story behind it, which needed uncovering. Such an account would perhaps help untangle the motive and the identity of the perpetrator of the attempted murder.

Sizwe decides to ask Dae to come to the police station for interrogation. She went on the second day after the incident.

"How do you know your neighbour Hussein?" an investigator, part of the Sizwe team, asks Dae.

"Not more than a neighbour, I suppose, though he invited me once to his first apartment party when he moved into the area. On another occasion, he had pleaded with me that he needed someone to socialise with, to get over any personal issues he had at the time. We went together to a restaurant. Then in a nightclub. On my part, it happened that in the same period, I missed going out. This time out with him came to be a one-off. The rest of the time, we greeted each other unceremoniously each time when our paths crossed," Dae explains how far her relationship with Hussein stood.

The inspector who interrogates Dae wonders if he should show her the picture they had found where she appeared with Hussein in a restaurant.

"Is this the restaurant you mentioned you went to together," the inspector pushed the picture towards Dae on the table?

"Yes, it is! Where did you get that picture?" Dae asked the investigator, with a little surprise on her face.

"Who took that picture?" Dae asks.

"The important consideration, in this case, appears to be that we have it. We try to put together the puzzle of the attempted murder of Hussein. As a consequence, we tap into every place where we could get information from," Inspector Sizwe replies. Dae, with some hindsight, remembered that she had given a copy of the picture to Florencia. Over the years, she remembered that she had given many of her photographs to Florencia when they became close friends.

"But in this picture, you and Hussein have the look of more than normal acquaintances," the inspector points to the photograph in the restaurant. Both pictures lie on the table in front of Dae's eyes. He observed her reaction, but she successfully remained composed.

"I don't deny that I know him, but not as you would want to think. He doesn't come close to my type if you presume that we have ever been boyfriend and girlfriend. Another trait of personality exists about him that everyone who knows him somehow will tell you. His abuse of women and arrogance stands incomparable. Additionally, on top of his unattractive personality, he seems too young for me. I prefer mature men," explained Dae while she spoke as convincingly as she could.

"Between midnight and two-thirty early Monday morning, what did you do?" asked the inspector. This question would be his final one.

"I think I went to bed immediately after the Night News at 10:00 pm. I had a tough day. As a consequence, I had a deep sleep. I didn't hear any suspicious noise the whole night," Dae explains.

"Is there anyone who can confirm your alibi," asks further the inspector.

"Unfortunately, no one. I live alone," said Dae.

Two investigators from Inspector Sizwe's team watched the interview with Dae from the interrogation room's other side. Their gut told them that Dae hadn't indicated the whole story about her relationship with Hussein. She undoubtedly lied about the part of her story he couldn't put his hand on.

"I promise you I will find the whole truth, whatever you stop from telling me," said Inspector Sizwe, who as well decided after the interview to seek a search warrant for her apartment. The search got performed on that same day, around four of the afternoon.

Inspector Sizwe believed in his gut more than his team's work, and he suspected that Dae could somehow be involved in the Hussein murder case, though he didn't have any evidence for his premonition.

As a detective, he thought of different ways a criminal could cover up their tracks after they committed their crime.

He had proof that the perpetrator, whoever this was, had wiped out their fingerprints from the crime scene. The pictures collected from Amina's apartment appeared to point at Dae as a possible suspect.

Once the general prosecutor got approached for a search warrant of Dae's apartment, he immediately signed it on the validity of the strong suspicion proven by the victim and their validated relation.

In Sizwe's understanding, a risk existed that if Dae took part in the incident, in such a case, it would be difficult to find evidence. The police would've taken too long to consider her involvement, and she would've had enough time to destroy any compromising signs.

A whole day had passed since the incident. The inspector in charge of the investigation feared the disappearance or destruction of any evidence used in the criminal operation.

Luckily, the company that collected the waste from the block of apartments went around the properties only on Tuesday mornings. Consequently, if the perpetrator had put any evidence in a rubbish bag, it could be traceable.

The investigators could analyse the vehicle's route if the concerned rubbish bags ended in the landfill. Inspector Sizwe ordered two investigators to identify and contact the company that collected the rubbish and determine where it took it once collected from the area.

SECTION 5. Investigation

Haile's Interrogation

The first round of interviews of the initial suspects for the attempted murder on Hussein ended rapidly. Two days had passed. Despite all the collected information from two critical witnesses and several suspects, inspector Sizwe didn't progress much with the case.

He learns that Haile attended Kyutsu University in Fukuida of Okyto like him. Also, he had found out that he lived in the neighbourhood where the inspector was doing his police investigation. Therefore, he decides to invite him for a meal, with an initial intention to talk about their lives as alumni from the same university, and secondly, the murder case.

Sizwe felt hesitant about getting any new element on the case that he didn't already know. Haile, on his part, though he didn't suffer any guilt about the issue, has to be careful while he talks to the inspector, in whatever circumstances this could be, private or official. He suspects Amina's involvement in the crime, but at the time, while strongly determined, he decides to protect her at any cost.

"Hi, Haile. I am Inspector Sizwe. I would like to invite you to share a meal for a strictly private get together meeting. Since you said we attended the same university, it would be appreciated to meet and chat. I don't every day meet people who also studied at the same place as I did. We could make it either tomorrow at 6:00 pm or the day after at the same time."

"I will do it the day after tomorrow as I already have another commitment for tomorrow."

"I will call early on the agreed day to remind you."

"Is there any document that I need to bring?"

"Only your ID. Though I won't need to see it."

324

They meet in a place on the Uhuru Road of Central Vodnak. In that area operates a Greek Restaurant. It doesn't look popular given the number of its clients and its overall outlook.

Despite that, it hosts many famous personalities who want to celebrate their achievements but don't want to show off. Haile arrives first. He waits approximately ten minutes, and then here comes the inspector Sizwe. Haile notices him near the receptionist at the entrance while Sizwe asks where to find his reserved table. He also enquiries if his guest has already arrived. Once he got his eyes directed at the other end of the room, he spotted Haile immediately after that, close to the principal and wide gothic window. He doesn't wait for the receptionist to finish her sentence. Instead, he heads towards Haile with an all smile on his face. When he gets in front of his chair, he pools it slightly towards him and sits down.

"Hi. Did you have to wait long?"

"Not much."

"I can see that you haven't ordered yet. What would you want to have?"

"As your guest, you can make suggestions. If it happens I don't like what you will order for me, they will take it away, and I will decide on an alternative of my choice."

"Ok, let's do that."

Sizwe calls the waitress to take their order. While they wait, they talk about their time in Niasan. Haile asks Sizwe if he had ever interacted with secret societies on campus in their university years. Though he didn't have any particular interest, nor did nobody try to sell him the concept.

The majority of first-year undergraduates slept in dormitories. Only a few from wealthy families rented or lived in studio apartments.

"Why did you choose to study maths?"

"From an early age, I liked the subject. Then I got a teacher in primary school who made me like maths even more. That's how I always got interested in maths. The more I got involved, the more I found it fascinating."

By that time, the waiter had served their meal. They dig in after two waitresses display all the ordered dishes on their table.

They empty their plates within less than fifteen minutes. The food merely appears delicious to both. They order dessert, then coffee afterwards. They have consciously opted to chat less at this stage while exchanging little on a variety of subjects.

Sizwe, as the host, gets short of stories to share. Haile doesn't help either as he never had that skill of storyteller. The inspector then suddenly brings up the subject of some interest for him that evening, the Hussein murder case. He has invited Haile with the pretence of a togetherness, consequent to a long period of separation, but he wants to carry on his investigation through his soft skills.

"Firstly, I don't want to talk about the case in our conversation, but, on the other hand, if unfortunately, it didn't happen, we wouldn't have ever met after our years at university. Therefore, I would like to ask you how you know the victim informally."

"To be frank, I don't know him except that I saw him around for a few months. I can't confirm whether he could be a resident or not because everyone who moves around in our neighbourhood can't necessarily be one. He might've been a visitor without a permanent residence status. Our paths have never crossed. Consequently, I will not say much about him."

"What about Amina?"

"Her apartment occupies the space located fifteen meters away from mine. She came to our estate a few years after me. She lives with her twin sister, who works in a restaurant. We regularly jog together. Comparatively, I know her more than I do regarding Hussein. The little information I have about him, I learned from her. Until recently, I got told that they spent time together. They behave like boyfriend and girlfriend, but I have never asked such a question to any of them to confirm."

"Let's talk about Amina. Have you ever had an interest in her?"

"Would there be any issue if I did?"

"As you both are singles, you could match each other. Amina, since she is attractive and intelligent, then why not get feelings for her?"

"She left me out to be with Hussein. On top of that, she doesn't fit my kind of girl."

"How did you start to jog together?"

"She asked if she could join me in my early hours' runs. I have for years practised fitness activities in the parks of the area. When she got in touch, at the time, while she showed anxiety about her weight, her doctor had recommended that running could help.

Their conversation didn't provide new clues about who might've attempted on the life of Hussein, but instead, carried on a different tangent. After they finished their meal, the waitresses removed the plates Haile and Sizwe had used. They ordered coffee that each sipped, while they only exchanged little. It had come to around 9:00 pm when they decided to leave the place and head home.

***

327

A quarter past six in the morning, with his co-runner, Amina speaks randomly, with no set agenda, about any topic that would come to her mind, on their way to the park for their run, or while they came back home. That almost consists of an unspoken ritual they agreed on. A commentary about Elmton Cemetery would pop up in Haile's mind and become the topic for their discussion of the next two to five minutes. On her side, Amina would explain her plans for a cruise vacation in East Qarfi, or savings for a trip to Sareponga would be another subject of their conversation.

Twenty four hours earlier, the murder incident in Hussein's apartment has occurred. Haile wants to investigate as deeply as possible and dig out the truth about Amina's presence in the open space of their block of flats that night. He saw someone with a lookalike profile and a similar overall demeanour.

The person looked as if she came from the victim's apartment. He intends to interrogate Amina informally to know how far she has known Hussein. Only then he would unveil what had been her level of involvement in what appeared to be a murder case, the way he saw it evolving.

"How long have you known Hussein?" Haile asks Amina.

She doesn't know if Haile is aware of her level of responsibility in Hussein's attempted murder. She has to reply quickly to help not raise speculation about her from the police and Haile. Her brain has to process many variables and reach a satisfactory answer, which doesn't compromise her, but at the same time, could make Haile more suspicious than he seems by then.

Haile had many unanswered questions. Amina knew that he had seen Florencia while she left Hussein's apartment. But she wasn't sure that Haile had confirmed to the police his suspicions about the person he saw that night.

This uncertainty was her understanding of the possible connection Haile had with the murder and what he had witnessed that night. Florencia had also explained her involvement in the crime. Consequently, Haile's guess about Amina had links with what she knew or did the night of the incident.

"I think the first time was around six months ago," she replies without any hint that she might think of any dubious motive behind Haile's question.

"I first met him on a night out. I went with a friend from work. We spent a few hours altogether, chatting; we drank and danced all of us as a group. He appeared to me as a guy of some interest, apparently from a wealthy Disau family," she adds. She tries to paint a portrait of him as comprehensive as possible from what she knows. She deliberately leaves out the negative side of their relationship, as she doesn't want to feed Haile with reasons to suspect her.

"How close to him could you be?" pursues Haile while he investigates his friend.

"We went out together from time to time, though our kind of intimacy didn't consist of boyfriend or girlfriend at all. However, I can assure you that we stand as close friends," replies Amina. Their interactions projected to those who looked at them as more than friends, though Amina unconsciously would tell a white lie, probably to protect herself - from some harm, challenging to discern -, since only Haile as a friend enquired about their relationship.

Haile sighs slightly and feels relieved a little since no strong commitment between the two exists. Once aware of that truth, he becomes interested in her to some extent. His apparent informal interrogation doesn't end there.

"Were you at Hussein's apartment on the day the attempted murder incident took place?" The question comes out as a bombshell. Amina has to respond by the negative whether or not someone saw her that night.

"No, I couldn't be there," she responds without much hesitation.

"I saw you that night. I returned from the 24/7 corner shop. I know it looked late, but I saw someone who looked like you," Haile explains. Amina felt cornered by that statement. Despite that, she didn't let him read her and instead wondered what Haile insinuated. Several questions hung in her mind while her anxiety level rose, unsure what to say immediately.

"What did you see?" Amina manages to ask.

"I saw the light at Hussein's apartment at that early hour of the morning. You walked near the entrance of his building. Moreover, you headed to your place," answers Haile, while he observes to see how Amina would take it. That looked like a clear and direct accusation of her involvement in a murder case from her best friend.

"At the time, when I got into my apartment, the thought of calling you crossed my mind, though I didn't want to sound dramatic, and it would've been the first time I would've called someone at that hour, while uncertain about the tragic nature of the related incident."

"I said to myself that I didn't need to worry much about it, and then calmed down. The next day, when I saw the ambulance and later on heard about the police's investigation, I regretted that I didn't call you," Haile explains to Amina how he processed the incident at the time it occurred.

With all this information at hand, while he talks to her, she has to decide and come clean about what happened effectively. Either she would continue to deny her implication or tell Haile what she did.

At this stage, she didn't even know if she had to confirm to him her non-involvement. Her twin sister had confessed. It must be her that Haile probably saw that night. If he ever did see anyone.

"Listen, I heard about an accident," she finally indicates. She decides to lie.

The implicit lie transpires from the conversation they both have.

"I visited Hussein yesterday, and he remains unconscious. I can't know what happened. Probably the police will unveil the truth," Amina elaborates before they separate.

They had arrived near the pond in Notgni Gardens, where they usually started their jogging, for each one to branch out towards their direction.

"I will go that way now, and when I finish my rounds, I will call you to meet up and return home," Haile indicates.

Once they finished, which meant after thirty minutes, they implicitly agreed on a specific point where to meet. The last response that Amina gave to Haile brought more confusion in his mind. It didn't provide the answers to the questions he had about her involvement in the attempted murder. At the time, they couldn't pursue the conversation because they had come out for their regular run. Further questioning, if any, would be for another time.

Though unsure of Amina's involvement in Hussein attempted murder, Haile had uncompromisingly decided to help her unconditionally and was even ready to exchange his freedom for her safety. He argued that without her simple existence, his life would've been long gone. Suppose Amina hadn't come to live in his neighbourhood and knocked on his door on that particular evening. As a consequence, he didn't see any problem pledging his humanity to protect his saviour.

331

If there could be some evidence to confirm the uncertainties Haile had, Amina would end up imprisoned. Whatever he had decided to do to help her, he opted to share only the minimum he considered necessary for her to know. The rest he would keep to himself, though she would know or not be aware of the results of his work behind the scenes as the investigation unfolded.

***

Two days have passed since the attempted murder of Hussein. Relatives have flown to Vodnak from Disau Aibara to find out what happened and eventually comfort the victim. Officially, his doctor had already declared him in a coma. Therefore it seemed impossible for them to talk to him.

One of Hussein's cousins came with Amina to the ward where Hussein lay on a hospital bed; respiratory machines supported him to stay officially alive.

"Do you think he will ever become conscious again and be the Hussein we know?" Hussein's cousin asks Amina.

"Let's only hope he will. Maybe the doctors could tell us more about the probable possibilities, but even then, I think that nobody can predict the outcomes in some situations," Amina explains her views.

But in her mind, she got deeply conflicted on the whole picture of the direction things seemed to take. The thought that Hussein could recover from the coma gave her goosebumps on her skin and butterflies in the stomach.

She got tormented at the unique mental process of that possibility.

From the explanation Florencia had given her the night of the incident, she could confirm to whoever she wanted that her sister had committed the attempted murder.

Amina was afraid that once Hussein would recover, he would straightforwardly indicate who he saw that had stabbed him. In his mind, he fell unconscious probably while he thought that it was Amina who was in the room, instead of Florencia, unless Hussein deceived the latter before he fell into the coma.

Sizwe's investigators also counted on his recovery to make tangible progress with their case. The inspector closely monitored the situation in the hospital.

The police feared that Hussein's assassin might strike him a second time while he would be in the hospital. As a consequence, one policeman stayed continuously there to check on the people who visited the victim. Unfortunately, such protection only lasted until the conclusion of the case, and the official culprit was apprehended.

Amina and Hussein's cousin knew each other from previous occasions. They continued to chat in his hospital room for thirty minutes. Their conversation covered Hussein's health situation, but also their past encounters. They recalled both the time when they had spent one Saturday, all of them together, including Hussein, in a central Vodnak pub in the Ohosh area.

'I will leave first. I have important academic assignments to submit next week, and I haven't made much progress,' Hussein's cousin excuses himself to say bye to Amina.

"Let's leave together. Staying here on my own and looking at the unconscious Hussein on his bed, 'we won't have much to share,'" Amina replies to Hussein's cousin.

They passed in front of the hospital reception area at the very time that they chatted.

The cousin seemed much older than Hussein but still younger than Amina.

They parted at the entrance and promised each other to call if they wanted a friend for chilling out.

Amina, on her way home, continued to reflect on the eventuality of Hussein recovering. She could foresee herself with handcuffs and enter jail as a consequence. She couldn't let it happen in any way.

"One way out of this quagmire exists," Amina talks to herself, almost whispering. At that moment, she doesn't see the end of the tunnel. Haile's name clicks in her mind. That's it. She goes to seek help from her unconditional friend Haile and find a solution together.

If the mentioned eventuality materialised, Amina could've found it unfair to become the official culprit of the attempted murder instead of her sister Florencia. On the other hand, she needed to try whatever possible to protect her.

A tacit kind of agreement between the two sisters existed, which indicated that whoever among them would become the accused, the innocent one would have to look after the other who would get in jail. Luckily things hadn't yet progressed up to that stage.

All this stood still as speculation about Hussein recovering or the direction of the investigation.

Media's Interest

When Sizwe's team arrived at the crime scene, two journalists from the tv channels X1 and YZ were already there talking to the residents. Their informants from the crime section unit at the police station had alerted them about the case. As soon as possible, the journalists rushed to Hussein's apartment. Unfortunately, police investigators arrived there first. The delay didn't allow anyone other than the police to have a close look at the body still in the apartment; only the investigators and other specialists needed for the investigation could get in. Journalists got a glimpse of the body only when the ambulance service took it away from the crime scene.

The journalists had no permission to enter the apartment. The investigators feared that unauthorised individuals on the scene might contaminate any evidence since they couldn't rightly appreciate the importance of clear evidence for police cases. Despite the interdiction, they could talk to a few onlookers who wondered what happened and saw several police officers in their area.

The news people learned about the victim's identity, provided even the name and address of her probable girlfriend, Amina, who lived in the immediate neighbourhood. Since they didn't find much after the ambulance had taken Hussein's body to the hospital, they tracked down the girlfriend for an interview. Luckily for her, they rang her doorbell after ten in the morning while she had left her apartment.

An hour later, after they tried her doorbell and couldn't reach her, they called her workplace, but she responded that she didn't want to talk to the media. She didn't tell them intentionally that, that day, she would go to the hospital to see Hussein.

In that whole day, she resisted talking to them; she had decided to only respond to the investigators' questions in charge of the case.

Amina wanted to delay such a predicament as long as she could because she was anxious about the public reaction to the media's statements. After the first phone call from a journalist, she received two more within three hours.

"In these tense moments of my life, I need to seek help from trusted friends. I don't see anybody else than Haile who could be of some assistance," Amina thought.

Thus, for her first time, she dealt with the media on a practical matter on which her future hung.

"Let me call Haile," she decides in her mind. He had offered to support her and her sister in these challenging times. Since she didn't want anyone among her colleagues to know about the police investigation, she went to the restroom, and once alone, she called him for advice.

The journalists who covered the incident published topical news about Hussein in the afternoon paper when they announced his body's discovery. The headline talked about a murder attempt on a Disau student in Vodnak. The article highlighted the identity of Hussein as a person, but without much information. They didn't mention any relatives he might have.

The newspaper had featured a family picture of the victim they had picked online. Another photo revealed the state of his wounds. The article indicates the body's discovery. It also announces the time when the victim fell into a coma and arrived at the hospital. It doesn't mention the girlfriend. Inspector Sizwe happened to not have yet any strong leads about the suspect for the crime. Another possibility could've been that he operated strategically and avoided revealing his prime suspect publicly.

News outlets in Vodnak city talked about the incident vividly.

The media highlighted how the caretaker noticed the unusual elements in front of the victim's apartment door. One paper reported the incident in the next way.

"Every Monday morning, the caretaker's task takes him on the stairs in front of Hussein's apartment. Contrary to other days when he worked in that area, he found the door slightly opened."

"At first, he thought the resident had left that door open because he had gone back to look for things he forgot inside when they had come out. The caretaker waited to do his work not too far from there, then after five minutes, he came back and found the door still in the same position. He became suspicious. He knocked on the door, but he didn't receive any reply. He makes sure he doesn't touch objects with measured caution; this could be important for future investigation; he pushes the door.

He immediately saw a body on the floor, at four metres approximately from where he stood near the apartment entrance. He stopped and decided not to get inside but anxiously inhaled and breathed in some air. He wasn't sure if the person was still alive or not. He looked around with no clue about what he expected to discover. After approximately one minute in which he didn't have all his senses functioning at their optimum, he called the police and reported the incident."

This newspaper highlighted that the public could hardly assume who the culprit could be without enough clues for guidance. It cited inspector Sizwe and indicated that the murderer had left behind the weapon probably used for the crime. He had also exited the scene by the main entrance to the apartment. On the tricky question about the door left open, could that be that the murderer wanted the crime discovered quickly? Or did that happen because of negligence? By that time, nobody had explained the motive behind it.

Journalists who reported on the case had already traced the girlfriend of the victim. They investigated the time Amina had left for work in the morning. Thus they had waited in front of her apartment the next day, and this time she somehow had prepared. Around seven forty-five, the doorbell rang, unusually for it to buzz that early. Amina went to check who this could be.

"Yes? What do you want?"

"Miss Amina?" The person at the other end ran to get to her door intercom. She looks and sounds like someone out of breath.

"Yes. It's me. How can I help you?" Amina replies and then asks.

"Rebecca from Channel X1," the journalist says.

"Please, can we talk about the incident which happened last night in this area?" the journalist asks.

She didn't expect the question to be so openly direct and challenging to answer, as it implied that she was perceived as a suspect by the public through the journalist's eyes. In her mind, she immediately thought that more people already linked her to Hussein's attempted murder. There had been firstly Haile, her neighbour and runner partner.

"What about that incident?" Amina retorted. She regretted afterwards that she responded that way. Her question sounded on the defensive as if she possibly felt guilty. That could've been one of the thoughts from anyone who would've heard her reply. Without waiting, she pushed the button on her intercom to get the journalist in.

Rebecca came with a colleague cameraman. After welcoming them, Amina instantly explained that she would answer any of their questions about the incident but didn't want to appear on any TV programs. She told them that she would sue them if they ever went against that understanding.

338

"No problem. We understand," Rebecca agrees to Amina's request.

"I've noticed some particular and strong interest from the media about me and the incident. I've contacted my lawyer to advise me on the right way to deal with the incident. The advice indicated that if I didn't want to talk to you journalists, I could. Now, you know where I stand," she clarifies.

"No pictures. Right! Consequently, your picture will not appear on our channel," Rebecca replies. Nevertheless, she predicted that someone in the general public would publish her photo and link it to the Hussein incident. She counted on that to have a complete story well put together.

"What type of relationship do you have with Mr Hussein?"

"In the state of our current relationship - not formally engaged to each other -, we stand only as close friends."

"Everyone who knows about your relationship with the victim longs to hear what you have to say about the incident," the journalist stated. Nonetheless, this statement pressured Amina to indicate her position, either as a victim or a potential suspect.

"I regret what happened to my friend and would like to see the culprit brought to justice," Amina explains with a sincere expression she has on her face. She knows the culprit, but she has decided to protect her as long as she can and no matter what.

"When did you last see Mr Hussein?"

"I explained that to the inspector who leads on the case. He advised me not to talk about my recent meetings with Hussein. In the interest of the investigation, I will not discuss that issue with the media."

"What type of person could Mr Hussein be?" This question seemed a tricky one. She didn't want to portray him the way he effectively was, an abuser of women, because that would have pointed to her as the culprit. She had taken revenge on him - her sister happens to be the one who punished Hussein -, because of the things he did to her. He had abused her countless times.

"He was and continued to be a dependable man. I visited him yesterday at the hospital. He lies in a coma. I pray he recovers quickly. His youth makes him behave like any other peer, but with more money to spend."

"Would you mean that he spends a lot? Could you provide examples," the journalist asked.

"On some occasions, we would go out, and he would pay for anyone in the pub and ask them to fill their glasses with whatever they drank at the time of his announcement. Such an incident happened twice while I accompanied him. I can't guess how often he did that in my absence."

"At times, we couldn't be together for any reason. Unless he paid for drinkers to impress me," Amina explains.

"So far, the general public thinks of you as the prime suspect. What do you say to that?" the journalist highlights.

"I can't control what people think of me. Deep down, I can only give my views. My innocence cries out loudly. I empathise with what Hussein goes through right now because of what happened. His being a crime's victim doesn't, however, make me the murderer that the investigation seems to look for," Amina explains.

"In your relationship with Hussein, did there exist any consistent tension between you both? Your neighbours told us that to be the case," the journalist persists in her questioning.

"No serious incident. Hussein speaks loudly, and that characterises him. His manly tone of voice adds to his charm. That's all I can say about him. If you don't have any other questions you think to be relevant, I would like to end this interview now," she stood up calmly and invited the TV crew to leave her apartment and showed them the door.

In the afternoon of her interview with Rebecca, the journalist, a friend of Amina who watched the news on channel X1 reported what they said. The presenter journalist hinted that Amina could be the police's prime suspect as the victim's girlfriend.

The news' presenter explained that the police had requested her not to reveal her recent meetings with Hussein, which constitutes part of their strategy to let Amina off her guards, and put her to think that they didn't consider her as their primary suspect. Thus, while the police would gather evidence against her, she would feel comfortable. That way, she would be caught while unprepared to be. The presenter's point of view made some sense. Her analysis of Amina's situation pressured the latter to be even more cautious than before.

Two policemen in a car followed her in all her movements. They had started from the time the police had asked Amina for an interview.

They didn't know that she had noticed them when she left the hospital. Haile had explained to her that she would be the primary suspect in the eyes of the police.

Consequently, she had to behave in a way that would not increase their suspicions. Though she had to be careful, Haile had told her not to change her routines. Only would she try to lose the police officers on her tracks when she would be doing things related to Hussein's case.

***

The investigation team had found several finger-prints and a set of hair samples in Hussein's apartment. They appeared in the bedroom, on cups and glasses in the kitchen.

"Please send the collected samples to the forensic lab. This evidence needs to be compared to the records in the Federal DNA Database and confirm if any match exists," Sizwe addresses his subordinates but also instructs his most experienced investigator of his team to be responsible for the assigned task.

Haile had sensed the urgency of the process of these different pieces of evidence. With a friend's hacker's help, he enters the Federal DNA Database and searches the records' online register. He intends to remove from the resources any information related to the twin sisters.

Haile's friend executed the required illegal intrusion within less than fifteen minutes, as he explained years later to a group of friends, who had appeared all implicated in the case. In that particular moment, the hacker displayed a high level of expertise in that field of knowledge; he had found the database not robustly protected to resist external attacks. When the Sizwe team brought collected samples to the Forensic Lab for analysis, they didn't find any match. Thus they had to resort to other directions to catch their culprit.

Beyond the twins' concerned case and comparing their DNA with the data kept on the Federal DNA Database, some ethical issues the public had raised over the years remained pending. As an illustration, by 1990, one year after creating such databases' legal framework by the Criminal Justice and Public Order Act that the QK Parliament had passed, five-point two per cent of the QK population had their DNA information recorded.

But the majority of the registered individuals had never been charged with or convicted of any offence. Jeopardising the lives of the twin sisters could be easily possible - if they weren't already if the database had recorded their details -, whatever the reasons.

For several years, and under the law of that time, the database's projection for the database estimated that it would increase up to twenty-five per cent of the QK adult male population and seven per cent of adult women. The database had raised public concerns of privacy, government surveillance and human rights because of its broad scope.

Despite the controversy around the database's aspects, this didn't stop the public authorities in different countries from emulating its significant importance in the criminal system. The initial Federal DNA Database, given the budget problems, included only offences related to violent and sexual crimes and domestic burglary. Unfortunately, violations that included begging, drunkenness and disorderly, and illegal demonstration, all these cases could also get recorded under the Federal DNA Database's directives.

Laws introduced previously at different periods allowed the police to take DNA samples without consent from anyone arrested in connection with a recordable offence, even if there were no charges. It could be disputable that the simple fact that, deliberately or not, they found themselves in contexts where they got arrested - from the law enforcement authority that included the police -, a high probability existed that they would be in a similar situation in the future.

Therefore, in the legislator's eyes, such ways of proceeding justified the reason to keep their DNA. Thus, the national database kept their records, though, in the initial instance, there had been no conviction.

With Hussein's case, finding forensic evidence on the crime scene would be helpful under specific contexts, enabling the police to compare the evidence with already available forensic data. Nonetheless, Haile had ensured the destruction of such information when the investigation team would come looking for it; this happened before analysing any forensic evidence. Even if that information had existed and consequently and positively proven matching with the evidence from the crime scene, the situation wouldn't have been enough to make the person that it belonged to responsible for the crime. Even so, Haile didn't want to take any chances. The only conclusion the police could come up with would only indicate that the person had been at the crime scene sometime in the past.

***

At the peak of the investigation, the Sizwe team consists of ten individuals: seven police officers and three experts in forensic science. On the day of the announcement of the attempted murder on Hussein, a local paper had printed an article on the incident. In the days that followed, the same newspaper also published a police appeal to the public to come forward and report whatever they knew about that case.

Sizwe interviewers started and went door-to-door in the vicinity of Hussein's apartment to ask questions about what they might know.

"We would like to ask you a few questions because of the investigation related to the crime committed in your area. That won't take more than five minutes of your time," they say to introduce themselves.

The investigation team did a re-enactment of the crime and several appeals at different periods of the inquiry.

After a month of investigation, the police sifted through all the gathered information. Without a clear indication of the real suspect, the woman or someone seen with a woman profile that night constituted the only plausible possibility. Two witnesses had come forward and confirmed that they saw her as if she came from the same area as Hussein's apartment, around the time of the attempted murder on his person.

The investigation had ended up inconclusive.

"The analysis of all the gathered evidence doesn't provide the culprit without any reasonable doubt," Sizwe reported to his superiors.

Two members of the investigation team decided to take blood samples from everyone, male and female, who lived in the apartments where two CCTV covered exit points in the immediate neighbourhood.

They extended their collection of evidence's pieces to anyone who could've left the vicinity of the considered area in the month that followed. The assumption was that no adult in good health could remain indoors for that whole period. They used the town hall register of voters that indicated how many people were in each recorded address. The police hoped to narrow down the number of people who would provide blood samples.

The final number of people they took blood samples from came down to twenty-five. Within two weeks after the sampling, the laboratory completed the process of tests against the evidence collected at the crime scene. They didn't find any matched samples. As it happened from time to time for some of the police's criminal investigations, the question was to wonder if the case would be closed as unsolved. The inspector, Sizwe, wouldn't give up yet.

SECTION 6. At The End

The Last Resort

Haile turns himself in when he realises that inspector Sizwe has nearly gathered all the evidence required to convict Amina.

"I don't have any other option. If I only turn myself in, Sizwe will certainly stop the investigation. I can't bear to see her in prison when I could change the variables of the equation and avoid her imprisonment," he reasons.

He has been in constant communication with her all along the entire investigation process. He closely monitored every step. The police strongly linked Amina to the murder case because of a bloodstain found on her sofa in the main room. A forensic examination of the evidence confirmed that the found sample of blood belonged to Hussein. The unclear part of the analysis concerned only about how long it had been there.

Nonetheless, with hard work, Sizwe's team of investigators had also already managed to trace from the landfill trainers with small particles of Hussein's blood that had stuck on the rubber underneath inadvertently. Dae had put those trainers in a rubbish bag collected the next day after the attempted murder. With that evidence, she got implicated as well. Clearly, at that stage, the investigators made a significant milestone to solve the case.

After the investigators found their most substantial evidence, they proceeded to further interrogations of the suspects. They questioned Amina and Dae several times to clarify certain aspects of their possible involvement. Between the accomplices of the crime and Amina, they had only made one call while they accomplished their operation.

346

Until then, the inspector had been unaware of Dae's involvement. Amina had assumed that Dae had called from her apartment. She imagined that her sister had gone there after she committed the crime.

Inspector Sizwe interlaced his fingers once he sat on the opposite side of the table in the interrogation room.

"How did Hussein blood end up in your apartment on the night of the attempted murder?" The inspector makes Amina believe that he got the evidence in question a moment before the interrogation. He pushes his luck with the interviewee, though no element proved the bloodstain's recent evidence scientifically. The forensics hadn't been able to determine how long that sample had been on that sofa in Amina's main room.

"I presume you don't pretend that the found bloodstain has been put there on the night of the murder. That would be preposterous to associate me with the incident. Hussein and I, because of our relationship, visit each other regularly. Probably, he came once with a cut on his skin and left blood on my sofa. Nobody noticed anything. That would be the only possibility. As I remember, such an incident happened more than a month ago. The rest would be pure speculation."

"Hussein didn't come to my place recently, nor did I go to his apartment that night," angrily reacted Amina to the inspector's allegations about the bloodstain. He touched his chin with the right thumb as he reflected before he put back his whole hand at the table.

"What an extremely well-planned murder!" Inspector Sizwe acknowledges the criminal skills of the murderer while he looks Amina in her eyes.

"The way fingerprints got wiped out from all the usual places someone can find them indicates a meticulous mind in action.

Despite that, what I don't understand, is why Hussein's door was left open. Did a distraction occur to make you leave the place in a hurry?"

"I don't know what you're talking about!" Amina replied with an exaggerated tone of surprise.

"As I told you in my previous interrogations, I haven't seen Hussein in days."

"The forensics indicate that Hussein got stabbed around 2:30 a.m. Whatever distraction occurred at that time, what would it be?"

"Visibly it made the assassin commit a mistake," continues the inspector at the attention of Amina, but also seemingly monologuing.

"Once I checked all the suspicious communications and somehow related to all potentially involved people, and conversations made close to that period, I found out that one critical exchange occurred between Dae and you at 2:35 a.m. It announced that Florencia would be at your place in a moment. That call proves that you didn't stay together at home as you allege. Thus your alibi doesn't stand any more at all. Your sister could've been elsewhere. You both lied all along about what you did that night. Nobody else, except you both, can confirm your alibi that says that you stayed asleep in your beds at the time," Inspector Sizwe elaborates for Amina to understand the sequence of what might've happened then.

"How did you tolerate his persistent abuse towards you?" Inspector Sizwe continues to ask Amina. He referred to her strained relationship with Hussein. He deliberately shifts the line of interrogation in a different direction.

"I see you've singled out that side of his personality. The reality comes to the fact that I had started to adjust myself to it."

"On his side, he received some specialist help," Amina tries to deflect the perspective of the case and ensures that her boyfriend would not be profiled mainly along with the considerations of his character.

"What could be your sister's view about his abuse of women?"

Inspector Sizwe had learned from everyone in the neighbourhood he had interviewed that Hussein had an impossible character to live with, given his persistent verbal abuse. Thus, surprisingly, the inspector could observe that his girlfriend didn't highlight his character's problems for some people.

According to the inspector, Amina could've at least confirmed the issue formally. Then she could've also pointed to how she dealt with it.

The way Amina leaned towards the defensive and acted indicated that she felt guilty of something.

"Who left the door of the apartment open?" Sizwe opts for a new line of questioning. He had noticed that Amina had become more and more reluctant to answer.

"You tell me! I spent time in my apartment; how could I - at the same time - go to close or leave his apartment open?"

"So you don't remember if you closed or left the door behind you?"

"Sorry, inspector. I didn't go to his apartment that whole evening, nor the previous two days. Hussein and I hadn't yet managed to get over a difficult period of our relationship, way back before the incident."

"And what did that situation relate to?" Inspector Sizwe asks. Before Amina replies - though he doesn't know if she would react - he pursues observing her intention.

"You forget that someone who knows you well saw you in the courtyard that night while you headed to your apartment."

"The witness says that he saw you with some assurance, but he can't confirm totally because of the lack of sufficient light in the area. Nevertheless, he categorically believes that the person, a woman with similar traits as yours, surprisingly resembled you more than anybody else. With all the evidence we have gathered, we can confirm that you are the only suspect with the strongest motive to kill the victim. The elements of conviction point at you as the perpetrator of the crime. Tomorrow I will take your case to the judge."

The inspector still had his doubts about the conviction. Further to that assumption, he decides to ask the judge to keep Amina in police custody for forty-eight hours.

He presented the motivation to uphold her to be the weakness of the evidence to sentence the accused; the inspector wanted to proceed to one more examination of the case. Once granted the authorisation, he calls his team of investigators.

"I want you to reexamine the case from every possible angle, revisit all the evidence we collected, talk to anyone we interviewed, or anybody else you think we missed, find more tangible elements," he asks them.

"We only have forty-eight hours," he adds.

"Please put aside all the other cases you have."

During the first twenty-four hours, all the members of his team got busy. They reviewed all the evidence available, but with a different look. The next day, inspector Sizwe instructs his team to reexamine the case and check the substances and steps that made Hussein unconscious.

He got inspired into that direction of his investigation while he took his breakfast. He usually liked to have a range of food supplements to compensate for his intake of food.

He had resorted to that option, as a workaholic, without much time away from his tasks; in his investigations, he could spend long hours without eating. He missed lunches or dinners, and that seemed part of his lifestyle. Once told that this could affect his long-term health, a doctor advised him to take vitamins to alleviate the consequences of his irregular meals.

He looked into the substances that led to Haile's unconsciousness while taking his vitamins' supplements from their bottles and other containers. In his investigation, he remembered that the lab's results had found Rohypnol traces at Amina's and the victim's apartments. He reflected that this would've been impossible if Amina didn't get involved. Unfortunately, though enough pointers showed her as the perpetrator, she didn't know about that rape drug. Her twin sister hadn't informed her about it until after the incident.

When confronted with the evidence, Amina became the official perpetrator who had attempted on the life of Hussein. However, whenever investigators had asked her to admit her responsibility in the offence, she refused. Deep down in herself, effectively, she hadn't committed the crime that would put her in prison.

Though in her case, the inspector Sizwe had more solid evidence than for other suspects, he still couldn't confirm Amina's full responsibility as the perpetrator.

"Does Amina try to cover up a crime she didn't commit to protect someone?" On the last day of the trial, Inspector Sizwe had this question on his mind.

Amina lets fate take its course at that moment. She decides to stop claiming her innocence. Her sister had confirmed her total responsibility in that crime. Dae knew as well. This secret that the three women shared now would bind them together for the rest of their lives.

Even so, as the subsequent events showed, Haile still believed that Amina, as the real perpetrator in his mind, committed the crime. He misjudged the character of her twin sister, Florencia. He would take in his grave such misconception of the sister's personality side. Though a criminal, she would never face justice. Time and fate had decided to protect her and conceal her crime forever.

***

Despite her conviction and sentence followed by her imprisonment, Amina fears that he might reveal the real culprit if Hussein comes out of the coma. She knows at what lengths Haile went to cover up her involvement in the crime. Therefore, once he became her friend, though Amina didn't seek their friendship, there wasn't any doubt in her mind that he would remain close. With such trust in their closeness, she seeks his assistance to clear the persistent fear she has about her boyfriend, who by then lives in a vegetative state.

Close to the day of the month when Haile visits Amina in prison, he wears a casual dress typical of his personality. After he puts down his details in the register for visitors, he waits in the hall. The correctional officer calls him and invites him to take a seat in front of the glass where Amina expects to be in a moment, on the other side.

By then, they often see each other that way. Consequently, they leave out the formalities. She has an important task that demands a perfect execution to succeed, and she wants him to accomplish it for her. She manages to pass the message, despite the guardian's vigilance. She might've hinted that she effectively did it but immediately regretted what she said. On Haile's side, despite Amina's worries, he didn't overthink about what she asked him to do for her.

He has always been blinded in a way by the affection he has for her to reason logically.

"I will think about it. Give me some time, I will let you know in which way I can help you," he replies, but surprisingly not phased out by the suggestion of killing someone, even if the target lives in a vegetative state of total coma.

***

After three years from the time Amina got imprisoned, Hussein comes out of the coma. But, unfortunately for him, he doesn't have the time to enjoy his recovery. Amina thinks that this should be the right time to murder Hussein, this time for good.

"I will do it," Haile told Amina on his next visit to the prison.

"Don't worry about it. I've started the necessary preparations for the operation," Haile added.

"If my sister can be of any help, please let me know," Amina told Haile at the time.

"Effectively, I might need a second hand in my operation," Haile explains.

"I will tell her to get in touch," Amina says.

He devised a mask that looked like one of the doctors responsible for the patient.

He bribed a janitor who worked at the hospital that looked after Hussein to get two uniforms, one for a doctor and another for a nurse.

Three days after Hussein came out of the coma, but still, under the medical care of the hospital, Haile and his disguised nurse accomplice unnoticed entered the ward. Despite other medical staff in adjacent rooms, the intruders inject an undetectable poison in the victim's blood through the suspended fluid bag. Hussein didn't wake up from his deep sleep. He died within two hours of the injection.

While Amina prepared for the ultimate death of Hussein, Haile had done an initial inspection of the hospital. He had identified the location of the CCTV cameras. Though he and his accomplice wore disguised outfits while the operation of that night went on, they hid their faces from the cameras. A police team that investigated the crime could only confirm that the hospital's suspicious visit to Hussein's ward didn't come from their staff. No record mentioned when Hussein got supposedly injected with the poison in the scheduled visits to the wards.

Presumed Culprit

Sizwe perseveres and looks into the mindset of the perpetrator's psyche of the attempted murder. He carries on and tries to find out the reason the door of Hussein's apartment got left open. Still unclear, this could've been intentional or accidental. Given that only Hussein and Amina fingerprints seem identifiable in that space, suspicions ran high and more directed on the girlfriend than anybody else.

Every criminal wants to conceal their crime forever if they can. In the case of Hussein, if the door left open seemed intentional, Sizwe concluded that the perpetrator wanted the offence to be discovered quickly, and eventually, direct suspicion towards the most obvious culprit, the girlfriend. On the other hand, if the door left open would have been only an accident, and no different fingerprints than those of Hussein and Amina in the apartment existed. This situation complicates the search for the culprit.

No signs showed that somebody wiped out fingerprints or that, to cover their tracks, the murderer used gloves. Subsequently, it emerges that the investigation heads in the wrong direction on these two accounts. Florencia and Dae have been thorough when they cleaned and removed any possible evidence they might've left there.

Nonetheless, Sizwe had concluded that whoever could be the perpetrator, he or she must appear likely as the person who left the door open - whatever excuse there could be. No other exit from the apartment exists. Its windows located on the fifth floor remained closed. Nobody could've entered the apartment, opened it from outside, done whatever they came in to do and then closed the windows and left through them once they finished.

The glasses found and dried in the kitchen tray showed signs of clinical cleaning. As a consequence, it looked impossible to trace back the incomplete fingerprints to the owners.

When the investigators interviewed Amina at the police station, she had categorically denied that she had been to Hussein's apartment in the last three days before the incident. On the night of the murder attempt, she had a solid alibi. She slept in her room while her sister Florencia did the same in hers.

***

Inspector Sizwe has collected all the evidence that implicates Amina. She has been for a while the primary suspect the inspector had eyes on from the beginning. Now she has turned herself in. As soon as the case started, she had decided to protect her twin sister at any cost. Since they became orphans, she had implicitly taken on the responsibility to lead on their single unit of two instead of her sister. Touched by the intended sacrifice of Haile to cover up her crime, she considers that she can't let it be and continues the way it has been, while she knew who the real murderer was.

The investigator doesn't believe her to be the ultimate culprit for the attempted murder of Hussein. The prosecutor's file to put forward in front of the court includes a new witness' statement. Their testimony alleged that they saw a person who strongly resembled Amina and came from the area of Hussein's apartment. The person in question headed to Amina's place around the time of the murder.

Two days have passed since Amina turned herself in. The police held her in custody.

Though she admitted to having committed the crime, all the evidence gathered didn't single her out as the primary suspect without any reasonable doubt. Only the bloodstain found on her sofa bed links her to the attempted murder case.

The other pertinent evidence produced by the prosecutor concerned Haile Mohamed and his statement. In all the interrogations the police had made, the motive Amina had mentioned to kill Hussein appeared to be weak.

When the incident occurred, no irrefutable trace of her near the crime scene could be confirmed.

"Why would she kill him when she benefited from him in every regard as his girlfriend?" had the inspector tried to reflect on the motivations of the crime.

Amina had received many valuable gifts from him. They included a car from her last birthday. She couldn't be the perpetrator, given the evidence available to the investigators; instead, she could preferably or probably be seen as an accomplice more than anybody else in the case. Even in that situation, the argument sustaining any involvement couldn't convince enough.

The Sizwe team found inconclusive the fingerprints of Amina's they had collected in Hussein's place. Understandably, they could've been there because of their relationship. From that day onwards, the team's work couldn't progress because it couldn't reach a satisfactory outcome.

Both sisters had reliable alibis. They indicated how they stayed asleep in their apartment at the time of the attempted murder. When interrogated about the time they came home, they had confirmed that fact, though they lied. From the inspector's perspective, it became a challenge to prove them wrong, from whichever angle he had tried to test their alibis.

In his statement about the person he saw that night in the courtyard, and without any doubt, Haile couldn't validate the presence of Amina. He couldn't confirm because the lighting was weak in that location.

The panel of judges consists of three members in total. They all agree that Amina seemed the one whose motive could be the most plausible among the suspects. Their tumultuous relationship had a high level of abuse from Hussein to consider in the case.

This perspective led the panel to focus on the sentence or the time in jail for the accused. In the court hearing, the lead woman judge who conducts the court session intends to give a light sentence to address women's abuse from Hussein.

The defendant had strongly argued for her defence. The lawyer insisted on the fact that Amina had endured for a long time Hussein's abuse. Further to what he had done to her for a considerable amount of time, there was broad ground that she might try to kill him.

"The judge has arrived. Everybody rises," announces the court secretary.

After the three judges sat in their chairs and the lead judge introduced the case to the audience's attention, she called upon the prosecutor to present his accusation.

"Thank you, your Honour. The defendant you all see over there, Ms Amina, has attempted to kill someone; she happens to be no other than the girlfriend of the victim, Mr Hussein. Since the incident, the victim has been in a permanent coma state, almost living a vegetative life. Only a miracle could free him from that undignified sort of life. Whatever went on between the two, there would not be any circumstances somebody would be allowed to take the life of anyone without penal retributions. On the night of the attempted murder, the accused stayed with the victim in his apartment."

"Our investigation found that the committed offence came about after Hussein got deliberately made unconscious. Though the victim's blood sample shows that he had a high level of alcohol in his body, the expert also found that he got poisoned. Your Honour, this first exhibit indicates the drug used to make the victim unconscious. He got stabbed after the murderer injected the drug. Please also find exhibit number two, a kitchen knife that stabbed Hussein several times in the chest, with an intended objective to kill him. Unfortunately for the assassin, the murder didn't go as planned. While the stabs meant to cause the victim's death, they only put him in a coma."

"The analysis of fingerprints in Hussein's apartment couldn't determine the culprit. Though we found Amina's fingerprints there, this seemed only logical for them, given the relationship between the victim and the suspect."

"However, after we analysed a bloodstain pattern of samples collected from the surfaces and clothes found at Amina's apartment, we found fresh traces of Hussein's blood. I can conclude with certainty from that evidence that the night of the murder, Amina went to her boyfriend's apartment. She killed him for reasons we couldn't elucidate fully. Afterwards, she covered it up as much as she could, but the blood of Hussein in her place came as a significant element of her responsibility in that attempted murder. That's all, Your Honour," the prosecutor indicates.

"The defence, you can question the defendant," the lead judge points his hand towards the stand where Amina sits.

"No question for the defendant, Your Honour," the defence lawyer replies. After the latter heard the prosecution's arguments, the other side couldn't present any counter-argument, given that it was unprepared, it got surprised at the prosecution's revelation.

"We will make our decision known tomorrow at 11:00 am," the judge announces.

The defence didn't have any argument to oppose the evidence produced by the prosecution. If certified proof from a neutral forensic laboratory existed that showed that Hussein's blood was found in Amina's apartment, the discovery couldn't dismiss her culpability. The decision of the court about her sentence would come the day after. In the meantime, unresolved issues remained.

Florencia got devastated. Her impulsive action to break the relationship between Hussein and her sister didn't mean to end that way. It appears she had missed out on many variables in her planning. Her marriage had ended tragically.

She had now her sister's boyfriend almost killed and her sister imprisoned. Indisputably, she didn't regret what she did. However, she had some empathy towards her sister.

Haile got even more appalled by the entire proceedings of the court and the outcome of the investigation.

Given the efforts he had put in, not to implicate Amina - and now that she had become the attempted murderer officially - he felt pathetically disillusioned. In his cell, his future depended widely on the judge's decision about Amina.

He became angry at his fate, despite the fact he didn't believe in it. Whatever this looked like, his doubts concerned its inclination; what it did to him appeared unfair. He had planned to spend time in prison, as long as her life-saver would be happy and safe outside. Now that she became the one to be in jail, he didn't have much reason to stay alive. He appeared gracefully merciful for the period he had been able to live because of her. Without a purpose and hopelessness-bound, his life could become meaningless again.

The day of the court announcement on Amina's case arrives.

"The judge has entered the court. Everyone rises," the court secretary announces.

The three judges who preside over the case take their chairs.

"Before we announce the court decision, I invite the defence to present their final statement," the chairperson of the panel of judges announces. Though the judges had already made their decision, they, however, leaned towards a reduced sentence. Regarding women's abuse, the court's witnesses had characterised the victim with the public expected from the judges to consider that element.

The judges wanted to listen to what the defence brought up with their final statement and reinforce their position.

"Thank you. However, about your evidence's integrity, considering the mistakes forensic laboratories make with samples, it would be fair in this trial to have another opinion from a different and reliable forensic laboratory. People should remember that Amina turned herself in. At that exact moment, the prosecution presented the related and collected evidence."

"Nevertheless, one would question its importance since it lacked early on for the court to convict the same person. Finally, Haile, on the same investigation, whose case has not yet been closed, too did turn himself in. I end my statement on that, Your Honour," the defence pleaded and implored the judges.

Informed by the defence's request, members of the panel that presided over the case declared the court in recess. They would reconvene within twenty minutes to announce their decision. Once in their chambers, between themselves, they looked at the point raised by the defence: it wanted to reexamine the evidence of bloodstain collected from Amina's apartment.

It had been six months since the murder. Forensic laboratories suffered a high volume of backlog examinations of blood samples.

The judges had Haile's file; it showed inconsistent evidence for his guilt, even though he had turned himself in as the murderer. They considered the excellence of the forensic laboratory, which had provided the analysis for Amina's conviction. The results came in after they waited for four months. The lab featured as the top of the three renowned in the country. Its success rate scored above ninety per cent, the second on the list had eighty-one per cent.

The prosecutor had produced the forensic result only after Amina had turned herself in and it played in favour of the defence. The prosecution requested another analysis. The judges decided to go with their initial decision that aimed to give a reduced sentence. Nevertheless, before they announced it, they intended to seek further clarifications.

"The judge has arrived. Everyone rises," the court's secretary announces.

The whole judge bench took its seats.

"Before we announce the court's decision, we would like to hear the reason the prosecution had brought the result of bloodstain at the apartment of Amina only recently," the lead judge asked the prosecution's lawyer.

"Your Honour, we have verified the integrity of the evidence that convicts Haile. It took a while to go through the number of documents and other items that showed his guilt. Only when Amina turned herself in, we started and looked seriously into the evidence which stood against her. The motive and the bloodstain became stronger evidence day after day. Besides, we also considered the Rohypton rape drug at both Amina's and Hussein's apartments."

"These pieces of evidence overtook the significance of those that incriminated Haile. That's all, Your Honour," the prosecution explains.

"The court confirms and decides that Amina attempted to murder her boyfriend, Hussein. She will stay behind bars for four years without parole. Her sentence starts from the day she entered prison. This case has ended," the lead judge declares. Her judgment showed the critical and significant correlation between a primary suspect in an investigation case and the trial's guilt conclusion.

CHAPTER FIVE - Life Started Over

Interconnection

Dae has some interest in history, particularly about past relations between her country Pobe and Meng. She knows that at one time, Meng occupied Pobe. As a power that conquered the land, Meng committed many crimes against Pobean nationals and their country as a whole. She wants to find out from her friend Aimi what she thinks of the past conflictual relations between their two countries. She hopes to get out of the discussion a way to assess their mutual friendship. If they share similar views on the topic, their relationship could grow from there, but if they disagree, its strength could be shaken up, take a dent and would need to be mended for their friendship to carry on. They embark into the discussion one afternoon, the time of a picnic they organised in Shinjuku Gyoen National Garden."What do you think of the historical relations between our two countries?" Dae asks Aimi when they finish their sandwiches, a set of sushi rolls, some fruits and lemonade they had packed for their lunch in the park.

"Historical topics belong to the past. Therefore, please don't be surprised by my vague answers," Aimi replies.

"I hope you don't set me a trap!" she adds.

"Not at all! Why would I? As a friend, I only want to hear your interpretation of the relations that prevailed before world war two," Dae provides time-sensitive boundaries to help Aimi in her reply.

"But before I answer your question, can I ask one as well?" Aimi responds to Dae.

"Sure. Go ahead," Dae replies.

"Why history," Aimi asks.

"Some people like animals, enjoy swimming or singing; why shouldn't I like history? Interests come as diverse as nobody can imagine. If one can unleash the lid of taboos on human wants or desires, there would be some surprises," Dae explains her choice of interest.

"Interesting," as if Aimi felt that way as well.

"You must have a zeal for history. I suppose you might always see the world around you through the lens of the past," Aimi adds.

"But without a past, people have no reference to be proud of or hang on to move forward confidently," Dae elaborates for Aimi.

"We come from the past, and part of who we become today constitute luggage we carry consciously or without knowing," Dae continues.

"I don't think I have a passion as such for history, but only a vivid interest in the matter," Dae clarifies.

"Otherwise, I won't do film production as my specialisation."

"Right! To answer your initial question, from what I learned at school, read for my interest, plus a personal understanding, Meng has been a military and economic power for a long time in the region. Aware of such status of dominance, it used it to its advantage, sometimes abused it at the expense of the conquered people and nations it dealt with," Aimi explains. She tries to be broad, sound objective, and avoid specific details.

"I couldn't agree more. You should've become a diplomat. As I listen to your answer, it sounds typical of what my dad, a professional diplomat, would've given to a similar question," Dae replies.

Dae didn't pursue the discussion topic, as they moved to other subjects more mundane and less important. She was satisfied with Aimi's answer.

She didn't want to dwell on her ancestors' specific mistreatments in the hands of the Meng occupants.

She also belonged to the new generation, which had more interest in an optimistic future where sad occurrences of the past wouldn't take place. That was at least her expectation.

The bond between Dae and Aimi grew stronger with time. Their friendship continued even after they graduated.

When Dae moved to Vodnak, she stayed in touch with Aimi, and every two years, each time she travelled back to Okyto, which constituted her second home after Pobe, she ensured to visit her. It was true; she had spent an important part of her life mainly in Meng. Her parents lived and planned to retire in that country. Many of her friends lived there. Besides, even her changed social status, from single to married, followed by being a divorcee, almost as a natural sequence of life events, which all as well took place there, didn't modify the relationship with her closest friend.

***

Dae got drawn towards Aimi's family, firstly because of the friendship the two young ladies shared, although, most importantly, she got attracted like a magnet to the kindness she discovered in her friend's mother. The father seemed like a kind of a thinker, but he also ran a business. When Dae thought of Aimi's mother, she looked back and found that she had never seen a human being who cared as much as she did about people around them and those who came to them.

On their first visit, Dae and Aimi, whose surname is Sato, both arrived at the Taketoyo station of Kanage city at 4:00 p.m. Aimi's mother waited there to pick them.

On that occasion, Dae notices a unique trait about her. She projects around her a kind of aura challenging to describe. As a consequence, Dae comes to envy her friend. In comparison, her mother behaved like a tough woman cold-hearted without much sensitivity while dealing with human emotions.

"I would like you to stay home and practise your instrument over the weekend. Your school plan includes a music assessment for next week. For that reason, I will keep your mobile phone until I come back. In case of emergency, use the landline telephone. As for your dinner, you know where to find the food." Dae's mum usually gives her several instructions on most weekends.

In such absences, she attends functions, but at the same time, she wants to have a grip on her daughter's life as a way to guide her in her youth years, like any other teenager. Dae, at the time, felt eager to be with her friends. Instead, she thinks her mother keeps her held as a prisoner.

Though she didn't lack any material things while growing up, her parents didn't live with her all the time; consequently, a particular emotional gap had gradually developed. In the end, it affected their normal relationship. It didn't have to be that way between a parent and her child. Luckily, the overall outcome didn't lead to any abnormal situation, which would've fundamentally jeopardised her relationship with her parents. Despite the hardship, she feels in her heart occasionally, and though generally optimistic, Dae never contemplates giving up on life or getting suicidal thoughts.

However, she remembers once that she ran away from home. On that occasion, she stayed with a friend for three days, but when she finished her allowance, she timidly came back and apologised to her parents.

She said that she had let them down and made them worried. She showed them how much she regretted what she did and promised never to repeat it.

Aimi, on her part, doesn't have any siblings. Consequently, since she lives as one only child for her family, she got lucky that her parents channelled all their love into her.

The mother looks like a late forties' woman. Tall, athletic, she always wears trendy outfits. In the business circle of the district she lives in, her peers nicknamed her the Empress of Kanage. A born networker, she organises many business events related to her sector of activity. Somehow well known, and with an MBA qualification from a Gansian university on her belt, she helps her husband run their hospitality business. She supervises the department of strategy and development.

More of a charismatic person than her husband, she would be proven in the years to come when she would be in charge of the business.

Her family has its origins in the ancient Okyto. Part of the nobility of that city, her ancestors, had moved to the Kanage district when Okyto declined and lost its fame and preeminence to Takado.

A heated dispute about inheritance in the family had occurred; her direct ancestor, six generations before her, decided to come and settle in the current district where they lived. He willingly avoided Okyto because he wanted to be away from all the relatives who resided in that area.

The ancestor in question had grown up in a well-off family and married Aimi's mother's great-great-grandfather, the son of a great merchant in the Kanage district. The latter led, at the time, as chairman of the local chamber of commerce and owned several businesses.

She had initially met him at a function they both attended at the time. After one year of dating, they got married in front of their respective families and friends.

***

368

In those days, while Dae attended the Okyto University of the Arts, another girl initially became her acquaintance, her best friend. Aimi came from a Meng family.

A student with a model's body and gracious manners, with an average height for her age, her beauty and charm immediately strike; she grabbed Dae's attention when she first saw her. Over time, her character traits became more apparent once one came to know her more closely.

Her clothes generally had a casual outlook, without any specific style of reference. They appeared cheap and straightforward. Her make-up looked low-key yet sophisticated. Dae, too, didn't value the importance of appearances. However, she enjoyed the outlook of a nicely dressed woman.

Dae enjoyed reading. The range of books she had read seemed diverse. She had a particular interest in historical classics about ancient Pobe and Meng. She knew a lot about ancient Egyptian mythology and the emperors who oversaw the building of the majestic pyramids. Unlike her friend Aimi, she knew, for example, Cleopatra VII, the last Egyptian empress and talked broadly about Toutankhamon and his wife Ankhesenamun or their entourage, plus the main achievements of his rule.

She appeared confident but avoided expressing her confidence. She didn't want to attract people's attention, and consequently, this attitude meant she took time before she intervened in any situation. In her mind, she initially weighed the pros and cons.

As a result, she became respected among her peer group, which included boys and girls. They thought she always looked considerate of other people's feelings or views.

She had a birthmark in the form of a letter V, well graphically and naturally designed into her skin, located at the top of her chest.

If someone stood in front of her, they could see it slightly on the left side and one inch down from her chin. The mark had made her peers nickname her the V-Girl. That didn't embarrass her. Instead, she considered it a plus to her overall outlook, like a beauty mark. She didn't take any measures to hide it when she chose her clothes or necklaces to wear.

The first year, when Dae registered for uni, she decided to live in a student dorm near her campus, though she could've stayed with her parents if she wanted. She commuted for only one-hour maximum. She wanted to experience and live her adult freedom independently, away from the family. Despite her overall confident and assertive personality, she didn't make any new friends that year.

Aimi became Dae's classmate in her master's programme. Though the first year had ended without any particular or noticeable incident, she had used it to adapt herself to uni life.

Her experience as a high school boarder helped enormously, particularly with the necessary amount of discipline required to study, focus and succeed. Hence, she progressed in her university years without any significant problem.

Dae can't recall what initially attracted her to Aimi. However, some aspects could explain in a way part of the nature of their relationship. Except for two other girls, who also did the same courses as they did, the rest of their cohort did fewer subjects together. Only one academic subject they both didn't attend together.

Both girls scored above the average in their selected topics. However, they didn't share any lessons where they stood out, and people considered them top performers.

Of the same age, they had come into the universe in the same month, with a few days of difference. On top of that, Aimi stood as the kind of girl that others wanted to befriend.

Animals and their ways of life excited her. She would observe an ant on a table and the way it moves and not get rid of it, but instead, she would eventually focus and remove any obstacle which would affect its movement.

Since she also did her masters in film production, she dreamed of producing manga movies that featured Meng characters and Suan cowboys of the early years of SU's discovery by the Europeans. While still young, Aimi had been fascinated by Suan cowboys' movies.

Though not the type of beauty to turn heads, Aimi had that kind of attractiveness that widely compensated for any disadvantage she might have on other fronts of her personality. She played exceptionally well as the moderator in conversations. She made everyone who participated in a discussion feel essential. Charismatic and liked by some girls, many of her friends considered her reliable and independently minded. She let nobody walk over her, whoever they could be. She knew how to set boundaries for anyone who would approach her, whatever their appearance.

On some free weekends, Dae and Aimi would travel together to Kanage, where the latter grew up. On a Saturday, they both took the train from Okyto to the city where her parents lived. Aimi had told them that she would come home with a Pobean friend. The trip lasted only one hour. Her mother went to the Taketoyo station to pick them up when they arrived.

In Okyto, where Dae and Aimi live while studying, one stays in student accommodation, affordable, but without all the comfort that private apartments offer. Dae students' rooms accommodate three to four students each. All the first-year students live in those.

The congested character of the atmosphere doesn't allow a lot of closeness between residents. Though girls live separated from boys. In the second year, students move into the studios of two residents each.

Dae chose to live in a students' dorm, not because her parents, who worked as diplomats, couldn't afford a private studio for their daughter. She wanted to know more about the majority of the university students' real-life conditions, not those of the wealthy minority to which she belonged.

Her peer student could have thought that she and her friend Aimi didn't have much of a concern. Unfortunately, like anybody else human, they couldn't be worry-free. Everyone only carries on and does their best to keep on living.

***

Asahi Aratani, Aimi's father, owns and manages a local hospitality company in Kanage. The family had run that business for three generations. That evening, the whole family has dinner together with Dae as their guest.

"So you work as well in films like our Aimi?" Asahi Aratani asks. He sounds optimistic about the profession his daughter pursues, and he somehow shows his pride in that.

Dae's academic interests coincided with those of Aimi, his daughter.

"Yes, I am," Dae replies without hesitation.

"What do you want to specialise in to further your career in that sector," Asahi asks again.

"I would like to actualise the traditions that modernity tries to erase either intentionally or ignore," Dae replies.

"It's the same as Aimi, who wants to incorporate Suan cowboys characteristics in our manga. Don't you think so?" Asahi seeks approval from the guest Dae.

"Yes, it is, but with a twist," Dae replies.

"Let me explain. I wouldn't do that personally. I fear or predict a shock of cultures of which it would be difficult to measure the impact. On the other hand, such a culture shock would not occur if one brings back Meng strong values or artefacts from the past and revives and or adapts them to the present times. Contemporary culture has those elements already available but in a dormant state; the spotlight would focus on their comeback. There won't be any major cultural conflict to make them accepted or acceptable by the younger generation because the old one has been around as a keeper. The process could smoothen the betterment of that past or facilitate the transition. What had been absent until then seems to be the lack of a channel for expression or a voice," Dae explains how she sees her strong interest in the regeneration of the traditions in the film production sector that evolves continuously.

"Allow me to agree and disagree at the same time," Aimi intervenes while she looks at Dae.

"The old generation could play an important role, as a solid bridge to facilitate the transition from the past to the present. This understanding seems equally accurate for national traditions. In the case of foreign traditions to incorporate in our contemporary artwork - I mean manga in my circumstances -, from the shock of culture you mentioned, what would emerge seems unknown with certainty, at least at my level.

Who knows if the outcome would be negative? No one. I value such risk, given the possible gains, if one could call the outcome that way.

Like for an exploratory journey, the project leader or the commissioner can't be certain about what to expect, though, through the effort and the risk taken, new channels to advance humankind would emerge," Aimi responds broadly to Dae's views.

***

In the first and timely encounter that initiated their relationship, Dae approached Aimi and asked if they could exchange their contact details. They gave them out to each other without hesitation. They both eagerly expected, as divinely instructed, for that moment. Past their exchange, they talked about many things that got forgotten with time.

Dae safeguarded in her memory - cautiously and with much clarity - the atmosphere of their conversation. They remembered how enthusiastic they had felt when they had finally connected. It looked like an opportunity that was meant to happen and grow in happiness when that time materialised. When they separated after that moment, they looked positively forward to the blossom of their newly found friendship.

When Aimi started to like Dae, she got interested in the fact that their personalities appeared compatible and complementary.

They seemed to like similar things. When their parents' pocket money allowed, they offered themselves a lovely meal in some chic restaurants of Okyto in the Ganzi district once in a while. Though they both studied film production, they didn't excessively enjoy watching movies because their teachers recommended learning purposely. That meant that they had watched a lot of films as part of their studies.

They only went to watch a movie when a close friend insisted and wanted them around.

They liked the arts in general, particularly film production, and the ingenuity that characterised its processes to capture human sensitivities and communicate specific messages to audiences.

"Have you seen Jack's typewriter from The Shining, a film by Stanley Kubrick?" Aimi asks suddenly.

"Unfortunately, I have not. What does it talk about?" Dae replies but shows as well some interest in the question.

"Human creativity has reached extraordinary heights in this particular case when one looks at that described machine and considers where the world stands today in terms of tools and signs to communicate. We can enjoy all the benefits from such technological advances," Aimi expresses her amazement and reflects on the impression that the view of the machine in that movie gave her.

"But typewriters or their contemporary replacements don't constitute the only sophisticated inventions around," Dae refutes.

"I concede that but when I saw it in that movie, a kind of interest rose in me about the object and where we came from in terms of communication through written symbols," Aimi replies.

Some distance away from a french-style restaurant where they had agreed to have their dinner separated the two friends, Dae and Aimi. The place stood as the cosmopolitan part of Okyto in the Ganzi district.

"Yesterday I reserved a table for two, but I forgot, and I had a late lunch today. I want to skip dinner," Dae announces on the phone to Aimi, who, in the meantime, prepares herself to leave her apartment and meet her for their planned outing.

"You should cancel the reservation since I don't feel hungry. Let's meet and find where to have a light cocktail with snacks instead," Aimi suggests.

Their friendship grew as they spent more time together. From time to time, Dae invites Aimi to her parents' house in Ebisu. She has already been there twice.

Aimi has also hosted her friend once at their home in Kanage. Since it's far away from Okyto, they can't visit each other as often as they want. Aimi wishes her friend to discover all the right places and things about her city of birth.

***

Aimi graduates and enters the Meng film production sector as she has planned for many years. Her sublime work would use manga to tell stories of the shared loneliness and the alleviation of isolation. She wants such stories to transcend cultural barriers; convey thoughts and ideas far more refined than words alone would come to the global audience.

Manga specialists at the time immensely innovated in creativity and took risky jumps into new territories. Some specialised studios produce animated versions of the work of creators of stories. Other niches focus on books that narrate the same stories and get this time distributed as visual materials. The most acclaimed manga producers of the new era manage to combine current affairs and fiction. In specific contexts, the audience - viewers and readers - can hardly separate the two worlds. Both genres look cleverly intertwined.

They can tap into their creativity for targeted issues, if necessary, and make manga producers easily influence or manipulate the collective national conscience towards a desirable direction.

They could see the possibility they carried, with its social and political impacts. Consequently, Meng powerful interest groups bought major and influential studios to control them; they intended to use the power of persuasion of their productions to manipulate opinions for their interests.

After three years of graduating, Aimi has accumulated significant intelligence and experience from her sector.

With the money from her parents, she bought most shares in a small but specialised manga studio through which she creates, develops her brand and markets her craft.

Aimi was in her sixth year after graduation and worked in the film sector. With her manga release of 'Kanage,' a title borrowed from the name of her native city, and features Meng cowboys at the conquest of the Raassa desert and countries in Qarfi, she won the first prize of the film industry in Meng. With such acclaim on her belt, she didn't look back. She experienced success after success year after year. When her father retires, she decides to appoint a cousin to run the family hospitality business.

All those years, Dae, who hasn't been as successful as her friend in her field of work, has in the meantime encountered difficult times, which have seen her marriage fall apart. Luckily, a Vodnak police investigation in a criminal incident she had participated in left her off the hook, despite her active involvement. That investigation failed technically to link her to an attempted murder in which she had been a critical accomplice.

From The Closet

That weekend comes as one of many that Hussein and Amina have spent time together. There has been the death of an aunt in the boyfriend's family. His mother calls him, and he gets the sad news. Amina knows well how Hussein lived in close relation with the deceased, despite the distance which occasionally separates them at moments. She decides to call and comfort him.

"Did you know that our colleague lost a close relative two days ago?" Amina heard from a mutual friend at the start of that week.

Two weeks have passed since, and the official grief period has ended. Hussein, who has grown up firmly attached to her aunt, finds it hard to let it go. The death of the deceased takes a toll on him unexpectedly. It's unusual. Among his friends, they picture him as usually emotionless. Amina suggests an outing.

She takes him to visit a place in the east part of Vodnak city. They can see all the important landmarks the QK capital offers to its cosmopolitan visitors from that location. With a relaxed and joyful gaze on his face, while he looks at the scenery, Hussein appears as if he genuinely enjoys the moment. In a way, that's the aim for them to come out as Amina envisaged it. After the viewing, they went to relax in a coffee bar close to where they were.

"I know you feel sad, but time has, time and time again, been the best cure for the human pain," Amina interrupts Hussein, whose mind shows some amazement through his face. She tries to uplift his spirit.

For Hussein, her deceased aunt featured in an ancient world where humans behaved as decent beings, a world different from his contemporary times. He had never seen her shout for whatever reason one could imagine.

Soft-spoken, she always praised her husband for all his endeavours. Hussein considered her close to sainthood when he didn't picture her as a living saint in his eyes.

"It's not that I struggle emotionally because of my aunt's passing, but the unfairness of life or death if you think about it. She's only fifty-four," Hussein lets out his regrets.

"I try to understand, though it could sound irrational to pretend that I do. Nevertheless, two things constitute milestones' in people's lives, and I think I fully grasp the central part of their meaning, and for both, nobody can't plan or control. Birth and death live on an unexplored island in the universe. Understandably, things would be different if people commit suicide and pretend to control how and when they die. Although death manifests itself under that format, individual fate has taken over the handle and manoeuvres on peoples' behalf. Even if these two components of our human nature stand out of our reach, though we could not try to master them, we should not let ourselves be over-preoccupied with them," Amina tries to reason with Hussein on his grief.

After they finished their chat about that issue, they appeared not to have any other topic to discuss. Amina tries to come up with different themes without much success. Hussein seems absent-minded. On this occasion, he has no interest in the centre stage. Within ten minutes, they empty their glasses and head home. Hussein drives Amina to her place and says goodbye, unceremoniously. The next few days he becomes more and more introverted. He starts to drink at home and avoids his friends who want to comfort him.

He calls in instead a woman he had known for a while. Out of respect for Amina, he ensures that she doesn't become suspicious of what goes on.

In the four weeks between his aunt's death and the day he falls victim to attempted murder on his person, he has been incapable of finding a mentally comfortable place for himself. The new woman he sleeps with or the alcohol he takes intensively doesn't help reduce his deep sadness as the days pass, his dejection of life as a whole increase.

Surprisingly, it's on one of such days that Amina's sister visited him for the second time, with an objective to deadly punish him for his abuses against women, and from which her twin sister has suffered as well.

***

Florencia comes out as lesbian one night, half drunk and half asleep. She does it for herself, to feel at ease from then on. The attitude of the general public towards people like her, still hostile, had gradually changed favourably. A few years back, she had entered into an unofficial marriage with a male husband, who turned out to be indifferent to the necessary care for his spouse. From her adoptive Muslim family, she understood that getting married and having children was the only right path to pursue in life for a normal and respectable woman.

Once she becomes an adult, for years, she suffers privately and struggles with her sexuality. Not to have children, she takes it as a blessing. At times she wonders how she would've coped if she had to take care of children and deal at the same time with her insecurities.

To have failed in her heterosexual marriage, she wants to explore other parts of her personality. In the past, she felt compelled to suppress her attraction to women because of the social stigma attached to intimacy manifesting between individuals of the same gender. To move in and live with Dae has been the initial step to self-affirmation.

380

Luckily she doesn't get harassed because of who she represents. She lives in a western country where a minimum of human rights to abide by, and overall tolerance towards diversity in people prevail. The law, through the state's institutions, almost guarantees and enforces them in practice.

After some years, Florencia and Dae become close friends. They decide to live together as partners. They find love away from men and live happily while counting on the accumulated wisdom gained over the years.

Dae has matured. Henceforth, after her divorce, she knows what she wants from life. Florencia occasionally uses her listener's personality type and appreciates her broad knowledge about some areas no one could imagine. That weekend, Haile spends time with the two women on a night out.

"This time, you sound like a philosopher," Florencia expresses the depth of her partner's reflection. While Haile speaks to her, he had elaborated on a point they both had different views.

"Listen. I could effectively be one. Who knows?"

"Proud as an ex somebody's wife, I once got married in a heterosexual couple, and have now turned partner in a same-sex relationship. The wealth of knowledge I accumulated in those different life experiences effectively puts me on the same pedestal as the one for philosophers or thinkers," she explains.

***

Though he recalls his rare interactions with Florencia and reflects on some people's significant character traits, Haile remembers that she could demonstrate acute excellence in liars' type without any remorse.

He has his lunch with his colleague Sarah in the college cafeteria where both teach. He discusses her views about the issue of lying.

"What do you think of liars as people," Sarah asks suddenly.

"They have chosen a way to communicate with the rest of us - in case I don't seem to belong to their group - which makes them untrustworthy.

Consequently, to try and listen to them could be a waste of someone's time and theirs as well. Hence, the best solution to live in contexts where they navigate would be to cut off any interaction with them," Haile explains.

"And what if the liar appeared to be a close relative someone lives with!" Sarah highlights.

"In those circumstances, you must only count on the hope that perhaps the expected lies would turn out to be truths. Hence one needs to constantly look out and scrutinise what they put on the arena of truth. In the case someone has been seriously harmed as a consequence of the lies from a relative, there should be a time when they cut all relations with them becomes the ultimate solution," Haile replies.

The time to go back to their classrooms has come. Haile and Sarah returned in front of their students for the afternoon session.

In the case of Florencia that Haile knows through Amina - the latter talked about her twin while they jog together -, one would sum up that more lies than truths thrive in whatever she says. Numerous instances abound where Amina has, for example, caught her while she expressed unthinkable or unverifiable facts to deceive her listeners. It became nearly impossible for anyone besides her to distinguish truth from lies she speaks out.

"I lost connection and full sense about whatever I say," she uttered once. Her assertion didn't refer to how she forgot about something, but the truthfulness of what she said.

At one point in time, she must've also been confused herself when she felt obliged to distinguish what she has put out as truths and keep them as such with time. Consequently, what happens with constant liars, translates in that they lose track of things they lied about and when they come back to them. Instead, they went along because they feared losing the friendship they shared.

The liars had been in bed with the lie for an extended period that the truth for them had become foreign or strange, like a young man who experiences war their entire life and then one-day peace comes. It becomes hard for them to adjust. They have to unlearn many things for them to survive. The process appears as hard as when it's in troubled times, if not more.

In the past, the liars who, by the intensity of their lies, had astonished Haile. These liars appear to possess in their brain a continuous and unbreakable operation centre to fabricate them. He shared that opinion with his friends in the academic world who worked in psychological studies.

He learned that the monstrosity or lightness of expressed lies depends on many variables from his trusted sources. These include the liar's unique personality, their ultimate intention of self-preservation or harm to others, the context in which they tell their lies, and how they get worded or vocally expressed.

Florencia features in the category of those liars who lie about important things and for whom lie detectors become ineffective in front of the displayed prowess in that matter. Sometimes they don't mean to lie, but lies come naturally to them. That group of liars can also lie about small things.

Since they excel in the former type of lies, they also perform more comfortably when it comes to the latter.

The difficulty in identifying and denouncing those lies resides in their repetitive frequency and deliberate or almost conscious expression by their authors. A costly system to monitor, uncover and punish to enforce right-eousness against the perpetrators would be required to deter anyone of that category from lying. People general-ly accept to live in a world of lies and almost deliberately decline to consider their deterrence to be a priority in the face of their other primary existential needs.

The liars Haile have encountered in his not yet extended life have no guilty conscience at all. They lie about all considerations of life. Stories of lies that hap-pen in a variety of settings populate their periods of sleep. Issues highlighted in those moments cover a broad spectrum of themes. There, people lie continuously to and about others. They don't show any signs of caring about the consequences of their selfish wrongdoings.

Their victims - disempowered or only dead as one unfortunate outcome - often amount to millions of peo-ple. Such situations occur when the perpetrators lie from important positions of political, economic or religious authority. These lies with deadly consequences seem sometimes not confined to specific countries' bound-aries.

They also appear in every category of society, rich or poor, educated or illiterate, male or female, religious or atheist, and foreign or resident. From this understand-ing, to lie could be seen as one of the critical common denominators among human beings. Even those institu-tions of which official missions set to root out lies ap-pear corrupted to the extent that their responsible use covert tactics - which transpire as a kind of lies by omis-sion - hide their inefficiencies.

Florencia lies about time and promises. Though, for example, she can announce to accomplish a specific task at any given time, she would complete it at some other time whenever she chooses or ignores it completely. She doesn't care, like many self-centred personalities. Amina complains all the time about her because of her lies. They appear to be her way of life. Her sister has lost any trust in her. One of the many consequences of those lies was that Amina herself started to copy her, live and lie as a modus operandi. In the confined world of the two twin sisters, lying appeared to be contagious.

***

On an ordinary Sunday, free from any urgent academic assignment, Dae decides to visit Aimi. She takes the train to Ueno Station and arrives at the nearest station thirty minutes later. Aimi lives in a private studio. Her father, an average businessman, rents it at half the market price. Aimi's uncle has an estate business, and that's how the studio can be cheap to accommodate his niece.

When Dae enters her apartment, she immediately expresses her surprise.

"How could someone of my age rent such a luxurious place. Your family must be in the money."

"Not true! Though I consider myself and our family as working-class people. Neither rich nor poor, we can't afford to buy property in the Ganzi district. To be frank with you, my father comes from a modest background. I think he has enough money saved up, but he lives a frugal life. As for this studio, he made a deal with my uncle, who runs an estate business. As a result, we only pay him half of the market rent price."

"I see," Dae replies as if she understands to what extent her father went while he negotiated the rent deal with her uncle.

"Will you inherit your father's business when he retires?" Dae asks Aimi suddenly.

"I can't tell since I haven't read his dispositions on the matter. At this stage, I hesitate about his intentions. The business itself looks complex and constitutes a challenge for an outsider. If you think about it, no aspect of life comes ever simple. It's all about the capacity to overcome personal struggles. My plan about what you said consists initially in pursuing my interests, especially with my studies. At the same time, I will spend some time at my father's business and learn about it. If my interest area doesn't work out as expected - I will give it five to ten years after graduation, then I will stop and join the family business.

In the opposite scenario, where I might do well with the film production, I will inherit the family company but appoint professional managers to run it. I wouldn't want to sell the legacy to outsiders," Aimi responds.

"That sounds like a well thought through plan," Dae replies, impressed by the clarity of her friend's foresight. On her side, she thinks of what she will inherit from her own family. She knows that they own some properties: land and estates, but in Pobe. Surprisingly, they have only one two-bedroom apartment in Okyto that they rent out. They have spent thirty years in Niasan. When they retire, they plan to live the rest of their lives in that country.

She promises to ask the difficult question about inheritance to her father in due course.

"Have you ever imagined your name not being in the will of your parents as their heir?" Dae asks after a short period of pausing.

"What a silly question you ask there!"

"No. Seriously! I haven't heard of anyone I know or from my family who didn't inherit from their parents. Though we read or watch on television and in movies about such situations," Dae clarifies for her friend.

"I don't expect my name not to be in my dad's will. Why should I imagine such a scenario? I don't either see him with such thoughts or even dream about that," Aimi reacts and argues thoroughly with her friend.

"When that happens, it generally emerges as a consequence of a bad relationship between the supposed heir and the parent," Dae highlights. In this scenario, she assumes that there hadn't been any problem between Aimi and her father.

"I can predict what might happen in particular circumstances; a parent can disown a child in the interests of the latter and put the management of the inheritance in the hands of a third party to ensure that the heir gets all that they need for their primary needs.

The third-party only gets involved if the heir has some proven incapacity to look after themselves and their assets, but this doesn't look like my case," Aimi puts forward a strong argument to prove her point.

"Let's agree that generally when a parent leaves a child out of their will, it's because their consideration of the child's competence to look after their future has become questionable. Extreme cases occur when the child gets completely disowned, most of the time, this comes as a sort of punishment for their damageable behaviour for the family," Dae explains and refers to cases she remembered from related movies she watched.

They don't talk only about inheritance during Dae's visit. They agreed that they would return together to the campus the next day. They had plenty of time to chill out in Aimi's neighbourhood. After they visit a local park and take a small snack nearby, they decide to go further and spend a few hours at an Iwaeton nightclub in the multicultural district of Kuoel.

They enjoy their late night out with drinks, and they dance moderately as well. By 11:00 pm, they return to Aimi's studio to rest for the next day. The earliest lecture started at 10:00 am.

Life And Death

Dae's birthday was approaching. Invitations to old and new friends had been already out. A week or so has passed. The story of Amina's release from prison features far in the past. It looks as if it didn't happen since many have forgotten what it entailed, particularly the twists in the guilty plea from different and involved personalities interested as outcomes' beneficiaries.

More than a year has passed. A life post-imprisonment appears to take place steadily. She has opted to become more of a housewife who supports and enjoys her partner Haile's success. Two of his books became bestsellers, with a million copies sold each. He has bought a big mansion in the Vodnak suburb where he invites and entertains his guests.

However, there seems to be no special ceremony for Dae's anniversary, despite the invitations. She has invited her guests to come and enjoy time together. It's a social event like any other. She wants it to be like a party where guests end up in one's mood because they are in that space and enjoy each other's company. Birthdays weren't her thing, though many people do consider them to be. Some of her past anniversaries had passed without her noticing. On such occasions, it had been her friends who reminded her about them. Between conversations, the host approaches Amina.

"Hey, I've known you for many years, but we've never been close. Not intentionally, please believe me. I have been more attracted to your sister. By special connection," she chats with her mainly while she refers to the bond that she and Florencia share.

"Yes, I know this has been the case. I don't have any issue with that. Things ended the way they came to be. Frankly, nobody should worry if they think they need to," Amina soothes the atmosphere, though she sounds a little bold but also indifferent.

She recalls from her memory how Dae has been the accomplice of her sister in her boyfriend's attempted murder. She still has some unfounded resentment at the back of her mind.

Several years have undoubtedly passed.

"Could whatever go on in the past and related to that matter be forever buried?" This quest remains one unclear point Amina has on her mind while she talks to Dae. Nonetheless, she can't stop herself to consider that if Florencia hadn't found encouragement and support from Dae, maybe the attempted murder on Hussein and then his ultimate death would've never happened. Her whole life had taken a radical transformation after the turn of all those events. She couldn't help it, not come back to that sad past; it happened each time she interacted with her. Though they had both made up, Florencia was one of the people who, at one time, had negatively impacted her life.

"Let's not dwell on the past too much. I only made a blunt statement on our relationship, if I could call it that way. No bad feelings at all," Dae replies calmly. She slowly directs her attention to a couple that stood and chatted at her right. The couple held their glasses of wine and were in the middle of their conversation.

"Excuse me, I need to talk to that friend I used to work with," Dae tells Amina, though she tries only to get away from her.

***

When Aimi's father dies, Dae becomes the first Aimi informed outside the family circle, as her best friend. By that time, Dae lived in Vodnak with her partner Florencia.

"For many years, I have been close to Aimi's family. Practically, it has been since our time together at the university," she had once told a friend. The latter seemed interested in her relationship with Aimi.

More than ten years had passed.

When Dae graduated, she worked in Okyto for a few years before she moved to Vodnak. After her relocation, every two years without failure, Dae returned to Niasan to visit her parents and childhood's acquaintances. They included Aimi's family.

Dae and Florencia, her life partner for a few years, agreed to attend the funeral together. They would have to travel to Kanage, Chita District. As a business owner, the business community of that city knew Aimi's father well.

Further to her successful work in the manga production sector, Aimi had already made her name in the entire Niasan. She was only in her thirties. Both his father and herself had connections with different broad networks, and as a result of that, the funeral would be a big event. To cope with its size and importance, the family called upon a specialised agency to help arrange it to make things run smoothly.

After the funeral, Aimi stays at the family home for a few days. She made arrangements to ensure that Dae and her partner Florencia remained comfortably there as well. It's on the first day after the funeral, around 4:00 pm. Aimi joins the couple in the family's garden. They take tea and biscuits, chat and wait for dinner in a few hours.

The events of the previous day hang on everyone's mind. On their part, Florencia and Dae have both been involved personally with death when they attempted to murder Hussein. They got close, but they got him in a permanent coma, though he died later on under different circumstances.

Understandably, they don't go around and talk to strangers about their criminal record, but those close to them know well how this whole story affected their lives.

"What do you think of death?" Aimi throws the question to anyone ready to answer but avoids indicating who should respond to it specifically. She didn't proceed that way intentionally.

"Most people find it unfair when one dies young, but also unfair to those who remain when one dies old. The loss in all circumstances can be fundamentally disruptive.

The level of distress depends on the significance of the connections the departed had with the survivors. Age of the departed doesn't enter into the equation in this latter consideration," Amina explains how she understands the question.

"I agree that death constitutes a loss, but not necessarily only in physical terms, though it commonly goes hand in hand with that. I consider that each time we lose an entity we depended on, be it tangible or invisible to the naked eye, an entity that added to our wellbeing, we can also consider it as death. In the particular situation of my first marriage, I can rightly say that I lived with a partner romantically dead. Though I can't tell if he ever lived romantically with anyone else before me," Florencia adds her understanding.

"Generally, our people consider death only as a transition to an afterlife, but which manifests itself in a different form. We presume that our dead carry on living and need food regularly. Not caring for one's death, society considers it a failure of the ancestors' filial duty. From the little I know about other cultures, I think we have the most respectful and considerate people who honour the dead," Aimi explains to her friends. They carried on drinking their tea and chatting about other varied subjects until dark when it became necessary to get inside the house and wait for dinner.

The next day, at dinner time, the whole family gathers. Aimi, her mother, the cousin who runs the hospitality family business, another cousin, both with their wives, Dae and Florencia, take all part.

Though Aimi had inherited the family business from her father, the deed that entitles her to the leading shareholder position also stated that her mother would always be the company's chairwoman as long as she would be alive.

This statement implied that she was the one to authorise issues related to ownership.

It also meant that practically, with the father's death, the mother automatically became the family's head and the ultimate leader of its hospitality business.

That evening, participants at their dinner altogether avoided discussing topics of significant interest. Expect the information Aimi's mother gives out when she mentions that the family business would from then on expand more globally than it did before. That came as unusual. In the past, the father had categorically prohibited talking about the family business while they had their dinner. Thus she already departed from the habits of the household.

She wants to seek future assistance from both Dae and Florencia, who already live in Vodnak, a country featured among the richest on the planet. They willingly accept help in due course. Random jokes about people who lived in different places also got exchanged—how Dae and Florencia had met to become a couple appeared to be the only subject of interest. Their story started an inquiry into how anyone around the table had met their partner.

One of Aimi's cousins first saw her wife at a train station while heading to a public toilet. He, too, on his part, was going to the men's restroom.

He recalled love at first sight. Though he feared that he couldn't find her since she rapidly entered the women's public toilets. Therefore, the cousin held it in and remained at the entrance and waited for her to come out. Luckily for him, she didn't stay long. He approached her and talked to her. At the time, he marketed products and did public surveys for a big Malaysian pharmaceutical company.

"Excuse me. My parents named me Kim Ji-Hoo. We currently run a public survey. We pay fifty dollars to anyone who answers a few questions related to our study," he said while he handed a survey form to the young woman.

"How long does it take to fill it in?"

"Five minutes while totally focused, and ten minutes while not, then consider the fact that in those few minutes, you could earn five times what the average worker earns within a whole hour."

The woman didn't give it a second thought. She immediately took the form from the hands of Kim Ji-Hoo, almost as if she feared that he might change his mind and not let her have it. That became their first encounter, and their relationship took off from there. They then got married. One child now. They have been together for five years.

***

Few years have passed. Within all that time, Amina and Haile have been neighbours. The friendship they developed has been like therapy for each one involved. The openness that transpired through their conversation touched their well-being positively. "Give and take" kind of lifestyle characterised their relationship.

They learn from each other and help one another. Amina appears lacking in following through with her personally prescribed diet. Haile, on his part, struggles with his eating, but in reverse order. He lacks appetite, while Amina has a lot of it. He benefits from her advice on how to improve his eating.

"I've missed you. What has been happening? You have given many excuses to not come out for our regular walks in the park," Haile sermons Amina when she skips, for example, for a week or more their routines together in the park.

For an entire month, Amina doesn't reply to Haile's calls every other day to go jogging. She responds - when she does from time to time - and says that she suffered some depression.

Since Amina lives alone and occasionally gets visits from a relative who would sleep over once in a while, all this situation didn't constitute a practical arrangement to address her emotional vulnerability. She grew up in an environment characterised by not enough love from her parents. Thus, she always needed someone to keep her company to feel mentally stable and safe.

"Is there any support that I could provide if need be?" Haile offers in those particular periods when she feels stressed. He fears that some dire predicament could happen.

"I will let you know, but for now, I feel alright. Still, you can come for a cup of coffee, and if you want, we will watch a movie together," Amina often replies to Haile's concern about her.

In the past, Haile had requested from Amina a copy of her keys. It was further to the story of a friend whose relative had been found dead in his apartment after six days. He took those measures to prevent a similar incident from happening.

If he called Amina and didn't respond after several calls over a reasonable time, he envisaged going and opening her apartment to find out her situation. To address her loneliness, she finds different alternatives.

Amina reads regularly good newspapers; she avoids tabloids deliberately as much as she could. The content from the latter adds to her level of anxiety. She goes out to a restaurant with her paper in hand, orders a cup of tea, then spends a whole half-day there. Her attractiveness prompts the clients' restaurant to come to where she sits and initiate a conversation with her. On other occasions, it's the other way around.

While she jogs with Haile, she likes to share with him stories from her conversations with strangers. He would listen attentively for minutes and wouldn't most of the time comment at all. Out of ignorance, in some cases, many topics didn't arouse any interest in his mind. He rarely participated actively in those conversations that they shared between five-thirty and seven-thirty in the morning.

CHAPTER SIX - The Circle Continues

A Future Unfolds

New relationships between those who, in a certain way, got involved in Hussein's attempted murder start to emerge and develop. This change happens when inspector Sizwe and the prosecutor send Amina to prison, and Haile gets released. He remembers the crime that put him in jail and its transfer to a different culprit. The police cleared his name.

While Amina stays in prison, Florencia acquires and runs a prosperous restaurant. She attends several personal development programmes. However, her bad experience with her ex-husband makes her develop a fear of men. Dae, her friend, visits her restaurant regularly to help on days when there are many clients.

Within a few weeks, after the announcement of Amina's sentence and either because of it, Florencia and Dae begin to develop an intimate relationship. The imprisoned twin sister, probably because she wasn't around in her life as before. Florencia's personality became more expressive, showing more openly and freely its inner feelings she had unconsciously hidden to outsiders. She spends her time with Dae and goes out to restaurants and movies. Together they attend a variety of public events and travel to places they have never been before. Life appears more worth its enjoyment than it has been so far. Thus, within a year after Amina's imprisonment, Florencia discussed with her sister if they couldn't rent out the apartment they both owned and in which they had been living. Her desire to move in to live with Dae seems strong at the time. Not like in the case of her ex-husband, it took her enough time to know her partner. In her mind, she could rightly assume knowing her well and trusting her for a life together.

On one Saturday, Dae and Florencia have their dinner in the renovated restaurant that the latter owns and manages. Given the customers' number, Dae doesn't hesitate to put on a prone and help in the kitchen.

Later on, she would work with the waitresses to serve the ordered meals. Once the last customer is out, they go home and arrive at their apartment past ten in the evening. They prepare themselves a tasty meal—a bottle of an excellent Rhenish wine comes along. The next day, Florencia plans to reopen her restaurant after ten in the morning; they agree to have a few more glasses.

"You know what I think when I get drunk! It's late. Let's sleep."

"Will you sleep with me?"

"If you've missed someone in bed, I don't mind becoming your valuable alternative."

"It's true I haven't slept with anyone for many years."

Dae and Florencia had been heterosexual until a few months before. Almost gradually, they had, however, both discovered how comfortable they could be together intimately. Dae had already been into two solid relationships with men. They hadn't ended well for a variety of reasons. In her mind, they constituted something meant to happen, and her life had only been the timeframe for its performance. She doesn't emphasise much that past when someone trustworthy asks her about it. That whole experience remained at the back of her mind all the time, despite her decision to move on.

Her complicity with Florencia in the attempted murder against Hussein has brought them closer to each other. In one of their encounters at Dae's main room, the latter seriously felt her heart race when she looked at Florencia, a few more seconds than usual.

At the time, they watched a tv programme together.

"Please, could you not stare at me like that? You make me feel uncomfortable," Florencia whines.

"Sorry. Please don't feel offended when I say what I have to say," Dae replies.

"I can't get enough of you. You look undeniably beautiful. I think I like you. It's now crystal clearer in my mind than it has ever been in the past. I get flustered by the simple fact of your presence in front of me," Dae adds.

The TV programme while still on, Florencia had asked Dae the initial question, then moved back to focus on the tv screen. She did as if she didn't hear or listen to what Dae said. Every word from their conversation fell clearly in Dae's ears. However, the latter tried to keep it temporarily hidden. She lets it pass and doesn't respond at all to the apparent flattery that came from her friend - she takes it as a kind of seduction attempt. She doesn't even say the usual thank you for the part that requires such a response. Visibly she doesn't want her friend to think that she agrees to whatever she said. Hence she somehow opts to look indifferent, and that offends Dae a little. She reluctantly accepts such an attitude from her friend because she doesn't want to look aggressive to pursue or express her heart's desires or feelings selfishly. If she acted that way, that would jeopardise their strong friendship.

"Forget about what I said. Do as if I didn't mention any of the nonsense I brought out," Dae finally says after she notices that Florencia doesn't want to comment at all about her confession.

After that experience, they have dinner together, then Florencia leaves and goes back to her sister's apartment. The more Dae tries to restrain herself from how she feels about Florencia, the more the feelings stick solidly into her mind.

Only after a few days, did her discomfort ease. From that time onward, she accepts for her benefit that other women attract her more than men do, and she has to live with that part of herself. She doesn't have to try to fight it. She knows there have been some new leaps to accept same-sex partnerships in society.

Dae's romantic fantasies with Florencia have not gone yet by their next encounter. Two weeks have passed. When Dae analysed how her friend had reacted then, she thought that she could only be straight.

They have both failed in their marriages. They don't have children. Without a husband or children, their feelings of love haven't any other target than themselves, and occasionally their other friends. Therefore, they can't indefinitely bury those kinds of emotions. This time they have decided to go for a picnic together.

On the summer day they picked, the sun and a blue sky suck out from people the happiness that good weather provides.

"What do you think about my sexuality? Do you count me among straight people, Florencia?" Dae asks her friend suddenly.

"I suppose so since you got married and into men and boyfriends after your divorce," Florencia replies but similarly surprised.

"But why such a question at this particular time of your life? Do you have a problem with your sexuality?" she adds while asking.

"That doesn't sound right. I found myself inclined toward lesbians, though I have only been into men until now. I have only found out recently. Thanks to my confession to you the last time, I revisited my past relationships and reevaluated my different moments of discomfort in those times. I relate such bad memories to the gender of the partner I had, instead of their personality," Dae replies.

"If I had developed similar relations with women, the consequences would have certainly been different."

"On my part, uncertainty rooms. Though the last time we got together, you and I in your apartment - and you didn't come out as the first woman to do that to me - I felt some insights in me afterwards, which made me question my sexuality as well. I have tried to silence or suppress such feelings because of how taboo or unacceptable our society has made everyone think about them. What if people decide not to feel guilty and express them openly as you did two weeks ago. I suppose you felt liberated," Florencia replies and elaborates on the subject.

For their lunch, they have brought a variety of dishes: sushi, sandwiches, cakes, fruits, chocolates, and concentrated juices. With the lot they have, they could feed two more people. Their lunch goes on for approximately forty-five minutes. They agree to pack their items then walk around the vast park of Kimbeni they came to enjoy instead of remaining in one place. When they start walking, they pursue their conversation from where they had left it before lunch.

"I think we sacrifice our happiness on the altar of society," Dae argues.

"But society doesn't constitute an abstract construct. It encompasses people, either collectively or individuals, as separate entities. When they come out together in their distinctive individualities, that is what forms the makeup of society," she adds.

Though the concept of straight or heterosexual people come to the mind of many naturally, with no need for drugs or other motivators and incentives, those who are gay or lesbian openly require some encouragement and or understanding to come out publicly. Dae had already reached that level. She expresses her inner sexual feelings to the right person without external assistance or fear to be ostracised.

Florencia lags far behind. She still has a distance to feel comfortable with her sexuality and tell someone about her intimate sexual orientation. She stays with Dae for part of the evening before she returns home.

While at Dae's place, they pursue their discussion on sexuality.

"Could we have some wine again like the last time?" Florencia asks Dae. She goes to her special storage for wine, where she keeps her best red and white collection. She bought a good selection in her different trips around the world, not cheap nor expensive, each time she came across a special one.

"I hope this will do," Dae shows Florencia a bottle of Champagne Bollinger Special Cuvee Brut. She holds it in one hand and an opener and two wine glasses in the other.

Dae offers champagne to Florencia, who wonders the motive of the celebration. Though the surprise doesn't relate to them, they both drink that special wine together -, and it constituted their first occasion to do so -, Florencia didn't miss to appreciate the highly valued drink.

"Sometimes, people forget that Champagne comes from the same family of wines. As for the occasion, I want to enjoy the time we spend together."

Dae pools the drink in their glasses.

"Cheers."

"Thanks."

"Can I put on a short erotic movie if you don't mind?" Dae asks.

"We could enjoy both the movie and the drink."

"No problem. Hopefully, I won't get drunk," immediately and excitedly Florencia says.

"Even if you did, you could spend the night here. It would not be your first. I will wake you up on time for your work."

"I will also prepare you a hangover soup to refresh you before I send you off," Dae tries whatever she can to make her friend at ease. She brought cheese and nuts, even crackers.

They have to move out of the kitchen table and go on the sofa in the main room to watch their movie. Halfway through the film, they had started to enjoy themselves while they kissed each other, and their hearts raced at an increased speed. To be more comfortable, they had to move to the bedroom.

Dae likes Florencia dearly. Among the different things she likes about her are the cruelty and the rudeness she exhibits while interacting with people. She has similar beauty traits as her twin sister Amina. Unfortunately, she lacks her refinement. The fact that she knows her for some time makes it easy to read her mood.

An empirical observation highlighted that adults who have attended private schools while they grew up - where they spent months away from their families - generally seem challenging to read.

Therefore, one could take advantage of Florencia's vulnerabilities. Dae has started to like her sincerely and intends to protect her for the long haul.

***

Once released from prison, Amina decides to marry Haile. She had come to like him. Their complicity in crime had made him likeable despite his physical unattractiveness. In the meantime, he has become a bestseller writer, slash murderer. The police had recorded among unsolved cases his involvement in Hussein's death in a hospital.

Amina and Haile organise their marriage as a low profile standard event. They invite only close friends who have known them for years.

The small circle of friends know their story. They gather in Florencia's restaurant for the occasion to exchange vows and rings.

After her release, she meets her best friend, who still works at the PR company that employed her some years back. That friend attends as well among the guests of the event.

She visited Amina regularly in prison. She thinks that, in the case of the attempted murder of Hussein, the victim also had some responsibility. Hussein appeared as guilty as those who tried to kill him.

In that friend's view, he had become a public danger for women's wellness in general and those close to him in particular. After being a victim of an attempt on his life, the court didn't allow any judicial pursuit against him. Many among the people who had followed the case found it unbelievable that none of the women he had abused had ever reported him to the police.

"What do you plan to do in the future?" her friend asks, at the same time as she refers to what she intends to do in the future. She would have liked to see her come back to her previous employer, but this would less likely happen for multiple reasons.

Probably her employer would be reluctant about her return. An eventual discomfort could rise among all the staff on her redeployment.

"My partner earns good money with his writing. I will give it some time before I settle for any activity to earn an income."

"But all these years, I thought about your case. I remember the numerous situations where your ex-boyfriend got involved in women's abuse and made the victims doubtful about themselves and became insecure. As a consequence, he jeopardised their future. I realised that, though he got what he deserved, the real victims in the situation constituted those women he abused.

Considering that you got sentenced to imprisonment for a long time, in my view, you should not have gone into jail in the first place. Your actions helped society get rid of a human nuisance that threatened and endangered women's lives. As a consequence, I will seek - on your behalf - revenge on officials who didn't assess your case correctly, and start with the inspector Sizwe," the friend pursues and explains how Hussein's abuses had impacted many women's lives. She decided not to let that case rest.

"What do you plan to do?" Amina finally asks her friend.

"Uncertainty still exists. Once I have a solid action plan, I will inform you."

***

In that week, Dae received a promotion from her employer. Her new role saw her salary increase by twenty-five per cent. She wants to celebrate the occasion with her friends the following Saturday, but she mainly wants Florencia to be there. The whole Saturday, she doesn't do much except prepare for the event, meant to start around 6:00 pm. When the guests arrive, they begin with a variety of cocktails she has engineered.

They then eat and dance. Later on, they watched a movie together, though two of the guests chose to play a table game while drinking.

By 11:00 pm, the first guest asks permission to leave because of a significant commitment the next day, but by midnight, all the guests have left except Florencia. In the meantime, Dae has asked her to stay for the night. She has promised her she has a special gift for her. It wouldn't be the first time she would spend time with her under similar circumstances.

They both know for a while now that they constitute an item, attracted to each other, and only need space
to freely. By 1:00 am, they had finished clearing the tables used for the celebration. They put dishes in need of
washing together in a pile close to the kitchen sink. They
agreed that they would clean them the next day before
their breakfast. Before they go to bed, they take a shower
together, dry each other's bodies. They massage each
other in bed; when they finish and feel relaxed enough,
Dae and Florencia go under the sheets, pooling them
until they reach their necks.

"You know what. Could you get your hand and
touch me here," Florencia suddenly took Dae's left hand
and directed it between her legs, under her pants.

"It's true you seem horny."

As she intends to take away her hand, Florencia
holds it on the spot of her body she has touched, as if
she somehow invites her to do more than that.

The atmosphere in the room feels warm enough,
with no need to turn on the heater. That summer night,
Dae's body projects its tenderness. Florencia takes advantage of that when she starts to caress her. Her pace
of air in and out changes a little towards the upside. She
brings her right arm under Florence's neck, intending to
support her, as she sleeps on her back somehow comfortably. Her left hand at this time holds Florencia's right
one on her tummy. She starts to tell her a story of a sexual encounter with a friend she knew in her secondary
school years.

"Her sex partner had helped her remove her
clothes gradually and slowly while he kissed her on different parts of her body, which included her neck, lips,
nipples and tummy, in such a way that the whole process
got her wet. At first, she felt embarrassed. That constituted the first time someone did it to her, and she enjoyed it."

"If I tell you this makes you feel annoyed, please don't hesitate. You can stop me any time you want."

"Not at all. Please go ahead."

"So my friend went on saying, "after she took off all my clothes, he went inside me. He started slowly, but when he tried to penetrate deeply, it hurt. I felt embarrassed. How could I explain to him that I can't perform the sexual ritual that constitutes the essence of any normal and naturally built woman? I couldn't tell him to stop. He noticed it hurt me a lot. The more I hurt, the more he, however, looked excited to get inside me faster and deeper.""

"My entire body and my brain didn't take it well. He seemed as if he forced a nail into a sensitive concrete where the latter would choose to die instead of continuing and suffering the persistent and painful penetration. Bang. I passed out and fell unconscious. The guy continued somehow his rape until he came. I recovered from the temporary coma a few hours later, with my uterus damaged. It had bled throughout the act, but it had stopped," she elaborated about the whole sexual encounter. The first action she did next consisted in a quick consultation with a health specialist and explaining what had happened to her."

Dae had told this story to Florencia to turn her on. Instead, it ended up with an opposite result and its sad outcome. To make up for that, she started to look into her eyes tenderly. She initiated kisses on her body wherever she sensed that she could change her mood. Within three minutes, she got back and wet.

For the next ten minutes or so, they both visited nirvana. The guide took them from place to place though they didn't leave their bed.

At the end of the climbing, they found themselves with a lookdown of the valleys they had left behind.

"While much younger and I looked at middle-aged women in their forties, I didn't know that at that age, one could fall in love. I don't yet fit in that age range, but despite that, now look at me, I feel deeply into it like when I lived my twenties," Dae reflects for herself at the momentary intimacy she experiences with Florencia.

***

Dae suddenly puts her hand on her stomach. She complains about sharp pain. Haile, Florencia and Amina, all four travel in the same car while they come from the prison, on the day the latter gets released.

"It's painful. Please, I need help. Could you take me to the nearest hospital?" Dae cries out to her friends.

Within an hour, the hospital admitted her to the emergency services for a general checkup. A few hours later, the diagnosis says that she has cancer. With a probability of eighty per cent, she could be operated on and treated successfully. The other twenty per cent counts as a risk that she could die on the operation table. Her arranged surgery would take place within two days.

For the last few years since Hussein's attempted murder, Dae's conscience has always made her feel somehow guilty about what happened. Her initial involvement has been incidentally guided by severe anger against the victim who abused women, although, with time, she wondered how to clear her mind of that sense of guilt.

When she learns that she could die in her surgery, she decides to talk to Amina, Haile and her partner Florencia one day before the operation. At six in the evening, Dae lies on a hospital bed while her friends stand beside her comforting her.

"I know the operation I will have tomorrow. As my doctor said, I should not be overly anxious, but you never know."

"I would like to share with you, as my closest friends, a side of me you might not be aware of so far. It weighed on me for some time and was related to the Hussein case. Everybody knows. We all got in some way connected to it. The role I played in it, I don't think I have ever told everyone. I have shared it with my partner, but as I had asked her not to tell anyone else, I suppose we both kept the full story to ourselves.

"When Florencia came and asked how to deal with Hussein, I had long decided to handle him on my own and in my way. I would not have imagined that there could be other people as like-minded as I was, concerned with his case. His apartment and mine featuring in the same block meant that his abuse towards me was frequent. I had reported him several times, but the property management company looked as if they didn't care."

"I had begged the managers to talk to Hussein, but to no avail. I owned my apartment. I wouldn't have traded it and sold it because of the nuisance of a mentally sick neighbour. Consequently, I decided to take things into my own hands. I managed to get a copy of his house keys. Please don't ask me how I did it. I could go in whenever I liked as long as he would be elsewhere. I had opted for a slow death, the same as he inflicted it on me through his abuses. I had identified chemical substances I put in his food and drinks. Their effect would've taken longer to manifest their impact."

"When Florencia approached me and suggested a faster solution to get rid of him, I willingly agreed to help. I think the rest of the story, everyone knows. That consists of all that I wanted to share."

"Hence if I die tomorrow on the operation table, at least you will all be aware of how lucky the world will get rid of that evil person that I have been."

Dae's friends who had listened to her involvement in the Hussein case had their evil conscience about it and dealt with it in their way. Perhaps, when they too will be near death, they will share it willingly. Suppose they have time for it.

At that particular moment, they only focused their efforts on comforting their friend whose surgical operation was on the next day.

That night before Dae falls asleep, she calls her friend Aimi in Okyto.

"Listen. Tomorrow I will have an operation. I only wanted to inform you in case any unexpected hazard happens after tomorrow. Please, in the meantime, take care of yourself."

"I will call in two days to find out how the operation went. I will even visit you before your full recovery. GoodBye."

Dae considers herself as an everyday human being, mentally and physically healthy. When she gets informed about her surgery, she consequently develops some sort of moderate level of anxiety. She has never had any major operation of any kind. Overall, she feels averagely optimistic about the outcome.

When Dae comes out of the surgery, the lead surgeon announces that all went well. Her friends felt relieved because of the anxiety she had shown days before.

A few months later, she feels another severe and persistent pain in her abdomen. When she goes to her doctor and proceeds with multiple tests to diagnose her illness, the specialists tell her that she has extensive endometriosis.

It's a disease characterised by cells from the uterus that spread in other parts of the body where they don't belong, but despite that fact, it grows there and causes painful bleeding.

"Heaven punishes me for my sins. I should blame nobody. I have to pay while still alive. Until one pays their debt, the universe shouldn't leave them in peace. I will only request from the master the power to endure the punishment," Dae deeply reflects on what affected her wellness in recent months.

Meaningful Memorials

From an individual point of view, or on a national level, memorials have and should have strong meanings when people connect with their past. The problem arises when some past events become officially banned from personal or collective memory for political reasons. However, even for the remembered past, the accompanying rituals are restrictive to a certain degree since they pursue the authorised policy's discriminative character on the issue.

Haile doesn't feature among those who fall victim to the restrictions, but he suffers from the shortcomings of a different nature. He doesn't have any pictures to refer to when he thinks about his late mother in his everyday vocabulary. His mother grew up when photography didn't constitute a common feature of lifestyle in her remote community. Thus, even in Haile's young age, no photographer existed around to capture visual memories for posterity or himself when he would get older.

For that reason, no family album shows where he can see photos of his parents or himself while in his childhood. Consequently, his only way to remember the parents consists in an immersion of himself into any possible memories he hardly borrows from his brain, wherever his neurones have safeguarded their traces.

Regardless, he wonders why when he wants to remember his parents, his mother shows up in his mind more frequently than his father. Could it be because humans generally spend more time with their mothers than their fathers? That could be a plausible explanation. People tend to remember things and people they have been most familiar with and have marked them in a particular way.

"Without memorials - these are objects or symbols that make people visit their past - what do they look for or which reference guides them when such need occurs and becomes a critical existential question?" Haile navigates in his mind after he considers his circumstances.

He wonders what has been the consequences of not having such memories that some lucky people display with strong emotions. Those who don't have such shortcomings hold a privilege they ignore. They have something valuable they might not treasure enough.

Given such consideration, one would wonder the purpose of a memorial. In non-expert terms, it helps remember and communicate with the past. Though the past can talk to the posterity, the latter can not talk back. The situation looks like a monologue or a one-way conversation, indeed with many understandings. Despite such an unbalanced relationship to the past, another related question that leaves many unresolved issues would be this: if memorials concern the departed, or the foregone circumstances worth capturing, there must be many victims or significant occurrences out there without them.

"There seem plenty," Haile confirms for himself. He remembers his history classes on many hugely and deadly conflicts that humanity experienced in its hundreds and thousand years of existence.

"Perhaps millions in every corner of the world and from different times of humankind's history," he adds. While he reflects on these existential questions, he took some time and wrote down a related poem. A story of a memorial built in 1996 in Washington DC inspired his piece of writing. He had read in a magazine an opinion/article that talked about that memorial.

"Another fervent advocate of capitalism," with this first verse, Haile referred to some writers he had come across in his broad reading. However, one would ask if he had some negative views of the capitalist system to start his poem that way. Indeed, no element in the mentioned article pointed out that the central theme described a situation unique or typical to capitalism, given that memorials existed in all human civilisations.

"He referred to the 1996 edition," the second verse goes—the referred occurrence related to a contemporary historical fact at the time.

"Which edition could it be about?" Amina asks Haile when he reads the poem from his collection written over several years. The question comes about.

"The Time Magazine of that year," he explains.

"It could eventually be The Economist as well, or some other magazine," he goes on. It has been a long way to remember without failure which publication Haile had read.

"I can't remember either," the next verse goes on. At the time, Haile used to get several specialist western magazines, and sometimes he would flip through to find out the most talked-about news in world affairs.

"About the victims of communism," his poem ensues. The reference to communism in such terms seems to dehumanise that political ideology. In the writer's mind, supposedly, the initial understanding was that no positive aspect seemed present in the communist societies' experiences.

"Confirmed I got at my first reading," Haile finds evidence of what he has always believed to be correct about the highlighted subject. He felt like someone what his stomach or mind craved for, his food's desires fulfilled expectedly, when the entire experience became a complete delight.

"Who would be interested in and talk about the victims of communism to justify the elevation of a Jewish memorial, not in Israel, but the US?" Haile has this question on his mind. He doesn't voice it out. While he composes his poem, he initially thinks that the memorial relates to Jewish people, but in reality, it doesn't.

"Memorial dedication in Washington DC," Haile's poem goes on.

"For victims of Marx and Lenin disciples," the next verse says. The two names stand portrayed as the culprits that need hanging, if they didn't already feature on crosses readied for them, to get their blood sucked out of their bodies.

"Why not build memorials where the victims fell instead, because the majority of them suffered in the vicinity of territories controlled by that ideology?" Haile wonders.

"I had and still have the same question as you have," he comments.

"Was it for propaganda or the use of the victim card, to render insignificant the plight of victims of other ideologies, different from communism?" Haile still wonders about that memorial. He gazes towards a distant point outside the apartment through the window. A total silence around him prevails.

"They had ruled and overruled," the poem goes on. The rule in question had risen at the expense of or as a consequence to fight communism.

"I agree that in places where communism gained strong political influence, it made sure the leaders to rule would be on their side as long as possible," Haile highlights. Countless victims had fallen to strengthen and dominate the conquests.

"But this seemed, and it remains the modus operandi of any oppressive ideological external power in conquered territories," Haile elaborates.

"Seen as victims of the Communist order."

415

"Why did the communist ideology come to be in the first place? Didn't that constitute an outcome of the failures that previous leaderships had avoided to take responsibility for?" Haile argues. Nobody dares to give a counter-argument.

"In places like Russia, Cuba, China, Wethi," the poem carries on.

"These belong to countries where historically communism became the political ideology that ruled for a significant period," Haile clarifies.

"Under Stalin, Castro, Mao and Mengistu." History books talk widely about these personalities.

"But surprisingly, no memorial for other victims," Haile points out.

He thinks about those back home - whichever home it could be for anyone, as his ancestral land of Wethi - whose bodies he passed by when he couldn't pay attention to them because far too many of them abounded nearly everywhere. His victims looked like they constituted part of his natural landscape as a re-designed space for their impressive display.

"Fallen under a relentless Capitalism reign," he continues with the poem.

"The same way some wanted to build a memorial for victims of communism, the same way even more victims of capitalism required one," Haile thinks.

"All victims of Human nature," here goes on the poem.

"Interestingly, and generally, humans must be the only species which deliberately takes on its peers and makes them suffer intentionally for the only purpose of the power to dominate them," Haile comments. He expresses his comprehension of why people kill or oppress and exploit each other, sometimes massively and atrociously.

"Crippled once, a lifetime, for generations," he pursues.

416

"Such suffering, once done or inflicted, impacts for a long time if not forever. It appears somehow and, in some cases, impossible to reverse. Many generations that follow experience the impact," Haile feels. That impact appears real in victims' daily lives. At times, some behaviours they adopt unconsciously as a consequence."

"Occasionally these seem detrimental to their well-being. In other situations, victims rationalise their plight and take it to the extremes whereby they see the world around them as if it owes them something, like an obligatory favour, because they suffered. As if they existed as the only people among the human race to have experienced their peers' cruelty.

"They kneel at the cruelty of the fittest," Haile elaborated and thought about the survival of the strongest in the animals' kingdom.

"Oppressed for lack of muscles to resist," he carries on and explains why weakness seems a deadly sin. The expression goes like this: "challenges in life make us stronger."

"Instead, think about all these victims," he continues.

"No need for memorials," he explains that such reality invades spaces and becomes visible to whoever would want to see and or forces itself through an implicit flirtation with the onlookers.

"Humans appear as only different animals," he clarifies to translate what the reality of humankind is.

"No need to be hypocrites," he despises those in denial.

"Let's be more human and less animal," he advises people to be on the side of what differentiates humans from animals.

This advice could be aspirational only because if no planned action comes along and some sort of accountability requested to get to such a transformative shift, the process wouldn't achieve any result.

"That should be the real memorial," he defines the ultimate aspiration for humanity if each member could put themselves in others' shoes.

"If we see ourselves in others," he insists on the main predicament from the animals' kingdom.

"As victims of our orders," he finally describes the consequences of when the world refuses to care for humankind. He concedes that what happens to the human race emanates from its own making. They shouldn't blame anyone but themselves. No need for scapegoats to make some people feel good about themselves.

Unpredictability And Wisdom

Amina and her twin sister lost their parents while young. That early death robbed them of their happy childhood and adolescence. Each time Amina remembers that period without them, it stays alive in her head and creates a permanent wind between her and the world that suffocates her. What that means embodies the fact that she lacks the exact words to explain it. Further to that situation, she has for her life struggled to understand or figure out what difference her parents' presence would've brought to her existence. Such absence brings out an empty zone that no imagination can fill.

Firstly, their father, a soldier in the Occorz army, died in a military expedition in the Southern Rhaasa while fighting the Rouha rebels. He ended up in the military because no other employment options existed in his village. If it hadn't been for the help received from a relative who worked in the capital Tabor at a government office, he could've missed his enrollment. After completing his military programme at the Academie Royale Militaire Senkes, he moves around among Occorz battalions in the occupied territory; he finally gets sent to Tifari, where he dies in an ambush during a major military battle between the two sides to the conflict.

Amina, who once an adult learns about what the mission of that expedition entailed, gets disapproval of the Occorz leadership who went to colonise those territories. She doesn't become contrariant of her father, who obeyed his superiors' orders, but in the excuse that anyone generally uses to blame somebody else for their actions. Southern Rhaasa had remained the last colony their continent continued to have in the 70s from another Qarfi country.

Amina's father left her mother pregnant. When the twins came into the world, they, unfortunately, lost her as well when they only reached their fifth anniversary.

They grow up looked after by an aunt and one of their grandmothers.

The family originates from Mesied and has its records there for more than seven generations. The area has all the hallmarks of a small village in the South East of Occorz. The population amounts to no more than two thousand people. The family's ancient history says that their ancestors and descendants belong to a Birbar clan found in the Rhaasa desert.

When they turn ten, an uncle who had settled in the QK for more than two decades asks the broader family if he can look after them as their guardian and support them for their future education. He brought them to the QK in the summer of 1996. They arrive in QK and settle with their uncle's family until they become adults and live independently.

After she graduates from the University of Kankan Moussa in the Nebdre city, Amina finds work and comes to live in Vodnak. Her twin sister poses as not bright. She works in a local restaurant as a deputy Chef. They both live together in one of the apartments along Wright's Drive. Not as close as twins would usually behave, at times, they confront each other fiercely as rivals, particularly when it comes to men. Despite that, they care uniquely for each other instinctively.

"You must've had a good time with your prince," Florencia utters to Amina sarcastically. This conversation occurs after one of the evenings Hussein had with Amina.

"He carries himself as usual, with his unsupportable manners," she replies.

"I understand you want to become his friend badly. Nevertheless, at what price! You always come home complaining. Unhappy as it could be. It seems like you never have a good time with him."

"I do have good times. But_"

"Yes, that - but - makes it a problem."

"My dear sister, your relationship with him gets on my nerves. How long do you think I will tolerate living with that situation?"

The twin sister knew Hussein well. She had seen his relationship with Amina developing, and her jealousy increased as time passed. She couldn't get over it. Partially jealous of the way Hussein materially cared for her sister, she seriously and unexpectedly became unhappy about how he mistreated her.

Occasionally, people who didn't know the two sisters wondered and couldn't differentiate them. As identical twins, From afar, the twins appeared even more identical for those who knew them enough to point precisely at each of both.

Florencia had planned Hussein's murder, but it didn't get executed as she expected. Many outcomes of her act took her life and that of her sister into uncertain and unchartered territories. Even so, overall, this defined a part of her journey in the universe, its unpredictability.

***

That spring, Dae turned thirty-two. Her life appears dull and uneventful at the time, to the point that she worries about her future.

"I don't see any change," she asserts and analyses her life's direction. Objectively, no solid argumentation supported that subjective statement.

Despite Dae's conviction to the contrary, almost everything with proof of life in their essence changed around her.

Climate change campaigners loudly claimed to anyone ready to listen to them that the world would end in destruction if people didn't radically modify their consumption habits. Engineers of artificial intelligence introduced robots in relationships, cooperation, and trust between human beings.

Interactions of machines or robots with humans had been tested and measured the evaluated results that promised better futures.

The QK that Dae lived in became gradually protectionist. It cut its direct trade ties with the rest of the world, pretending that its problems were caused by others.

Understandably, the country's leadership couldn't blame itself for anything. It also got untangled into an open crisis of political conflict where protagonists frequently disagreed on the best approaches to become more independent from other nations or blocs of countries. The country feared, unwillingly, to isolate itself. Besides, new global political and economically powerful nations emerged at the time, and the balance of influence shifted towards these new players.

In a moment of clarity in her mind, Dae remembers some profound meditations Aimi's father had once shared with her when she had visited the family years back. They had both gone together for a picnic in a public garden close to the ocean. They had brought a musical soundtrack, "Enjoy before it happens", to help regenerate the mind. While they listened, the shared reflection tried to convey the joy and power of patience.

> A kind of a journey.
> What could it entail?
> Experience it!
> Think about it!
> Only as a real doer
> Seriously,

What the hell!
I mean it.
They look back
They experience
In no more or less
An almost physical
A draining exercise
A mental gymnastic
Emotionally,
Highly motivated
On oneself
Between two people
Even more
Possibly remotely
Different
From other exercises
Physical or mental
At its climax
Most enjoyable moments
Their occurrence
Before accomplishment
Occur before
Its accomplishment
Once the end rises to

Imagine that moment
A second
A minute
An hour
A day
A week
A month
A year
And more
Before they have it
Thrilled they feel
Imagine

Experienced feeling
In a slow-motion
Never-ending

They don't get it
Physical or mental
Charged exercise
They become

The created connection
Become established
Between two people
Even more
Dependency
Experiencing
The enjoyment

The different bond
If cared for
No cause of trauma

Once completed
The next thing
A different connection
A kind of bond
Ownership
Partnership
Truly different

Positives and negatives
Firm pedestal
Destructive energy
Tragedy

Enjoyment
Given
Before

Lost
Distorted

Master oneself
Intentionally
Avoid losing
Overwhelmingly

Demonstrate
Character
Strong impact
Before
Things
Happen

Enjoy.

Dae recalled this meditation that Aimi's father led while at that picnic, and it calmed her dullness and her different fears that life exposed her to from time to time. They had previously affected her in a certain way. She could henceforth confront difficulties more positively. Her anxiety level had declined; she didn't worry anymore when she looked at how happy she felt. She had stopped the chase of happiness into others, particularly men. A sense of fulfilment had made Dae settle with Florencia, her female friend. It wasn't because of the intimacy they shared occasionally. Florencia enabled her to achieve any pursuit - either while around or away - when she only thought of her. She had discovered that happiness drew breath from a state of mind that no external reality could help get. It only became an outcome of an inner exercise to oneself.

Raped Victims

Two runners, husband and wife, participate as one of the couples in the host family's small group that night. They appear to be in their late twenties. The family has decided to convene the gathering to honour the guests. This organised event was after the couple had made a journey of several hours and thousands of kilometres. It had used different means of transport to reach that place.

That weekend, Amina and her twin sister visit their remote relatives they have not seen since their young age. Haile has offered to accompany them, mainly for touristic reasons, and discover the part of Occorz where the sisters were born. The family host and the relatives the twin sisters visit don't live too far from each other.

The couple and everybody else, including Haile and the twin sisters, travel to the same destination. Haile surprisingly finally ends up staying with the husband and wife in the host family. He could've also gone with the twin sisters but chose to join them a few days later. For unclear reasons, he felt attracted to the welcoming atmosphere and changed his mind about spending his time on that trip.

The guests and the hosting family chat and exchange hospitality while they wait for the evening meal. Haile initiated a discussion on the benefit of exercising.

"I try to run three times a week and ensure I do thirty-five miles a month," the husband from the couple had responded to show and impress about his presumed fitness. He glanced, from time to time, to his partner while he talked. It appeared that he almost sought approval for what he said. Haile had travelled with the couple from Vodnak to Mesied, a remote village in the vast South Eastern region of Occorz.

It has been hard to get there. Haile learns about the couple's hobby while on the train when he asks the man how, as a family, they spend their quality time.

Unintentionally, the conversation started when Haile indicated to the husband what he read when the latter asked. The exchange between them happens before the couple reaches the airport to fly home to visit their family. The couple comes from this same region. The twin sisters are as well on the same trip.

Haile thinks of how their community generally hosts male guests. He had heard the story from an elder of the community. He excitedly expects to receive similar hospitality. The couple had joked about it when they explained to Haile such a tradition. They requested that he doesn't get surprised or laugh when asked which woman to accompany him in bed. It's part of the gestures of welcoming guests the host family wants to bond with for future relationships.

"I don't expect the host to give me his wife as a partner for the night," he seriously considers that possibility, but he doesn't announce it openly. Contrary to the custom, nobody has yet to tell him discreetly or show him which woman would be his companion for the next few hours.

The broad family has a few young unmarried women who would get involved and help around. The family chief wants to extend his social status and influence through possible marriages. While the whole family has its dinner, Haile had one chance to wink at one woman in her thirties and say a few words at her address, but without much promise on her part.

He wonders with mixed feelings. His mind takes him then to alternative worlds of different times. It moved several thousand miles in space while the rest of the group continued their conversation.

"Will I be moved like I did on that day when I saw the model in our office? She moved around somehow naked," Haile's conscience makes a fast-paced flashback in a recent past he had experienced at work. He tries to paint a picture of what to expect in the host family.

As part of a group of girls Haile saw then, the model worked for a beauty magazine.

Despite the uneasiness of the moment, he had enjoyed that experience. For a long time, he hadn't seen a woman with the least clothes on her body.

Haile goes back to the realm of memory, like absent-minded, as he doesn't participate in the conversation around him. It appears like yesterday. Nevertheless, twenty years have passed since that precise moment of his past. When the story unfolds, he remembers while still young and sitting not far from the elders.

His father and another guest much older tell the group a terrible foregone period their respective families went through. A significant fraction of their people died a horrible death.

"You, people - those with whom they share the meal -, can hardly put yourselves in the shoes of those who left us behind without a proper farewell," at the time, Haile's father reflects, looking at their group of guests and hosts.

"Experience stands out on any journey in the universe. The experience happens to be the only key to understanding; without it, people only go about and pretend to grasp the wholeness of contexts," the old man keeps on and rumbles in his head.

Haile realises that he has been mentally far away and then joins the conversation in the host family. He refers to the last bit of the conversation, which carries on.

"Great that you could do that many miles in such a short period," Haile replies to the guest. He has travelled with him from Vodnak.

"I struggle to do even fifteen a month," he adds.

"It's not easy when you start to get older."

Haile gets back into his past where he remembers what happened to his people. He navigates those places unconsciously.

The moves get out of his control, and he doesn't have the willingness or the power to stop it.

"It must've been horrible," a family acquaintance said. He profoundly scrutinised the facial expression of the older adult in the room.

"You can't measure how tragic it must have been for those on the ground," the old man finally says.

The two interlocutors had a subconscious conversation about events that occurred to their people in a different part of the world. Haile also participates in the discussion from a different angle and location, though he appears only as an observer interested in all the details. He tries to make sense of the bits from his past he gets told. He doesn't ask any questions.

The next scene that comes to him as another flashback from that period gets marked and safeguarded forever in Haile's mind. Though it appears as a product of his imagination, it lacks crucial details, like a dream when the dreamer wakes up. He wonders if the long period which has elapsed since the real events took place doesn't play with his conscience. However, he can't guess the purpose of the game.

"Haile, please help. They came for me," a neighbour they stayed together for two hours earlier loudly calls him on his landline. His voice implores over the phone. Before Haile says anything, he hears several shots from guns before the neighbour finishes his implosion."

"The lousy shouts from the perpetrators resonate from afar; they don't take any precautions to ensure that nobody outside the room hears them. Their victim couldn't hang up the telephone properly. Whatever noise emerges from the room, they shoot members of the household and get retransmitted at the other end of the line. At the time, the war had erupted. Gunshots constituted common occurrences.

An extended period has passed when Haile wonders how the victim at the time knew him. He didn't help in any way. He almost justifies his non-intervention, arguing that at the time, he could risk his life and that of his small family for someone he didn't know much. They had only been neighbours who occasionally greeted each other when they met. Haile knew where that neighbour worked. His father had told him that he had seen him on national television.

He supervised football matches as a referee of the Premier League. They had never sat together to share genuinely as real friends do. The call he received from him on that tragic day became the first and last between them ever.

Haile had learned about the murder of his brother in law, his wife and their two children. The incident had occurred in a different part of the village. At the time, Haile's family lived what everyone in the country experienced on a bigger scale. Chaos and desolation occurred unpredictably.

They had broad up unspeakable situations and considerations of dire morality.

One such topic concerned how rape victims imagined their new humanity once they experienced the traumatic incident.

"Victims of rape would wish to see all women raped by the conquerors; that way, they would not be ashamed alone by what had happened to them."

"In case they would manage to have life partners, the latter would come from the demographics of men at the bottom of the societal hierarchy. In general, the community shames those women because they got raped as if they called it on themselves willingly," the old man reflects in absolute privacy since he doesn't speak out his thoughts in the open. Such thinking was an opinion's summary he heard from a rape victim whispering to a friend. The point of view appears too outrageous, given the fact that even the person in question doesn't want to stand up for it.

That thought, once heard, made Haile think.

Like a non-linear tread, it navigated in his head without a specific purpose. However, it seemed to rationalise such consideration.

"If their wish to see every woman raped materialised, in their view, only such a situation could be an act of fair revenge to their misfortune."

"Understandably, while they saw such context as a possibility, they didn't care much about the fate of the children who would come into the world in those circumstances, let alone the collective psyche of a society where rape would've been a commonly accepted fact."

"Undoubtedly, - though no fact indicates that this constituted a shared view - this translated only a wish from some victims. Fortunately, it couldn't become a reality of any sort, though there had been in contemporary history, places where conquered communities had seen their women raped massively. As a consequence, issues of post-rape trauma and children born from rape could become taboo topics, like societal minefields."

The rape left its victims overwhelmingly shamed and pained. What they didn't know - and they would never realise - indicated that the physical and mental scars inflicted by their aggressors would have a profound and long-term impact on their wellbeing.

They would be in a near-constant state of fight and flight. They would suffer from physical pain, of which doctors can't detect the origin, from time to time. Even after a period of, let's say, ten years from the incident, the victims would still experience the symptoms of shame, such as a chest that hurts, overactive sweat glands or tunnel vision, all of which come near-identical to those of untreated post-traumatic stress disorder.

These constituted the facts about their war. It had different facets. Overall, some view it as a forbidden fantasy, where someone plays with people's lives, while others die because of it, or live or die slowly, and the former benefits from the entire criminal scheme.

Unfortunately, this fantasy has constituted one integral part of the DNA of humankind since immemorial times.

On that summer night, the conversation turned to other subjects as well.

Climate change has made a big part of the world exceptionally hot. Tens of people in Kagri and Cafordomo had died caught in the middle of fires caused by the level of heat the earth had endured. Consequently, Haile had decided to sleep without wearing his pyjamas. He couldn't find the right position to sleep comfortably. Either on his tummy or back down, it was difficult to rest immediately. He happened to explore his body unconsciously. The bedsheets touched his penis and made him think of a desire to have a woman next to him. He regretted not having someone to lean on in those critical emotional times. Tired of the long journey of the day, he went into a deep sleep, within twenty minutes in bed, until he woke up at his usual time.

Before the whole group travelled to the remote ancestral village in Occorz, Amina had been on a week-long seminar away from home.

At the time, before she fell asleep, Haile had wondered if it would appear wise to call her. He hadn't seen her since their jog a week earlier. Haile resisted and remembered that they hadn't talked to each other while away. He gave up on the idea. By the time of that trip, Haile hadn't confessed his love for her. Also, he didn't want her to know at that particular period of his life. He waited for the right time to reveal his true feelings to her, though he appeared apprehensive about her reaction.

A Marvelous Morning

The talk and the air in the block feel familiar. People that count in Haile's life all seem to know him well. Though they resonated as disconnected at first, these two random thoughts cross his mind when he considers to set out. They leave their randomness the same way they had entered it, inadvertently. Haile can't, however, follow their thread for some inexplicable reasons.

Outside, it appears as an ordinary early day like any other. The sky displays moody clouds typical for July. Though that month had recorded unusual rainfalls, it would've been sunny given the season.

He decides to go out for his jog on his own. He mulls over the weather, which prevails once he gets out of his door. While he does his usual rounds along the pond located in the park, he feels poetically more inspired than any other day. At moments, poetry has been on his mind as a means of expression of his inner feelings. His muse meets him on his way to his everyday spot where his exercising starts. It feeds him a title for a poem he decides to call "A Marvelous Morning."

Understandably, such a title would summarise his overall state of mind only after the run. He takes an all-around look at different corners of the sky, as far as his eyes can see on the horizon. The rain has begun to drizzle when he finishes stretching his legs and arms' muscles before jogging.

Luckily, he has never encountered or met cats and dogs that fall like rain in his early hours' sessions since he started exercising. He promises himself to thank the universe at the end of his run if they don't come around.

"Still a little dark it showed," he finds out once he opens his curtains. Outside looks virtually still dark, and that actual state of the time would and will, occasionally and time and time again, put in jeopardy his jogging sessions. The night before sets for him the plan to exercise the following morning.

He doesn't want to be disturbed while in the flow. That makes him prepare beforehand. The weather ends up disobeying its master, though he would've liked it to behave.

"But the time comes," he admits to certain things despite the circumstances. To find the outside still dark doesn't come out as a challenge to overcome because he has the necessary authority to take action.

"This became like a routine," he imagines the sun or the moon when they perform the same activity every day or night and don't realise that they act unconsciously - if one could lend them a conscience. He performs some actions in his daily life without thinking, like even the related process, to open his eyes, breathe, feel hungry or thirsty. They come up whenever needed to appear when particular circumstances trigger them, and all this happens because of the wiring up of his brain.

It comes to him as a surprise when he discovers that ninety per cent of human actions don't call upon people's willpower and that only the last five provide outcomes from people's conscious decisions to make them happen. He has never wondered how the world would look if that distribution of consciousness and unconsciousness changed and conscious choices became predominant. Some of the outcomes, instinctively, could range among, for example, things like "I decide not to think, to love, to hate, to kill or not to kill, or to drink." However, his primary source doesn't reveal which category of decisions fall only under the remit of consciousness.

Haile doesn't want to venture in that direction and take the challenge because the exercise would put him on the agenda, pointing to other fundamental considerations about other issues. The engineers of the universe have their reasons to make what does exist operate the way it does.

Those who pretend to know his ways can only fool themselves. Intelligent people acknowledge what their limited competence and knowledge don't grasp. The muse continues its glittering on Haile's mind.

"Wake up early for a run" occurrence triggers a particular purpose. To run on one's own could, in some communities, relate to craziness. These communities don't generally see much connection between running and being fit or having overall well-being. It comes mainly close to the concept of time as a measurement. One example illustrating that would be the importance of being early to an appointment or imperatively avoiding a dangerous situation because it constitutes the only logical perspective. All these considerations suffer from the ignorance of those who cannot grasp their extensive uncharted territories. Haile has before faced similar moments in his runs.

"Make plans to be changed," he draws towards that end, while already some justifications rush to visit his mind. Two excuses might have been sufficient or not to get out of bed. In the still-dark hours of the early morning, then cloudy skies outside announced the possibility of rain. His conscience plays a game that tests his determination for his exercising.

"An hour and a half later it would be," once Haile has overcome all the hurdles to his fitness routine.

"Rain continues; it's drizzling," this paints one part of the overall picture on that morning. It shows its true nature at that moment. Even so, Haile seems convinced that he could still endure without much pain or regrets.

"The usual sixty-plus hadn't missed the early Rendez-Vous of runners." Visibly, despite the momentarily adverse weather, Haile features among all those who confront it vigorously in that morning. He doesn't even imagine that others have gone through similar mental torture, at the very same period of the day, before they open their front door.

Sometimes people jump into situations and only realise afterwards the real context they entered. Their struggle overcoming any misfortune or getting out of it happens to be more challenging than for those who assess the context rightly beforehand.

"He had changed his route." Haile doesn't find any reason the concerned individual comes from another direction at that early time of the day than the usual one. He has no answer to the question which pops into his mind when he sees him. Even so, his mental process could've been applied to any being, alive or not, at any particular time. He thinks of the factors that initiate change in people's behaviour. Though he understands that the readiness and the requirement to move towards specific directions also characterise part of the nature of things that change.

"The walk occurred on the high street," thus the change of direction takes place in a particular location. Without prior knowledge of the motive, Haile can only observe the way the older adult walks passively. Until he understands the intricacies of the occurrence, at the moment, he decides to become an indifferent spectator.

"Contrary to its paced speed in the park," he doesn't understand why his subject of observation walks much slower than usual. Perhaps this relates to the way the runner has momentarily organised his exercising. Haile, generally, walks as well at a slower pace while on the high street.

With the cars that pass, he considers that he could take in polluted substances in high volume when he speeds up his pace and breathes or inhales the air around. The decision of not exercising on pavements, near or along with the cars on the move, was there for a while. He had made such a decision a long time before. His resolution considered his jogging as a practice for the long haul. In the same line of thinking, he occasionally avoided walking on the main high street. He instead used parallel streets to get to his destination.

"Rain that drizzles looks marvellous," he feels that way once he starts his jog in the park and gets tiny drops of rain on his face. Unexpectedly warm, they seem to come from a cooled space in the skies. Haile wonders if the rain has as well decided to join in the mood of change.

"That promises an incredible bonus," his body and the weather conditions all came together to enable him to perform better than usual. The predisposition highlights the value put into hope. Moreover, such an approach guides people to perform actions they wouldn't have imagined if they had known beforehand. Hope, in some regards, tends to be the most precious currency in humankind history. It has made nations conquer others, enslave their real owners, or people marry others while relying only on the power of their instantaneous love.

"The run would reach new heights." This hope translates to motivation for that morning. The mood of that moment anticipates positive outcomes.

"Ten versus six rounds pounded," Haile remembers not to stop when he reached his usual target of rounds. He doesn't feel tired at all. He went on and on until he could get back to his place by seven in the morning. His schedule dictates him to leave the apartment for work at a particular hour.

"Rain drizzling, pond, grey sky," these three elements of mother nature work hand in hand in harmony with each other. They like to meet around an unspoken agreement between them to adopt a confident attitude conducive to a good run. When nature takes somebody's side, they can only do tremendous work and enjoy the moment.

"Wild ducks, besides young people carrying their twenties," while the exuberant nature, part of the scenery accompanied with a representation of the new generation, seems prepared to see through the rites of passage.

"Three on the bench chatting," they have visibly come out early for a purpose different from running. Nobody can tell the subject of their conversation. As all of them appear as girls in their twenties, Haile presumes that they might talk about their new lovers or plan to conquer new territories. Haile will never know since he doesn't envisage to stop or have the audacity to ask them when he passes in front of their bench.

Haile finishes the ninth of his rounds around the pond. He doesn't remember how many he did on that occasion because there was no register for his jog records for posterity. Some days he recalled performances close to thirty rounds in a row around the pond.

"Muslims deep in their prayers," runners see them in such a posture. In contrast, the time indicates to be close to seven in the morning. They seem to have come out in the park to talk with their god. They kneel on mats especially brought there for prayers. That presumption doesn't come with any other argument that could support it. It finds its justification in the fact that those mats seem to serve only for praying.

The discussion group that would come together to pray in the park must have been unusual given the location and the arranged time.

Undoubtedly, they want to have the upper hand about the outcome. They have had to sacrifice a worthy element - their sleep until dawn -, to gain what they pursued.

"Black girl while she cares for her healthy look," she displays a well-shaped, neither fat nor skinny body. In that early hour, she visibly exercises as someone who runs for a purpose and is determined to get it. Haile can guess from the level of her commitment to her jogging. He doesn't see her in any of the weeks that follow.

Haile wonders if she went on to exercise only on the days when he skipped his jogging. That could've been a possibility, or she might've stopped for good after that one-off. He has done similarly in the past. He would never know at that moment. He couldn't read much into what his mind told him.

"Asians who discover the park early" wore traditional outfits that made Haile presume about their origins. They could've been locals who had settled in the country already for a few generations. Although he learnt from Amina that cohorts of Asian tourists came to that park to enjoy its beauty in some periods of the year.

The park has that magic "je ne sais quoi", which draws people to its contemplation.

Haile could feature as one of such people. He never hypothetically marvels at the reason that has made him choose that park at the expense of others in his vicinity.

In July, for the early weeks of the summer, several Asian women, young and old, walk with the one only boy of the family around, while the latter looks bored or annoyed because he forcibly got there. Those Muslim women, particularly those with a Barka that cover their faces, can't get out of their houses without a male representative, however young he might be.

Their tradition dictates, and they have to abide by it, even when they travel as tourists. Haile would've liked a challenge on such affirmations.

"Forty-plus after a clear target," his pace is fast because the speed seems similar to that of runners for fifteen hundred meters or five kilometres. He appears to be from a different league than Haile.

"All fits a marvellous moment," the painted picture characterises all these runners, joggers, and walkers on those early hours of the day around the pond. Such joyful weather and scenery look staggering.

About The Author

Kanage Kanyamanza is a writer from the Great Lakes. Trained as an economist and engineer, he paints and cares for plants. The Neptersine is a dialogue between the main character, Haile Mohammed, and the universal mind, translated through a range of people's interactions. Written at a time the author's life stumbled on a challenge of possibilities, the book explores what it means to relate to each other, how we deal with friendship and the nature of our interconnectedness. Through a regular jogging routine with his neighbour Amina Ye, Haile Mohammed navigates a fictitious narrative of moral transgression, abuse, and ultimately, redemption.

The crime novel offers a vehicle to discover the hidden aspects of the human soul. What are the spaces of love and friendship? How does intimacy develop? When does love dissipate and turn into complicity or violence? How do we reconcile the violence we inflict upon each other? In between these diverse questions and many unspoken others, life pursues its timeless course.

Review Request

If you enjoyed this book,
And learnt something,
Why not write a sweet review
And send it to this email

kanage.kanyamanza@gmail.com

A reward of a free collection of poems will be yours.

Thank you!

Books I Enjoyed Reading

A certain amount of madness: the life, politics and legacies of Thomas Sankara - Edited by Amber Murrey

Never let me go - Kazuo Ishiguro

Norwegian Wood - Haruki Murakami

The devotion of suspect X - Keigo Higashino

The girl who played with fire - Stieg Larsson

The tipping point: how little things can make a big difference - Malcolm Gladwell

In The Pipeline

The Kanagean (July 2023) - a series to follow the crime fiction "The Neptersine," with *Kanage Postal Code* as the epicentre of action.

The Immortal Wind (July 2024) - a reincarnation story which recreates an active relationship between ancestors and the living descendants.

Memory and Liberation (July 2026) - or how the connection to one's home can be a strong motivation to become and feel freer.